FIGHTING FOR THE CROWN

(ARK ROYAL, BOOK XVI)

CHRISTOPHER G. NUTTALL

Text copyright © 2021 Christopher G. Nuttall

Printed in the United States of America.

ISBN: 9798586917836

Imprint: Independently pubished

Cover by Justin Adams

http://www.variastudios.com/

http://www.chrishanger.net
http://chrishanger.wordpress.com/
http://www.facebook.com/ChristopherGNuttall
All Comments Welcome!

CONTENTS

PROLOGUE

FROM: Admiral Paul Mason, Director of Alpha Black, Special Projects

TO: Admiral Susan Onarina, CO Operation Lightning Strike

ADMIRAL SUSAN ONARINA,

As per your request, my department has spent the last two weeks conducting an extensive post-battle analysis of Operation Thunderchild. This has not been an easy task. The much-touted bioscanners were nowhere near as efficient as we were assured—surprise, surprise—and the urgent need for a retreat from the targeted system ensured a significant lack of late-stage data. In short, there is a sizable question mark over both the data we collected and our conclusions and I would be remiss in my duties if I did not bring that to your attention.

However, a number of things can be said with a fair degree of certainty.

The BioBombs were less effective than we had hoped. They certainly lacked the punch of an enhanced radiation weapon. However, once the biological agent had established itself on the planetary surface it spread rapidly. We believe it achieved effective continental saturation within two or three days of its deployment, destroying the virus's chain of communication as it spread. It took longer for the viral package within the infected hosts to break down, but it is clear that the BioBombs took their toll. The infection was uncontainable without extreme measures. We assume the virus was as reluctant to cut off a limb to save the body—if I may use a crude metaphor—as ourselves.

It cannot be denied, as some officers pointed out, that the BioBombs are weapons of genocide. The counter-viral package is far more effective, and dangerous, than the tailored viruses released on Earth during the Age of Unrest. It is also clear that *the* virus is unable to counter the infection without doing immense damage to its organisation and communication. In short, unless the virus finds a way to counter the threat, we can expect to eliminate the infection from our worlds in very short order. This will, however, condemn the virus's hosts to death. Our attempts to save hosts under laboratory conditions have had mixed results. We cannot offer any sort of guarantee the host will survive, even in ideal circumstances. The infected hosts on occupied worlds are certain to die, if we release the BioBombs. Frankly, if our backs were not already pressed firmly against the wall, I would urge the PM and the other world leaders not to deploy the BioBombs. We will be killing millions so billions might live.

That said, I am not sanguine about the virus's inability to devise a response. Biological weapons do not survive, obviously, in the vacuum of space. The virus can rearrange its ships along more human lines, relying on communications networks and datanodes to handle matters rather than blending viral matter into the control systems. We expect some degree of early awkwardness, if the virus tries, but it does have access to experts! If nothing else, it can simply copy our designs and integrate human systems—and our electronic servants—into its fleet. I don't know if there would be some improvement in efficiency—the virus does not appear to have problems handling its fleets, despite relying on biological networks—but it would certainly make it harder to get the biobombs onboard. The marines might have to storm the entire ship to wipe out the enemy presence. It would be considerably easier to simply insert nuclear bombs, then detonate them as soon as the marines withdraw.

A more serious possibility is the virus copying the biobombs and deploying biological weapons of its own. It has, so far, been reluctant to commit population-destroying atrocities—although it has shown a frightening lack of concern for civilian casualties—but that may change if it feels truly threatened. As strange as it may seem, the virus may well regard its losses so far as effectively immaterial; a real threat to its very survival may provoke a nastier response. We simply don't know. But, as I said, our backs are against the wall. We have no choice. We must use every weapon at our command to win before we lose everything.

It is my very strong feeling, Susan, that we should launch Operation Lightning Strike as quickly as possible.

Yours,
Paul.

CHAPTER ONE

"DO YOU HEAR THAT?"

Richard Tobias Gurnard turned over, momentarily unsure of where he was. In bed, with Marigold...they were in London, he recalled suddenly, visiting the capital city before they reported back to HMS *Lion*. He sat up, blinking in confusion as the emergency lighting came on. The hotel room, a grotty singleton that was all they could afford, had an air of unreality, as if he was still asleep. He glanced at his wristcom and frowned. It was the middle of the night and yet...

He felt a frisson of fear as he heard the scraping sound in the corridor outside. The hotel was relatively quiet, he'd been assured; the manager had made a point of assuring his guests that the walls were completely soundproofed. It wasn't the sort of place that served breakfast in bed, or did *anything* beyond the bare minimum. The peeling paint on the walls, and the scent in the toilet, suggested the owner simply didn't give a damn. And yet...

"I can hear an alarm," Marigold said. She sat up next to him, arms crossed over her breasts. "Can't you?"

Tobias listened, carefully. The alarm was very faint, if indeed it *was* an alarm. He wished, suddenly, that he'd paid more attention to the emergency procedures displayed on the wall. His CO would have a lot of sharp things to say, if he knew; he'd insisted the gunboat pilots had to learn as much as possible, even if—technically- they didn't have to know anything outside the scope of their duties. Tobias felt his ears prickle as the scraping sound grew louder, wondering—suddenly—if the manager was trying to sneak into the room. It was possible. He'd certainly heard a lot of rumours about cheap hotels in London. And yet…

The wristcom bleeped an alert. Tobias glanced at it and froze. BIOLOGICAL CONTAMINATION DETECTED, LONDON. Sheer horror held him paralysed for a long chilling moment. Biological contamination meant that someone had deployed a biological weapon…no, that the virus had gotten loose in London. He remembered the sensor recordings from the previous mission and shuddered, helplessly. If the entire city had been infected, they were screwed. They had no weapons, nothing beyond their masks. He hadn't thought to bring an emergency kit. It had never crossed his mind he'd need it.

Marigold swung her legs over the side of the bed and stood, hastily donning her clothes. Tobias followed suit, eying the wristcom as if it were a poisonous snake. He wanted to believe it was a false alarm, but…his mind raced, trying to determine what they should do. The room wasn't airtight. It certainly wasn't isolated from the remainder of the hotel. A viral outbreak in the right place—or, rather, the wrong place—would spread through the hotel very quickly. The scraping sound grew louder. Tobias cursed under his breath, wishing—for the first time—that Colin had accompanied them. His former bully turned marine would have been very helpful in a tight spot. But Tobias had never even *thought* of inviting him.

"Someone is right outside," Marigold said, so quietly she was almost subvocalising. "That lock isn't going to hold up for long."

Tobias nodded, curtly. He was brave, as brave as brave could be, behind a computer terminal…or, he admitted to himself, when he put his hands on his gunboat's controls. It was easy, somehow, to pretend he was still playing a game even when he flew the gunboat into combat with a fleet of enemy ships. But in the real world, he knew he was a coward. He'd put on some muscle since joining the navy—Marigold and his CO had convinced him to spend more time in the gym—but he was all too aware he couldn't push *anyone* around. Sweat trickled down his back as he donned his mask. No one, absolutely no one, had a legitimate reason to break into their room in the middle of the night. The manager—or the police—would bang on the door, then wait for the occupants to open it. Whoever was on the far side, they weren't friendly.

The lights went out. Darkness, warm darkness, enveloped them. Tobias sucked in a breath as Marigold activated her wristcom, using it as a makeshift torch. They hadn't thought to bring flashlights either. Tobias hesitated, then picked up a chair as he heard the lock starting to give way. It wasn't an electronic lock. The lock and key were something out of a period drama. Tobias suspected, in hindsight, that it wasn't as charming as he'd thought. The lock could be opened by anyone who had the key, a copy of the key or the tools and skill to simply pick the lock.

He took his mask and pressed it against his face, then held the chair at the ready and waited. In hindsight, he should have brought his pistol. Military personnel were required to be armed at all times, in a world that could shift from peaceful harmony to screaming chaos in the blink of an eye. His CO would probably scold him for not being armed...Tobias prayed, as the lock clicked, that the CO would have the chance. The door opened, so violently Tobias almost dropped the chair. A shadowy figure rushed into the room, running towards Marigold. No, towards the *light*. Tobias panicked, bringing the chair down on top of the figure's head. It crashed to the ground, then kept crawling forward like a giant crab. Tobias stared in disbelief—blood was leaking from a nasty wound to the head— and then brought the chair down again. The figure—the zombie—didn't seem to notice.

Tobias realised his mistake, a second too late. The zombie infection was in complete control of the host's body. Crushing the zombie's head wouldn't kill the host. The host had died when the infection had taken root, then built control structures within the body. He felt a stab of pity as the zombie reared up, hands lashing out towards him. He kicked the zombie as hard as he could—not hard—and then brought the chair down again and again, breaking the zombie's legs. It wasn't enough to do more than slow it down.

"That was the manager," Marigold said. The man had once been jovial—and sleazy enough to make Tobias want to take a shower after shaking his hand. Now, his body was a mangled pulp that was somehow, absurdly, still trying to advance on them. "We have to get out of here."

"Got it," Tobias agreed. He checked that his wallet was still in his pocket—he had a feeling he'd need ID, when they ran into the police or the military—then keyed his wristcom. There was no update, nothing to indicate the authorities were already moving to contain the threat. He hoped—prayed—they were. They should be. The military had plenty of experience deploying troops to counter everything from riots and terrorism to outright viral infections. "Where do we go?

"Out of here," Marigold said. "Quickly."

Tobias nodded as he made his way to the door and peered outside. The corridor was dark and silent. His imagination insisted it was as dark and silent as the grave. He told that part of him to shut the fuck up, then forced himself to think. The hotel wasn't *that* big. If the manager had been infected…it was possible the other guests had *also* been infected. If there were other guests…it was that sort of hotel. Tobias cursed under his breath. He didn't have any night-vision gear, no way to see in the dark. And even if he could, the viral particles were too small to see with the naked eye. He touched his mask, checking—again and again—that it was firmly in place. Breathing deeply might be enough to get him infected. He wouldn't even *know* until it was far too late.

And the moment they see our lights, they'll know we're there, he thought. The virus didn't even need to do *that*. If there was a sufficient concentration of viral matter in the air, the virus would be aware of their presence even if it couldn't infect them. He wanted to go back to the room, barricade the door and wait for the police, but he knew that might just get them killed—or worse. The zombie behind them was—somehow—still alive. *We have to move fast.*

He glanced at Marigold, her face pale and worried, then told himself to be brave as he inched down the corridor. The carpet felt soft under his feet, their passage making no sound at all. He thought, just for a moment, that he could hear men and machines in the distance—helicopter blades clattering against the humid summer air—but the sound didn't seem to be coming any closer. Ice washed down his spine as he remembered the reports from the last mission. The infected world had been hot, very hot. The virus had been able to survive in the open air, to the point that opening one's mask was effectively committing suicide. He found it impossible to believe the virus could last indefinitely in the British weather—it would rain sooner rather than later, if he was any judge—but it could do a lot of damage before it died. Someone who got infected, without ever knowing they were infected, could do one hell of a lot of damage before they were tracked down.

The air grew warmer as they reached the stairwell and looked up and down. Tobias tried to think what to do. In a video game, they would head upwards and find their way to the roof and then jump from rooftop to rooftop until they reached safety. The real world was much less obliging. Colin and his comrades might be able to get out of the trap that way, but Tobias had no illusions about his lack of physical prowess. He'd always been picked last for games…he put the memory out of his mind as he started to make his way down to the ground floor. The stairwell was cramped, narrow enough to make him feel almost claustrophobic. The darkness seemed to reach out and touch him, as if monsters were lurking within the shadows. He shuddered, helplessly, promising himself he'd move to a lunar city or an asteroid settlement as soon as his enlistment was up. His country hadn't treated him very kindly.

Lights flared, outside. Tobias flinched, hefting the chair as if he expected someone to come crashing through the windows. He'd known the windows were there, but…he stared into the darkness. The lights just added to the air of unreality. He forced himself to move faster, reaching the bottom of the stairs as the sound of helicopters grew louder. The building rattled as the aircraft flew over the hotel. It felt as if they were only an inch or two above the rooftops.

Marigold shined the makeshift torch ahead of them, then froze. A body was lying on the ground, a child…Tobias stumbled backwards, swallowing desperately to keep from throwing up inside the mask. The body was a shifting mass of…he recoiled, unwilling to look at the figure. It had to have been a child, but the body was so badly warped that he couldn't tell if it had been male or female. The darkness swallowed the body as they picked up speed, hurrying towards the door. It was closed and locked. Tobias gritted his teeth, suddenly *very* sure there was something nasty right behind them, and hit the door as hard as he could. The lock shattered. Tobias blinked, then stumbled outside. Blinding lights struck them a second later, so bright his eyes hurt even after he squeezed them tightly shut. Marigold whimpered.

"DO NOT MOVE," a voice bellowed. "DO NOT MOVE!"

Tobias froze. His eyes were still closed, but he could hear men running towards them. The light dimmed suddenly. He risked opening his eyes and saw three men in heavy-duty HAZMAT suits. Their eyes were hidden behind their masks. He shuddered, suddenly all too aware that the troops could be infected themselves. And yet…he couldn't move. He could see more troops on the other side of the road, guns pointed directly at Tobias and Marigold. He wanted to scream at them, to insist they were pointing their guns at friends, but he couldn't say a word. The troops didn't know any better. Tobias *himself* didn't know any better. The virus might have already gotten its hooks in them.

He offered no resistance as they were shackled, then pushed towards a large open-topped lorry. The troops pressed samplers against their necks, testing their blood for any traces of infection. They relaxed, slightly, when the tests came back negative. Tobias wanted to suggest they be unshackled, but the words caught in his mouth. A handful of other people were already in the lorry, their arms and legs shackled to metal railings. They looked as shell-shocked as Tobias himself. The troops half-pushed, half-lifted him into the lorry and shackled him beside the others. Marigold followed a second later. Tobias gritted his teeth as the UV lights grew stronger. In theory, if one of them were infected, the infection wouldn't spread to the rest. In theory...

The virus managed to get a foothold in the city, he thought, numbly. A pair of helicopters flew overhead, spotlights stabbing down at the ground. *What else has it done?*

The lorry lurched into life. Tobias gritted his teeth as the vehicle rumbled down the eerie street. The sky was still dark, but the spotlights lit up the community with a blinding light that cast out the shadows. There were hundreds—perhaps thousands—of troops on the streets, all wearing masks if they weren't wearing HAZMAT gear. A row of AFVs sat beside a barricade, one clearly thrown up in a hurry. Tobias shivered. He'd walked past the barricade only a few short hours ago, back when the world had made sense. The barricade hadn't even been *there*. London had shifted from an old city, repaired and rebuilt after the Troubles and the Bombardment, into a Lovecraftian nightmare, a horror from the days biological weapons had been deployed by terrorists and rogue states alike. He'd heard the stories—he'd studied the official version in history class and the unofficial version on the dark web—but he'd never really understood the reality. It had been nothing more than *history* to him, until now. He shuddered, again and again, as they drove past more troops. They looked ready for anything. Tobias devoutly hoped that was true.

"STAY IN YOUR HOMES." A police car drove past, blue lights flashing as the message was repeated time and time again. The racket was so loud Tobias was morbidly certain no one, absolutely no one, was still asleep. They'd be having nightmares long after the night was over. "STAY IN YOUR HOMES. STAY OFF THE STREETS. IF YOU FEEL UNWELL, CALL US IMMEDIATELY..."

"No one will listen," an older man predicted. He looked to be the sort of person Tobias had disliked once upon a time, a schoolyard bully grown up into a manager bully. His walrus moustache wriggled as he spoke. "They'll all be trying to get out before the infection gets them."

Tobias said nothing, but he feared the older man was right. The infection had clearly gotten its hooks into the district. He'd heard rumours about emergency plans, from the careful evacuation and sterilization of the infected area to its complete destruction by nuclear weapons. Tobias doubted that any British Government would authorise the use of nuclear weapons on British cities, but the government might be desperate. The Prime Minister was in a precarious position. Tobias didn't follow politics and even *he* knew that. Decisive action against the virus, at the cost of hundreds of innocent lives, would either boost the man's career into the stratosphere or utterly destroy it. In this day and age, it was hard to tell which.

The vehicle rattled to a halt. Tobias watched, grimly, as the soldiers unhooked the rear of the lorry and started dragging the prisoners out. He'd been through mil-grade decontamination procedures before, when there hadn't been any real threat. The process had been strict, but not *that* strict. This time, they could take nothing for granted. Tobias doubted they'd see their clothes again, after they went through decontamination. It was rather more likely that everything they wore—and carried—would be incinerated. The military wouldn't take chances, not now.

"I'm not infected," the older man protested, as he was half-carried out of the lorry. "I'm not infected!"

"Be quiet," a soldier growled.

"Do you know who I am?" The older man glared at the soldier, trying to stand upright in shackles. It would have been comical if it hadn't been so serious. "I'm the managing director of Drills Incorporated and…"

"I said, be quiet," the soldier repeated. He hefted his shockrod menacingly. "You'll be checked as quickly as possible and released as soon as we're sure you're uninfected."

Tobias kept his thoughts to himself as the older man quietened. He wanted to protest, but he understood. The soldiers *really* couldn't take anything for granted. For all they knew, the entire lorry-load of prisoners was infected. They had to be careful, very careful. And if that meant treating civilians—as well as Tobias and Marigold—like dangerous terrorists…

They don't have a choice, Tobias thought, glumly. *They don't have any way to be sure we're not infected. Nor do we.*

CHAPTER TWO

"THEY'RE SAYING IT'S THE END OF DAYS."

Admiral Lady Susan Onarina kept her face expressionless as the official car made its way through a military checkpoint before turning onto Whitehall and heading towards Number Ten Downing Street. The driver, who'd been a cabbie before being recalled to the colours in the wake of the latest string of disasters, had kept up a cheerfully irrelevant conversation that—under other circumstances—would have charmed her. Some of her relatives were cabbies, men and women who specialised in putting their passengers at ease as they drove through the winding streets of the capital city. But now, with a viral infection blighting London itself, she found it hard to listen. The world had just shifted on its axis. Again. As a younger officer, she'd wondered why her superiors had been slow to adapt to a whole new world; now, older and wiser, she thought she understood. Everything she'd known before the war had begun was now obsolete.

The car passed through the gates and came to a halt in front of Ten Downing Street. A uniformed policeman hurried to open the door for her, allowing Susan to bid the cabbie goodbye and clamber onto the street. Her skin prickled, a grim reminder that she was under close observation. She might be a Peer of the Realm, and a Lady of the Garter, but she couldn't be trusted completely. No one could, not when the virus could turn a loyal officer into an unwitting traitor overnight. It rankled, even though she understood. She'd worked long and hard to overcome the stigma of her birth, skin colour and everything else that had threatened to bar her from command rank. To be distrusted so openly…

It happens to everyone, she thought, as the doorman welcomed her into the building. A pair of guards, just inside the entrance, pressed a sampler against her neck to check her blood. It hurt, more than she'd expected. They'd improved upon the design. She made a face as she passed through a set of sealed doors, into the next chamber. *They've been tightening the defences ever since they discovered the virus could infect the brain—and the brain alone.*

"Admiral," Simon Portage said. The PM's aide nodded politely. "He's waiting for you."

"Thank you," Susan said. She knew she was running late, although the PM was unlikely to make something of it. She'd half-expected the meeting to be cancelled. The PM had ordered COBRA convened, according to the BBC; he'd be expected to chair the meeting personally, even though there was little he could do. He'd given the right orders and all he could reasonably do now was wait. "Just take me straight through."

She glanced at her reflection in the mirror as they climbed up the stairs and walked through two more checkpoints. Her skin was as dark as ever, her hair threatening to turn grey under the weight of the world. She wasn't the young woman she'd been, back when the hardest task she'd faced had been to break into a world dominated by the Old Boys Network and riven with suspicion and fear of anyone who couldn't trace their bloodline back to the Norman Conquest. One didn't have to be aristocratic, perish the thought, but one had to be British. The hypocrisy had irked her, once upon a time. The Royal Family was *German* in origin, something that had been more than a little embarrassing during the world wars. Now, she would have sold her soul to go back to those days. The entire world wasn't at risk of a fate worse than death.

The PM's office had always struck her as surprisingly small, for all its importance. It was decorated in a style that had been gone out of fashion long before the Troubles, although the original owners would have been alternatively baffled and horrified by the terminal resting on the heavy wooden desk and the security screens worked into the walls and windows. There was something unassuming about the entire building—it was hard, sometimes, to believe that it was the heart of a Great Power—but she had to admit it appealed to her. It kept its occupants humble.

Prime Minister Arthur Harrison rose to greet her. He was a middle-aged man, going prematurely grey under the stresses of his office. Susan disliked politics, but—in her post—she had no choice but to follow them. She knew Harrison's position was weaker than it seemed, despite the War Cabinet and the Government of National Unity. The viral outbreak in London had made the government look like fools, even though it had been swiftly contained. If matters didn't get any better, it was quite possible the government would fracture as the opposition parties struggled to avoid a share of the blame. Susan understood the system—she appreciated that it worked better than some foreign systems—but she wasn't blind to its weaknesses. No one really wanted to take collective responsibility—otherwise known as sharing the blame—for anything.

"Susan," Harrison said. He shook her hand, firmly. "Thank you for coming."

"Thank you for seeing me," Susan replied. "I'm sorry to be the bearer of bad tidings."

The PM grimaced. "Please, take a seat," he said, indicating the armchairs in the corner. "We have much to discuss."

Susan sat and composed herself as Harrison ordered tea. His accent was so strongly aristocratic that, once upon a time, it would have made her clench her teeth. Even now, it grated. She knew from experience that not *all* aristocrats were worthless pimples on the body politic—technically, she was an aristocrat herself—but it was hard to shake the old prejudices. No doubt they felt the same way about her. She told herself, firmly, that it was unfair to blame them for their ancestors. She'd been judged by hers often enough to know how profoundly unfair it was.

A maid appeared with a tea tray, which she placed on a small table next to the armchairs and withdrew as silently as she'd come. Harrison sat, his fingers lingering on the teapot as he counted the seconds. Susan watched, feeling torn between amusement and grim understanding. She'd grown up in a world of instant tea and coffee, but…she had to admit there was something about the ritual that was almost soothing. The PM was using the pause to gather his thoughts, without seeming rude. She smiled inwardly and waited as he poured the tea, then held out the biscuit tray. He needed the pause. If she was any judge, the entire world was demanding answers. And there were none to be had.

Not yet, she told herself. The viral package had spread quickly, too quickly. That bothered her. The virus presumably understood its cellular structure a great deal better than the human xenospecialists. If it had found a way to survive England's weather, and spread right across the globe, the war was within shouting distance of being lost. *If Lightning Strike fails, we may have to start preparing for a full-scale evacuation of Earth.*

She glanced at her teacup. It wasn't going to happen. There was no way they could evacuate an entire planet. The combined carrying capacity of every starship in human service wouldn't even scratch the surface. Susan had seen some of the emergency plans, the ones drawn up to meet a threat no one had ever really believed existed. Their most optimistic estimates suggested that only a small percentage of the planet's population could be saved.

The PM took a sip of his tea, then cleared his throat. "We don't have much time, as I'm sure you're aware," he said. "Can we move to the point?"

Susan nodded, concealing her relief. She was well aware of the urgency, but she was also aware that most politicians preferred not to come straight to the point. There were political implications to everything, even something as simple as ordering dinner. The pettiness of the political mind, particularly a mind belonging to someone who would never be offered a seat on the cabinet or party leadership committee, could never be overstated. And *this* was something with *real* political implications. If the PM made the wrong call, or even the right call if things went wrong, it would blow up in his face and destroy his career.

If there's anyone left to land the fatal blow, Susan mused. British political history was full of elder statesmen who'd told serving prime ministers that it was time for them to go—sometimes overtly, sometimes not—but that rather depended on parliament surviving long enough to do it. *We could lose the war overnight if the operation goes badly wrong.*

"Yes, Prime Minister," she said. She straightened, putting her cup to one side so she could rest her hands in her lap. "Operation Thunder Child was a moderate success. The biobombs were effective, although not as effective as we had hoped. Given the nature of the viral command and control system, the virus would be faced with a serious problem if the counter-virus got a solid foothold. It would either have to shatter the command network itself, thus weakening its ability to coordinate operations, or risk losing everything to the counter-virus."

"It would have to cut off its nose to spite its face," the PM said, quietly.

"More like cut off its own arm to keep the infection from spreading," Susan said. She'd read the reports from the bioweapon research labs. A handful of researchers had faced the blunt choice between mutilating themselves or being infected and sentenced to almost certain death. The thought was enough to make her shudder. The idea of cutting off her own arm...she knew she was no coward, but she honestly wasn't sure she could do it. She wouldn't *know* until it was too late. "The virus doesn't think the way we do, Prime Minister, but we find it hard to believe that mutilating itself wouldn't cause some qualms."

The Prime Minister nodded, slowly. "Is it even intelligent, as we understand the term?"

"We don't know," Susan said. "It's certainly capable of reading memories from infected hosts and using them against us. That suggests a certain intelligence, but it hasn't made any move to open communications or even demand a surrender. Opinion is divided on why it hasn't tried to come to terms with us. One group thinks the virus knows we wouldn't surrender,

15

another thinks we just haven't hurt it badly enough to force it to come to the negotiations table."

She grimaced. She'd played plenty of computer games, as a schoolgirl, where the player just couldn't win until she'd hunted down and destroyed the last of the AI-controlled units. The battle had been fought and won, but the AI had refused to admit defeat. It hadn't had a hope of winning and yet it had prolonged the battle for hours, forcing her to search the entire level for the last remaining enemy unit. Human opponents were far easier to defeat. They tended to accept that a battle had been lost and surrender, then insist on restarting the game. The virus didn't seem to be capable of admitting defeat either. It had certainly never made any attempt to surrender.

"It isn't as if it could offer reasonable terms," the PM said. He sipped his tea, thoughtfully. "I assume you want to proceed with Lightning Strike."

"Yes, Prime Minister," Susan said. "When the operation was first discussed, it was one of a multitude of options for later consideration. There was no sense that it was any more urgent than any of the other possible operations. Now, however, things have changed. Long-range survey missions have revealed that the virus…"

"I've been briefed," the PM said, curtly. "The Admiralty was divided on the merits of the operation."

"It was a risky concept, when it was first discussed," Susan said. "Now, it may be our only hope."

The Prime Minister said nothing for a long moment. Susan understood. The buck stopped with him, him and the war cabinet and GATO. The Global Alliance Treaty Organisation would have the final call, on paper, but everyone knew that the PM could have said no—and refused to allow British forces to take part—if he'd wished. There would be enough blame to go around, Susan reflected, if there was anyone left to point the finger. Operation Lightning Strike promised either total victory... or defeat. There was no middle ground.

"You are sure about the survey reports?" The PM sounded quietly desperate. "And about the need for such an immense commitment?"

"Yes, Prime Minister," Susan said. "In theory, we could carry out phase one with only a squadron of warships. We could handle it ourselves. In practice, we'd need a major deployment if we wanted to move straight to phase two. The window of opportunity will not remain open for long."

"If you manage to open it at all," the PM pointed out. "The virus must be aware of the dangers."

Susan felt a hot flash of irritation, which she hastily suppressed. The red teams at the Admiralty had been working overtime, trying to list all the ways Lightning Strike I and II could go horrifically wrong. It was their job, and she didn't fault them for drawing up contingency plans, but...she resisted the urge to shake her head. In her experience, there was a difference between considering the worst that could happen and allowing oneself to be hypnotised by it. There were always risks to everything, including doing nothing. The virus wasn't a normal opponent. There was no hope of peace.

And if only one of us can survive, she thought sourly, *I will do everything in my power to ensure it's us.*

"We don't know for sure," she admitted. "Prime Minister, carrying out phase one will win us some time, even if we cannot move directly to phase two. And we are desperately short of time."

The PM nodded, curtly. He'd have to make the calls himself. There were some things that simply couldn't be left to the Foreign Office mandarins. They had their uses, but they also had a tendency to soften diplomatic messages until they no longer carried their original urgency. Susan had studied history. A great many problems might have been avoided if ultimatums hadn't been watered down by the diplomats. She smiled at the thought. It was equally possible the problems might have been made a great deal worse. Very few governments could afford to back down at gunpoint, for fear it would give their opponents ideas.

They should understand what's at stake, she thought. The Great Powers often disliked each other, but they'd learnt the hard way that they had to work together. Humanity was surrounded by alien races, some of them extremely hostile. The Great Powers had to hang together or hang separately. There was no choice. *London wasn't the only city that suffered a biological attack.*

"If the GATO powers agree to back the plan, I'm sure the war cabinet will also agree," the Prime Minister said. "However, it may take some time to organise the deployment."

"Yes, Prime Minister," Susan said. "Time is not on our side. If the virus manages to deploy its forces before we mount the operation, we'll be staring down the barrel of a gun."

"I know," the Prime Minister said. "But if the operation fails, or if it even works a little *too* well, we'll be cut off from our ships. And that would be disastrous, too."

Susan nodded. "We have contingency plans, but something must be left to chance."

"And no warship can do very wrong that fires on the enemy," the Prime Minister misquoted, dryly. He'd have studied Nelson in school, just like Susan herself. The post-Troubles government had no time for suggestions that Nelson, a great naval hero, had been a cad, a bounder, an adulterer and father of an illegitimate child. "I dislike relying on luck. It has a habit of being unreliable."

He put his cup on the tray, signalling the interview was over. "I'll speak to the world leaders," he said. "For now, you are authorised to begin planning for the deployment on the assumption they'll agree. If they don't… you can proceed with phase one."

"There'd be no way we can move to phase two," Susan warned. "Not alone. Not unless we commit the entire navy to the mission."

"Which isn't going to happen," the PM said. "There's no way we could authorise such a deployment."

"No, Prime Minister," Susan agreed. "However, without phase two…"

The PM stood. "I understand the risks," he said, as Susan stood too. "I'll do everything in my power to convince the rest of the world to join us. If not…we can at least win some time."

"But not enough," Susan said. "It won't take the virus long to rebuild."

"It really is terrifyingly efficient," the PM said. "If only *we* had such budgets…"

Susan nodded as the PM's aide materialised at her shoulder, ready to show her out. The virus had no need, as far as anyone could tell, to provide even a basic standard of living to its hosts. It didn't even seem to *care* about them. Rotting bodies didn't matter, once the virus had built its control structures within the walking corpses. And that meant it could devote everything to making war. Susan shuddered as she was escorted back to her car. The virus didn't *need* a bigger industrial base than the human race. It just had to commit it all to war production.

She took a breath as she stepped into the warm summer air. The air stank faintly of disinfectant, a grim reminder that London had been scarred by the virus. And that nowhere was truly safe…

The driver had been right, she decided as she climbed into the car. It *was* the end of days.

CHAPTER THREE

"THEY'RE SAYING THAT ALL OF LONDON IS GONE," some dimwit said. "And that it's just a matter of time before the virus gets here."

Captain the Honourable Lord Thomas Hammond gritted his teeth, trying to remember the dimwit's *name*. The man was a few years older than him, just old enough to ensure Thomas hadn't had the pleasure of knowing him at school or university, but still…if he'd been invited to the party, Thomas should know him. Or maybe not. It had been Lady Charlotte Hammond, Thomas's wife, who'd put the entire party together on short notice. She'd done everything, from hiring the servants to dispatching invitations to everyone who was anyone in the aristocracy. Thomas was sure she'd even sent invitations to aristocrats who physically *couldn't* attend. They might have a good excuse—military service was practically compulsory, for aristocrats and commoners alike—but Thomas was damn sure they'd *remember* not being invited. It was the kind of social *faux pas* that could be relied upon to spark an entire string of demented feuds.

It was a great deal simpler when we settled such matters with swords, he thought. The idea of cutting the dimwit's head off was growing more and more attractive by the second. *It probably helped cut down on insults and suchlike, too.*

He scowled, inwardly, as the man went on and on, talking endlessly about a subject he knew nothing about. The dimwit didn't know the slightest thing about the virus, let alone how it spread. The party itself would have been cancelled at short notice, if the virus had blanketed the entire country. Thomas—and everyone else—would have been infected. The virus didn't care for parties or anything, really, beyond spreading as far as it could. It certainly wouldn't bother to uphold the society Thomas had sworn to defend.

"The government should be telling us more," the dimwit continued. "We *run* the country."

Thomas sighed, inwardly. He had to admit the lack of information was troubling—the BBC's broadcasts had been long on exhortations to remain calm and short on actual data—but he was all too aware that unfriendly ears might be listening. No one was entirely sure of just how much the virus understood, when it intercepted human transmissions, but there was no point in taking chances. Better to assume that everything broadcast in the clear was intercepted and relayed to the alien homeworld than wind up being surprised by the virus knowing something it shouldn't.

Not that there was much more on the military channels, he mused. He'd tried to access the military datanet as soon as he'd heard the news, and he'd checked back throughout the day, but his clearance wasn't high enough to get more than the very basics. Army personnel had been recalled to their garrisons, naval personnel were expected to sit on their arses and do nothing. *That doesn't bode well for the future.*

He allowed his eyes to wander over the crowd as the dimwit wittered on and on. His lips thinned in disapproval as he spotted a handful of army officers, all of whom should be elsewhere. They were probably useless bean-counters, rather than officers who led men into battle, but still...a good organiser would probably be very helpful in London. Beyond them, there was the usual mixture of older women, debs and a smattering of young men intent on courting the girls. There were fewer of *them* than Thomas had expected. The war had taken many young men from their homes and thrown them into the storm...

A middle-aged woman caught his eye. Thomas turned from the dimwit and marched towards her. Charlotte would make him pay for that later, he was sure, but he found it hard to care. A few more moments of listening to the babble would have him contemplating homicide…or, perhaps, retreating to his rooms far too early in the evening. Charlotte wouldn't be happy about that either. Leaving the party wasn't a harmless little prank like spiking the drinks. It would be a sign he simply didn't care about the guests.

And I don't, Thomas thought, crossly. He had no objection to the real work that came with his title, what little he had to do personally. Charlotte ran the estate while he was on active duty and did it very well. The parties, on the other hand, were just boring. Thomas would almost sooner have been a midshipman again. At least he'd done something useful with his time. *Does anything that happens at this party truly matter?*

"My Lord," Lady Bracknell said. She had a large handbag under one arm, something that had always amused Thomas more than he could say. "I trust you're having a pleasant evening?"

"It has its moments," Thomas said. He spotted a waitress carrying a tray of drinks across the room and sighed, inwardly. Getting thoroughly drunk would make the evening go quicker, but there would be hell to pay afterwards. "And yourself?"

"I must say you always put on the best parties," Lady Bracknell said. "My husband was quite impressed."

"I'm glad to hear that," Thomas lied. He was fairly sure she was lying, too. Lord Bracknell lived for hunting and nothing else, as far as he could tell. He wouldn't enjoy the party any more than Thomas did. "And how is your son coping with his new career?"

"He says his captain is a very understanding man," Lady Bracknell said. "He's already made First Middy."

"Impressive," Thomas said. Lady Bracknell's son wasn't *that* senior, was he? It was unlikely he had enough time in grade to outrank the rest of the middies. A toadying captain, promoting a well-connected young man above the rest? Or was he doing Lady Bracknell's son a disservice? It was hard to believe, sometimes, that his own little girls were adults in their own right. Part of him would always think of them as children. "I'm sure that speaks well of him."

"I'm glad you think so," Lady Bracknell said. She put a hand on his arm, steering him into a corner. "I wanted to discuss a possible match between my son and your daughter."

Thomas called on all his years of naval service to keep his face carefully blank. "I think that's something best discussed with my daughter in person," he said. Charlotte would have mentioned it, wouldn't she, if someone had been sniffing around for a marriage alliance. He'd known it was coming, but it was still a shock. "And perhaps in a more private time."

"He's due to get a week's leave, next month," Lady Bracknell said. "He could meet your daughter…"

Thomas had to smile. "*Which* daughter?"

"It does not matter to us," Lady Bracknell said. Thomas couldn't tell if she remembered either of his daughters or not. "We're interested in a marriage alliance."

"I shall discuss it with my wife and daughters," Thomas said, stiffly. "Have you discussed it with your son?"

Lady Bracknell looked blank. Thomas sighed inwardly, feeling a stab of sympathy for the young man. It had been a long time since he'd met the brat, long enough to recall him as a teenager rather than a grown adult. He made a mental note to discuss the matter with his daughters *first*, before his wife got wind of the affair. Their match had worked out well, he supposed, but they'd been lucky. He cared for her. He wasn't sure, at times, if he loved her. But then, marriages amongst the aristocracy weren't meant to be about *love*.

She probably hasn't even told him about her plans, he thought. *She's deciding his future for him, leaving him in the dark as long as possible.*

"We'll discuss the matter later," he said, hoping she'd drop it and knowing she wouldn't. Not yet, perhaps not ever. Elizabeth and Lucille were heirs to one of the largest fortunes in England. Elizabeth would inherit the estate itself—that was entailed, ensuring it couldn't be broken into smaller chunks—but Lucille would hardly be destitute. "And then we'll be in touch."

His stomach churned as Lady Bracknell strode away, every inch the matriarch. Thomas wondered, idly, if she'd discussed the matter with her *husband*, let alone her son. It was very typical for social matrons to march ahead, daring anyone to be so unbearably rude as to say no. Thomas had no patience for them and yet…he *would* have to ensure his girls married well. His lips quirked. If he recommended a young man to his daughters, either of his daughters, it would probably prejudice them against him. He made a mental note to check the young man's record. His captain might not write down anything too dreadful—Lady Bracknell and her clan had a long reach—but Thomas was quite experienced at reading between the lines. If nothing else, he could take the man out for a drink and ask him questions completely off the record. He might get some honest answers if the captain thought he could speak freely.

The dreadful evening wore on. Thomas forced himself to be polite to a couple of retired admirals, both of whom had served their time during the First Interstellar War and refused to believe that naval combat had moved on. One of them was smart enough to accept that Thomas knew what he was doing, if only because he'd returned alive; the other seemed to think Thomas had escaped certain death by sheer damned luck. Thomas bit his lip to keep from telling them precisely what he thought of their feelings, all too aware his wife was watching him. She'd put a lot of effort into the evening.

Damn it, Thomas thought. He glanced at his wristcom, wishing the Admiralty would recall him. Or something. He'd been told he had to report back to Nelson Base in two days, but…he would almost have welcomed an alien attack. Not, he supposed, that he would have been able to get back to his ship. There simply wouldn't be time. Commander Donker, his XO, would have to take command. *We wouldn't even have time to call off the party.*

He forced himself to keep moving. A pair of young debs wittered to him about nothing in particular, suggesting they'd gone to a finishing school that specialised in turning a young lady's head into mush. Thomas wasn't sure if they were hitting on him or just trying to make pointless conversation. There was no sign of a chaperone. The dresses they wore, all too revealing, suggested they'd come alone. An older man babbled endlessly about the horses, while drinking glass after glass of expensive wine. Thomas tried to hide his disgust. The intelligent aristocrats, the ones with working brains, were serving their country. The ones who couldn't count past ten without taking off their socks—and thought that taking down their pants, instead, was the height of humour—were infesting his estate. He wanted them all gone.

Charlotte joined him as the butler called the crowd in for dinner. Thomas glanced at her, wondering—again—why she cared. She'd gone to some trouble to dress up, donning a long pink outfit that gave the impression of being translucent without revealing anything and tying up her hair into buns that made her look mature and yet strikingly young. He supposed it meant something to her, but what? It wasn't as if she was a prisoner on the estate. She *ran* the place. She could take a trip to London any time she liked…

"You're seated next to Lord Aleman," Charlotte said, pitching her voice so low Thomas could barely hear her over the babble. "Try and keep him onside."

Thomas sighed. Lord Aleman wasn't as bad as the dimwit—he was currently flirting with one of the debs, who looked as if she wanted to gut him with her bare hands—but he wasn't Thomas's idea of a good dinner companion. He caught sight of Captain Campbell, looking completely out of place, and winced inwardly. The lucky bastard didn't have to worry about maintaining an estate. Or pretending to like someone he wanted to strangle.

"I'll try," he said.

"Lord Aleman has the Prime Minister's ear," Charlotte added. "We don't want him saying the wrong things, do we?"

"No," Thomas said. "I suppose we don't."

• • •

If the general public knew about this, Captain Mitch Campbell thought sourly, *they'd drag the entire aristocracy to the guillotines and behead them.*

He tried to keep his face under tight control as he took his seat—at the lower table, naturally—and looked around the giant hall. There was so much wealth and power concentrated in a single room that it was a marvel it didn't go supercritical and explode, or that he hadn't been unceremoniously ejected for being a very blatant commoner. His dress uniform itched like mad—whoever had designed the outfit had been a sadist—and he had every right to wear it, but the mere act of wearing an untailored uniform was clear proof he wasn't rich enough to afford a private tailor. The debs—young women entering their seasons, now they were old enough to marry—might be willing to flirt with him in private, but not in public. And hardly anyone else was interested in him at all.

Mitch felt his heart sink still further as the servants brought dinner into the hall and started to serve the first course. There was so much food…a commoner family on rations wouldn't get anything *like* as much. It had been a long time since anyone had actually starved in Britain—ration bars were free, on the grounds no one would actually pay for them—but they tasted of cardboard, when they tasted of anything at all. He tried not to show his envy as he saw the roast haunches of meat, shining platters of vegetables and giant tureens of gravy. He hadn't eaten so well since…since ever. The bright young things all around him had no idea how lucky they were. London was infected, under quarantine, and the lords and masters of the universe didn't give a damn.

He gritted his teeth as he saw Captain Hammond, chatting happily with an older man in a fancy suit. Captain Hammond wasn't a bad officer, but he was conservative to a fault. Mitch was *sure* they could have done more damage to the enemy, if they'd continued the fight. But Hammond had wanted to quit while they were ahead…Mitch snorted in disgust. He should never have accepted the invitation. He wasn't even sure why it had been made. God knew Captain Hammond was probably sick of him, too.

The dreadful evening continued as course after course was served. Mitch heard a middle-aged man braying like a bull, the girl beside him looking more and more embarrassed until she *accidentally* knocked her wineglass into his lap. Mitch had the feeling it might be worth getting to know her, but she left in a hurry as the servants helped the man sort himself out. He couldn't help feeling sorry for them. It couldn't be easy to work in an aristocratic household. He knew *he* would have gone mad—or gotten himself arrested—very quickly.

He breathed a sigh of relief as the dinner finally came to an end and the guests started flowing into the dance hall or spilling out onto the lawn. The staff had set up dozens of tiny lights, turning the garden into a maze that would have been romantic under other circumstances. It was impossible to believe they'd put so much effort into a party. Mitch had arranged gatherings and staff meetings, when he'd been a junior officer, and they'd been far simpler. It helped, he supposed, that everyone had been in the navy. They'd known how to put their egos aside and work together for the greater good.

Mitch stood and headed up the stairs, back to the balcony. He knew he should join the dancing, but what was the point? No one would notice his absence. He didn't belong on the estate. His presence was a reminder that there was a world beyond the distant walls, a world where people without connections and estates and limitless bank accounts struggled for survival. Not for the first time, Mitch considered applying to emigrate to Britannia or another colony world. There was a great deal more social mobility on a world that was desperately short on settlers.

He reached the top of the stairs and peered into the darkness. There were no lanterns on *this* side of the estate. The darkness seemed almost a living thing. He looked up at the stars overhead, wondering just how many of them were space stations and orbital industrial nodes and everything else that kept human society going. *Unicorn* was up there somewhere, too small to be seen with the naked eye. He felt a twinge of guilt. He'd desperately needed leave, but...

"You left early," a feminine voice said. "Don't want to dance?"

"No," Mitch said. He turned to see Charlotte Hammond standing by the door. "I don't think anyone wants to dance with me."

28

"You might be surprised," Charlotte said. It was hard to make out her expression in the gloom. "You're a legitimate war hero."

"Yes," Mitch agreed. "And that and five pounds will buy me a cup of tea."

Charlotte laughed, but there was a hint of nervousness in the sound. "You don't like the party?"

Mitch decided to be honest. "No," he said. "I don't know anyone here."

"It's a good chance to make connections," Charlotte said. She stepped closer. He was suddenly aware, very aware, of her body. The dress concealed her bare skin while leaving little to the imagination. "You never know who you might meet here."

"I'm no good at making connections," Mitch said. "It feels too much like kissing ass."

Charlotte giggled. "That's true," she said. "But that's not why I invited you."

And she leaned forward and kissed him. Hard.

CHAPTER FOUR

MITCH AWOKE, SUDDENLY.

He was in his room, the giant suite that wouldn't have shamed an admiral, and he wasn't alone. Someone was sleeping in the bed next to him, snoring loudly...he sat up and saw dark hair spilling over the pillow. A flash of alarm ran through him. What the hell had he done? Had he lured one of the debs into bed? Or...he froze, torn between hope and fear, as he remembered the previous night. Charlotte had seduced him. No, she'd kissed him and he'd kissed her back and...they'd wound up in bed together. He tried to tell himself that it was still evening, that he'd only slept for a few moments, but the light streaming through the windows was a grim reminder that it was morning. The following morning. They were going to be caught at any second...

Panic washed through him, followed by grim amusement. Duelling wasn't legal. Not *really*. He'd heard stories, but...he shook his head. He'd bet his life—he *was* betting his life—that he could outdraw and outshoot Captain Hammond. Mitch had spent his entire career on small ships, where every-one—even the captain—had to get his hands dirty. He'd kept up with his shooting whenever he'd had the chance, while Captain Hammond had Royal Marines to do the dirty work for him. Mitch could win a duel...he cursed under his breath as more and more memories surfaced. Captain Hammond could *really* screw with his career. The Admiralty would not be amused.

Fucking a captain's wife is bound to be against some kind of regulation, Mitch thought, with a flicker of humour. A wife who cheated on her husband when he was away on military service would be lucky if she was just sent to Coventry. It was socially unacceptable, even if the husband was an abusive piece of shit. *I'm sure they can come up with something if they try.*

He stared down at Charlotte. She wasn't his usual type. She was easily ten years older than him, perhaps more; her body was pleasantly plump, with a hint she might become genuinely obese if she didn't take care of herself. She'd had two children, he recalled, both in their late teens. And yet...the memories mocked him. How many times had they done it? Three? Four? It was hard to believe she was *that* much of a tiger between the sheets, but the memories didn't lie. He'd heard stories about older women, when he'd been a teenager. He'd always assumed they'd been made up, just like every other locker room story. He wasn't so sure now. Charlotte hadn't played coy and waited for him to make the first move. She'd been the one who'd kissed him. It had been one hell of a turn-on.

Charlotte opened her eyes and smiled. "Good morning."

Mitch glanced at the clock. "It's seven," he said, as she sat upright. Her breasts bobbled in front of his eyes. It was hard to raise his gaze to meet hers. "Shouldn't you...?"

His words caught in his throat. Charlotte had been with him all night. Her husband was in the same goddamned house! Surely, he'd have noticed something. Captain Hammond had a lack of imagination, Mitch knew from their disagreements, but surely he wouldn't have missed his wife not coming to bed. And what about the guests? Mitch couldn't believe Charlotte had chased them all out, before coming to him. The party had been planned to last into the wee small hours. For all he knew, the guests might be still downstairs. A couple had been drunk enough to pass out well before the party came to an end.

"Not really," Charlotte said. Her eyes moved to his crotch. "Thomas and I don't sleep together."

Mitch stared at her, unsure what he'd gotten himself into in every sense of the word. Charlotte was naked, gloriously naked. She wasn't making any attempt to cover herself. Mitch had spent his entire adult life in the navy, where privacy was non-existent, but still…he'd never known a girl who'd been so comfortable naked. It wasn't as if they'd spent weeks or months or years together. His relationships rarely lasted so long. It had bothered him, sometimes, that he didn't have a permanent girl back home. And yet…he felt cold at the thought. *Unicorn* was tiny, compared to a fleet carrier or battleship. A handful of missiles would be more than enough to blow her into dust.

"You don't?" Mitch's voice seemed strange, even to him. "You don't… not at all?"

Charlotte stood, knelt by the side of the bed and took him into her mouth. Mitch stiffened, automatically, as her tongue started provoking him. It was suddenly very hard to think straight, let alone stand, bend her over the bed and enter her from the rear. It crossed his mind to wonder, a second too late, if one of the servants would hear them. Charlotte seemed completely abandoned, lost in pleasure. Mitch gave himself up to her, knowing—even as he lost control—that he was making a mistake. But he'd always known his life was going to be short.

Afterwards, they stood on wobbly legs and headed into the shower. Mitch was used to communal showers, but he still felt odd showering with her. Charlotte looked stunning as water ran down her body, washing away all traces of their lovemaking…Mitch tried to force himself to relax, praying to God she knew what she was doing. Her husband might come looking for her at any moment, if it crossed his mind to wonder where the hell she was. It was weird to think of a husband not sharing his bed with his wife. Mitch couldn't understand it. He'd always liked spending time with his girlfriends.

"I…" He stopped suddenly, unsure how he should address her. He'd just been inside her! "I…how do you know Captain Hammond won't find us?"

Charlotte shrugged. "We always sleep in, after a party," she said. "Thomas has no engagements today. He can spend the entire morning in bed, if he likes. The maids will bring him coffee, and breakfast, when he wakes. We're not due to have lunch until one."

"After which we're expected to head back to London," Mitch said. He wondered, suddenly, if the plans had changed. It wouldn't be the first time the military bureaucracy had mindlessly tried to follow an outdated plan. "Will you…why?"

Charlotte looked at him. Mitch reminded himself, sharply, that she was a very intelligent woman. She ran the estate, when her husband was on active service. The party had probably been harder to arrange than he'd thought, given how many high-ranking or well-connected people had attended. And…he wondered, suddenly, how many other guests she'd dragged into bed. She'd been alone for months…no, not alone. She'd been surrounded by servants.

"Because I get bored easily," Charlotte said. "Does that answer your question?"

Mitch shrugged. "And the servants won't talk?"

Charlotte smiled. There was a very sharp edge to the expression. "They're loyal to me, not to Thomas," she said. "Even the oldest of old retainers knows better than to pick a fight with his mistress. If they talked…I'd fire them. I wouldn't have to blacklist them. The mere act of tattling on me would be quite enough to blacklist them from any respectable work. No one would trust them. How could they?"

Her voice hardened. "As far as anyone knows, I spent the night in my own room," she added, dryly. "No one will care enough to investigate."

"I hope you're right," Mitch said. Her comment about servants blacklisting themselves had unsettled him. "Can I ask a question?"

"Of course," Charlotte said. She picked up the shampoo and lathered it into her hair. "Go ahead."

"You went to a lot of trouble to arrange a party," Mitch said. He bit down the urge to point out just how much money had been wasted on the party. Hundreds, perhaps thousands, of families could have been fed for the same amount. "Why?"

Charlotte said nothing as she washed the soap out of her hair. "Politics," she said, finally. "It isn't *just* telling people what to do, you know?"

She grinned. "Think of politics, and social interaction, as a battlefield and you won't be far wrong."

"How so?" Mitch found it hard to believe. "A regular battle would leave hundreds of people dead or bleeding or…"

"Social death is death, without an end," Charlotte said, suddenly serious. "Someone who makes a serious mistake, one they don't have the social capital to avoid, is likely to wind up in big trouble."

She turned off the tap and reached for a towel. "On your ship, you give the orders and people snap to obey, right?"

"More or less," Mitch said. A good captain, one who understood his men weren't machines, could get more out of them than a martinet. "But that's the basics."

"Not here," Charlotte said. She waved a hand at the wall. "The people I invited are well-connected, either directly or indirectly; owners of the land, titans of industry, men of wealth and power…some of the women I invited have little formal power, but considerable influence. None of them would react well if anyone, even the monarch, was to give them a direct order and expect them to follow it. Instead, they come here—and to other parties—where they are convinced to support the government and ruling factions."

Mitch frowned. "You make it sound like a game."

"It is," Charlotte said. "And one played for the very highest stakes."

She shrugged. "Lady Bracknell wants her son to marry well," she said. "She's got multiple irons in the fire, trying to determine which bride would be in the best interests of the family. Lord Darlington owns title to a bunch of asteroids, which are worthless unless he manages to sell mining rights to someone prepared to pay for them; Lord Roderick is hoping to convince the social queens to make his creations fashionable so his dressmaking shop becomes profitable…"

"You're kidding me," Mitch said. "He makes *dresses*!"

Charlotte laughed. "There are men who wouldn't be seen dead cooking for their wives," she said. "And yet, at the same time, those men are professional cooks."

"It's the same thing," Mitch said.

"It's a matter of presentation," Charlotte said. "Point is, you cannot expect these people to unthinkingly do as they're told. You have to convince them that it's in their best interests to support you. Even if you have formal authority, you still want them on your side. It'll save trouble in the long run."

Mitch was torn between fascination and an odd sense they were talking about different things. It was hard to understand what she was saying, even though it...he shook his head as he towelled himself down. The aristocracy was a whole other world. He'd been in foreign parts, but... he'd never felt so alienated. Perhaps it wasn't a surprise. America and France had been foreign. He'd known they'd be different. But the British aristocracy was British.

Charlotte strode back into the bedroom and opened the chest of drawers. Mitch watched the sight, admiringly. Charlotte was striking. He knew it was partly the hormones talking, but...he felt himself stiffen again. He forced himself to look away. It was nearly eight. They were pushing it. God alone knew what the guests had thought, when Charlotte vanished...

He turned away to pick up his own clothes. "What about the guests? You left them alone."

"Unsupervised, you mean?" Charlotte shot him a wink. "By tradition, the hostess is meant to leave the party shortly after dinner. It's a way of saying the party is now over and the guests can leave without causing offense. You left early, did you not?"

Mitch sighed. "Does anyone here really care about me?"

"Consider yourself lucky," Charlotte told him. "If you were one of the young bucks, or the debs, you'd be watched like a hawk at all times."

I notice you didn't deny it, Mitch thought, as he watched her dress. There was something oddly enticing about watching her put on her clothes, even though—with every movement—she raised a barrier between them. Her dress was a uniform, in every way that mattered. It struck him, suddenly, that she'd planned the whole affair right from the start. How else would she have known to preposition clothes in his room? His lips quirked at the thought. *I've known logistics officers who wouldn't have done so well.*

He frowned as she stood, brushed down her dress, and stepped through the door. The room felt bigger without her, as if her personality had pervaded the chamber. It was hard to believe, somehow, that she and Captain Hammond's wife were the same person. Mitch wasn't unused to the slight confusion that came with seeing senior officers out of uniform, but…he shook his head. Common sense said he should say nothing, go back to London, rejoin his ship and forget her. He'd never been very good at listening to his common sense.

This isn't the first time she's done this, Mitch thought. It was hardly the kind of risk anyone would take on a whim. Charlotte would have to be very certain the servants wouldn't rat her out. Who really owned the estate? Mitch had always had the impression it was Captain Hammond, but… what if he was wrong? What if it was Charlotte? What if…?

There was a knock at the door. Mitch hastily finished putting on his trousers and shirt, then raised his voice. "Come in!"

A maid stepped into the room, carrying a breakfast tray with practised ease. She was a slight girl, wearing a uniform from a bygone era that exposed the tops of her breasts. Mitch felt oddly creeped out by the display. It was unlikely the maid had been allowed to choose her uniform. She certainly didn't have the raw sensuality Charlotte had displayed…he pointed to the table, silently indicating she should put the tray there and leave. It was hard not to feel sorry for the girl. If she was so short of career options, she had to go into service…

He felt an odd stab of resentment. It wasn't fair. The world wasn't fair—he knew the world wasn't fair—and yet it still stung. He was a firm believer that everyone should have the right to climb as high as they could and…it was a sick joke to remember the guests from the previous evening and realise that doors were opened to them simply because of who and what they were. Admiral Onarina had cut her way to the top through sheer brilliance, but how many other senior commanders owed everything to a name? Mitch himself knew he was unlikely to be offered command of a battleship, let alone a promotion to admiral. Not, he supposed, that he'd want either. A frigate might be small, but she could go places no one would dare take a battleship.

The breakfast was perfect, of course. The cook hadn't been content to make *simple* scrambled eggs. She'd worked chopped bacon and herbs into the mix, then poured it onto fancy bread. Mitch wondered, once again, just how much money had been wasted on the breakfast. Eggs weren't expensive, even during the war. Bread was even cheaper. But that would have been far too plebeian for the estate. The cooks would sooner have died than work with cheap ingredients.

He picked up his wristcom and skimmed through the messages as soon as he'd finished his breakfast. There was nothing new, save for a handful of general alerts. The BBC didn't seem to have sent out any new updates, nor had the handful of news services he followed. He wondered just what they thought he was paying for, if not the news. There were people who followed the comings and goings of aristocrats and rock stars with surprising interest, but he didn't care who was cheating on who…

You might have to care, he thought, sourly. *Are you going to say no if she invites you into her bed again?*

He tried to convince himself that the answer was yes. He didn't have to come back to the estate. It wasn't as if there weren't a hundred and one tasks waiting for him when he returned to his ship. He could make an excuse, if he was invited; he could claim everything from urgent repairs to a prior engagement. And yet…he shook his head. Charlotte had been good, very good. He didn't want to turn his back. The sheer risk involved, to both of them, was part of the fun. What was the point of gambling if you could afford to lose?

And she's probably bored with her husband, Mitch thought. It was an unworthy sentiment, one he knew he shouldn't allow himself to hold, but it was impossible to brush it away. *He's not the type to be adventurous in bed.*

There was another knock at the door. "Come in!"

The maid stepped into the room. "Captain, Lord Thomas has been ordered back to Nelson Base," she said. "A shuttle has been dispatched to transport him. He requests the pleasure of your company for the trip."

Mitch glanced at his wristcom. There were no new messages. Did Captain Hammond suspect something? Did he know he'd been cuckolded? Or did he merely want to assist Mitch in returning to his ship? Hell, for all he knew, they'd *both* been invited to the base. HMS *Lion* and HMS *Unicorn* were supposed to operate in tandem. Neither ship was really designed to operate alone.

"Inform him I would be honoured," Mitch said. In a way, it was almost a relief. He'd be out of temptation's way. And it wasn't as if it would take long to pack. "I'll be down in five minutes."

The maid curtsied. "Yes, Captain."

CHAPTER FIVE

"SO," DOCTOR FARAH SAID. "How do you feel?"

Tobias tried not to glare at the older woman. "If I wasn't ill when I was escorted into this facility," he said, "I sure as hell am now."

The doctor gave him a sharp look. "Explain."

"I've been here for days," Tobias said. He thought it had actually been hours, but it was hard to be sure. "You have poked me and prodded me and jabbed me with needles and injected me with so many different drugs that it's a wonder I haven't bled to death."

His stomach growled, menacingly. "And you haven't given me anything to eat."

"Yes," the doctor said. "As you may recall, you were near the epicentre of a biological attack. Ground zero, to all intents and purposes. If you had been infected, we might have been able to do something if the infection hadn't already reached your brain and taken control. Denying you food also denied the infection resources it needed to turn you into a zombie."

Tobias shivered. The doctor was right, but he still felt abused. "And am I infected? Is Marigold infected?"

"Not as far as we can tell," the doctor said. "You were lucky you thought to put on your masks. We found traces of viral particles in your hair and clothes. Thankfully, the UV lights kept them from spreading once you were out of the hotel. You two were the only survivors from that building."

"Shit," Tobias said. "Why did it happen so *fast*?"

"As near as we can tell, you faced an enhanced viral package," the doctor said. "Perversely, it is actually *too* lethal. The infection killed a number of victims *before* they could become zombies, burning through their bodies so quickly they didn't even become contagious. We're sweeping the area now, with UV lights and flamethrowers, but we think we have the outbreak under control."

"You think," Tobias said. He rubbed his forehead. The shackles had been removed once they'd passed the first battery of tests, but the room still felt like a prison cell. The walls were bare, the lights were too bright... his skin itched under the glare. He was imagining it—he knew he was imagining it—but it felt real. "How can you be sure?"

"We can't," the doctor admitted. "Not completely. However, the viral package doesn't seem *designed* to step down so it can perform a stealth takeover. If you were infected, you would either be dead or a zombie by now. There's certainly no trace of viral matter in your bloodstream."

"Thank God," Tobias muttered. "What an end to vacation."

"It could be worse," the doctor said. "You'll never guess where I spent my honeymoon."

Tobias shrugged. The days when the average citizen had travelled halfway around the world for a quick holiday, or a honeymoon, were long gone. He didn't recall any of his schoolmates ever going on a foreign holiday, although he supposed that shouldn't have surprised him. Getting to Europe or America had been tricky even before the virus had shown the human race that it needed to tighten the borders, again. It would be a long time before anyone went to North Africa or Turkey for a simple vacation.

"We were in Bournemouth," the doctor said. "It wasn't so bad, but the company..."

"The rain must have been lovely and warm," Tobias said. "Or did you get some sun?"

"We did," the doctor said. She let out a heavy sigh. "You're cleared to leave. Make sure you have tracker packages enabled on your wristcoms, at least for the next forty-eight hours or so. I'd prefer you didn't deactivate them until you report back to your ship. The ship's doctor will probably insist on checking you out, just to be sure there's no problem. Give them as much time as they need. They can't risk a viral outbreak on a starship."

"Even though it should be easy to contain, on a starship," Tobias said. "I thought that's what all the emergency drills were for."

"In theory, yes," the doctor said. "In practice…we weren't expecting a fast-burning viral outbreak. It's either evolving or modifying itself to present us with a harder challenge. It's quite possible it'll find a way to hide within the human body, sooner or later, and remain undetected long enough to get onto a starship and spread widely. There's no point in sealing off a compartment if the infection is already on the wrong side of the airlocks."

She stood. "The orderly will escort you down to the lobby," she said. "Make sure you have your wristcom enabled before you go."

Tobias nodded. "Yes, doctor."

He frowned as he keyed his wristcom. It was hard to forget, sometimes, that the wristcom was a very effective tracking device. It wasn't as obvious as the standard ankle-bracelet provided for prisoners on parole, a device designed to be as uncomfortable as possible just to remind the wearer it was there, but…it was far more effective. Tobias was all too aware that it could be used to track him, or to allow the government to trace his movements back in time to the moment he'd first purchased the device. It bothered him, more than he dared say out loud. Sure, he'd been *told* the device didn't broadcast location data unless the function was enabled, but was that actually true? He doubted it. Even if the locator beacon itself was turned off, the wristcom announced its location every time it checked the datanet for new messages or accepted an incoming call.

And no one really knows where all the data is going, he thought, grimly. *Who's really tracking my every move?*

He brought up the menu and enabled the tracker package. In theory, if he was infected, the wristcom would sound the alarm. He wasn't sure that was true—the wristcom wasn't designed to serve as a biological sampler—and he'd heard horror stories of armed police turning up to arrest people who'd accidentally triggered the alarm. The device was designed to monitor someone's vital signs. It wouldn't take more than an unaccustomed jog to speed up one's heartbeat beyond the norm... he shook his head. He'd just have to make sure he took it off before he did anything too strenuous. The thought made him smile. One thing he liked about being an adult, and a gunboat pilot, was that no one made him go to PE class any longer.

The orderly poked his head into the room. "Richard Gurnard?"

"Tobias, please," Tobias said. There were times when he cursed his parents for naming him Richard. The jokes had practically written themselves. "I can't wait to get out of here."

The orderly grinned. "I know how you feel," he said. "I can't wait for my shift to be over too."

Tobias nodded as he stood and followed the orderly down a long white corridor. The medical centre felt like a maze, as if a dozen buildings had been woven together into a single complex. Doctors and nurses hurried past on urgent business, the orderly motioning Tobias against the wall whenever a trolley or stretcher was rolled past. A handful looked completely sealed, their occupant little more than a dark shadow behind the translucent cover. Tobias shivered, remembering the body bags he'd seen on *Lion*. It was hard not to believe he'd wind up in one himself, one day. Cold logic insisted he'd be blown to bits, if his gunboat was hit, without enough left to fill a teaspoon—let alone a coffin—but the thought refused to leave.

He cheered up as the orderly showed him into a small cafe. Marigold was sitting at a table, looking frazzled. Tobias waved and ran towards her, giving her a quick hug before sitting down. She looked as if she hadn't slept or showered or so much as brushed her long hair in hours. Tobias doubted he'd win any awards either. He wasn't sure just how long they'd been in the medical complex, but he was fairly certain it had been more than a day or two. It was easy to lose track of time in a hospital.

"I feel rotten," Marigold said. An empty paper mug rested in front of her. "I…fuck."

Tobias nodded. He didn't feel great either. He wanted to find a hotel and sleep until the time came to report back to the spaceport…he swallowed, hard, as he checked his wristcom. They'd been in the medical centre for a day and they were expected to return to the ship tomorrow. He checked his bank balance, already knowing what he'd see. He didn't have the money to book a hotel in London. His lips twisted. There was little hope of recovering the money they'd paid the *last* hotel. God alone knew if the insurance company would pay out or not. Even if it did—and he was morbidly sure the firm would fight tooth and nail to keep from paying a penny—it would be weeks, if not months, before everything was processed. It wasn't as if the company would be able to visit the hotel and perform an investigation. For all he knew, the hotel had been burned to the ground.

And we were the only survivors, Tobias thought. He hadn't seen *many* of the other guests—it was that sort of hotel—but he'd seen a couple. A middle-aged man with a young woman—a girl, really—no older than Tobias himself. Tobias had been sure he'd been a sugar daddy with his sugar baby…his stomach churned in disgust. Wherever they'd been, they were dead now. Dead, or worse. *We got incredibly lucky.*

He felt sick as he stood and poured himself a cup of coffee. It tasted ghastly, but it helped to wake him up. He'd thought himself used to flying a gunboat, to pretending—in the privacy of his own mind—that the starfighters and capital ships he engaged were nothing more than lights on the display, no more real than opponents in computer games. He'd never seen himself as a groundpounder, he'd never dared imagine himself fighting hand-to-hand…it had been easier to pretend he had superpowers than the muscles or training to stand up for himself. And he'd hated it and…his head spun. He hadn't wanted to *really* hurt someone. He hadn't wanted to…

"I killed him," he muttered. "Fuck."

"The virus killed him," Marigold pointed out. "If he hadn't been infected, he wouldn't have threatened us."

"I know that," Tobias said. He swallowed, hard. "I just don't believe it."

He swallowed, again. There'd been a child, a dead child. The manager's kid? Or a guest? Or...it didn't matter. The poor kid was dead, dead and gone...their body might never be identified. He'd told the doctors what he'd seen, but...for all he knew, the body had got up and walked away before the armed police and soldiers arrived. It wasn't impossible. He'd hit the manager's body several times, hard enough to stop a regular human in his tracks. And yet the zombie had tried to keep coming...

Marigold touched his hand. "It wasn't your fault," she said. "If we'd had the money..."

"...We'd have gone somewhere else," Tobias finished. He shook his head. "I don't know what we're going to do tonight."

He glanced at his wristcom. There was no point in asking for an advance on his next paycheck. The military disliked offering advances, from what he'd heard; it was far too easy for a CO to find himself acting as an unpaid collections agent when a soldier or spacer had bought something he couldn't afford. His mother didn't have the money to loan, even if he wanted to ask her...he cursed under his breath. It was starting to look as though they'd have to risk the spaceport barracks. They were free to military personnel, but...he couldn't think of anything else. He certainly didn't want to ask *Marigold's* family to pay.

"We'll have to go to the barracks," Marigold said. She'd clearly been thinking along the same lines. "Unless you know anyone in London who'd put us up for the night."

Tobias shook his head. He didn't know anyone who'd put him up anywhere, except perhaps his mother. If they were in Birmingham...he considered, briefly, catching the monorail to Birmingham and asking his mother to let them stay the night, but the timing wouldn't work out. The only reason they'd booked a hotel in London was so they could head to the spaceport in the morning, without using the barracks or spending most of the day travelling back to the ship.

"Joy," he said. His stomach growled. "Do you think we can get something to eat before we head to the barracks or...should we just go?"

Marigold keyed her wristcom. "I'll let the barracks know we're coming," she said. "You check to see if there's anywhere open right now."

Tobias nodded, cursing his luck under his breath. He'd hoped they'd have one more day in bed together. There were privacy tubes on the ship, but...it wasn't quite the same. He *liked* waking up in bed with her, as well as everything else. It was hard to believe she felt the same about him. A wave of despondency threatened to overwhelm him as he keyed his wristcom once again. It was just a matter of time before she found a far superior man and left. He was sure of it.

Don't be a wanker, he told himself, sharply. *She could have had her pick of men if she'd wanted. And she chose you.*

He frowned as the wristcom bleeped. "The city is still in lockdown," he said. It looked as if they'd have to travel quite some distance, just to get something to eat. He eyed the rows of ration bars on the counter, free to all comers. It was easy to see that none had been taken in the last few hours, if at all. "Essential services only."

"We might be able to get something to eat at the barracks," Marigold said. "Or find somewhere open closer to the spaceport. We can probably find a taxi outside."

"Lockdown or no lockdown," Tobias muttered. He stood, walked over to the counter and collected a handful of ration bars. They might taste like cardboard—the *good* ones, at least—but they were short on options. They'd be glad to have the ration bars if they couldn't find somewhere better to eat. "Shall we go?"

He held her hand as they walked out of the medical complex. It felt like a military base—or a prison. Armed guards stood everywhere, their eyes sweeping from side to side as if they expected to be jumped at any moment. Tobias shivered as he noted their uniforms. They weren't reservists, but regulars. The medical complex was either a military facility in all but name or…someone thought it might come under attack at any moment. A chill ran through him as they made their way through the gate and the check-point beyond, the guards waving them through after a cursory look at their naval IDs. Tobias was entirely sure it would be a great deal harder to get *into* the complex. The guards probably had orders to shoot first, if they had any doubts, and ask questions later.

"There." Marigold pointed to a taxi waiting by the road. "Let's go."

Tobias nodded and followed her to the taxi. The driver looked relieved to see them. Tobias wasn't too surprised. There were too many soldiers on the streets for anyone to have any doubts about the potential danger. Soldiers in public view had been common, since the Troubles and the Bombardment, but…he shook his head. Anyone could be a zombie, these days. Anyone could turn into a lethal enemy…

The taxi hummed into life and drove away from the medical complex. Tobias hadn't been to London very often, and he hadn't spent much time in the city, but even *he* could tell the capital was oddly subdued. The streets were largely empty, save for soldiers, policemen and a handful of civilians. The latter wore masks, some of which looked as if they'd come straight out of the Second World War. Tobias wasn't too impressed. A man might rely on a mask to save his life, but a zombie could also use one to hide his true nature. He'd heard rumours that police checkpoints were making people lift their masks, as well as submit to blood screenings. It would certainly make a great deal of sense.

He shivered as a pair of helicopters clattered through the air. Police or military? It didn't really matter. London had been a no-fly zone for every-one else for decades, ever since the Troubles. The PDCs on the far side of the city had authorisation to shoot down aircraft that ventured into the secure airspace, perhaps without warning. Tobias tried not to think about the shuttle that would be taking them back to the ship, passing too close to the PDC for comfort. He understood the logic—a zombie would have no qualms about crashing an airliner into the city—but it still chilled him to the bone. They might wind up doing more damage to themselves, through paranoia, than the virus could do.

You know better than that, he told himself, as they passed through a checkpoint and drove onto the motorway. There were only a handful of vehicles, civilian or military, heading in or out of the city. *The threat is very real.*

But he couldn't help feeling relieved that they were going back into space, leaving the world behind.

CHAPTER SIX

CAPTAIN CAMPBELL HAD BEEN ODDLY QUIET during the flight from the estate to Nelson Base. He'd seemed almost relieved that they were on their way back to space. Thomas tended to agree with him. Deep-space combat was relatively simple, compared to the genteel battle-grounds of the country's aristocracy. Thomas was glad to be away, despite spending the morning going through letters and missives from mothers who wanted to arrange good matches for their sons. It was a pain in the arse, he'd decided. There was no way he was going to *push* his daughters into marrying someone they barely knew.

He kept the thought to himself as the shuttle docked, the airlock hissing open to allow them to stumble out and into the security checkpoint. The blood test was as unpleasant as always, although they both knew the importance of ensuring everyone was in their right mind. The aide on the far side saluted them, then led them through a maze of corridors into a giant auditorium. Thomas felt his heart begin to race as he glanced around the chamber. There were at least thirty captains and other officers in the compartment, including a number of American, French and Chinese personnel. Something big was afoot. There wouldn't have been so much tension in the air if they were planning something simple. An aide offered him a mug of tea, which he accepted. Captain Campbell was already heading down to the front row.

We wouldn't be meeting in person if it wasn't very important, Thomas thought. He was a big fan of holocommunications and conferences—there was nothing to be gained by meeting in person, if it could be handled over the datanet instead—but face-to-face discussions were good for actually getting to *know* people. *What are we planning?*

He took his seat and waited, eyes flickering around the giant compartment. He knew a handful of officers, some personally and some by reputation, but the remainder were strangers. The war had taken one hell of a toll on humanity's space navies, grinding down the pre-war establishments and forcing the militaries to promote younger officers into suddenly-empty billets. Thomas grimaced at the thought. The war had smoothed out the cracks, teaching the various navies how to work together, but...it could not be denied that a great deal of institutional knowledge had been lost. It was hard to believe, sometimes, that things would ever go back to normal.

A rustle ran through the room as Admiral Lady Susan Onarina walked up to the podium, followed by a pair of staff officers. She looked little different from when they'd last met, after *Lion* had returned from Operation Thunder Child, but there was a hint of anticipation on her face that suggested the fleet was *really* going to head into the fire. Thomas silently counted the commanding officers, noting there were now over forty starship captains and a handful of groundpounders. Royal Marines, United States Marine Corps, Russian Naval Infantry...it was impossible to believe they were assembling for something minor. He felt a thrill, despite his natural caution. They might be preparing for a *decisive* operation.

"At ease," Admiral Onarina said. She spoke in English, the shared language of multinational operations. "Welcome to Operation Lightning Strike."

Her words hung in the air. Thomas leaned forward. Thunder Child, Lightning Strike...someone was a fan of old movies and serials. The admiral? Or one of her aides? It was hard to be sure. The MOD preferred to name operations something innocuous, in the hopes of avoiding media attention if the codename leaked out. Thunder Child hinted at too much, in his opinion. Anyone who ran the name through a search engine would find more than enough reasons to suspect the truth.

"The operation has been authorised by the world governments," Admiral Onarina continued, calmly. "The precise details of the concept have been classified, as will the outcome of our planning sessions. I should not have to remind you, but I am obliged to do so, that sharing anything with anyone outside the info-compartment will result in national and/or global charges being brought against you. Your governments will not be amused if the secret leaks ahead of time. These days, bulkheads have ears."

Thomas nodded. The virus had access to countless human prisoners. Worse, it could turn them into traitors. It was quite possible the virus was monitoring human communications, trying to keep track of human politics. There was certainly no way to prove it *wasn't*. It hadn't been such a concern in the First and Second Interstellar Wars—the Tadpoles and the Foxes had lacked any insight into human society, and vice versa—but the virus had a Rosetta Stone. It could spy on the human race from a distance. They had to assume it was.

"We have a great deal of ground to cover," Admiral Onarina said. "With no further ado, I'll turn you over to Commander Vicar."

Vicar stepped forward. He was a small bespectacled man, wearing a uniform in a manner that suggested he wasn't used to wearing it. Thomas guessed he was an analyst, rather than a proper staff officer or military beancounter. That might be good or bad. An analyst who didn't give a damn about his career, and had no qualms about speaking truth to power, might be very useful. But, at the same time, his lack of military background would work against him. Thomas knew there were thousands of officers who thought less of civilians. They just didn't understand what it was like to be in the military.

A holographic starchart appeared in the centre of the chamber. Thomas studied it thoughtfully, noting the cluster of green, blue, red and orange stars, all linked together by glowing tramlines. There were two more orange—infected—stars than he remembered, although he hadn't heard anything about more systems falling to the virus. He made a mental note to check on that as quickly as possible. The public might not have been told the entire truth, but he wasn't a member of the public. He was a naval officer and an aristocrat with a seat in the House of Lords. He *needed* to know the full situation, damn it.

Vicar spoke with a calm confidence that belied his appearance. "Two months ago, long-range gravimetric sensors detected gravity waves propagating at FTL speeds, emanating from UAS-4832," he said. A red star blinked once. "The star system, as you can see, is in a curious position. It is no less than fifty light years from Sol, but—thanks to the idiosyncrasies of the tramline network—is actually impossible to reach directly. As the old joke puts it, the Scots must march *north* to reach England because there's no way to travel south."

Thomas frowned as the starchart zeroed in on UAS-4832. The problem was obvious. Anyone who wanted to reach UAS-4832, a dim red star of no interest to anyone, would have to travel quite some distance along the tramline network before doubling back to reach their final destination. The star hadn't even been surveyed before the First Interstellar War, if only because it couldn't be reached without alien-grade drives. Orbital telescopes had inspected the system, concluded it was largely useless and no one had bothered to visit. Officially, at least. The system was so barren it was unlikely to host a covert colony.

"The gravity waves were strong enough to convince the navy to dispatch a survey ship to UAS-4832," Vicar continued. "They reported that the virus was establishing no less than *twenty* catapults, within easy striking distance of Sol. Given the..."

A rustle ran around the compartment as his words sank in. Thomas felt as if he'd been punched in the belly. A single catapult was so expensive that even a Great Power would hesitate to build it. Twenty of them...Britain's entire GNP wouldn't be enough to produce *twenty* catapults. It sounded more like a fantasy fleet dream than anything else, along the same lines as planners who insisted Britain could deploy a thousand fleet carriers...

if, of course, the country didn't want to produce anything else. He shook his head in disbelief. Every time he thought he'd come to grips with the true scale of the threat, something happened to convince him that he'd barely begun.

"Jesus," Captain Campbell said, quietly.

For once, Thomas agreed wholeheartedly. Twenty catapults...he thought he knew, now, how the long-gone Roman Emperors had felt when they'd seen the barbarian hordes riding over the plains towards them. The tramlines forced invading fleets to stick to a predictable course, giving the defenders time to redeploy their forces to meet the threat, but now...if the entire sky could become a tramline, humanity's defences would become worse than useless. The ships holding the line would be hopelessly out of position...

"Our best-case scenario is that the catapults will be ready within two months," Vicar said. "They are one-shot weapons, thankfully, but that's small consolation. Our calculations suggest they can throw enough ships at Sol, in a single transit, to overwhelm the defences and destroy our industrial base. At that point, it will be just a matter of time before they finish the job. Imagine a boot stamping on a human face for the rest of eternity."

The virus doesn't need to oppress anyone, Thomas thought. *There'll be no one left who'll need oppressing.*

Vicar stepped down. Admiral Onarina stepped forward.

"The situation is grim," she said. "On the face of it, as you can see, if we do not take out those catapults quickly we will be defeated. There will be no hope of holding the line. Either we call our ships back to Earth, allowing the virus to claim the remainder of the human sphere or we risk ignoring the threat and losing Earth when they put the catapults into service. However, it does offer us an opportunity as well as a threat. Sally?"

Another officer—a young woman—stepped forward. "Operation Lightning Strike is divided into two sections," she said. "Phase One involves capturing or destroying the catapults before they can be put into service. Phase Two involves making use of the catapults ourselves. As you can see"—the starchart changed, again—"the catapults could easily be used to put a fleet in the *enemy's* rear. If we can make use of the catapults ourselves, we can strike the enemy in the back and—hopefully—do immense damage to their industrial base."

Thomas frowned. The concept seemed solid, on paper, but it sounded like a plan dreamed up by an armchair admiral. There was no way to be *sure* they could capture the catapults, let alone put them to use. And even if they did, there would be no way to jump *back*. They'd have to fight their way through the tramlines, all too aware the enemy would be straining every sinew to block their retreat. He looked around, silently gauging how many starships were going to be thrown into enemy territory. The human race could win the battle, but lose the war.

An American had the same thought. "How do we know we can use the catapults?"

"The virus's tech is odd, by our standards," Sally said. Thomas had the impression she'd anticipated the question. "A lot of their control systems are blurred into its biological network, rather as we use command and control implants. Its processing power is so great, compared to a merely *human* brain, that it is capable of multitasking on an incredible scale. However, the systems themselves are solid tech. In some ways, they're actually *simpler* than ours. We cannot expect them to do something that requires long-term effort, according to the techs, but we should be able to get them up and running long enough to make transit. We only need them to work once."

"And then we'll be trapped behind enemy lines," Thomas pointed out.

"Yes," a French-accented voice said. "How do we even know we'll be making transit into enemy space?"

"Intelligence has been studying the remnants of infected ships for the last decade, ever since the war began," Admiral Onarina said. If she was annoyed by the question, she didn't show it. "The precise details are classified, but suffice it to say that we have a rough idea of the size of enemy-held space. It looks odd by our standards, suggesting the virus has overwhelmed at least four interstellar powers, yet...we think we've pinpointed a handful of alien industrial nodes. We make transit, we blow the nodes to dust and head home as quickly as possible."

Her voice hardened. "We don't know, yet, if we'll be able to proceed to Phase Two. There is a chance the catapults will be destroyed or discovered to be unusable, when we hit the system and try to capture them. It's quite possible we'll accomplish nothing more than buying time to develop new weapons and put them into mass production. And yes, there's a chance we'll be trapped behind enemy lines. The GATO council would not have authorised the mission if they hadn't been certain we have no choice. If the virus brings those catapults online, it will win."

She paused. "Defeat means the end of the world. There will be no hope of resistance, no hope of mounting a war of liberation...nothing, apart from the virus. Bear that in mind."

"If nothing else, we can force it to start rebuilding the catapults from scratch," Captain Campbell said. He sounded as if he was certain the plan would succeed. "That will buy us some more time."

Admiral Onarina nodded. "And all of this leads to a second point."

Her eyes swept the compartment. "The BioBombs were not as effective as we had hoped, but they *were* effective. Accordingly, we will be deploying them wherever possible. Our goal will be to destroy the infection wherever we find it, regardless of the cost. The host bodies are beyond recovery. We will seek to give them a clean end, rather than remain trapped in a living death. Many people will argue that we're planning to commit genocide"— she held up a hand to stave off protests—"but we have no choice. We must destroy the infection, root and branch, or it will destroy us."

Thomas shuddered, remembering the sensor images from the last mission. They'd sentenced an entire colony world to death. Cold logic told him the colonists had been dead from the moment they'd been infected, when their minds had been raped and their bodies had been stolen, but it was hard to believe. The Royal Navy was supposed to prevent atrocities, not commit them. And yet...he felt sick as he contemplated the reports from London. Very little had been released publicly, but he knew how to read between the lines. A little less luck, and worse timing, might have resulted in a far greater loss of life. He wondered, grimly, if someone would have insisted on dropping a BioBomb on London. The cure might have been worse than the disease.

Or a nuke, he thought. There'd been plans to use atomic bombs in the hopes of wiping out a handful of deadly diseases. None of them had ever been put into practice, but…now, that might change. *We might have to wipe out an entire city to save the rest of the country.*

Admiral Onarina tapped a control. The display vanished. "The provisional operational plan has been sent to your terminals," she said. "Please inspect them, then feel free to propose alternatives. The plans will not be finalised until the allied contingents arrive. Once they do, we'll depart Earth and commence the operation as quickly as possible."

Allied contingents? Thomas blinked. *Tadpoles? Or Foxes?*

The thought bothered him. He had nothing against humanity's enemies-turned-allies, although he knew there were millions of humans who disliked the Tadpoles after the Bombardment of Earth, but it would be extremely difficult to coordinate a large multiracial fleet. He wasn't even sure human and alien ships could work together, let alone lock their individual datanets into a single entity. There'd be all sorts of problems, from computers that wouldn't work together to cultural assumptions and blindspots and…

They said the same about multinational formations too, he reminded himself. *And we worked out all the kinks eventually.*

Sure, his own thoughts answered. *And how many people died while we were learning how to do it?*

He put the thought out of his head as he keyed his terminal, bringing up the operational plan. It was surprisingly simple, for a concept devised by a desk jockey. Thomas guessed that Admiral Onarina had outlined the basic idea, then given it to her staff to develop. There were a number of question marks—the outline was honest about the things the planners didn't know, starting with how many ships would be assigned to the mission—but there

58

were no obvious flaws. The notes insisted that the entire operation had been wargamed, with the good guys winning more often than they'd lost. Thomas wasn't impressed by *that*. There were so many unknowns, particularly on the far side of enemy-held space, that the wargame parameters were little more than uneducated guesses. For all he knew, the virus was fighting on multiple fronts and the fleets humanity had destroyed were little more than a drop in the bucket. There was just no way to be sure.

Not until we go find out, he thought. *If they're building catapults on such a scale...*

"This should be fun," Captain Campbell said. "A strike right into the heart of the evil empire itself."

"No doubt," Thomas thought, with a flicker of irritation. He just didn't *like* the younger officer. "And total defeat staring us right in the face if we lose."

CHAPTER SEVEN

"WAKE UP," MARIGOLD SAID, URGENTLY. "We've arrived."

Tobias gritted his teeth as he sat up, rubbing sleep from his eyes. The barracks hadn't been comfortable. He'd never liked sharing a compartment with his fellow gunboat crew, let alone a bunch of strangers from a dozen different military branches. And being in the male barracks had been the worst of it. Marigold had been on the other side of the complex. Tobias understood the logic, but it still galled him.

He felt oddly naked even though he was in his shipsuit. His carryall had been lost in the hotel, contents thrown into the fire rather than decontaminated and returned. He hadn't had *much* with him, beyond several sets of clothes and a couple of souvenirs that hadn't been worth the money he'd paid for them, but it was still annoying. Thankfully, his uniforms had been left onboard ship. He could purchase most of what he needed when he returned to the planet…

If I ever do, he thought, as they headed to the airlock. *I might not come back.*

He tried not to think about it as the gravity field twisted under his feet. The air smelt familiar, as if he were coming home. *Lion* wasn't his home and yet, in a way, she was. He flew his gunboat away from the battlecruiser and then returned to a welcome bunk and a rest before doing it again and again…he shook his head. He'd been told it would be a while before the

Royal Navy put more missile-heavy battlecruisers into production, even though *Lion* had proved herself. He was quite likely to spend the rest of his career on the battlecruiser.

The thought mocked him as he stepped into the checkpoint. A pair of marines stood there, wearing masks and spacesuits. Tobias tensed, recognising Colin even through the mask. He knew his old bully too well to mistake him for anyone else, despite the protective garb. It was all he could do to stand still as Colin pressed a sampler against his neck, then did the same to Marigold. Tobias had to fight not to say something in protest. Colin was only carrying out his orders…

He's grown up, Tobias told himself. Colin and he had reached an understanding, he supposed, and yet…there were times when he wished he'd taken the shot that would have blown Colin into atoms. It wasn't as if he wouldn't have gotten away with it. There'd been so much confusion that it was unlikely anyone would have realised the accident hadn't been an accident at all. *He's changed, for the better.*

"You're clear," Colin said. The voice was the same, even though the suit. Colin's insults had never been very clever, but they'd never had to be. "I have orders to see you two to sickbay."

Tobias nodded, not trusting himself to speak. There'd been a time when Colin would have happily humiliated him in front of Marigold. The only reason Colin hadn't done it in front of his girlfriend at school was that he hadn't *had* a girlfriend. There was nothing like being a useless cowardly wimp to convince the girls to look somewhere—anywhere—else. Now…Tobias tried not to flinch as they started to walk. The starship was clearly preparing for a hasty departure. Hundreds of crew—and yarddogs—thronged the corridors, carrying out repairs or transporting spare parts to the hold. Tobias stepped to one side as a trio of marines ran past, carrying a device that looked like a portable mecha. He hadn't seen anything like it outside a video game.

"We've been placed on twenty-four-hour warning to depart," Colin said. He sounded a little calmer now they were alone. "Did you hear the news from London?"

"We were there," Tobias said. He wondered, suddenly, how many people Colin had killed. Hundreds, probably, if not thousands. He'd bet good money Colin slept well, too. Tobias had had nightmares about the man he'd killed, even if it had been in self-defence. "It was pretty bad."

"No way!" It was hard to be sure, but Colin sounded impressed. "Really?"

"Yes." Marigold's voice was flat. "We were there."

Tobias said nothing as they reached sickbay and stepped through the hatch. The air was bright with U V lights, his skin itching under the glare. Doctor Patty Haugen waved to them, then pointed to a pair of chairs. She didn't seem to be taking the risk of infection seriously, Tobias decided, although he supposed she had a point. There was no reason to think that either Marigold or himself were infected. Their wristcoms certainly hadn't signalled an alert to anyone.

"I'll see you later," Colin said. "Good luck."

"Yeah," Tobias said. "Later."

The doctor tested their blood, then nodded thoughtfully. "Clean," she said, as she pushed more sensors against their bare skin. "No hints you might have been infected, or otherwise influenced. Quite clear, all things considered."

Tobias breathed a sigh of relief. He'd known he hadn't been infected... no, he hadn't really known. How could he? It wasn't as if it was something he could control. There was no way he could have been entirely sure he was uninfected. A person could become contagious long before they started to show symptoms, spreading the disease without ever knowing what they were doing. His blood ran cold. The virus had found a way to speed the infection up. What if it had found a way to slow things down?

"Thank you," Marigold said. "Are we really going to depart tomorrow?"

"We've been placed on alert, but it's meaningless," the doctor said. "Realistically, we could be leaving any time from tomorrow to next week. I suspect it means the brass themselves aren't sure when we'll be leaving."

"Hurry up and wait," Tobias said.

"Quite," the doctor agreed. "Better to be ready to go—and not need to go—then to be unready to depart."

She made a shoeing motion at the hatch. "I've performed the basic scans. There's no hint you need anything more complex for your routine physicals. I'll be seeing you again, but right now you're at the back of the list. Hopefully, nothing will happen to change that."

Tobias nodded as he stood and headed for the hatch. He'd never liked the routine medical examinations that had been a part of his life since childhood, even when they'd been conducted by professional doctors rather than underpaid nurses. The school had always been more interested in boys who were fit enough to play football and other games…he shook his head. It had been pointless then and it was even more pointless now. Colin had been a sporty bastard at school, and what had he become? A Royal Marine! Tobias would have been more impressed if he hadn't been sure Colin had been conscripted into the bootnecks.

"It could be worse," Marigold said, as they walked down the corridor. "If either of us had been infected…"

"I know." Tobias didn't want to think about it. "We were lucky."

He shivered, again, as they reached gunboat country. The compartment seemed largely empty, somewhat to his surprise. They'd taken the early shuttle, but he'd always had the impression that half the squadron had remained on duty. The bunk beds looked unclaimed, the nametags on the headboards blank…he shrugged as he put his jacket on the bunk nearest the washroom, then headed down to check the storage compartment. His handful of possessions should have been left there.

"Tobias," a voice said. "And Marigold. Welcome home."

"Thank you, sir," Tobias said. Colonel Richard Bagehot—they shared the same first name, but Tobias was sure no one had tried to make fun of the colonel's name—was an odd duck, a strange mixture of drill instructor, cheerleader and father-figure. He could switch from being warm, friendly and approachable to stern and cold in the blink of an eye. "What happened to the others?"

"The squadrons are being reorganised," Bagehot informed him. "Two-thirds of the original group have already been reassigned, to share their knowledge elsewhere. You two will be in charge of the new pilots, when they arrive. I expect you to show them the ropes."

"We'll do our best, sir," Marigold said. "Does the assignment come with extra pay?"

"No, but it does come with a commendation for good work," Bagehot said. "If, of course, you do a good job. You're not going to replace me—at least, not *yet*—and we're not asking you to train new pilots from scratch, but we do want you to answer the questions *your* instructors didn't know to ask."

Tobias smiled to hide his consternation. "What is the price of sliced ham, per portion?"

Bagehot fixed him with a stern look. "*Relevant* questions."

"We'll do our best," Marigold said, again. "When will the newcomers arrive?"

"This afternoon, unless their shuttle gets retasked again on short notice," Bagehot said, a hint of irritation entering his voice. "There haven't been any formal orders, not yet, but—from what I've heard—we're going to be departing in a fortnight. And we're not the only ones. Flights from Luna have been rescheduled or cancelled or..."

He shook his head. "That's well above your pay grade," he said. "Don't worry about it. Get some rest, spend some time thinking about what you wish you'd known, when you became gunboat pilots. Make sure you add it to your reports, too. People who've never flown a gunboat in their lives are so ignorant that they're ignorant of their own ignorance. You have to make sure they know, at least on paper, what to expect."

Tobias frowned as Bagehot left the room, the hatch hissing closed behind him. "What do we know that we don't know?"

"I don't know." Marigold laughed. "What do you wish you'd known before you started?"

"I don't know!" Tobias shook his head. "But seriously..."

He considered it for a long moment. He wasn't sure what he could tell the newcomers that they didn't already know. They'd slept in barracks while they'd been at the academy, unless they'd been permitted to commute from Clarke or one of the other lunar cities. It didn't seem likely, somehow. Luna Academy was on the moon, but not *of* it. Flying gunboats? The new cadets would have practiced on simulations based on their first missions. Relationships with the rest of the ship's crew? Somehow, Tobias doubted *his* experience was the sort of experience the newcomers should emulate. What were the odds of another bullied schoolboy finding his bully assigned to the same ship?

Not as low as one might wish, Tobias thought. *It wasn't as if the navy gave much of a damn about our childhoods.*

"My mind has gone blank," he confessed. "I can't think of anything worth mentioning."

"We can show them around our compartment, if nothing else," Marigold said, after a moment's thought. "And we can show them how to tend to their craft."

Tobias nodded. Gunboat maintenance hadn't been part of the training course. They'd had to pick the basics up from the engineering teams, when it had become apparent that the starship's crew would be overstretched. Tobias knew he couldn't build a drive system from scratch or repair a targeting system, but he could replace a damaged section—if he had a spare component on hand—or jury-rig a spare part intended for the battlecruiser if there was no other choice. Everything was designed to be modular anyway. And, in theory, he knew how to do a great deal more.

In theory, he reminded himself. *You've never done it in the real world.*

"True," he said, finally. "And their questions might lead us to the answers."

He keyed the wall-mounted terminal, checking for orders. There were none, beyond the command to prepare for departure. Anything else was clearly classified well above him...probably. It was unlikely Captain Hammond or his XO would have decided to prepare the ship for a hurried departure on a whim. The wear and tear on the equipment, and the crew, would be quite substantial.

"No orders," he said. "Where do you think we're going?"

"I have no idea," Marigold said, primly. She picked up a datapad and looked up the records from the first few weeks onboard ship. "And, right now, I think it isn't our problem."

. . .

"I trust you had a good leave?"

Corporal Colin Lancaster straightened to attention as he followed Sergeant Ron Bowman into the officer's compartment. It belonged to Captain Curt McConnell, but there was no sign of their superior officer. Colin was still very new to the Royal Marines—he was surprised he'd been allowed to keep his stripe, which he'd earned on his first deployment—yet he'd seen enough to be sure the ship was preparing for something important, perhaps even decisive.

"It was...interesting, Sarge," Colin said. He'd resisted the temptation to go home, after discovering what had become of his old school friends. Cronies, as Tobias would probably have put it. "I went mountaineering instead."

"A good idea," Bowman agreed. "And did anything interesting happen?"

Colin smiled. "I rescued a girl called Clementine from certain death. She was very unhappy and said she didn't need my help. But her father treated me to enough drinks to make up for it, so I went climbing with him the following day instead."

Bowman laughed. "Next time, tell a more convincing lie, or at least come up with some more interesting bullshit," he said. "I know the song too."

"I met a mountaineering band," Colin said. "It was one of their songs."

"Good, good," Bowman said. He met Colin's eyes, signalling they were about to get serious. "We don't have any solid confirmation yet—everything keeps being changed—but it looks as if we're going to get a full company of marines. The unit will end up at full strength, when all the movements have been completed. A handful of sections will be rotated out to share their experience. It's quite possible we will be hitting another alien world."

Colin grimaced. "Shit."

"Quite." Bowman looked him in the eye. "If everything goes as the CO plans, your platoon will be—technically—detached from the rest of the company. On paper, you'll be a reserve unit. In practice, you have a very special duty."

"I see," Colin lied. It wasn't like the sergeant to dance around the subject. It suggested bad news. Ceremonial duties? It didn't seem likely. Colin knew he wasn't very photogenic. The guards outside Buckingham Palace, he'd been told, had all been chosen for their looks as well as their fighting skill. "Sarge…"

"You'll have to integrate a very special soldier into your platoon," Bowman explained. "And treat him as one of your own."

Colin blinked. "A foreigner?"

It was possible, he supposed. American and French officers had been integrated into British military formations before, and vice versa. He'd never heard of one being integrated into the Royal Marines, although he supposed it was possible. Foreign officers and soldiers *had* been trained in British facilities…he doubted, somehow, that the newcomer was American or French. They had their own training facilities. An Arab? That was going to be interesting.

"In a manner of speaking," Bowman said. He picked up a datapad and held it out. "His real name is something none of us can pronounce, but we're calling him Kevin."

Colin stared as he opened the file. The face wasn't human. Very definitely not human. "A Vesy?"

"Yes," Bowman said. "Kevin—and no, I don't know who suggested the name—has been assigned to the ship. There's a complicated political *quid pro quo* involved, from what I've heard. He's trained on human equipment, tactics and protocols…according to the paperwork, he's no better or worse than the average boot who'd just completed commando training."

"Fuck," Colin said. "How the…"

"Read the file," Bowman said. "Kevin has been assigned to your platoon. He'll get a taste of modern war, without being expected to do anything *too* important. If things go well, it will prove that Vesy can handle modern society. If they don't…"

"Fuck," Colin repeated. "With all due respect, Sergeant, we're heading into harm's way."

"Quite," Bowman agreed. "Kevin is not onboard to serve as a diplomatic rep or anything other than a marine. He's quite willing to go in harm's way and understands that yes, he might not be coming back from this. I expect you to treat him as one of your own. If he does turn into a problem, or if you can't integrate him into the platoon, he'll be confined to quarters for the duration, but…realistically, we expect you to handle him like any other boot."

"Yes, Sarge," Colin said, automatically. He had the nasty feeling he'd just been given a poisoned chalice. It was hard enough to integrate women, or foreigners, into a tight-knit military unit. Integrating an outright *alien*… he wasn't sure it could be done. The Vesy weren't human. The reptilian face staring up at him was *very* inhuman. "Does he even eat the same food?"

"He eats the same as us, and quite a bit more," Bowman said. "Good luck."

"I think I'll need it," Colin said, darkly. "When's he due to arrive?"

"Unless things change, again, you have a couple of days to read the file and make preparations," Bowman said. "You're keeping the rest of your platoon, so—if things go well—you'll have an oversized unit under your command."

Sure, Colin thought. It was a challenge. He wanted to succeed. But, at the same time, he was very aware of the risks. *And if things don't go well, I'll find myself holding the bag.*

CHAPTER EIGHT

"OVERALL, CAPTAIN, WE'RE READY TO DEPART," Commander Staci Templeton said. "When are you coming back onboard?"

Mitch felt a pang of guilt. The last two days had been hectic. They'd been back and forth between Earth and Nelson Base twice, moving between military and diplomatic conferences to private political briefings that didn't—as far as he could tell—require his presence. The operation might have been authorised, according to the admiral, but it felt as though the politicians were having second and third thoughts about the entire thing. Mitch couldn't believe it. The alien catapults were a knife pointed at their heart. They had to be taken out, at the very least. And the admiral's plan to capture and use them instead appealed to his tactical mind. The human race was losing the war. It was time to stake everything on a single desperate gamble.

And that's something Captain Hammond will never understand, he thought, sourly. *There comes a time when prudence must be put aside.*

He dismissed the thought with a flicker of irritation. "I'm hoping to be back onboard in a couple of days," he said. He'd been *meant* to return to his ship yesterday. "Have you had any issues you can't handle?"

"Well, I can't carry out the coup without someone to launch a coup against," Staci said, deadpan. "Other than that, we're ready to go. We could leave tonight if we wanted."

Mitch nodded. Staci was an extremely competent XO. She was also in line for command of the next frigate, when it was finally released into active service. It wouldn't be that difficult a transition for her. Frigate crews had always had a degree of informality the larger ships lacked. She'd have more problems if she had to take command of a battleship or fleet carrier. Her role, and that of her new XO, would be far more sharply defined.

"I'm sorry to leave you in command," he said. He meant it, too. It was one thing to put her in command when they were on active service, when she could gain valuable experience for her next promotion, but leaving her in command while the ship was floating in orbit wasn't quite the same. It was more like leaving her holding the bag while he enjoyed a relaxing shore leave. "I'll be back up as soon as possible."

"Don't worry about it," Staci said. "We'll *try* not to leave without you."

Mitch laughed as he keyed the terminal, closing the connection. It was hard not to envy his XO. He was a captain, commanding officer of a starship, but here—in the Admiralty Building—he was one of the *lower-ranked* officers. It was hard to believe, yet it was true. The pen-pushers and data-miners infesting the building actually outranked him, when he wasn't on his ship. A captain could issue orders to an admiral when they were on the bridge, but not on the planet. And it would be a brave or foolish captain who tried.

He smiled, humourlessly, as he made his way back into the conference room. He'd had the impression that only a few officers knew the whole plan, but...it was clear that hundreds of personnel knew aspects of the truth. It didn't strike him as being very secure. The MOD staffers might have passed repeated polygraph tests, just to make sure they were loyal, but the virus laughed at such precautions. A man could be turned into an unwitting traitor overnight and no one would so much as suspect a thing until it was too late. The latest reports from the viral attack were terrifying. If there was another attack in the heart of London, it was quite possible it could take out much of the government before anyone could react.

Which isn't too likely to happen, he thought. *But there's no way we can be sure.*

He sighed, inwardly, as he slipped back into his seat. An admiral—someone who'd never commanded a ship in battle, if Mitch was any judge—was discoursing rapidly on something he didn't understand. Mitch tried not to look contemptuous as the desk jockey went on and on, feeling rather like a schoolboy forced to sit through a boring assembly. His old headmaster had been remarkably fond of the sound of his own voice…no doubt, Mitch reflected, a legacy from his bid to become an MP. Thankfully, he hadn't been elected. It had probably never crossed his mind that his constituents weren't a captive audience.

I don't need to be here, he thought, sourly. He really was a junior officer. Admiral Onarina and her staff would make the decisions, then send the orders to their subordinates. Mitch would snap to attention, salute and do as he was told. *Why do they even want me here?*

He tried not to sigh again as his eyes wandered the room. A handful of foreign officers, their faces masks that suggested they were as bored as he was; a cluster of British officers who were paying rapt attention. Captain Hammond was sitting on the other side of the room, his fingers dancing on a datapad. Taking notes, the little swot. Mitch knew he was being unfair, but it was hard to care. He really didn't have a place in the chamber. He should be back on his ship, preparing for departure. His XO wouldn't *really* mount a coup, but…it looked bad to leave *everything* to her. There was nothing like arranging and supervising everything to give you a solid idea precisely how things stood upon departure.

Admiral Onarina called a halt, what felt like days later. Mitch stood and joined the exodus of officers, some not even *pretending* they weren't hurrying to the toilets. His lips twitched in amusement. It really *was* like school. Leaving the assembly ahead of time was a serious crime, according to the headmaster. Bastard had never really considered that his pupils had small bladders and short attention spans.

His wristcom bleeped. Mitch glanced at the incoming message and blinked. An invitation to walk out of the Admiralty Building and meet... meet who? His eyes narrowed. It wasn't as if he'd expected to meet someone in London. It wasn't as if he'd so much as known he'd be going back to London until the orders had arrived. He'd thought he'd be heading straight to his ship...he frowned, turning the matter over and over in his head. Who had his private comcode? There weren't many people who did, most of whom would sooner use the military net. Mitch's family wouldn't come to London to see him. And that left...who?

A reporter, perhaps, Mitch thought. He wouldn't put it past a particularly unscrupulous reporter to obtain his comcode, either from his family or one of his lady friends. *Or...who?*

He was halfway towards the door before he'd quite realised he was going to meet the mystery person. It was something to do, something different before he boarded the shuttle back to his ship...assuming, of course, he wasn't recalled to London again. And again...a flash of irritation shot through him. Spaceflight might be routine, these days, but it wasn't as if travelling backwards and forwards wasn't a major commitment. Nelson Base wasn't in Tottenham Court Road, a short walk from Whitehall. He'd spent more time in transit than he'd spent doing something useful. He checked his schedule, just to be sure nothing was booked for later. The last thing he needed was for someone to declare him AWOL.

The streets were dull, the dark clouds throwing shadow over the city. The weather had never been quite the same since the Bombardment, Mitch had been told, although he'd read complaints about the English weather that dated all the way back to Julius Caesar. He glanced upwards, silently gauging the likelihood of rain, then hurried down the street. A dark car sat at the end, waiting for him. If it was a reporter, he could have the pleasure of telling him to fuck off. Politely, of course. The admiral would not be pleased if the reporter filed an official complaint. It wouldn't look good on his record.

He slowed as he approached the car. There were no visible number plates, suggesting...what? An official vehicle? Or...or what? He didn't know. Cars had to have number plates in clear view, if he recalled correctly. The window opened, revealing…Mitch blinked in shock. Charlotte was sitting in the car, waiting for him.

"Well, don't just stand there," Charlotte said. The door opened, revealing an interior compartment that seemed surprisingly roomy. "Come on in."

Mitch had to smile as he climbed inside. The interior was larger than his first cabin, back when he'd been promoted to lieutenant. There was a single large sofa, a small drinks cabinet…he shook his head in astonishment. It felt more like a luxury shuttle than a groundcar. The door closed behind him, the vehicle moving away from the curb. It crossed Mitch's mind to wonder if he'd been kidnapped. He certainly hadn't expected to meet Charlotte in London. He hadn't expected to meet her at all.

He studied her as the vehicle picked up speed, passing through the security checkpoints and merging with the traffic without being stopped. Charlotte wore a long fur coat that rose from her ankles to her neckline, concealing everything behind a wall of white fluff. She looked as if she'd spent hours getting ready to come out…she looked like a respectable lady, out for tea with her friends. Mitch had seen women like her, drinking daintily in teahouses as they alternatively welcomed their friends or cut them dead. He'd disliked and envied them in equal measure. And yet, Charlotte wasn't quite what she seemed. How many others had lived a double life?

Mitch found his voice. "What are you doing here?"

Charlotte mimed being hurt. "And there I was thinking you'd be pleased to see me."

"I am," Mitch said, too quickly. He wasn't sure that was true. He might not have anything on his schedule, now the meeting was over, but the admiral could call on him at any moment. She would not be pleased if he was unavailable. And yet, why would she want him? It wasn't as if she needed his advice. "I'm just wondering…"

"I came to London to shop," Charlotte said, favouring him with a smile. "And I just thought it would be nice to see you again."

Mitch had to smile. "It is"—he swallowed hard, suddenly unsure of himself—"it is nice to see you again too."

Charlotte nodded and started to open her coat. Mitch stared, feeling his manhood stir as she undressed piece by piece. He started to fumble with his dress uniform, cursing—once again—the sadist who'd designed it. It wasn't easy to undress in the car, but...he couldn't believe what they were doing. His heart raced as he glanced at the front. Making love on the backseat of a car was one thing—he'd done that when he'd been younger—but the car hadn't been moving at the time. And he'd been the driver.

He indicated the front. "What about...?"

"Brinkley won't say anything," Charlotte said. She pulled down her underwear and stood, magnificently naked, in front of him. "Come here."

Mitch stared, drinking in the sight. She was...she wasn't the perfect girl of his imagination, when he'd been a teenager; she wasn't the ideal woman of everything from adverts to porn films. She wasn't...and yet, he found her arousing beyond words. He wasn't sure what drew her to him, what pushed common sense out of his mind. She knew what she wanted and she worked to get it, putting her dignity aside along with her clothes. Cold logic told him he was risking everything, by sleeping with an aristocrat's wife. But cold logic was nothing faced with the reality of her body. He wanted her. And that was all there was to it.

He stood and stumbled towards her, feeling like a horny teenager again. Charlotte reached for him and pulled him to her. And then there was nothing but her...

• • •

"The Tadpoles are due to arrive tomorrow," Admiral Onarina said. They stood together in a small office, briefly assigned to the admiral. "Once they're embedded in the formation, we'll be departing."

Thomas nodded, wondering—idly—where Captain Campbell had gone. The younger man wasn't needed—Thomas himself wouldn't be needed if he hadn't had powerful connections—but it was still annoying not to have him around. The staff officers were starting to grate on Thomas's nerves. They didn't seem sure how they should treat him. And the officers who didn't have any real combat experience were worse.

"It should be interesting, Admiral," Thomas said. *That* was an understatement. Human navies shared the same command and control protocols, along with a great deal of technology. Three brutal interstellar wars had taught the human race the importance of ensuring their systems were as compatible as possible. But the Tadpoles weren't human. Everything about them was different. "How are we going to get everyone moving in the same direction?"

"It won't be easy," Admiral Onarina said, grimly. "Even now that we know the stakes…"

She shook her head. Thomas could fill in the blanks. The foreign governments weren't *entirely* keen on their ships operating under British command. God knew the British government would feel the same, if things were reversed. There were times when it felt as if GATO, and the planned Amalgamation, was so fragile that the slightest misstep could bring the whole edifice tumbling down. There was no shortage of naysayers, just waiting for an excuse to say "I told you so." The more Thomas thought about it, the more he wondered if they were right. Globalisation had led to a whole string of disasters, including some that had almost destroyed civilisation. Who could say Amalgamation wouldn't lead to similar issues?

He banished the thought with a flicker of irritation. It wasn't *his* job to question his political superiors, not in his role as naval officer. He had to carry out his orders to the best of his ability, or—if he found himself unable to do so—to resign. And yet, not for the first time, he found himself caught between two roles. Charlotte had been nagging him to resign from the navy and go into politics for years. Thomas knew he'd hate it, but he was starting to think it was his duty. The House of Lords needed naval officers who knew how things really worked.

And if Nelson himself had survived the years, Thomas mused, *would his experience be any use to us now?*

"I'll be greeting the Tadpoles personally, in my role as Fleet Commander," Admiral Onarina said. "We'll depart immediately afterwards, as planned, and do most of the shakedown work as we head to the target star."

Thomas grimaced. The individual ships were in good condition, or so he'd been assured, but none of the ships and their crews had experience working together. It would take time, and days upon days of exercises, to discover any problems and smooth them out. The idea of taking an unprepared fleet into battle chilled him to the bone. Under normal circumstances, they would have spent weeks getting to know one another, learning what their comrades could and couldn't do. Now...

He shook his head. There was no point in debating the issue. The fleet just didn't have *time* to settle down, not when the enemy were preparing their final blow. They had to take out the catapults before it was too late or lose the war. There were no other options. Thomas would be surprised if there weren't plans to preserve something of humanity, but such plans would be incredibly risky. There was no guarantee the human race would survive.

And the virus will just keep coming and coming until the entire galaxy is infested, he thought, grimly. There were people who thought the virus was a weapon of war, one that had escaped its creators and started to spread uncontrollably. Others thought it was laying the groundwork for its creators to take over, once all active spacefaring races had been infected and subdued. And still others thought it was just something truly alien. *We have to win completely or lose.*

"You'll be the senior British officer, after me," Admiral Onarina warned. "If something happens to me"—her dark eyes narrowed—"I want you to start thinking about contingency plans. The chain of command is clear, but..."

Thomas nodded. The Russian and Chinese officers wouldn't be happy serving under an American officer. The French—and the other lesser powers—wouldn't be happy, either. Charlotte had told him just how much horse-trading had gone on, behind the scenes, to convince the world governments to accept Admiral Onarina as fleet commander. Hopefully, they wouldn't make an issue of it if Admiral Onarina was killed in battle. They were all experienced officers. They should know better.

"Yes, Admiral," he said. The admiral's command staff might well be killed with her. Even if they weren't, the fleet's commander and second-in-command could hardly come from the same country. "I'll be ready."

"I have no doubt of it," Admiral Onarina said. "Just remember, we cannot afford a war of attrition."

"Yes, Admiral," Thomas said. "But I do feel we're risking everything on one throw of the dice."

"We are," Admiral Onarina said, bluntly. There was no doubt in her voice, for she knew, possibly better than he did, just how much could go wrong. "And if there was any other choice…believe me, I'd take it."

CHAPTER NINE

I SHOULD HAVE REMAINED ON A STARSHIP'S BRIDGE, Susan thought, as her shuttle flew towards the alien ship. *If I hadn't let them promote me...*

She rubbed her forehead, feeling a dull ache behind her temples. She'd barely gotten any sleep, between holding meetings, smoothing out minor details that really should have been left to her staff and giving reassuring briefings to old ladies of both genders. There was an endless list of orders she needed to approve, items she had to handle personally...she shook her head. She'd thought there was too much paperwork when she'd been in command of a ship, but she hadn't known the half of it. An admiral didn't even have the satisfaction of knowing she was in command.

The shuttle quivered, slightly, as it altered course. Susan turned, clearing her mind as the display updated rapidly. The Tadpole superdreadnaught—the term had stuck—looked very much like a battleship, but there was something weirdly *melted* about the design. Human ships were crude boxy shapes, thrown together from modular components; Tadpole ships looked as if they were made out of melted wax. It wasn't easy to pick out the weapons emplacements, or the sensor nodes buried within the hull. Susan admired it absently, even as she contemplated how well she stacked up against a human ship. The Tadpoles were the most advanced race in the known universe. And if they decided to fight the human race for a second time...

You're being paranoid, she told herself. *The war started because of a misunderstanding.*

She groaned, inwardly. It was easy enough to predict, with a reasonable degree of certainty, what a human would do in any given situation. As long as one had a shared understanding of the situation, it was possible to calculate contingencies and lay plans to handle any *reasonable* response. But aliens were *alien*. Susan was all too aware that it was simply impossible to do more than guess at their thinking, let alone predict their actions. The Tadpoles, the Foxes, the Cows and the Vesy had their own ways of thinking. The only consolation was that they understood humans as poorly as humans understood them.

The intercom bleeped. "Admiral," the pilot said. "We will match docking ports in two minutes."

"Understood," Susan said. "Keep the airlock sealed until I signal."

She stood, feeling faintly absurd as she stripped and changed into her bathing suit. The idea of going to a diplomatic conference naked...she'd had nightmares about being naked in front of the class, the first time she'd had to give a presentation, but actually doing it...? She supposed it might have enlivened proceedings, at the cost of utterly destroying her reputation once and for all. Here, though...she shook her head as she tied back her hair, carefully locked her facemask into place and headed for the airlock. The Tadpoles didn't give a damn what she wore. They probably didn't care if she visited in person. But she owed it to them to show the same courtesy she'd shown the others.

The airlock felt oddly warm as she stepped inside, the hatch hissing closed behind her. Susan took a breath, tasting something unpleasant at the back of her throat. The facemask hadn't been used for quite some time. She put the minor discomfort out of her mind as the inner hatch started to open, feeling a frisson of panic as yellowish water spilled into the airlock compartment. It felt warm, against her bare feet. Susan calmed herself as the water rose rapidly, reminding herself she was perfectly safe. She couldn't help checking and rechecking the facemask, just to make sure it was firmly in place. If it came off, while she was in the alien ship, she would drown. Drowning in space...her lips quirked. *That* would look bloody stupid when someone wrote her obituary.

She padded forward as the gravity field shifted, then faded completely. The Tadpoles preferred zero-g to artificial gravity, probably because they spent most of their lives in the ocean rather than on the land. The water seemed to brighten as she swam into the alien ship, an eerie biolumines-cence pulsing from everywhere and nowhere...as if the water itself was glowing. She took a long breath as she spotted the Tadpoles waiting for her, three of them. It was easy to see why the first humans to meet them face to face had thought they were nothing more than beasts. On land, they looked like shambling parodies of humanity; in the water, they looked almost completely different. It was hard to believe they weren't two dif-ferent species.

"We greet you," the Tadpoles said in unison. Susan's facemask picked up the words and transmitted them to her. It had been over two decades since the war and yet...it was hard to be entirely *sure* the translation was accurate. The Tadpoles lacked concepts humans considered important and vice versa. "Welcome."

"I thank you, in the name of the human race," Susan said, carefully. The diplomats had had headaches, when they tried to put together a com-mon language. The more they tried to dance around an issue, the harder it became to translate. "We request that you approve our plan."

The Tadpoles moved suddenly, spinning around each other in a com-plicated dance that wouldn't be possible in normal gravity. Susan shivered, despite the warmth. The Tadpoles were less...individualistic than humans, she'd been told. They did everything in groups...factions. She didn't really understand it. No one did. Her training told her that a starship couldn't be run by council, that the crew couldn't vote on anything, but...the Tadpoles made it work. Somehow. She supposed it was hard for them to conceal their thinking from their fellows. A human dictatorship could convince each and every dissident that they were completely alone. The Tadpoles couldn't do that.

"Your plan is sound." The dance came to an end. Susan couldn't tell if the Tadpoles had switched places or not. They all looked the same to her. No doubt they thought the same of their human allies. "We will assist with Phase One and proceed to Phase Two if it appears workable."

Susan breathed a sigh of relief. "I thank you," she said, again. She hadn't dared hold out hope for anything more. The Tadpoles wouldn't commit themselves to striking deep into enemy territory until they knew it was possible. "We can ask for no more."

The aliens withdrew, moving back into the shadows. It was rude, by human standards, but...she shook her head. The interview was over. She found it oddly refreshing. She'd had to spend too much time making small talk with people she detested, people who didn't give a damn about her or...anything, really, beyond their own power. The Tadpoles didn't care about human etiquette. She wondered, as she turned and swam back to the airlock, why they'd agreed to the meeting in the first place. Had they considered it a diplomatic requirement? Or were they trying to humour their human allies?

She shelved the question as she swam back into the airlock, then keyed the hatch closed. The water level dropped sharply as it was pumped out, into the tanks. Susan ran her hands through her hair, promising herself a shower as the shuttle headed back to the flagship. Her hair hadn't felt so grimy since the Second Interstellar War. Back then, the universe had seemed much simpler. They hadn't known about the virus or what it could do.

The intercom bleeped as she hurried into the washroom. "Admiral?"

"Take us back to the flagship," Susan ordered. She should have enough time for a quick shower. "And inform the Admiralty that the meeting was a success."

Her lips curved into a smile as she stepped into the washroom and turned on the shower. It hadn't been a long meeting, but she hadn't expected it to last more than a few minutes at most. They never did. The Tadpoles understood humans found their native environment as unsettling and uncomfortable as they did the surface world. Susan nodded to herself as she undressed and stepped into the warm shower. Humans and Tadpoles didn't *need* to fight over anything. They could share entire worlds without any real contact.

And the virus threatens us all, she mused. *They may not think like us, but they understand the danger as well as we do.*

• • •

"I got to say," Private Scott Davies said as they waited by the airlock, "I thought this was someone's idea of a joke."

Colin gave him a sharp look. It was impossible to imagine Sergeant Bowman playing a joke on anyone, let alone his subordinates. The man had rotated between active service and training duties for longer than Colin had been alive. He was strict—and no one crossed him twice—but fair. He wouldn't set someone up for a pratfall.

And certainly not like this, Colin thought. He'd read the files very carefully, then read them again just to be sure he'd hit the high points. It was clear that whoever was behind the assignment wanted it to succeed. Perhaps. The cynic in Colin knew there were people who would openly promise the moon while covertly sabotaging their own efforts. *He wouldn't have volunteered me for the post if he didn't have faith in me.*

He sucked in his breath. The Vesy had been a primitive race when they'd been discovered by a bunch of Russian deserters. The deserters had thought, at first, that they were the last remnants of humanity and set out to turn the Vesy into allies for a war of revenge. And then they'd discovered they weren't the last after all, which meant they'd be hung for desertion when their countrymen caught up with them. They'd become space pirates—the first and only known space pirates in history—until HMS *Warspite* had stumbled across their operations and liberated the system from their control. The Vesy had become, to all intents and purposes, a client race. No one was very comfortable with the situation.

The airlock hissed as it started to open. Colin tensed. The files had made it clear that the human settlers were trying to uplift the Vesy, without making them into pale copies of humanity or shattering their spirit once and for all. They'd been finding ways for the Vesy to earn money...Colin wasn't sure what he thought of *that*. It was a good way to make someone dependent, without making it so obvious it couldn't be ignored. And yet, what did they have to sell? Only themselves.

He sucked in his breath as he saw the alien for the first time. Kevin—he promised himself he'd have a few sharp words with whoever had suggested the name—was alien. He kicked himself, mentally. Of *course* Kevin was alien. It was just hard to believe. He hadn't seen many aliens in his career, unless one counted the zombies. And they'd been human before they'd been infected.

Colin forced himself to look the alien up and down. The Vesy struck him as fundamentally *wrong*. He was humanoid, wearing a standard battle-dress tailored to his body, but his proportions were all...strange. Alien. He was tall, with scaly skin and a nose that looked as if it was a weird cross between a lizard's nose and a pig's snout. A handful of feathers seemed to be growing out of his head. Colin couldn't help thinking of them as a mane.

Kevin saluted. "Permission to come aboard, sir?"

"Granted," Colin said, automatically. The alien's voice was strange—no one would be mistaking him for human any time soon—but understand-able. "Welcome onboard."

He watched the alien walk out of the shuttlecraft and onto the ship. Kevin moved like a dancer...like a *lizard*, Colin's brain pointed out. It looked as if he could run a great deal faster than the average human, something Colin vaguely remembered from the files. He made a mental note to go through them again, just in case he'd missed something. God alone knew how the attachment was going to work out. The only thing he knew for sure was that there were surprises in store.

"Come with me," he ordered. His orders were to treat the alien like any other newcomer to the section. "This way."

He turned, all too aware of the alien at his back. Whatever his orders said, it was hard to accept the alien as one of his men. He gritted his teeth, telling himself that the Vesy had gone through the same commando training as he had. And yet…he hadn't heard of the program until now. He was surprised he hadn't heard so much as a whisper, even from the older marines and officers. Someone had probably worked overtime to make sure no one spoke out of turn.

They walked past a handful of crewmen, all of whom gaped at the newcomer. Colin smiled, despite himself. They'd have to get used to seeing the alien, somehow. Kevin would have to jog with the other marines, as well as carrying out hundreds of emergency drills until he could perform his duties in his sleep. Colin grimaced as he remembered just how much anti-alien feeling there was, down on Earth. The Bombardment had hardened a *lot* of attitudes. The Vesy weren't responsible for that—they couldn't so much as leave their homeworld without help—but he couldn't count on people being smart enough to believe it. They'd probably find it easier to think one alien looked just like another…

Never mind that they're two different species, Colin thought. *Idiots.*

He sighed, inwardly, as he led the way into the tiny briefing compartment. Bowman had assigned it to the platoon, a favour Colin was *sure* came with invisible strings attached. The rest of his men stood to attention as he entered, something that surprised him. He was only a very junior corporal, not a lieutenant or a captain or…he shook his head. Right now, it didn't matter. He'd worry about it later.

And if a junior screws up, he thought morbidly, *everything can be blamed on him.*

"Stand at ease," he ordered, watching Kevin out of the corner of his eye. The alien relaxed slightly, very slightly. It was hard to tell if the Vesy was actually standing at ease or not. "This is Kevin and…"

"Hey," Private Adams said. "What's your real name?"

Kevin produced a hissing sound that reminded Colin of a teakettle on the brink of boiling. He wasn't sure how Kevin made the noise and he was *sure* he couldn't make it himself. The planners had been right, he decided, to give Kevin a human name. He made a mental note to have a series of long conversations with the alien, just to test his command of the English language. Kevin shouldn't have any real problems, if he'd been through commando training, but it was well to be sure. Commando training was brutal, harsh enough to sort the men from the boys, yet it had one glaring weakness. Like all emergency training, it left out the emergency.

Colin cleared his throat. "We will be running training sims from now until departure," he said. If there was one advantage to being on semi-detached duty, it was a certain freedom to run his training exercises the way he wanted them. "I expect each and every one of you to work towards our development. If the rumours are true"—he'd heard all sorts of rumours, some so insane he couldn't even begin to believe them—"we're heading deep into enemy space. I want to be ready to give the virus hell, when we meet it again. Any questions?"

There were none. Colin breathed a sigh of relief. Life hadn't been easy for an immigrant family in Birmingham—he cursed himself under his breath, remembering that he'd been just as much of an arsehole as everyone else—and *they'd* been human. The girl he'd sneered at had grown into an exotic young woman...he shook his head. He really *had* been an arsehole when he'd been a kid. Perhaps he should write her a note of apology, if he could find her again. He didn't have the slightest idea where she'd gone. It was hard to believe she'd wanted to stay in Birmingham...

"Good," he said. He motioned for Kevin to sling his carryall under the table—thankfully, he could fit in a human-sized bunk—and then led the way to the training room. "Let's go."

Sergeant Bowman passed them as they entered the chamber. Colin was sure he'd be watching through the concealed pickups, gauging Colin's performance as well as the newcomer's. Colin wasn't sure how he felt about *that*. The assignment might see him promoted, if things went well, or it might cost him his shot at a commission and company command. He groaned, inwardly, as he activated the simulators. Promotion was swift in wartime—the war killed far too many promising young officers—but it wouldn't come if he had a major black mark on his record. And who knew what he'd do with himself then?

I'll think of something, he thought. *Until then...I'll give it my best shot.*

The simulation came online, projecting a handful of holographic targets. His stomach churned as he saw women and children in the infected horde. Ten years ago, accidentally hitting a civilian would have meant a beasting from the instructors. Now, infected civilians could be as dangerous as everyone else. He wondered, idly, what Kevin thought of firing on humans. It was hard to believe the Vesy *loved* their human patrons. Colin had had enough experience with do-gooders who thought they were helping to loathe them without reservation.

A problem for another time, he mused. A holographic image leapt at him and he stopped it with a holographic bullet. *Right now, we have other problems.*

CHAPTER TEN

"WELCOME BACK, SIR," Staci said. "Had a good leave?"

Mitch frowned, all too aware he looked like a man who'd spent the previous night with his girlfriend. He had, he supposed. By the time Charlotte had dropped him off at the barracks, they'd done it four times…he still couldn't believe they'd made love in a moving vehicle on the streets of London. The thought of being stopped by the police, or the army, had added a spice to their lovemaking he hadn't thought possible. And yet, he had no intention of talking about it to anyone. If the truth ever came out…

Staci cocked her head. "Did she dump you?"

"Nothing like that," Mitch said, wryly. "Did we receive our final orders?"

"They're in the datacore, waiting for you," Staci said. "And they've settled our final departure time. We'll be leaving in four hours."

Mitch nodded, cursing the politicians and diplomats and armchair admirals under his breath. They hadn't *needed* him in London, damn it. Nothing he'd done over the last two days had really needed him, except making love to Charlotte. He smiled, remembering her final kisses, the way she'd given herself to him with complete abandon. The thought warmed him, even though he knew he shouldn't have been there. He should have been on his ship, readying her for departure. It wasn't fair to leave everything to his XO. Staci was an experienced officer, and they were as close to friends as their respective positions would allow, but it was easy to miss something important in the rush to prepare the ship. He'd have to go through everything with a fine-toothed comb, yet he'd never be sure he hadn't missed something. He was surprised Admiral Onarina had gone along with it. *She* was no armchair admiral.

He put the thought out of his head as they strolled through the corridors and up to the bridge. *Unicorn* was tiny, compared to a battleship; he had no problems greeting his crew by name in a manner that would never have passed muster on a larger ship. The handful of newcomers would have to be greeted personally, once they were underway. There was no room for slackers on *Unicorn*. Everyone had to pull their weight. He made a mental note to make sure they had enough cross-trained personnel onboard. His engineering and weapons departments didn't have the manpower to cope with serious losses.

Not that it matters, he thought. *Anything that hits us hard enough to do real damage is likely to blow up the whole ship.*

He felt his smile grow wider as he walked onto the bridge. It was as tiny as the rest of the ship, a cramped compartment that felt smaller when all the consoles were manned, but it was *his*. He didn't really *want* a battleship or a fleet carrier, a capital ship that was rarely allowed to travel without a squadron of escorts. They weren't *independent* commands, not in the truest sense. *Unicorn* could go places—alone—that larger ships could not. He hoped, as he took his seat, that the mission would provide plenty of room for independent operations. *Someone* would have to do the scouting.

"Signal from the flag, sir," Lieutenant Hannah Avis said. "They're ordering the fleet to prepare for departure as planned."

Finally, Mitch thought. He'd never had any real doubts the operation was going to take place, but...there'd been so many stops and starts that he hadn't been entirely sure. It was all too easy to let a window of opportunity slip by, just through an excess of caution. It was bad enough, he reflected crossly, when they passed up on a chance to give the enemy a well-deserved thrashing. It was a great deal worse when they ran the risk of letting the enemy get into position to put a knife in one's back. *Once we're underway, the real work begins.*

He smiled at the display. "Inform the flag that we will be ready to depart as planned," he ordered. "And update them on our current status."

"Aye, Captain."

Mitch nodded as he keyed his console, bringing up the starchart. The timing was awkward, to say the least. The first phase of the mission would've been a great deal easier if the Royal Navy had twenty catapults of its own. Hell, he'd settle for just three or four. The boffins claimed the transit shock could be mitigated, now they knew it existed. Mitch wasn't so sure. Jump shock itself wasn't very well understood. He'd met doctors who insisted it was real, an effect of jumping through the tramlines, and others who swore blind it was all in their heads. The truth might be beyond human comprehension. All that mattered, from his point of view, was that the effect was real.

It'll take us nearly a month to reach the target star, he mused. For a moment, he thought he understood the government's reluctance to embrace the operation. The largest fleet humanity had deployed for years, sent so far into deep space that it couldn't be recalled in a hurry…he could see their point. *And yet, we have no choice.*

Staci looked up from her console. "Do you think we'll go all the way?"

"Yes," Mitch said, with more confidence than he felt. Admiral Onarina had done something similar, back when she'd been a battleship captain. Her experience had probably given her the idea. She might even have pushed for building additional human catapults before she'd realised there was a chance to steal a set of *alien* catapults. "I think this could win us the war."

He sat back in his chair and forced himself to wait. The flagship would send the order soon enough, then they'd be on their way. He'd be master of his own ship once again, scouting out alien systems and locating targets for the bigger ships. And then…he smiled. If the mission lived up to its promise, the end of the war could be at hand. If nothing else, hitting every infected world with a cluster of BioBombs would *have* to force the virus to sit up and take notice. Who knew what it would think when its own nature started working against it?

We have to take it out or be taken out, he thought, curtly. *There are no alternatives. Not any longer.*

. . .

Thomas barely noticed the midshipwoman until she held out a datapad for his inspection. He glanced at it, scanned the lines of text and pressed his finger against the scanner, authorising the request. A minor matter, one not normally deserving of his attention. He would normally have left it to Commander Donker, but the XO was in his cabin catching up with his sleep. Thomas didn't blame him. The entire crew had been working like demons to prepare for the mission.

It was hard not to feel a little unsure of himself as he studied the updates from the admiral. He understood the logic—they'd gone over it again and again until he could make the arguments in his sleep—but it still nagged at him. The cluster of green icons on the display marked the largest fleet humanity had ever dispatched into enemy territory, easily the most powerful force ever assembled. Admiral Onarina's fleet could crush the Royal Navy of twenty years ago and never know it had been in a fight. It represented a force that could win a war—or lose it, if the fleet itself was lost. Thomas understood that, sometimes, one had to gamble. He just didn't like the idea of gambling everything on one throw of the dice.

You said that to the admiral and she overruled you, he thought, curtly. *And now you have to carry out your orders.*

He felt cold. Charlotte was back on Earth, as were their daughters. He knew, like everyone else who'd joined the navy, that there was a very real chance he wouldn't come home. *Lion* was tough, and the battleships were tougher, but their weapons and armour were no longer a surprise. The virus had had months to devise countermeasures, as well as an industrial base that wasn't limited by economic necessity. Thomas had insisted on going through simulation after simulation, trying to deduce what the virus would deploy against them. It could easily deploy missiles and gunboats of its own...hell, it already had both concepts. Marrying them together wouldn't be hard. Or it might come up with something new. The virus was hardly ingenious, but it had a *lot* of processing power. It was quite possible it would plod its way to victory.

Dismissing the thought, he turned his attention to the final reports. The Royal Marines were settling in nicely, along with their alien...comrade. Thomas wasn't sure how he felt about *that*. He understood the importance of trying to ensure the Vesy knew they'd earned their place in the galaxy, to try to avoid damaging their pride, but there was a time and a place and that was *not* on a starship that was going into harm's way. Combined deployments were always a pain, even when everyone was *human*. Thomas was sure there would be problems, as the fleet shook itself down. He feared there was a very real chance some of the squadrons would head to the wrong star...

Everyone knows what is at stake, he told himself. *There may be problems, but they won't be deliberate problems.*

He frowned as he scanned the next set of reports. The gunboat crews had spent the last few days in the simulators. The CAG believed they'd be ready to take their gunboats into open space in a couple of days, unless an alien fleet arrived with blood in its eye. Thomas would have preferred more time, but...it wasn't going to happen. The entire operation had been thrown together at terrifying speed. They were lucky to secure as many experienced officers and crew as they had. And he knew it, too.

"Captain," Lieutenant Nathaniel Cook said. "Signal from the flag. We are to ready ourselves to depart as planned."

"Power up the drives," Thomas ordered, putting his doubts aside. "And inform the crew that this is their last chance to write home before we jump out."

"Aye, Captain."

Thomas glanced at his console. He'd somehow found the time to record messages for Charlotte and his daughters, although he hadn't said much. His girls were still at school...his heart clenched at the thought of one of them being called out of class to hear about their father's death. It had happened before, to countless children. Why couldn't it happen to *his* girls? He tried to tell himself that they were young women now, but it was hard to believe. They were still, in his heart, the girls he'd dandled on his knee.

And there's no point in recording another message, he thought. It would be an abuse of authority to send a final message, not when a goodly percentage of the crew couldn't do anything of the sort. It would send entirely the wrong message to the men and women under his command. *All I can do is hope for the best.*

A dull quiver ran through *Lion* as her drives powered up. Thomas forced himself to sit back in his chair, watching as the fleet carefully organised itself into formation. They were going to alter course sharply, once they'd passed through Terra Nova and started flying towards the front. A careful deception operation had already been planned, in hopes of deceiving any watching eyes, but it was impossible to be certain of escaping detection. There weren't many targets along their projected path. The virus would be foolish not to at least *consider* the possibility the fleet was heading for the catapults.

And it might speed up its plans, Thomas mused. Long-range recon flights had revealed major enemy formations keeping up the pressure on the human defences. It was just a matter of time, everyone thought, before they punched through. The delay had puzzled the analysts, once upon a time. It didn't now. *If it uses the catapults first, it might win the war.*

His gaze wandered to the halo of green and blue icons surrounding Earth. There'd always been a remarkable amount of firepower dedicated to protecting the homeworld, even before the true nature of the threat had been realized. It was hard to believe that anything, even the fleet shifting into departure formation, could punch through the defences and lay waste to the planet. Even the Tadpoles would have problems. And yet, the virus wasn't a conventional foe. If it started to deploy biobombs of its own...

And if we're caught short, weeks from Earth, he thought grimly, *we might return to a devastated homeworld.*

. . .

"I hope you haven't lost your touch," Admiral Paul Mason said. His holographic image stood in the centre of Susan's cabin. "Remember, port is starboard and left is right."

Susan had to laugh. "As long as I can do better than *that*," she said, "I will be happy."

"Yeah." Paul sobered. "Just remember you have to keep a hundred and one other things straight in your mind."

"Yeah," Susan echoed. She wished her old friend was accompanying her. She'd gone to some trouble to try to get him as her second, but the Director of the Alpha Black project could not be risked. He knew too much. She had strict orders to ensure she—and the other senior commanders—didn't fall into enemy hands, but her superiors understood the orders might be impossible to carry out. "It hasn't been *that* long since I stood on a flag deck and commanded a fleet."

"And you've remained at the cutting edge of naval technology ever since," Paul Mason said, calmly. "Just remember not to lose your cool if things go wrong."

"I won't," Susan assured him. "Try and come up with a silver bullet, while I'm gone."

"I've got people working on teleporters, force shields and time travel," Paul Mason said, with a grin. "And we might just come up with *something* brilliant if we put our minds together."

Susan laughed. She'd always liked Paul Mason's sense of humour. "I'll see you on the far side."

She raised a hand in farewell, then closed the channel. The holographic image vanished. Susan stared at where it had been, trying to keep her rolling emotions under control. It would be nice to think the boffins would come up with a war-winning weapon, then put it into mass production and start churning it out overnight. It would be nice...but the real world didn't work that way. New technology always had bugs, little flaws that had to be worked out to keep them from becoming a major problem. For every good idea that became a piece of new technology, there were a hundred concepts that proved impractical. She smiled, rather wanly. The boffins had been promising force shields for decades. So far, they'd produced precisely *nothing* in the form of usable hardware.

The intercom bleeped. "Admiral, the fleet is ready to depart."

Susan stepped back, pasting a calm and composed expression on her face. She'd barely gotten any sleep over the last two days, as she'd sorted out everything from minor disputes to disagreements that could have convinced the foreign governments to take their ships and go home. If there were so many problems when humanity was staring at total destruction, she dreaded to think what would happen when they weren't. God knew there were no shortage of people who hated foreigners or aliens or...

She put the thought out of her head as she stepped through the hatch and onto the flag bridge. Her staff kept their eyes on their consoles, as she'd taught them; she'd been very insistent she didn't want or need the excessive respect offered to other senior officers. She needed them to go the extra mile for her, not become bitter and resentful; she needed them to feel they could speak freely. It was all too easy, when one was in command, to decide that one didn't need to listen to one's subordinates. She'd served under officers like that. Never again.

"Elliot," she said. Her aide straightened to attention. "Is everything in readiness?"

"Yes, Admiral," Commander Elliot Richardson said. He'd wrangled the post through family connections, something that puzzled his superior. It had looked as if his family had thought Susan was based on Earth, instead of taking a fleet into danger. "The fleet is ready to depart."

Susan nodded as she took her chair. The battleship's drives were thrumming as she prepared to depart. Susan felt a moment of *déjà vu*, mingled with a faint bitterness. She really *shouldn't* have let them promote her out of *Vanguard*, even though she'd known it was just a matter of time before she was told to accept promotion or retire. *Thunderous* was the same class as *Vanguard*, so akin to her first command that she brought back memories...

"Signal the fleet," she ordered. The drives were getting louder. She didn't have to ask to know the battleship was ready to depart. "All ships are to commence departure proceedings on my mark."

"Aye, Admiral."

The die is cast, Susan thought. Once they were through the tramlines, and beyond the flicker network, there would be no chance of a recall until they completed their mission and returned home. She studied the display for a long moment, all too aware just how much trust had been vested in her. The sheer enormity of what she'd done swept over her. She understood, now, just how Admiral Jellicoe had thought at Jutland. He could have won or lost the war in an afternoon. So could she. *It's time to go.*

"Mark," she said, quietly. "Take us out of here."

CHAPTER ELEVEN

"INCOMING," MARIGOLD SNAPPED. "Form defensive formation!"

Tobias cursed under his breath as the gunboats formed up, too late. The enemy starfighters had appeared out of nowhere, lying doggo between the enemy fleet and the gunboats until the gunboats were too close to avoid engagement. Tobias watched grimly as the space between the two formations started to sparkle with plasma fire, the starfighters showing a terrifying lack of concern for their own survival as they closed the range. He could understand their logic—the starfighters were doomed, if their motherships were destroyed by the missile strike—but it still bothered him. It was a grim reminder that the virus considered each and every one of its hosts to be expendable.

The gunboats linked up, their point defence weapons merging into a single entity to force the enemy craft to fight their way through a hail of fire. Tobias allowed himself a cold smile as a handful of enemy icons vanished from the display, only to sober again as the remainder of the starfighters just kept coming. It looked as if someone had tinkered with the simulation, setting the enemy numbers to infinite. He gritted his teeth as plasma bolts started to zero in on their targets. The gunboats carried more armour than the average starfighter, but not enough to give them a realistic chance of surviving a single hit. He'd been warned, time and time again, that the best they could hope for was bailing out before the gunboat exploded.

He felt a curious sense of detachment as the enemy craft closed in on the squadron. The point defence was working well, but the enemy were ducking and weaving seemingly at random. It was unusually efficient for the virus, suggesting there was a brainship somewhere within the enemy fleet. The fleet itself was hidden behind a haze of ECM, denying Tobias any hard data beyond the simple fact it was there. His heart sank as gunboats started to vanish, icon after icon vanishing from the display. The enemy shooting wasn't very accurate, but they were pumping out so much fire it hardly mattered. The missile run had failed so badly...

The gunboat shook. The screens went blank. Tobias sagged in his chair as the simulation—their part of it, at least—came to an end. He keyed an override code into the console, in hopes of watching the remainder of the fleet score a victory, but it was starting to look as though it wasn't going to be *their* victory. He shook his head in dismay. He'd been told it was important to overestimate the enemy—better to prepare for the worst than be caught by surprise—but it was demoralising. They'd done everything right up until the moment the enemy had sprung their surprise.

"For you, the war is over," Marigold said, dryly. "We lost."

Tobias winced. His father had gone to war and never returned. He'd grown up in world where countless windows displayed black ribbons, a testament to fathers, husbands and sons lost to war. A surge of bitterness overwhelmed him, undimmed by the grim knowledge the war *had* to be fought. What did it matter, he asked himself, when he'd grown up without a father? When countless other boys and girls had lost parents to the war? When it was no longer clear that *anything* would survive, even if the war was won tomorrow?

And if we lose the war, he thought grimly, *there'll be nothing left of us.*

He gritted his teeth. He'd watched countless period dramas, alternate histories of how terrible life would have been in Occupied Britain. They'd been nothing more than bad propaganda, he'd always thought. Napoleonic Britain, Nazi Britain, Caliphate Britain...a country dominated by foreigners, until brave, super and noble Britons remembered who their forefathers had been and rose up against the occupiers. He'd never liked them, not least because watching had been compulsory at school. And pointing out the historical inaccuracies had always gotten him in trouble. And yet...

The hatch popped open. Tobias glanced at the remainder of the exercise, then stood and gave Marigold a quick hug. They hadn't had much time for themselves over the past fortnight. They'd been too busy training the newcomers and running endless simulations. Tobias was gloomily aware a *lot* of shit was going to be running downhill and pooling in their boots, when the admiral and her staff finally finished assessing the results. The entire fleet had been caught with its pants down, given the enemy a chance to put a boot up its collective arse...no, the admiral was not going to be pleased. The thought of learning from their mistakes wouldn't improve her mood.

He yawned and tried to hide it as they stumbled out the hatch. His legs felt unsteady, even though he *knew* they'd never left the battlecruiser. The simulations were so good it was easy to forget they weren't real, not least because the training officers wouldn't have hesitated to make an issue of it if the pilots treated the simulations like a computer game. One could do things in games one simply couldn't in real life. There was certainly no such thing as bonus lives. The pilots had to count themselves fortunate they'd have a chance to learn from their mistakes afterwards.

Marigold wiped sweat from her brow as the rest of the pilots exited the simulators and headed to the washroom. Tobias felt a stab of worry, even though he knew she was a better pilot than he. God knew she'd kicked his arse on the computer...he shook his head, looking away to give her what privacy he could. He wanted to urge her to stay home, where she was safe, but he knew she would take it the wrong way. His lips quirked at the thought. Was there a *right* way to take it?

Bagehot stuck his head into the compartment. "Briefing Room, ten minutes."

Tobias nodded—he was too tired to salute—and stumbled into the washroom himself. It had taken months for him to get used to sharing bathrooms and toilets with anyone, male or female, but right now…he was just too exhausted to give much of a damn. He splashed water on his face, made use of the facilities and then washed himself again before heading down to the briefing room. There was no one inside, when he entered. That was meaningless. The analysis deck had been watching. They were probably composing a truly savage piece of criticism, listing all the mistakes the gunboat squadron had made since the simulation had begun. Tobias wondered, idly, if they'd be making the same effort for the admiral. *She'd* been the one who'd issued the engagement orders.

He poured two cups of coffee, then sat down. Marigold joined him a moment later, her hair looking slightly damp. Had she had time for a quick shower? It was possible. Tobias loved to luxuriate under the water, but the military had taught him to wash efficiently in less than five minutes. Commandos, he'd been told, could wash in less than a *single* minute. He wasn't sure he believed that, although Colin had never shown any regard for personal hygiene. His body had always stunk of sweat and…

Put that behind you, he told himself, severely. *Colin's grown up.*

He forced himself to relax as the rest of the squadron joined them. Tobias couldn't help feeling as though the newcomers were intruders, forcing their way into a space that belonged to others. They shouldn't be there at all, but…he'd found it hard to memorise their names. It would just cause heartache if they died…when they died. The original squadron members were dead or reassigned. Tobias knew he'd been too attached to them. He didn't want to repeat the same mistake.

Marigold and I will die together, he thought. It was the sort of silly concept that idiots would declare romantic, except…it was pointless. *If only she would go home…*

"Well, that could have gone better." Bagehot entered and swept up to the front of the compartment. "What did we do wrong?"

"Everything," Tobias muttered.

Marigold shot him a sharp look. "We let ourselves get jumped," she said. "We didn't realise the enemy starfighters had powered down, pretending to be holes in space until we got too close. We didn't realise what we were seeing until it was too late."

"Starfighters can't flash-wake their systems so violently," another pilot objected. "They should have burned out their drives *trying*."

"It is possible, theoretically," Bagehot disagreed. His eyes swept the room. "Statistically, yes; you're right. A number of enemy craft should have rendered themselves powerless just by trying. But the odds were stacked against you."

Tobias nodded. He knew the score. As long as there was a *chance*, however slight, that the enemy would hit their targets, they would. The simulated starfighters had *all* survived their stunt, even though…he looked at the display, which was showing the remnants of the engagement. They'd fucked up. There was no point in trying to hide from the truth. They'd flown right into a trap because they hadn't given any real thought to what the enemy could do to *them*.

"We kept our active sensors offline," he said, thoughtfully. "And that gave them a chance to jump us."

"But if we'd put the sensors online," another pilot argued, "we'd have signed our own death warrants."

"We got our arses kicked anyway," a third pilot growled.

"We certainly need to deploy more sensor drones with the squadron," Bagehot said. "But even that carries its own risks."

"Our sensor pulses might reveal our positions to the enemy," Marigold said. "That would be awkward."

"A bit of an own goal," Bagehot agreed. "Perhaps if we were to adjust…"

Tobias leaned forward as the discussion continued, Bagehot trying to encourage all the pilots to offer their thoughts. There was no easy answer. Turning on their active sensors would allow the enemy to pinpoint their locations, yet not using the sensors…he considered the possibilities as the discussion went on and on. There weren't many. Military tactics were an endless succession of trade-offs, with each new tactic or piece of technology bringing its own difficulties in its wake. He hoped, desperately, that the virus's brainships hadn't been devising newer and better tactics, although he was sure that was nothing more than wishful thinking. The enemy had seen the gunboats and missiles in action. It *had* to start thinking about countermeasures.

"Dismissed," Bagehot said, when the discussion came to an end. "We'll continue our simulations tomorrow."

At which time, the flag staff will have completed their analysis of just what went wrong, Tobias thought, as he stood. *And they'll be ready to start pointing fingers and placing the blame.*

• • •

Colin tried not to grunt as he hotfooted it down the corridor, Kevin on his heels. The protective suit was uncomfortably hot, and he felt sweat trickling down his legs and staining his trousers. The plasma rifle in his hands felt uncomfortably heavy as they reached the airlock, taking up positions on each side as Colin hit the override. The airlock opened, revealing an empty corridor. Colin was torn between relief and disappointment. It would have been a damn sight easier to track down the zombie—and anyone else who might have been infected—if the wretched creature had stood in the centre of the corridor and waited for them.

He might also have tossed a grenade through the airlock as soon as it started opening, he thought, keying his throatmike to make a quick report. *And that would have killed the pair of us.*

Colin glanced at Kevin, who'd taken position on the nearside of the hatch. The Vesy was wrapped in a protective suit, hiding his face behind a mask, but he was still very clearly alien. The proportions were all wrong. Colin held up a hand, marking out a countdown, and got a nod in return. Kevin might be alien, but there was nothing wrong with his training. It remained to be seen how he'd perform in *real* combat. Colin wasn't looking forward to *that*. He'd sooner work the kinks out when no one was actually at risk of death—or worse.

Warning icons flashed up in his HUD as they slipped through the airlock and inched down the corridor. There were traces of viral matter in the air, suggesting the zombie had entered the infectious stage. Colin guessed the poor bastard—or the alien intelligence that had taking over his body—knew he'd been isolated. It was just a matter of time before the host was tracked down, either by the bioscanners or the compartment to compartment search. The virus was trying to do as much damage as it could before it was too late. Colin gritted his teeth as they kept moving. There was no hope of saving the host. All they could do was avenge him.

He frowned as he spotted an open hatch ahead of him, leading into a crewmen's compartment. He sucked in his breath. It was a rule of thumb that the larger the ship, the less space there was for the junior crewmen and officers. If there'd been a bunch of sleeping personnel in that compartment, they were almost certainly infected. They might survive, if they received immediate treatment, but…Colin's eyes narrowed. The scene might as well have T-R-A-P painted on it. He wasn't willing to throw explosive grenades through the hatch when he'd be killing men he could save. And that would give the original host a chance to get the drop on the marines when they crashed through the hatch.

His hand dropped to his belt, removing the UV flashbang. It would give everyone a shock, particularly if they weren't infected, but…it was survivable. They'd get a sunburn, nothing more. He hefted the flashbang, glanced at Kevin to make sure the alien was ready, then hurled the flashbang into the compartment. A brilliant flash of light pulsed through the air. His mask darkened, automatically, as he hurled himself into the compartment and looked around. A handful of men lay on the bunks, groaning theatrically. They looked to be in the early stages of infection. There was no sign of the original zombie. His eyes swept around, looking for the host. The poor bastard was nowhere to be seen. The wardrobe compartments lay open, revealing a collection of protective shipsuits. Alarm bells rang in his mind, too late, as one of the shipsuits moved of its own accord.

"Fuck!"

He lifted his rifle, too late. The zombie threw himself forward, crashing into Colin with all the power he could muster. Colin stumbled back and crashed to the floor, his rifle clattering down beside him. The zombie had hidden inside the suit, using the protective layers to shield himself from the flashbang. Good thinking, Colin acknowledged sourly, as they struggled. The zombie fought with inhuman strength, trying desperately to rip Colin's mask off his face. That might not be fatal, but it would certainly land him in sickbay for a few days. And his comrades would always wonder if he'd been infected...

The zombie jerked, then lay still. Colin pushed the body aside and looked up. Kevin was standing there, holding a shockrod in one hand. The zombies would, according to the boffins, be royally fucked if they were zapped with a shockrod, although Colin had no idea if that was true. No one had dared try, when shooting them was a great deal easier and safer. He certainly had no intention of risking his life trying to test the theory. If the boffins wanted to test it, they could try it themselves.

"Good work," he said, standing. His suit was intact, thankfully. The zombie had come very close to tearing off his mask. "That was far too close."

"I didn't dare try to shoot him," Kevin said. It was hard to be sure, given his accent, but there seemed to be a hint of humour in his voice. "That would have looked very bad on my record."

Colin nodded as he removed his mask, signalling the end of the exercise. Shooting one's commanding officer in a simulation was a good way to end up in real trouble, even if there was a shortage of other options. Kevin would have had to knock him out if the mask had come off, in hopes of slowing the infection long enough to get him to safety. Colin had known officers who would have understood and officers who would have demanded harsh punishment for the bootneck who'd clobbered them. They probably felt it set a bad precedent. Colin had heard whispers of officers who'd bitched and moaned about going through blood screenings, even though *everyone* knew the risks. He was just glad he didn't have to serve under one of them.

His earpiece buzzed. "Good work, Corporal."

"Thank you, sir," Colin said. He'd been caught by surprise—he'd never heard of a zombie donning protective gear before, not when the poor bastard was trying to infect the entire ship—but they'd recovered nicely. "It was almost fun."

He sobered as they left the compartment and headed back to Marine Country. It had been fun, but it was also deadly serious. They were preparing for war, against an enemy that—all too often—wore a human face. The next time it might be real. The next time...

We'll be ready, he promised himself. The analysts were still drawing up their concepts of what the marines would find, when they boarded the alien catapults. *And we'll give them the fight of their lives.*

CHAPTER TWELVE

SUSAN HAD NEVER REALLY LIKED FORMAL BANQUETS, even when she was the hostess. She would have preferred to handle all discussions via holocommunications, if only to ensure her commanding officers were on their ships if—when—the shit hit the fan. The last thing anyone wanted, particularly her, was to be caught on the hop by a maundering alien fleet. The spooks swore blind there were no major enemy formations between Earth and New Washington, but Susan knew she couldn't take it for granted. There was just no way to be sure the virus wasn't already mobilising every ship it could muster to intercept and destroy her fleet before it reached the target star.

She sat at the table, forcing herself to sit through an endless round of toasts to the king, the queen, a dozen world leaders and victory. She'd never been much of a drinker—she'd only been drunk once, an experience she remembered with a combination of embarrassment and horror—and the wine tasted oddly flat without alcohol. The handful of officers tossing the wine back like it was water bothered her, although she understood the impulse. She'd once served under an admiral who'd complained about the problem of getting everyone moving in the same direction at the same time. She'd thought he was moaning about nothing until she'd tried it for herself.

And it would be a great deal harder if we hadn't been forced to work together, she thought, sourly. *The virus taught us a great many lessons.*

The thought sobered her as she ran her eye over the guests. Admiral Herman Vermeulen, a French naval officer despite the Flemish name. He had to be competent if he'd risen so high. Belgium had been effectively annexed by France after the Troubles, after his country had been unable to cope with civil unrest that had turned to revolution and mass slaughter. No one had protested at the time—French troops had imposed order, at a cost—but she'd heard rumours of discontent. She hoped it wouldn't be a problem. The virus wouldn't give a damn about human political factions. It certainly hadn't shown any ability to manipulate them for its own purposes. Yet.

She scowled, then looked at General Garth Sampan, USMC and overall landing force commander. The Americans had contributed the largest marine force to the fleet and thus exercised their right to name the ground commander. Sampan was big and beefy, with a military record longer than Susan's arm. He was deep in conversation with Admiral Li, a Chinese officer who was second-in-command of the fleet. Susan cursed the politicians under her breath. She would sooner have had an American or French officer as her second. As it was…it was unlikely anyone would be particularly happy if Li succeeded to overall command. She could only hope they'd hang together long enough to avoid hanging separately.

Her lips quirked at the thought as her eyes wandered over the junior officers. Captain Hammond and Captain Campbell were talking to the other captains, carefully keeping their distance from each other. It was a shame, Susan reflected, that they were so different there was little common ground. As a team, a combination of aggression and common sense, they would have been unbeatable. And yet, their personalities made it harder for them to get along. They were just too different. Thankfully, they had enough sense to shelve their personality conflicts for the duration.

She smiled, then picked up her fork and tapped it against her glass. Silence fell, so quickly one might think it had been rehearsed. She'd chosen many of her officers for their determination to win, not for their love of ceremony. They didn't want to waste their time eating and drinking as the fleet steadily crawled towards enemy territory. She was fairly sure that at least two-thirds of her guests were counting down until the time they could head back to their ships without giving offense.

"Our first exercise, as a fleet, could have gone better," she said, with studied understatement. She'd gone to some trouble to make it as difficult as possible, with as many plausible command mistakes as she could devise. It was easy to do something stupid, but harder to do something that looked reasonable until the shit hit the fan. "We will be spending the rest of the voyage working on our tactics, analysing what we did wrong and correcting our mistakes before we run into the enemy. It is just a matter of time until we do."

She paused, long enough to let her meaning sink in. The flicker network was only a decade old, more or less. Many of the officers under her command had done their training in the days when it took weeks or months for messages to travel from Earth to the edge of the Human Sphere and back again. They'd been lucky no one had accidentally recreated the Battle of New Orleans, which had been fought—unintentionally—shortly *after* the peace treaty had been signed. It would have been very embarrassing, Susan had thought, if the British had won. Keeping the city would have been a breach of the treaty, and certainly restarted the war, but withdrawing would have caused political problems of its own. Susan liked to think *she* would have accepted the orders without protest, yet…she wasn't sure. A victory was something that should never be thrown away.

And the virus may already know we're coming, she thought. *Where does it think we're going?*

"We will be deploying scouts, once we pass through the New Washington defence line," she continued. "Assuming we have a clear path to the target star, we will make our way there as quickly as possible. There will be no time for more than a cursory examination of the sensor records, when we meet up with the scouts once again. The enemy may already have us under observation. They will not be in any doubt of our intentions when we alter course and head down the chain to the catapults. We must assume they will do everything in their power to stop us."

She looked from face to face. "This fleet is the largest, the most powerful force ever deployed from Earth," she concluded. "We must not fail. We *will* not fail."

A rustle ran through the compartment. Susan spotted the reporters in the rear, a handful of men and women brought along by the promise of a scoop…when the operation was completed and the reporters were free to tell the story. She grimaced inwardly, all too aware it was just a matter of time until she'd have to sit down with them for a background interview. God knew the bastards had done enough digging into her past, when her exploits on *Vanguard* had become public knowledge. She wasn't sure there was anything they didn't know. She'd never really had time for anything but her duty.

I should have come up with something more dramatic to say, she thought. *Or hired a scriptwriter to think of something for me.*

Instead, she leaned forward. "I have confidence in each and every one of you," she said. "And I know that, when we encounter the enemy, we will be ready."

She stood. The senior officers would join her in the antechamber for coffee and a final discussion, before they returned to their ships. The junior officers would remain the dining compartment, slowly heading back to their shuttles…her lips quirked in irritation. It would be so much *simpler* to handle everything via holocommunications. The idea of something going wrong, or an enemy fleet appearing out of nowhere, refused to go away. She'd read countless jokes about senior officers being killed—and unit efficiency doubling—but they weren't funny. Confusion over who was in command could be lethal. She'd worked out as many contingency plans as she could, but…she shook her head as she headed for the hatch. They'd just have to hope their plans worked when the enemy started lobbing missiles at the fleet. Losing too many nodes in the communications network could be just as disastrous, even if the senior officers remained alive.

And that's always the problem with emergency drills, she thought. She stepped into the antechamber, where stewards were waiting with tea and coffee. *The drills always leave out the emergency.*

• • •

It was a truism, Thomas had been taught by his governess, that certain events were public even if they seemed private. It was impossible not to invite everyone who was anyone to the events, not unless one wanted to give offense and make enemies. He'd often thought it was silly, but he understood the underlying logic. Opponents were one thing, deadly enemies who felt slighted were quite another. Better to put up with one's rivals for a few hours than risk starting a feud.

He took a sip of his wine, carefully gauging how much he'd drunk. The aristocracy might not say anything, out loud, if he drank himself into a stupor, but everyone would *remember.* The days when he'd sown his wild oats were gone, if indeed they'd ever been; the days when he'd had the excuse of being young had never truly been at all. His family had drilled proper conduct into him from birth, making it abundantly clear that the slightest misstep could result in social disgrace—or worse. He was fairly sure it was true of naval dinners too, although a good two-thirds of the attendees were foreigners. The Admiralty would make sure he never saw promotion again if he made a fool of himself in public.

As opposed to making a fool of myself in private, he thought, sourly. *That's a great deal easier to cover up.*

His thoughts mocked him as he stood and followed his admiral through the hatch. He wasn't the youngest officer amongst the fleet commanders, but he was certainly the *junior* one. He wouldn't even have been invited, if the admiral hadn't asked him to serve as her second. And yet…it was hard not to see how little she cared for the dinner party. She regarded it as a waste of time, as a distraction from her duties. Thomas knew better. The more the fleet commanders knew and trusted each other, the more they'd be able to work together when all hell broke loose. They all knew it wouldn't be long before the fleet was put to the test.

He caught sight of Captain Campbell, talking animatedly to a destroyer captain. It looked as if they were getting along like a house on fire. Thomas felt a flicker of irritation. Campbell had constantly proposed the most aggressive tactics, tactics that offered the prospect of total victory or total defeat. Thomas understood the situation was dire, that the human race was steadily being ground down, but…he tried not to scowl as the two junior captains glanced at him. Perhaps they were planning to make their way to the privacy tubes. He wouldn't put it past Campbell. The man clearly didn't have the discretion God gave a fly.

It isn't as if they're in the same chain of command, Thomas reminded himself. *It would be a great deal more problematic if one of them was superior to the other.*

He dismissed the thought as unworthy of him as he stepped through the hatch. A steward came forward, offering a mug of tea. Thomas took it, nodding gratefully. He'd drunk enough coffee, over the course of the day, to feel as if it was sloshing around his insides. It would make him look bad if he had to visit the washroom in the middle of the debate, although a handful of officers were already heading to the facilities. He smiled in amusement. Some of them had probably crossed their legs rather than show any signs of humanity in front of their juniors.

Just like school, he thought, dryly. He'd done well at boarding school, but he didn't remember it with any fondness. *How could anyone be allowed to believe the staff were actually human?*

He mingled with the other officers, memorising names and faces for later consideration. The admiral would want his impressions, he was sure. She'd presumably know some of the foreigners from her earlier command—he'd looked her career up, when he'd been assigned to her command—but others would be strangers. They all seemed competent, he supposed; they all had good records. And yet, there was no way to know how they would react when the missiles started flying. The fleet had never been tested in battle.

"The exercise could have gone better," the admiral said, drawing their attention to her. "What did we do wrong?"

"We lost our datanet midway through the battle," Admiral Li said. "And by the time we got it back up again, it was too late."

Thomas kept his face impassive. The Royal Navy trained on the assumption the fleet command network was unreliable. Any opponent worthy of the name would do their level best to knock it down as quickly as possible, forcing each ship to fall back on its own resources. The exercise had ended in disaster, at least in part, because the virus had wiped out most of the escort ships while the fleet struggled to get the network back on line, stripping the capital ships of their cover. If the engagement had been real, it would have been the biggest disaster since the Battle of New Russia. And that had been one of the most one-sided battles in human history.

"Your ships aren't trained to reboot the network themselves," Admiral Vermeulen pointed out, dryly. "Too much top-down command, that's your problem."

Li's eyes narrowed. "And too many ships trying to reboot the network individually," he countered, "made it impossible to get the network back up in time."

"We'll be working on that," Admiral Onarina said. "But we also have to prepare for the moments when the network is effectively beyond repair."

Which isn't going to be easy, Thomas admitted. As much as he cordially disliked Captain Campbell, he couldn't deny the man had the nerve to act without orders. The Chinese and Russian officers didn't have the same freedom. If his briefing notes were accurate, it was rare for Chinese officers to act without orders. They'd be punished even if they did the right thing at the right time. *We're going to have to train them to act without fear of punishment.*

"What else?" Admiral Onarina's eyes swept the room. "What went wrong?"

"We overcommitted the gunboats," Thomas said. He'd hoped *Lion* and her gunboats would demonstrate their value, but instead the gunboats had been wiped out without so much as scratching the enemy's paint. "Our plan to hit the enemy with a massive missile barrage was a total failure."

He sighed, inwardly. The concept had looked good on paper. The fleet's fifteen battleships were crammed to the gunwales with missiles. They just lacked effective long-range targeting, something he'd hoped the gunboats would provide. It would have worked, if the planners hadn't fucked around with the simulation…he shook his head in annoyance. He'd been lucky he and his crew had a chance to learn from their mistakes. They wouldn't have that chance in a real fight. There was no way they could push the reset switch and start again.

"It should have worked," an officer he didn't recognise pointed out. "We could have wiped out their entire fleet."

"We would have, if the missiles had had proper targeting data," Thomas said. "But they didn't."

He kept his face under tight control. Long-range missiles were no longer as ineffective as they'd been, with the recent improvements in drives and targeting systems, but they still had their weaknesses. Any missile that brought up an active seeker head would be revealing its position to the enemy, allowing them to target the missile and destroy it well before it entered attack range. And…they simply didn't have enough missiles to fire more than two or three massive barrages before they shot themselves dry. The combined navies couldn't produce anything like enough to meet demand.

"We'll work on that," Admiral Onarina said. "General?"

The American cleared his throat. "Preliminary reports indicate the landing parties know their stuff," he said. "However, there is a certain degree of uncertainty about what we'll face once we land on the catapults. The long-range sensor images we obtained tell us nothing about their close-range defences or their interiors. We're not even entirely sure where their command and control systems *are*."

"And they could be decentralised, because the virus doesn't need command centres," Admiral Onarina observed. "Can you take the catapults?"

"We can board them, yes," General Sampan said. "It's taking them in a usable condition that might be difficult."

"At the very least, we'll take them out," Li said. "That *must* slow them down."

"We don't know enough to be sure," Admiral Onarina said. "For all we know, the catapults represent a tiny percentage of their GNP."

And the virus doesn't need to spend its resources on anything else, Thomas added, silently. It was hard to believe, but it was true. *There's no way we can win a war of attrition.*

He stayed quiet as the admirals discussed the exercise, then started to lay plans for the remainder of the voyage. He could understand why Admiral Onarina and her fellows wanted to take the catapults and turn them against their creators, but…if they failed, the cost would be unbearably high. The fleet would be lost and the war would be lost with it. And yet, did they have a choice?

If we succeed, we might just win the war, he thought. *But is it worth the risk?*

CHAPTER THIRTEEN

"I WAS STARTING TO THINK YOU WEREN'T COMING," Colin said. He stood in the shooting range, holding a half-dismantled rifle in one hand. "And that I'd reserved the range for nothing."

"It's been a long week," Tobias said. Six months ago, the idea of being so close to Colin would have given him the shakes. Now…it was different, he supposed. "I was surprised you got the day off."

"It's more like an hour or two," Colin said. He sounded almost apologetic. "The platoon leader decided we needed some downtime."

Tobias frowned. "Aren't *you* the platoon leader?"

Colin laughed. "I'll speak to myself very sharply later," he promised. "More seriously"—he shrugged—"we pushed ourselves pretty hard, with no hope of relief. We needed a couple of hours to relax, even if it's just lying back with a good book or wanking or whatever."

"I hope you don't get in trouble for it," Tobias said. There were things no one should think about and wanking was one of them. The idea of Colin… he pushed the thought out of his head so hard his thoughts spun in circles. "Where do you think we should start?"

"Right here," Colin said. He placed the rifle carefully on the table, then picked up a box and pressed his thumb against the reader. "Didn't they teach you how to shoot when you were at the academy?"

"Only the very basics," Tobias said. He'd never joined the CCF or one of the shooting clubs in the city. The idea had never been tempting. "I don't have a shooting permit."

"You do," Colin corrected. "As long as you're in the military, you have an open permit to carry a weapon anywhere they're not explicitly banned. Didn't they explain that to you?"

Tobias shook his head. He hadn't paid that much attention. He'd always assumed he'd be in his gunboat, when the shit hit the fan; he'd never cared for the idea of fighting off a boarding party or landing on a hostile world. And he'd certainly never believed he could defend himself. He could carry a gun, yet...he was sure he'd simply have it taken away and turned against him. He was one of nature's wimps. He could no more fight to defend himself than he could defend his girlfriend.

And they sensed it in you, a nasty little voice whispered at the back of his head. *Why do you think they kept picking on you?*

"Fuck," he muttered.

"You'd better look up the rules," Colin said. "For the moment"—he opened the box—"we'll be working with a standard naval-issue handgun. There's a bunch of technical detail you can read later, if you wish, but all you really need to know right now is that it's an automatic pistol. It's designed for simplicity, allowing the owner to reload the clip manually if they don't want to use a machine. There are variants on the design that take rifle ammunition, but we're not going to be worrying about them today. They're pretty rare outside the military."

Tobias had to smile. Colin sounded a different person when he talked about guns. Or...or about something he was genuinely interested in. Tobias supposed he shouldn't have been surprised. Colin's marks at school had been terrible, in everything apart from PE and the CCF. No wonder he knew so much about guns. He could probably quote chapter and verse from memory.

"I see," he said, carefully. "Why are they rare?"

"Increased penetrating power," Colin said. He pulled the handgun free and held it up for inspection. "Standard army-issue body armour could dull the impact, if you shot the wearer from a decent distance. A rifle round…it would probably go *through* the armour, depending on various factors. You might not kill the victim, but you'd certainly do a great deal of harm that would require urgent medical attention."

"Ouch," Tobias said.

Colin smiled. "That, and you also put a lot of stress on the gun," he added. "There's a pretty good chance you'd fuck up your weapon if you used the wrong ammunition."

He dismantled the gun with practiced ease, then put it back together again. "This is the clip," he said, pointing to a row of bullets. "It slots into here"—he snapped it into position—"and the gun is now loaded. The safety catch is on, and the gun shouldn't be able to fire, but I expect you to remember the rules and follow them anyway. Just in case. The gun should never be pointed at anyone unless you intend to kill them."

Tobias swallowed as the explanation went on and on. How often had he lain awake at night, dreaming of the power to kill Colin? How often had he begged God for superpowers or something, anything, that would make him strong enough to fight without fear? He'd prayed for money and power, enough to hire a mercenary to beat Colin to death…he swallowed, again, as Colin held out the gun. It felt heavy in his hands, pregnant with possibility…it was all he could do to step up to the wall and peer towards the targets. The holographic images looked humanoid, without any real details. It was hard to believe they were *real* targets.

A thought struck him. "What's to stop the bullet bouncing off the far bulkhead and coming back at us?"

"The bulkhead is designed to prevent it," Colin said, vaguely. "I'd be a little more concerned if we were firing GPMGs in here."

He motioned towards the targets. "You'll see a mark when you hit the target," he said, calmly. "The range will also point out your mistakes."

Tobias nodded as he raised the gun, took aim and pulled the trigger. It wasn't the first time he'd fired a gun, but the bang was louder than he remembered. The holographic image seemed undisturbed. Tobias frowned as he saw a glowing light close to the image. He'd missed by several inches. And yet...

"I was aiming perfectly," he said, in protest. "How did I miss?"

"Handguns are not the most accurate weapons in the world," Colin said, dryly. "It takes time to learn how to fire properly. That's why most shooters are urged to aim for the target's centre of mass. Given time, you'll learn to overcome it and produce some reasonably accurate fire."

He nodded towards the target. "Try again. Please."

Tobias nodded and pulled the trigger. It clicked. "What?"

"You have to eject the last cartridge," Colin pointed out. "Or switch the pistol to auto."

"I see," Tobias said. He pointed and fired again. This time, he fired nine shots in quick succession before the pistol ran dry. "I hit him!"

"Two hits out of ten," Colin said. "You want the good news or the bad news?"

Tobias sighed. "Both."

"The good news is that, if you hit a human like that, you'd send him to hospital," Colin said, deadpan. He affected a teacher-like manner. "If there was no hospital within reach, he'd die. Probably. There's a reasonable chance you'd put a bullet through his heart or his lung, either one of which would prove life-threatening. The bad news..."

He paused for dramatic effect. "The bad news, I'm afraid, is that you wouldn't kill a zombie if you hit him like that. He'd just stagger, then keep on coming."

Tobias shivered. "How do you stop a zombie?"

"It depends," Colin admitted. He took the gun back, slotted a new clip into place and opened fire. Red marks appeared around the target's knees, with a single mark between the eyes. "If you're lucky, the original brain is still partly in control and killing it will take out the body too. If you're not, you have to make sure the body can't move again. Take out the knees and the body might collapse, at least for a while. The virus is good at working its way around damage. As long as there's a critical mass left in the body, it can regenerate and keep coming."

"Shit," Tobias said. "How do you stop *that*?"

"Fire, normally, or grenades," Colin said. He put the pistol back on the table. "You want to try again?"

Tobias nodded and started again from the beginning. It felt strange, to say the least, to be wielding a pistol. He wondered what he'd have done if, six months ago, Colin had given him the pistol and turned his back. The urge to put a bullet in his back would have been overpowering, muted only by the sense it wouldn't have worked. Colin could survive anything, while Tobias couldn't hope to defend himself...he shook his head. Those days were behind him, behind both of them. He owed it to himself to let the past go.

"Enough for the moment," Colin said. "You got a little better."

"A little," Tobias repeated. He'd hit the target four times. Just four. "I should have done more practicing."

"Yes," Colin agreed. "If you book the range when I'm not around, there'll be somcone on duty. Get them to supervise as you practice."

"Yes, sir," Tobias said, surprising himself. "I'll do my best."

Colin reached into his carryall and produced a flask, which he held out to Tobias. Tobias hesitated, then took a sip. It tasted like a demented cross between medicine and orange juice, as if someone had dissolved soluble painkillers in orange squash. He took another sip, trying not to grimace. He'd expected alcohol, but this was worse. The flavour made his tongue want to crawl up into a ball and die.

He passed the flask back. "What the...what is *that*?"

"Panda Orange," Colin said. "You put a tablet in a flask of water and— hey presto—orange-flavoured water."

"It's vile," Tobias said, with feeling. "Can't they give you something a little nicer?"

"Yeah," Colin said. He took a long swig, then wiped his mouth on his sleeve. "Point is, the juice is also purified. The tablet takes out anything that might harm us. There's no risk of the galloping shits if you put the tablet in the water first, then drink it."

Tobias grimaced. "Do you *have* to be so crude?"

Colin surprised him by taking the question seriously. "You know the difference between the very rich and the very poor?"

"They have more money?" Tobias couldn't remember who'd said that—he'd read it in a book somewhere, years ago—but it was true. "There isn't much of anything else."

"No," Colin said. "The very rich and powerful can afford to pretend the world isn't a stinking cesspit. They can pretend the garden is full of roses and ignore the thorns. They can tell themselves that things are perfect and, if they're not, they can just splash around enough money to make them perfect. Ugly mug? Cosmetic surgery. Bad grades? Hire a tutor. No place at university? Endow a research chair or something to encourage the university to make the right decision."

He shook his head. "The very poor cannot afford such delusions. They cannot afford to hide behind high walls and fancy words for blunt truths. They can't afford to pretend that things are perfect when they're not. And that's true of the military too. I am crude because I cannot let myself pretend things will always go my way."

"That's almost profound," Tobias said. "Who are you and what have you done with Colin?"

Colin flushed. "I've had to grow up a little," he said. "Either I learn to use my brain or I never get another stripe. I'll be lucky if I get to keep *this* one. If they hadn't wanted a semi-independent platoon…"

He shook his head. "Do you remember Ajeet?"

Tobias frowned. "Vaguely," he said, finally. Ajeet had been one of the few coloured students in Birmingham. His father had been a Gurkha or something, from what little Tobias remembered. He hadn't paid much attention. He'd had too many problems of his own. "What about him?"

"We gave him a hard time," Colin said. "And it never crossed our minds how difficult it must have been, for him, to come study with us."

"I suppose," Tobias said. "And yet, you accepted him when you discovered he was good at football."

He felt a flash of bitterness. It had been easy for Ajeet, hadn't it? It was astonishing what people would overlook, if they needed someone. The football team would have thumped anyone who gave Ajeet a hard time, after they discovered his talent. No one had ever defended Tobias that way, no one. Common sense told him Ajeet had had problems too, even after he gained a degree of acceptance, but…he ground his teeth. It was hard to take someone else's problems seriously when yours were so bad.

Grow the fuck up, he told himself. *Leave it in the past, where it belongs.*

"We did," Colin said, shortly. "Ajeet was human. Kevin is not."

Tobias was tempted to point out, despite everything, that he'd been treated as less than human for years. And yet…he told himself, again, to let it go.

"It can't be easy," he said, slowly. "Does it work?"

"It's hard to say," Colin said. "Kevin is a good bootneck. I have the feeling he had some experience on Vesy, prior to joining the program. There's no reason to think he's going to be a problem and I made sure the lads wouldn't give him a hard time, but…it just feels odd, as though a penny is waiting to drop. It feels weird."

"I imagine the first male soldiers who found themselves sharing duties with female soldiers felt the same way," Tobias said. "At least no one is trying to get into his pants."

"And you accuse *me* of being crude." Colin snickered. "No, I suppose we don't have *that* problem. But…maybe I'm just overthinking it."

Tobias flushed. He'd walked right into that one. "How different *is* he? I mean…does he have issues you don't understand? A religion? Or food? Or…or what?"

"I don't know," Colin said. "You know, back before the Troubles, there was a policy of embedding Western soldiers with foreign armies to teach their men how to fight?"

"I thought those policies were blamed for a lot of problems," Tobias said. "Or was that just propaganda?"

"A bit of both," Colin said. "I took the time to read some of the personal reports and memoirs from that era. Lots of them come from countries that don't really exist any longer, yet...most of the reports were written before things *really* got bad. They said..."

Tobias frowned. He'd never seen Colin as particularly studious. Six months ago, he hadn't even been sure Colin could *read*. "What did they say?"

"Their students were often different, culturally speaking," Colin said. "They'd do things the embedded officers found horrific or inexplicable. A lot of their conduct simply didn't make sense. There were moments that, in hindsight, should have been expected...but weren't, because the embeds couldn't wrap their heads around them. They were from different cultures. They didn't share our cultural assumptions. And the results were decidedly mixed."

Tobias silently reassessed his estimate of Colin's intelligence. Given a reason to study—and to learn—it was clear he was very far from stupid. And yet...Tobias couldn't imagine what it was like to be an alien amongst humans. Poor Kevin had to be feeling very alone. There were no other Vesy for hundreds of light years, unless there was one on the other ships. It didn't seem likely. Colin would have been told if there was...right? Probably. The chance to compare notes with someone undertaking the same task was not to be despised.

He felt an odd spark of sympathy. "And they expect you to handle everything yourself?"

His imagination provided a whole string of possible problems. He didn't know much about the Vesy, but...they were egg-layers, weren't they? Kevin might lay eggs at any moment...Kevin was a male name, yet who knew if the alien really *was* male? Or if there was something funny about their biology, something so alien the clues had been missed...he gritted his teeth. If humans had problems understanding their fellow humans, how could they understand aliens? He remembered some of the history books he'd read, the ones that looked back on the days of the British Empire and the Raj and frowned. He'd never been able to understand their mindset. The imperialists had belonged to a different century.

And yet they were human, he thought. *The Vesy are not.*

"We can't afford to bring a xenospecialist with us, not onto the battle-field," Colin pointed out, grimly. "We have to learn the hard way."

"They've left you holding the bag," Tobias pointed out. "What a fucking mess."

"We'll see," Colin said. He shrugged. "We could be overthinking it, you know. We might not have any major problems."

"I hope you're right," Tobias said. "If there's anything I can do to help…"

"Well, we could use a pair of outside eyes," Colin said. "Really, though, I don't think you could do much to help. We have to handle it ourselves."

"Good luck," Tobias said. His wristcom bleeped, reminding him that he was expected back in the briefing room in ten minutes. "What happens if the experiment fails?"

"Fucked if I know," Colin said. "Kevin will go home and…who knows?"

"We'll see," Tobias said. "Thank you for the lesson."

"Keep practicing," Colin said. He made a show of looking in all directions, as if he thought someone was sneaking up on them. "We might be boarded tomorrow."

"Yeah," Tobias said. He'd heard that before. "And we might not be boarded at all."

CHAPTER FOURTEEN

"CAPTAIN," MIDSHIPMAN DAVID CULVER SAID. "We have completed our download from New Washington."

Mitch nodded, thoughtfully. "Inform the flag that we are departing as planned," he said. "Helm, take us into cloak as soon as we enter the ECM haze."

"Aye, Captain," Lieutenant Sam Hinkson said. A low hum echoed through the frigate as she started to move away from the fleet. "Course laid in for Target One."

"Good," Mitch said. He felt a thrill of excitement. The moment they crossed the tramline, they would be in enemy territory. "Hold us on course."

He forced himself to relax as *Unicorn* picked up speed. The fleet had entered the New Washington system only a day ago, loudly announcing its intention to thrust its way up the chain towards Alien-One. It was impossible to tell if the virus was listening, or even if it cared enough to try, but it could hardly ignore the arrival of a sizable fleet. Any *sane* foe would be doing everything in its power to put together a blocking force, in hopes of preventing the fleet from grinding its way up the chain into enemy space. Alien-One might have been turned to radioactive ruins a decade ago, but the tramlines there provided access to the rest of enemy space. The virus *had* to stop them.

That's what we would do, he thought, grimly. *But the virus is inherently unpredictable.*

The thought nagged at his mind as his ship entered cloak. The Americans had already deployed a small fleet of decoy drones, intended to suggest the fleet was preparing to thrust up the chain even as it slipped out of New Washington and headed elsewhere. It wasn't easy to tell if anyone was fooled. New Washington had been settled for over a century and yet there was relatively little activity within the system, nowhere near enough to make life difficult for cloaked recon ships. The virus could have scattered thousands of stealthed sensor platforms across the system, relying on the vastness of space to hide them. Mitch had taken part in an exercise designed to track down and destroy primitive sensor platforms years ago. Hundreds of ships and thousands of starfighters had been devoted to the task, but it had been a complete failure. They'd buzzed within a few thousand kilometres of a couple of sensor platforms and suspected nothing.

He leaned forward as the tramline finally came into view. They'd planned to make transit well away from the system primary, to minimise the chances of being detected. The odds were very low, but if there was any power capable of emplacing sensor platforms right along the tramline it was the virus. Mitch wasn't blind to the implications of an entire economy devoted to making war, whatever Captain Hammond said. He just refused to let the prospect of being massively out-produced, then outgunned, intimidate him. They wouldn't have a hope in hell if they let themselves be hypnotised by the spectre of millions upon millions of battleships bearing down on them.

Although if the virus did have millions of battleships, the war would be over by now, he acknowledged, privately. *They could trade battleships for starfighters and still come out ahead.*

"Captain," Staci said, formally. "We are ready to make transit."

Mitch nodded, curtly. "Helm, take us through."

"Aye, Captain."

The display ticked down to zero, then blanked. Mitch felt something insubstantial hit his chest, as if he'd been hit without actually *being* hit. He gritted his teeth as the display hastily rebooted, knowing that they were within seconds of being blown to hell if there was an enemy squadron in firing range. They'd stepped down everything as much as possible when they'd readied themselves to make transit, but the cloaking device would have fluctuated the moment they jumped. If there was someone close enough to see them, they were dead.

"Captain," Staci said. "No active contacts detected within sensor range."

Mitch allowed himself a moment of relief. The display was filling rapidly, showing the positions of the primary star, a couple of planets and a handful of comets and asteroids. There was no sign of the enemy fleet, although he knew it had to be lurking somewhere between Tramline One and Tramline Two. The virus had tried using the system to stage an attack on New Washington, although it had added several weeks to its deployment time. In hindsight, Mitch suspected the virus had been really clearing the way to the catapult system. It had certainly taken pains to obliterate any human presence between Falkirk and New Washington. If anyone was still alive, it was unlikely they'd answer hails.

"Helm, take us on our planned course," he ordered.

"Aye, Captain."

Unicorn picked up speed, heading towards Tramline Three. The system had been largely classed as useless, back when it had been surveyed. The Americans hadn't known about alien-grade tramlines until the First Interstellar War. Even afterwards, the system hadn't been particularly useful. The tramline chain jumped from desolate star to desolate star until it finally terminated in the catapult system. Mitch had studied the reports, from the survey missions. If they'd missed something, it was very well hidden indeed.

He took a long breath as his ship circumvented the system. It was unlikely they'd be detected unless they got very unlucky, but they had to be careful. There was no hint the virus knew they'd detected the catapults, yet…Mitch shook his head. They had to take the catapults out, if they couldn't capture them. Leaving them in place would allow the virus to turn humanity's flank and win the war. Mitch had no illusions about the outcome, if the virus got into bombardment range of Earth. The virus would take root and spread so rapidly it couldn't be stopped. The human race would be cruelly and irrevocably doomed.

The display continued to update. Mitch frowned as the passive sensors finally picked up the alien ships. They were closer to Tramline Two than he'd expected, but far enough from his position for him to be reasonably sure he wouldn't be detected. He puzzled over the positioning for a moment, then decided the virus was waiting to see which way the human fleet intended to go. It was well-positioned to either slow the admiral down or break contact long enough to rendezvous with reinforcements further up the chain.

A shame the admiral doesn't intend to engage the fleet, Mitch thought. *We could sneak up and open fire before they even knew we were there.*

He stood. "XO, inform me when we approach the tramline," he ordered. "You have the bridge."

"Aye, Captain," Staci said. "I have the bridge."

Mitch wished, not for the first time, for a ready room of his own. It would have been nice to have a dedicated office right next to the bridge, although his cabin was only a few short metres away. *Unicorn* was too small to devote *two* compartments to the commanding officer, let alone anyone else. Mitch opened the hatch, then keyed his terminal to bring up the in-system display. It was reassuringly clear. If there was anything close enough to prove dangerous, his ship couldn't see it.

Which is meaningless, he reminded himself, as he sat on his chair and brought up the final list of messages from Earth. *They can't see us either.*

He frowned as he scanned the list. A handful of all-ships updates, none marked urgent…he made a mental note to go through them when he had a spare moment. They would have been flagged if there'd been something important, something that demanded immediate attention, but…he shook his head. The beancounters back home would bitch and moan if he didn't read their messages, even if they had a funny idea of what was important. It was all too clear they didn't have any naval experience of their own.

Idiots, he thought, with a twinge of contempt. *I'd sooner die than be trapped behind a desk.*

He put the thought out of his head as he read through the final messages. A bundle of e-newspaper subscriptions, forwarded from Earth. They dated back several months, suggesting the newspaper had decided to err on the side of thoroughness. Mitch had downloaded two thirds of the collection shortly before the fleet had made transit. A couple of messages from his family, an invitation to a party that had been and gone before he'd even seen the invite and…

Mitch blinked. *Charlotte sent me a message?*

He frowned as he read the header. Charlotte really shouldn't be sending him anything, beyond—he supposed—another invitation to the estate. She was a military wife. She had to know how unlikely it was that Mitch would be able to visit on short notice, even if he hadn't been serving with her husband. It crossed Mitch's mind to wonder if she had other lovers, other men—or women—in her life. It was far from impossible. The days when aristocratic women and princesses were locked up in towers and guarded by eunuchs were long gone. She didn't have to court disaster by messaging *him*. God alone knew how many filters the message had passed through before it had finally reached *Unicorn*.

Charlotte's face filled the screen. "Captain Campbell," she said, with heavy formality. Too heavy. "I trust this message finds you well. It is my pleasure to invite you to my daughter's coming out ball, to be held when her father returns from deployment. We would very much like to see you there."

She grinned, then lifted her shirt. Mitch stared, feeling a rush of arousal even though he knew she was light-years away. She was as bold and daring as himself, perhaps even more so…it occurred to him, in a moment of insight, that Charlotte would have made a great frigate captain. She had nerve and yet…he wondered, as Charlotte kept talking, if she truly understood what she was doing. He kicked himself a moment later. Of *course* she knew what she was doing. She'd grown up in the aristocracy.

Mitch swallowed, hard, as the message came to an end. Charlotte was no coy ingénue, no teenage girl unsure of what she wanted; Charlotte *knew* what she wanted. And she had no qualms about reaching for it. Mitch was torn between admiration, concern and desire. There was something about her that made him want her…it was exciting, in a way, to have a woman take the lead. And there was a thrill that came with sleeping with a married woman.

He reached for the terminal, then shook his head. There was no point in recording a reply, not now. It would just sit in the buffers until *Unicorn* linked up with the fleet, then remain in *their* buffers until the fleet returned home. Charlotte would probably get a dozen copies of the same message, if her inbox wasn't configured to detect and erase duplicates. It wasn't easy to trust online services, these days. There was no way to be sure a hacker wasn't screwing with the system.

Mitch stood, checked the terminal to make sure there was nothing that demanded his immediate attention and walked to the bed. It was small, barely large enough for a grown man. He'd known captains and admirals who would have thrown fits, if they were given such a small cabin and a tiny bed. Mitch snorted at the thought. Frigates just didn't have the room for anything bigger. He was lucky he wasn't sharing a cabin with his XO.

He found himself thinking of Charlotte, time and time again, as the ship continued her plodding way down the chain. There were no enemy contacts, not even a handful of freighters or warships making their way towards the catapults. Mitch was tempted to wonder if they'd been sent on a wild goose chase, although he knew it was unlikely. No one would devote so many starships to a giant waste of time. *That* only happened in bad movies and yet…it was *possible*, he supposed, that the admiral really intended to break into Alien-One and open the tramlines to the interior. No, she wouldn't have sent his ship so far away unless she thought it was worthwhile…

136

The thought gnawed at his mind as *Unicorn* transited into the final system. Mitch felt trapped, even though he knew it wasn't so. There was no reason to believe they were being tracked, let alone that they couldn't break contact and return through the tramline somewhere else. And yet, the thought bothered him. There was only one way in and out of the catapult system. It was easy to feel the door was slamming closed behind him.

"Captain," Staci said. "Long-range sensors are detecting *thirty* gravimetric sources."

Mitch stared at the display. "Thirty?"

"Yes, Captain," Staci said. "The spooks got it wrong."

"Or they assembled an additional ten catapults between the survey mission and our arrival," Mitch said. He would have preferred to believe the spooks were wrong. "Deploy probes as planned, then hold us here."

"Aye, Captain."

Mitch felt ice wash down his spine as more and more data flowed into the display. The catapults didn't *look* like catapults, certainly nothing like the conical device humanity had built to win the Second Interstellar War. They looked like giant spheres, each one a framework large enough for an entire fleet to nestle in. Mitch silently calculated just how many ships the catapults could hurl at Earth and shuddered at the answer. The virus could put together a fleet twice as large as Admiral Onarina's and practically *teleport* it to Earth.

And that would be the end, he thought. *They have to be stopped.*

His eyes moved to the cluster of warships holding position near the giant catapults. A fleet carrier, a trio of battleships, a handful of smaller ships and a brainship...he allowed himself a moment of relief. The fleet wasn't strong enough to punch through Earth's defences, let alone stand up to Admiral Onarina. The virus was still laying its plans, then. It wasn't on the verge of launching the invasion. And yet...he frowned, stroking his chin. There was something about their formation that bothered him. He couldn't put his finger on it.

"Captain," Lieutenant Jolly said. "I believe that nineteen of the catapults are ready for service."

Mitch frowned as a thought struck him. "Has their fleet already made transit?"

"I don't believe so, sir," Jolly said. "There's no hint they're refurbishing the catapults after use."

"Good," Mitch said. The original catapult had destroyed itself, spectacularly, after launching a human fleet into the enemy rear. The design had been improved, over the years, but even the latest catapults required such heavy refurbishment after use that no one considered them a worthy investment. The Royal Navy had applied, repeatedly, for permission to build one and the government had always refused. "Can you isolate their control nodes?"

Jolly worked his console for a long moment. "I think so, sir," he said. There was a hint of waspishness in his tone. "There's no way to be entirely sure."

Mitch nodded. If nothing else, taking out the catapults would force the virus to start again from scratch. It probably had the persistence to do just that, particularly as it didn't have to explain its expenditures to bean-counting bureaucrats, but it would give the human race a chance to start dropping BioBombs on every infected world. And put newer and better weapons into mass production. Mitch had seen the reports. There were all sorts of interesting ideas in the pipeline.

He keyed his console, bringing up the planned schedule. Admiral Onarina was no fool. She'd worked a great deal of leeway into the operational planning, pointing out that a fleet could hardly operate like a monorail. If everything had gone according to plan, there would be four days before *Unicorn* needed to return to the RV point and link up with the rest of the fleet. Mitch assumed Admiral Onarina had contingency plans for what she intended to do, if *Unicorn* never returned. He frowned as he looked back at the display. In her place, he would send two ships. And he'd make sure neither one knew about the other. The virus made a mockery of basic security precautions. Who knew what it might learn from capturing and infecting an entire crew?

"We'll keep our distance," he said. The virus didn't seem to be sweeping space as carefully as *he* would have done, if he was in command of the alien fleet, but there was no point in taking chances. It was quite possible space was seeded with hundreds of passive sensor platforms. The slightest glimmering of *Unicorn's* presence might be enough to bring the entire fleet down on her. The brainships were fearsomely good at turning a tiny sensor contact into a full-scale targeting solution. "I want everything noted and logged before we go."

"Aye, Captain."

Mitch nodded as he watched the display. He was no stranger to mega-projects—he'd watched giant fleet carriers and battleships take shape in the yards—and yet the sheer scale of the alien project stunned him. *Thirty* catapults? Even the *virus* had to quail at the thought of such a vast investment. It *had* to be running up against some pretty hard limits...surely. His skin crawled as it started to sink in. The virus wasn't *just* inhuman. It was...something terrible. The folks back home didn't know the true scale of the threat or they would have panicked and...

Perhaps that's why Charlotte threw herself at me, he thought. Charlotte played host to all sorts of government and military personnel. She might know the truth, even if the general population didn't. Hell, she might even know where the fleet was going. *She wanted to have fun before the world came to an end.*

CHAPTER FIFTEEN

"ADMIRAL?"

Susan jerked awake, half-convinced she hadn't been asleep at all. The flight from New Washington to the RV point had been a long slow crawl, enlivened only by a suggestion the fleet should feint at the alien blocking force before heading for the target star. Susan had overruled the officers who'd wanted to be aggressive, despite every instinct insisting they shouldn't leave such a fleet in their rear. The alien ships didn't have enough firepower to take her fleet, unless they'd invented something completely new, but they could harass her or take out the catapults to keep them from falling into her hands.

She rubbed her eyes as the lights brightened. "What?"

"*Unicorn* just made contact," Commander Elliot Richardson said. "She's transferring her sensor logs now."

Susan stood, grabbed her uniform trousers with one hand and hastily pulled them on. "I'm on my way," she said. "Put the coffee on."

"Aye, Admiral."

Susan took a moment to compose herself as she finished dressing, feeling a twinge of the old anticipation running through her. She might not be in command of a ship, but she was about to take an entire fleet into combat. Too much rode on the mission's success for her to be sanguine about the outcome, yet...she calmed herself with an effort as she ran her hands through her hair. She'd cropped it close to her scalp when she'd been a junior officer, only letting it grow out after she'd reached command rank. She kicked herself, mentally, for not cutting it short before departure. Right now, it only got in her way.

She glanced at herself in the mirror, then walked through the hatch and onto the CIC deck. Her aide already had a steaming mug of coffee in his hand, ready for her. Susan took it, nodded her thanks and hurried to the big display. *Unicorn* had done well and yet...Susan felt her heart sink as she realised just how many catapults were under construction. The virus could throw its entire fleet at Earth, if it wished...

And there could be more, deeper within enemy space, Susan mused. She was familiar with the basic economic calculus—it was the only way to avoid fantasy fleet syndrome—but the virus made a mockery of it. *How many catapults can it afford?*

She dismissed the thought as she studied the live feed. The fleet outnumbered and outgunned the defenders, but...the defenders would have a chance to destroy their own catapults rather than risk them falling into human hands. The devices were incredibly flimsy, if the sensor records were accurate. A handful of nukes would be more than enough to put them beyond repair. Susan knew she might hesitate, if she was asked to blow away trillions of pounds of investment, but she doubted the virus would react in quite the same way. It would just do it and worry about the costs later. She shook her head in dismay. The virus seemed to have too many advantages.

"There's no hint of any settlements on the planet," Richardson said. "If there's a black colony, it's keeping very quiet."

Susan nodded, tersely. The lone planet was cold enough to make *Mars* look warm and welcoming. There were no gas giants or asteroid belts, nothing that might provide fuel and resources for a space-based civilisation. It was possible that *someone* might have hidden a settlement on the surface, burrowing deep underground, but it was unlikely. They'd be so dependent on modern technology to survive that the odds of being detected, if someone troubled themselves to look, would be quite high.

"Right now, that's not our problem," Susan said. She tapped the console, bringing up the tactical concepts her staff had devised during the voyage. "I think we'll proceed with Lightning-III. Send the updated concept to the fleet."

Richardson nodded. "Aye, Admiral," he said. "I'll transmit the orders at once."

Susan could hear the doubt in his voice. They'd worked through hundreds of scenarios, from the destruction of the catapults to the arrival of the alien fleet before the catapults had been pressed into service. Lightning-III gave them the best chance to take out the enemy ships before they could destroy the catapults, but it also gave the enemy a chance to do just that if they realised what was coming before it was too late. Susan had agonised over the tactical problem, coming up with concept after concept she knew wouldn't have worked in the real world. They had to gamble. There was no hope of getting the entire fleet into attack range before it was too late.

She looked up. "Pass targeting orders to *Lion*," she said. "The brainship is the priority target."

"Aye, Admiral," Richardson said.

Susan grimaced. Standard tactical doctrine called for stripping away the escorts first, then targeting the capital ships. She was going to lose a bunch of gunboats...hell, she was probably going to waste a great deal of missiles. But the last thing she wanted was the enemy actually *thinking*. If she took out the brainship first, she might just wipe out the remainder of the enemy fleet before it started having ideas about destroying the catapults. And it should make it easier to take out the rest of the fleet.

She sat on her chair and watched, feeling oddly isolated, as her staff hurried to relay orders to her ships. The captains and their crews knew what to do. They'd gone through dozens of exercises, each one working out more and more of the kinks until the fleet was a finely-oiled machine. They'd learnt to work together as a team...she frowned as she studied the datanet taking shape and form. She hoped—prayed—that the datanet would stay intact, if—when—the enemy started trying to knock it down. And that the fleet would hold together if anything happened to her.

Her lips twitched. The flicker network had been in its infancy when she'd been a captain. She'd never really been *able* to phone home and request orders. Like most older officers, she'd regarded the network as a godsend *and* a bloody nuisance. There was nothing more dangerous than a politician who thought he knew what was going on, issuing orders that didn't quite fit the situation. And yet, independent command came with responsibility. She couldn't pass the buck up the chain of command. She could ask her subordinates for advice, but the final decision rested with her. She was solely responsible for the entire fleet. If the mission failed...

If the mission fails, I should probably not go home, she thought, ruefully. *I won't be very welcome back there.*

Richardson returned. "Admiral, the fleet is ready to make transit," he reported. "All ships report full readiness."

"Good," Susan said. She trusted her officers not to engage in creative editing. She understood the reluctance to declare one's ship unfit for combat, particularly in the more repressive navies, but a ship that wasn't capable of handling the mission risked everything. "Start the countdown."

"Aye, Admiral."

Susan sat back, crossing her legs and projecting an impression of calm. Her impassive face betrayed none of her inner turmoil. It had been years since she'd commanded ships in action...at least, outside an admiral-grade simulator. Something would go wrong. Something *always* went wrong. And it would be something unpredictable. Battles had been won or lost before on something as minor, something as simple, as the lookout needing to take a piss at the crucial moment. Or on a horse becoming lame as the rider was trying to summon reinforcements.

"Admiral," Richardson said. "The countdown has begun. Transit in ten minutes and counting."

"Good," Susan said. "And now, we wait."

• • •

Thomas knew himself, without exaggeration, to be a brave man. It would have been easy, with his connections, to ensure himself a posting to the orbital defences, or a desk job in London…perhaps even a regimental command in the Home Guard. There was no shortage of positions for officers a bit long in the tooth, officers smart enough to handle the ceremonial aspects of the job and leave any *real* fighting to his subordinates…hell, Thomas *had* been offered a post on his last visit to Earth. It was a way to look good without being in any actual danger…he shook his head. He doubted it would have fooled anyone who mattered. And he'd have been bored in a week.

And yet…he studied the sensor records, ice congealing in his heart. Thirty catapults…all hell was going to break loose, when the recordings reached Earth. He didn't have to check the live feed from the analysis deck to calculate just how much tonnage could be thrown hundreds of light years in the blink of an eye. He didn't want to think about it. At what point did resistance become futile? And at what point…

"Captain," Lieutenant Michael Fitzgerald said. "We will make transit in five minutes."

Thomas nodded, keying his console. "Commander Donker?"

"All decks report ready, Captain," he said. "The gunboats and marine shuttles are ready to launch as soon as we cross the tramline."

"Good," Thomas said.

He looked at the display. The line was growing closer and closer. It was easy to believe an entire fleet was waiting on the far side, ready to open fire the moment the human ships arrived. He would have preferred to make transit quite some distance from the primary star, but the admiral had decided speed had to be put ahead of stealth. Thomas had the feeling the resulting compromise pleased absolutely no one. They were going to make transit too far from the enemy fleet to catch them by surprise, yet too close to be assured of remaining undetected long enough to sneak up and open fire. Thomas understood the logic, and the importance of making sure the catapults were destroyed if they couldn't be captured, but…he shook his head as the countdown ticked mercilessly towards zero. They didn't have time for any more qualms. It was time to make war.

"Transit in twenty seconds," Fitzgerald reported. He started counting down the last few seconds. "Three…two…one…"

Lion shuddered as she made transit. Thomas gritted his teeth, ignoring the phantom pain in his chest as the display blanked and hastily started to reboot. Dozens of icons—enemy icons—blazed a brilliant red, as if the system had measles. He smirked at the whimsy, even though it wasn't funny. The system genuinely *was* infected. He felt as if he could *feel* the virus looking at him.

"Transit complete, Captain," Fitzgerald said.

"The enemy doesn't appear to have detected us," Lieutenant Commander Sean Sibley added, slowly. "There's no hint they're preparing for combat."

Thomas wasn't convinced. They'd made transit *far* too close to the enemy position for his peace of mind. If the virus's ships had spotted the fleet making transit, it might just try to get ready to repel attack without making it obvious. A nervy captain might stand his ground, relying on passive sensors to track the enemy fleet. Thomas wouldn't have taken the risk, not with such an important system, but who knew what the *virus* considered acceptable? Captain Campbell would have taken the risk. Thomas was morbidly sure of it.

"Launch gunboats," he ordered. The tactical concept was relatively simple. Like most simple concepts, execution would be quite complicated. "Prepare to fire missiles on ballistic trajectories."

"Aye, Captain," Sibley said. The display updated rapidly. "Gunboats…launching now."

Thomas nodded, curtly. The die was cast.

. . .

Tobias felt sick.

It wasn't the first time he'd been into combat, but…he still felt sick. He sat in his chair, straps around his wrist and arms, feeling as if he wanted to be somewhere—anywhere—else. The tactical sensors were passive only—turning on active sensors would tell the enemy precisely where to shoot—but they were still telling him things he didn't want to know about the enemy defences. Their battleships could pump out enough point defence fire to take out the entire gunboat squadron without even *noticing* while they were engaging *Lion* and the rest of the fleet. He'd seen the plan and thought it sucked. He and the gunboats were going to be frighteningly exposed...

He glanced at Marigold. Her head was hidden behind a helmet—they'd both donned shipsuits, ensuring their chances of survival rose from infinitesimal to microscopic—but he could tell she was tense. How could she *not* be? The slightest mishap would be enough to get them both blown to atoms, wiped out of existence in a moment so small he didn't have words for it. He wanted to run to the hatch, to throw it open and dive back into the ship... fear yammered at his mind, fear of death and destruction and...everything.

Tobias wondered, not for the first time, how Colin coped. He got down and dirty with the rest of the groundpounders. But then, Colin was used to it. He was probably too dumb to know he was in danger.

That's not fair, Tobias told himself, sharply. He'd seen enough of the *adult* Colin to know the bastard had grown up a *lot*. He was far from stupid, even if he lacked formal qualifications. *He probably just doesn't let it get to him.*

A low quiver ran through the craft. Tobias swallowed, nearly jumping out of his skin when something went *bang* behind him. His imagination supplied all kinds of possibilities, from accidentally swatting the battlecruiser's hull to crashing into a piece of debris. He'd been told the odds of collision were very low, but...hitting something as small as a screw at a sizable percentage of the speed of light would be utterly disastrous. He wished the boffins would hurry up and invent force fields. They were needed desperately. He'd seen enough movies where the starfighters had force shields protecting their hulls from enemy fire...

"We're loose," Marigold said. Her voice was quiet, even though she *knew* they couldn't be overheard. "We'll enter engagement range in thirty minutes."

Tobias nodded as he keyed his console. The laser network linking the gunboats together had been stepped down as much as possible, even though the odds of detection were very low. He wanted to talk to the others and he didn't want to talk…he knew, deep inside, that none of them would understand his feelings. How could they? They'd never flown a combat mission before. It wouldn't hit them until they returned to the battlecruiser, all too aware that some of their comrades would never return. Tobias swallowed, again. How many of the newcomers wouldn't come home?

The console bleeped. "The missiles are on their way," he said. His voice sounded raspy, even to himself. "They're ready to accept targeting data."

Marigold sounded tightly composed, so composed he knew she was nervous, too. "We'll be within engagement range in twenty-five minutes."

Tobias forced himself to take deep breaths and calm down as the timer continued to tick down to zero. He'd paid close attention in the briefing, then the endless simulations. He *knew* the closer they got to the enemy ships before they went active, the greater the chance of completing the mission and withdrawing without losses. And yet, the urge to activate the targeting sensors and send the missiles blazing into the heart of the enemy formation was almost overwhelming. His fingers twitched. He wanted to do it. He knew it would compromise the mission, to the point the entire operation might fail, but he wanted to do it. He wanted…

"When we get home," Marigold said, "where do you want to go?"

Tobias blinked at the question. He hadn't given the matter any thought. They'd been so busy, they hadn't been able to snatch more than an hour or two together since they'd departed New Washington. Back on Earth… what were the odds of getting back home? They struck him as very poor. Gunboats had a better chance of survival than starfighters, but not by much. He knew how close he'd come to death on the last mission and *that* hadn't included a headlong dive into enemy space.

"I don't know," he said. His chest hurt, as if Colin had hit it. Again. "Luna, again? Or somewhere new?"

"If we can go somewhere new, sure," Marigold said. "Is there anything open these days?"

Tobias shrugged. They'd had problems going places even before the London outbreak. The lunar settlements had decent checkpoints, with everyone who went in and out having their blood checked before they were allowed to proceed, but planetside it was a whole different game. It wasn't easy to move around in Britain, let alone the rest of the world. The days when one could take a flight to Ireland for the day were long gone.

"Mars, perhaps," he said, as they flashed closer to their targets. "Or maybe even further away."

It felt like the promise of a better world, a future they could share... later. Tobias allowed himself to dream, before the console bleeped an alert. The alien craft might have detected them. He forced himself to concentrate, hoping and praying it was just a random sensor fluctuation. If they could get a little closer...the display flashed red. They were out of luck.

"Fuck," he swore. The alien ships had brought their sensors on line. The gunboats were suddenly as naked as...a very naked person. He giggled at the absurd thought, even though they were in deep shit. "Go evasive!"

"Got it," Marigold said. "Get the missiles up and running."

Tobias nodded as he ran his hand down the console. "Going live...now!"

CHAPTER SIXTEEN

"CAPTAIN," SIBLEY SAID. "The missiles have gone active."

Thomas nodded, resisting the urge to curse under his breath. He'd hoped the missiles would get closer before the enemy started looking for them in earnest. The latest designs were hard to target precisely, when their drives were up and running, but when they were powered down—in ballistic mode—they were as easy to detect as anything when the enemy started sweeping for them. The virus's active sensors were at least as good as his own, he acknowledged, and the brainships were very capable. Given time, they'd wipe out the missiles before they became a threat.

"Deploy the second salvo," he ordered. It was hard to be *sure* they'd thrown enough missiles at the brainship to take it out. The brainship was crammed with point defence weapons and it was surrounded by a squadron of smaller ships. He was surprised the enemy carrier wasn't already launching its starfighters. "And prepare to pass control to the gunboats."

A shudder ran through the battlecruiser as she emptied her missile tubes. Thomas ignored the sound, trusting his officers to alert him if something required his attention. Instead, he watched the first wave as it converged on its target. The enemy was deploying one hell of a lot of ECM, enough to make it hard to get a clear bead on the brainship, but the gunboats were too close to be fooled effectively. Thomas allowed himself a moment of relief. The enemy was so intent on covering the brainship that the gunboats might get away before it was too late. They weren't easy to target either, but the battleships could fill space with one hell of a lot of firepower.

His eyes narrowed as he watched the first missiles starting to vanish. The brainship was firing madly, sweeping space with countless plasma bolts, but...had it scored more hits than anyone had expected? No one believed the virus would sit on its hands and do nothing, after it had seen *Lion* in action. Had it come up with a countermeasure? The xenospecialists claimed the virus was alien, and that it didn't think in ways a human could understand, but it couldn't be *that* alien. It had to have some sense of self-preservation. One might as well wander onto a shooting range clad only in one's socks.

Which didn't stop Great Uncle Aggie from meeting an unfortunate end while fox-hunting, Thomas thought. He'd never liked fox-hunting, even if it was an old tradition. *He really didn't know what he was doing.*

"Impact in twenty seconds," Sibley said. "The enemy carrier is launching starfighters."

Thomas nodded, tersely, as the surviving missiles started to slam home. The brainship was solidly built, easily tougher than a battlecruiser...or even the legendary *Ark Royal*. A dozen laser heads detonated, stabbing beams of deadly force into its armour; five contact nukes flew through the chinks in the defences and detonated against the hull. For a dreadful moment, Thomas thought the giant ship would survive. The hull had remained intact, despite everything. And then three more missiles plunged into the gashes and detonated deep inside the ship. The brainship fell out of formation, spewing superheated plasma in all directions. Thomas was morbidly impressed. The brainship was dead, yet the hull remained largely intact...

The heat must have killed the viral matter, he thought. The virus couldn't hope to seal *all* its compartments, not without cutting itself into smaller and smaller sections. It was just a matter of time, the analysts insisted, before the virus started copying the human solution to the problem. Thomas doubted it. The virus wouldn't find that very comforting, any more than a human would want to cut off his arm...even if he had no choice. *The brainship is no longer a problem.*

"Pass control over the second salvo to the gunboats, then prepare to fire a third," Thomas ordered. The enemy battleships were regaining control, their point defence network dented but not destroyed. Thomas scowled. He'd hoped the entire network would go down. Instead, the virus's computers had taken over. "And signal the flag. We have completed the first objective."

He leaned back in his chair as the enemy formation began to advance. The virus wasn't sitting still, waiting to be destroyed. Thomas rather suspected that meant it had loaded a considerable amount of viral matter onto the battleships, enough to allow them a degree of independence. They were certainly massive enough to provide storage...hell, they'd just need a tank to *store* the matter. It was bad, but not *all* bad. A laser warhead that burned through the hull would give the virus a nasty shock.

"Reduce speed," he ordered, calmly. "Let them come to us."

He smiled as the enemy formation picked up speed. The planners hadn't been sure just how much of the fleet the virus would actually *see*, between the cloaking devices, the ECM haze and the loss of the brainship, but it looked as if the alien battleships had only seen the tip of the spear. *Lion* and her escorts were visible—vulnerable—to their sensors, giving them a chance to run them down and extract revenge for the brainship. They couldn't see the trap beyond.

And if this goes wrong, he mused as the alien formation opened fire, *we won't live long enough to regret it.*

• • •

"The enemy starfighters are coming at us," Tobias said. The gunboats had reversed course and were accelerating away from the alien battleships, but there was no way to put enough distance between themselves and the starfighters before it was too late. "I think they're mad."

"We just killed their brainship," Marigold said. "Of *course* they're mad."

Tobias laughed despite the fear clenching his heart as the range closed with terrifying speed. The squadron had—somehow—survived the attack on the brainship, but the starfighters were a far more deadly threat. They couldn't put out as much firepower as the capital ships, yet they were considerably more accurate. The only upside was that the gunboats could return fire, blowing the starfighters out of space as they tried to close the range. Tobias feared it wouldn't be enough. The starfighters were also far more manoeuvrable than the gunboats.

He keyed his terminal, launching a nuclear-tipped shipkiller towards the oncoming swarm and priming it to detonate as soon as the starfighters were within the blast radius. It was impossible to tell if they'd try to shoot the missile down or not. They might assume a lone missile was no threat to the capital ships or they might simply blow it out of space, just to be sure. Tobias watched, feeling his heart skip a beat, as the missile darted into the cloud and detonated. A dozen starfighters vanished. The remainder kept coming.

"Good shot," Marigold said.

Tobias glanced at her. "When we get back to the ship, do you want to find a tube?"

Marigold laughed. "I think this is not the time and place."

"Hah." Tobias giggled as he ran his hand down the console, triggering the point defence weapons. "It's a more optimistic thought than anything else..."

He frowned as the point defence opened fire. No human could follow the action, let alone take opportunities that were open for only a fraction of a second. He'd been through hundreds of simulations that proved it beyond a shadow of a doubt, yet...he felt helpless, a spectator on his own craft as the weapons fired automatically. He wanted to take control himself, to fire back at the starfighters as they closed with terrifying speed...he knew he couldn't. All he could do was watch.

The compensator field seemed to shift, just slightly, as Marigold threw the gunboat into an evasive pattern. Tobias doubted it would be particularly effective. The gunboat was blindingly fast, compared to a battleship, but slow and inelegant next to a starfighter. His head started to pound as he watched the starfighters closing the range, plasma bolts zeroing in on them mercilessly; his fingers touched his mask, ready to snap it into place if they had to eject. Starfighter pilots had survived ejections, he'd been assured. There were no figures on how many had died in the attempt.

They'd be dead if they tried or just remained in their seats, waiting to die, part of his mind whispered. The display filled with new icons. *And…*

Marigold whooped, cutting off that line of thought. "They came! They came!"

Tobias blinked. Starfighters—human starfighters—had arrived, cutting a swath through the alien craft while they remained focused on the gunboats. Tobias let out a breath he hadn't realised he'd been holding, watching in awe as the alien starfighters—caught between two fires—were picked off before they could adapt to the new threat. Human pilots would have turned and fled, surrendering the chance to hurt the gunboats in exchange for survival; the virus, it seemed, didn't care.

"Keep us heading away from the titans," he ordered. His sensors were showing the human battleships now, spitting missiles towards the alien ships. "I'll check for orders."

His heart sank as they broke through into clear space. There'd been fourteen gunboats in the squadron, when they'd launched. Now, there were only ten. Eight people were dead…he tried to tell himself that they might have merely been separated from the rest of the squadron, but he knew it wasn't so. They were dead. He felt a wash of guilt that he'd never gotten to know them, mingled with relief. He wouldn't be mourning friends, merely…

No wonder fighter pilots are such arseholes, he thought. He'd met enough pilots to know he disliked them, even though he was technically a pilot himself. *They and their friends could die at any moment.*

He shook his head. *And so could we,* his thoughts added. *The battle isn't over yet.*

• • •

"Signal the fleet," Susan ordered. "All ships are to commence firing."

She allowed herself a wintry smile. She'd hoped the enemy would allow themselves to be lured into firing range and it looked as if it had worked. She knew, all too well, that it could easily be nothing more than a delaying tactic, to give them time to destroy the catapults, but there were ways to do that which didn't involve sacrificing a handful of battleships. No, they hadn't known the rest of her fleet was there until it was too late to avoid action. Her smile grew wider as the battleships opened fire. It felt *good* to have the firepower on her side.

A low rumble echoed through the ship as her main guns opened fire, sweeping plasma bursts over the alien hull. The alien battleships could take one hell of a beating—Susan knew that from countless sensor records—but their exposed sensor nodes and point defence weapons were far more vulnerable. A single hit would be enough to kill the nodes, allowing her weapons to pound the enemy ships without interference. The enemy was firing back, of course, but she had far more ships. They had to split their fire between multiple targets.

She nodded as a starfighter flew into the maelstrom and vanished. There was no way to tell if it had been human or alien, friendly or unfriendly. There was just too much interference. The pilot had either lost control of her craft or assumed, wrongly, that she could pick her way through the plasma bursts. Susan felt a stab of sympathy, which she ruthlessly suppressed. She didn't have time for anything but victory.

"Missiles away, Admiral," Richardson reported. "Impact in ten seconds…"

"Order *Lion* to target the alien carrier," Susan said. The alien fleet carrier was starting to reverse course, heading away from the battleships and back towards the catapults. The carrier wouldn't carry battleship-grade plasma cannons, but she could do one hell of a lot of damage if she wished. "Take her out before she gets out of range."

"Aye, Admiral."

Susan nodded, watching as missiles slammed into the alien battleship.

The ship was tough, the hull taking two nuclear strikes without serious damage. A missile detonated inside the battleship, but she kept coming. Susan would have been more impressed if the battleship hadn't been trying to kill her. The virus knew it had lost the battle. It also knew there was no hope of extracting the battleships. It might just decide to try to ram the battleships into their human counterparts. But if it wanted to try, it had left it too late.

She smiled, again, as the battleship finally gave up the ghost. The hulk fell out of formation as its drives failed, its weapons falling silent… Susan eyed the wreck for a moment, then dismissed it. It was harmless now. If there were any survivors, it was unlikely they posed any significant threat. They could be ignored, left alone…her heart clenched. She hated the thought of wanton slaughter, of killing people—aliens—who could no longer hurt her, but the hosts were already dead. Their bodies belonged to the virus. There was no hope of freeing them.

We'll destroy the hulks later, she promised herself. *Until then…*

• • •

"Captain," Sibley said. "I have a targeting lock on the alien carrier."

Thomas nodded. *Lion* had no place in a clash of the titans. The boffins swore his ship could survive a sustained barrage from the battleships, but he had no intention of putting that to the test. Better to circle around the engagement and engage the fleet carrier, rather than allowing his ship to be destroyed for nothing. The admiral clearly agreed.

"Fire," he ordered. They'd fired more missiles than he'd hoped, although not more than he'd feared. It wouldn't take *that* long to resupply, before they jumped into enemy space. "And order the gunboats to follow the missiles in."

"Aye, sir," Sibley said.

• • •

Tobias nodded to himself as the new orders flashed up on the display. The gunboats had been left alone since their side's starfighters had arrived. It looked as though the virus was having trouble reacting to multiple differ-ent problems, although he knew he could be completely wrong. The battle was spreading out of control, fought on such a scale he could barely keep track of his own, tiny aspect. He hoped the admiral was doing better. He'd heard good things about Admiral Onarina, but he'd also heard a lot of nasty things about admirals as a group.

"Here we go," Marigold said. "Make sure you take control of the missiles."

Tobias bit down on a sharp reply as the gunboats altered course, racing around the edge of the battle and zooming towards the enemy carrier. It took on shape and form rapidly, a cluster of boxy shapes surrounded by a handful of starfighters. There was something crude about the design, as if the designers had no sense of elegance. *Lion* wasn't the most elegant design in the navy—and she was far cruder than Stellar Star's personal ship, which was so futuristic she might as well be fantasy—but there was something neat about her. The alien carrier was so poorly designed that it was hard to believe the designers were actually intelligent.

Not that they care about my opinion, he thought, as he linked into the missile command network. The fleet carrier was already opening fire, its point defence forcing the gunboats to scatter as they closed in. *They certainly crammed a shitload of firepower into the hull.*

He gritted his teeth as he deployed a handful of ECM screamers. They wouldn't last for more than a few seconds—he'd be surprised if any of them lasted more than a minute or two—but they'd distract the point defence. He took control of the missiles, directed them through the haze and then logged out again. Marigold laughed as she reversed course, the compensa-tors straining as the gunboats roared away from the carrier. Tobias grinned as the missiles slammed home, unleashing a series of explosions that blew the carrier into a cloud of flaming debris.

"Scratch one flattop," Marigold carolled.

"Target destroyed," Tobias agreed. He couldn't see any more enemy starfighters—there was just too much electronic haze—but if they were still alive they were thoroughly screwed. Their mothership was dead. The rest of the fleet was dying. And there was no way their life support would last long enough for reinforcements to arrive. "What now?"

"I guess we'll find out," Marigold said.

• • •

Mitch smiled as the alien fleet died under human fire. He'd taken up overwatch position as soon as the shooting started, following orders he didn't particularly like…but understood. *Unicorn* had no place in a battleship engagement, even though her point defence might have made the difference between victory or defeat. He felt his smile grow wider as the last of the alien battleships exploded into a cloud of debris. The battle was effectively over. Humanity had given the aliens a solid thrashing.

He keyed his console as the remaining starfighters were wiped out, reviewing the engagement. It had been fairly one-sided, once the brainship had been taken out. And yet, the battleships had shown more independence than any of them had expected. He'd feared they'd stay too close to the catapults, forcing the admiral to risk a close-range engagement that could have destroyed the devices they'd come to steal. It would have been a victory, but…he shook his head. The operation had been a smashing success. It would do wonders for morale when the truth was released on Earth.

The battle isn't over yet, he reminded himself. There was one part of the plan that remained to be completed, before the surviving enemy did something stupid. *They haven't taken the catapults yet.*

CHAPTER SEVENTEEN

"IN SPACE," PRIVATE SCOTT DAVIES WHISPERED, "no one can hear you scream."

"Shut the fuck up," Colin snapped. The joke hadn't been funny the first time Davies had made it...probably not the first time *anyone* had made it. The idea of chasing aliens around a starship—or being chased by aliens around a starship—was the sort of thing that sounded cool in a universe where it didn't happen. "We'll be down in a moment."

He looked at his team, wishing he could see their faces behind the masks. They'd trained for the mission as best as they could, but he was all too aware that their planning rested on a great deal of guesswork. No one knew precisely what to expect when they burned their way into the control nodes, from a blob-filled compartment to a hive of host bodies fanatically determined to keep the marines from taking control. He studied the live feed from the shuttle's sensors as it coasted towards the nearest catapult, careful to stay well away from the titanic struggle between the fleets. Colin would have preferred to wait for a clear victor to emerge before jumping into the unknown, but General Sampan insisted the catapults be seized as quickly as possible. The last thing they wanted was for the virus to get any ideas about blowing them to dust, rather than let them fall into human hands.

His eyes lingered on Kevin. The alien's face was hidden too, but…Colin shook his head. It was impossible to tell what the alien was thinking. Colin knew what *he'd* been thinking, the first time *he'd* dropped into danger… he wondered, as the seconds ticked down, if the alien was thinking along the same lines. Pride in his skill, combined with fear of letting the side down…that attitude had been drilled into Colin well before he'd joined the marines. He'd spent most of his schooling playing football, or at least it felt that way. He certainly didn't remember much of his lessons. They'd been boring beyond words.

Conversation died away as the shuttle closed on its target. The catapult didn't *look* like a catapult. Colin was almost disappointed. He'd once owned a catapult that could probably have qualified as a deadly weapon, if someone had been inclined to press charges. The alien device was nothing more than a giant mesh, linked to generators and control nodes that were—presumably—charging up for the jump. The spooks hadn't been able to predict when the virus had actually intended to use the catapults, although Colin wouldn't have trusted them if they had. There were just too many institutional memories of the spooks being wrong with confidence.

They would have waited until they had everything ready for a knock-out punch, Colin thought, coldly. *And when they were ready, they would have moved without hesitation.*

"Ten seconds," the pilot called. "Get ready."

Colin tested his plasma rifle, one final time, as the countdown ticked towards zero. He preferred projectile weapons, but plasma weapons were more effective against the virus and its hosts. They were also more dangerous to their bearers, although…Colin gritted his teeth as he checked the grenades on his belt, readying himself for action. The boffins had been promising safer weapons for years, but nothing had ever materialised. The bootnecks would just have to be ready to hurl overheating weapons at the enemy, if their containment chambers threatened to explode. Who knew? The blast might destroy the enemy position and win the war.

The gravity field flickered as the shuttle latched onto the alien hull. Colin braced himself, wincing as a low whine echoed through the air. The cutters were going to work, slicing through the heavy metal and tearing deep into the alien hull. He would have preferred to use a plasma torch to burn their way into the alien structure, but they needed to avoid damaging the catapults as much as possible. No one had been able to calculate the odds of accidentally destroying the catapults as they tried to seize them, yet... he shook his head. There was no point in dwelling on it now. There'd be plenty of other people who'd be happy to second-guess him—and everyone up to General Sampan himself—if the mission failed.

"Go," he snapped, as the hatch crashed open. "Move!"

He led the way, hurling a flashbang through the gash in the alien hull and dropping through the hatch. The gravity field twisted, sending uncomfortable spasms through his neck as his perspective shifted. Down was suddenly up and...he pushed the thought out of his head as he landed neatly and looked around. The air was misty, heavy with dead or dying viral particles. His HUD flashed up a constant stream of alarms, warning him of the danger of removing his mask without going through a complete decontamination process. One breath would be more than enough to turn him into a mindless slave.

And not in the fun way, either, he thought, as the remainder of the platoon plunged into the catapult. He looked at the bulkheads, hoping to find something vaguely familiar. The boffins swore blind the marine techs could interface their systems with the alien catapult, but Colin had his doubts. The old movies featuring bold hackers who'd cracked alien computer systems had always had a friendly scriptwriter pulling the strings. *If they tear off our masks, we're dead.*

A shape loomed up in front of him. Colin didn't hesitate. He pulled the trigger, sending a plasma burst into the host body's chest. The poor bastard practically exploded, blood and gore flying in all directions. He'd been human once, Colin thought. It was hard to be sure. The remnants of the body were covered in so many pustules, it looked as though he was on the verge of giving birth to countless viral particles. Colin pushed through the mess, peering further into the mist. His mask's sensors were unreliable. He snapped a command, launching microscopic drones into the air. Hopefully, they'd plot out the interior and alert the marines before they walked into a trap. The virus hadn't known the shuttle was there, until it started to chop through the hull, but it sure as hell did now. It could hardly have missed the flashbang wiping out entire chunks of viral matter.

"We sweep the hull," he ordered, quietly. "Platoon One, with me. Platoon Two, secure the bridgehead. Kevin, take point."

"Aye, boss," Kevin said.

Colin watched as the alien led the way forward, moving with practiced ease. He'd definitely had *some* kind of experience before, Colin noted; he didn't move with the squeamish determination of young men facing combat for the first time. A marine could do well on the training field and yet freeze up when the bullets started flying. Colin knew he'd come close to freezing himself, that he would have if his sergeant hadn't planted a boot up his arse to keep him moving. He put the thought out of his mind as they slipped past devices of unknown purpose, half-hidden in the mist. The flashbang grenades cleared the way, wiping out huge chunks of viral matter without damaging any of the hardware. Colin hoped the blasts hurt. It was hard to be sure. Pulling out his nose hairs would also hurt, but it wouldn't do any real damage. The virus might be even less concerned with the individual particles.

The communicator bleeped. "Sir, we're losing recon drones."

Colin grimaced. The drones were practically invisible to the naked eye, but they were moving through a sea of viral matter. The virus was probably perfectly aware of their presence, even if it couldn't *see* them. Hell, it probably *could* see them. Colin didn't understand how the virus actually *saw*, when it wasn't within a host body, but it was clear it had *some* kind of awareness of its surroundings. It could probably congeal around the drones and weigh them down, eventually sending them tumbling to the deck. Or something. His mask darkened, automatically, as another flashbang detonated. The virus had to be on the back foot. It was his job to keep it that way.

"We'll sweep the floor, room by room," he said. "Prepare additional drones and sensor nodes to follow in our wake."

The sense of unreality grew stronger as they inched into an oversized corridor. It was weirdly proportioned, designed in a manner that made his head hurt. The host bodies weren't human, perhaps. The corridor certainly wasn't designed for humans. Or maybe the virus didn't care. It was just a giant living thing...he frowned as it dawned on him they were crawling through a host body, infecting the virus as it infected its victims. He had the strangest feeling they were being watched and judged by a vast intelligence, one so far above him that it was barely even aware of their presence. A chill ran down his spine, sweat prickling down his back. He'd never been quite so scared in his life...he snarled a curse, dismissing the warning icons that flashed up in his HUD. No one was ever *not* afraid, particularly when facing an enemy he couldn't see. He just refused to allow the fear to dominate him.

And yet...his eyes narrowed as they made their way through the giant complex. Where *was* the enemy? Colin knew what *he'd* be doing, if he was in charge of defending the catapult, and the virus wasn't doing any of it. Or was it? He could imagine the host bodies frantically arming a nuke, ready to blow the catapult and the boarding party to hell. And yet, it was wasteful. Surely, they'd at least *try* to repel boarders. Unless they felt there was no hope of saving anything. The fleet had practically won the engagement. It could blow the catapults away from a safe distance if the marines failed to keep them intact.

His concerns grew as the enemy remained unseen. Droplets of moisture formed on his mask, and he absently brushed them away as alerts flashed in front of his eyes. Where *were* they? The techs were trying to hack the network, but—apparently—not having much luck. The virus didn't bother with passwords and firewalls, not when it was the only intelligence on the station, yet it required a level of biomechanical interaction no human could match. Colin had seen enhanced soldiers, with implanted weapons and computer links, but none of them came close to the virus. Given time, it could turn its host bodies into super-soldiers out of science fiction nightmares. The only thing standing in its way, he thought, was a simple lack of concern. It cared as little for its host bodies as Colin cared for his skin cells.

"Sir," Kevin said. "The viral particles are growing stronger."

Colin frowned, holding up a hand to slow the team. The mist was wavering, as if the air circulation had just been turned up to the max. Streams of mist billowed towards him, somehow interfering with his mask's sensors. *Nothing* seemed to peer through the haze. He dropped to one knee, raising his rifle. There was no hope of hiding, not when the virus was practically crawling over their suits. He unhooked a flashbang grenade and hurled it into the mist, half-expecting to hit a wall of host bodies heading towards him. But there was nothing...

A tidal wave of liquid crashed down on him. Colin barely had a moment to realise the ceiling had caved in before he lost his footing, the yellowish liquid carrying him down the corridor and bashing him against the bulkhead. Alerts flared up as the suit's sensors realised it was under attack, the virus trying to find a way to break through the latches and worm its way into the suit. Colin felt the liquid start to congeal, threatening to pin him in place as the virus worked its way into the suit. Panic shot through him. He'd once rolled his eyes as a woman—a rape victim—had described feeling helpless as her attacker had started to remove her clothes. He'd thought she was a wimp, unable to stand up for herself. He understood now. God! He understood now.

He grasped hold of the final flashbang and detonated it. The jelly dissolved into liquid. Colin forced himself up, suddenly all too aware the remainder of the team was trapped. He snapped orders, looking around for his rifle. Sergeant Bowman would have a whole string of nasty things to say about a bootneck who lost his weapon in a combat zone, although Colin expected the sergeant would understand. They'd nearly been infected because...he picked up his rifle as the rest of the team broke free, dead viral matter dripping from their suits and pooling around their feet. Colin breathed a sigh of relief as he realised they were alive and uninfected. They'd have to go through decontamination before they were allowed to return home, but at least they were alive. Their minds were their own.

"Incoming," Kevin snapped. There was a hint of...*something* in his voice? Delight? Fear? Anticipation? It was impossible to be sure. "They're coming!"

Colin hefted his rifle as a shivering blob of viral matter advanced towards them. He had no idea how it was moving—it had no legs, as far as he could tell—but it moved with all the grace of a mid-sized tank. Giant tentacles reached out towards the marines, glimmering in the half-light as they snapped at the air. It was easy to believe they were harmless, but their appearance belied their strength. Colin had seen the recordings of marines torn apart by the blobs, armour or no armour. They could not be taken lightly.

He pointed his rifle and pulled the trigger. A stream of plasma pulses blew the blob into pieces, which picked themselves up and kept coming. Behind them, a line of host bodies appeared and ran at the marines. Colin keyed his radio, ordering more flashbang grenades from the second platoon as the marines opened fire. The host bodies looked nasty, their arms reaching out as if they intended to hug the marines to death, but they weren't the real threat. The viral particles in the air were the true danger. Given time, they would break through the line and crush the marines.

Colin gritted his teeth. He didn't want to use anything nastier than the flashbangs. The risk of damaging the catapult was just too high, particularly when they didn't have the slightest idea how the device worked. There was no way to be sure they weren't shooting at something vitally important, something that couldn't be replaced before the fleet ran out of time. The spooks hadn't been able to swear to anything, but Colin was morbidly sure time wasn't on their side. The virus wasn't known for wasting time. Once it had all of the catapults up and running, it would start the offensive.

"Open the airlocks," he ordered, curtly.

He braced himself. They'd planned to vent the atmosphere, as a last resort, but there was no way to be sure just how much damage they'd do to the device. It wouldn't trouble a human design, he'd been assured, but the virus handled most of the command and control tasks itself, rather than relying on proper datacores. The sudden drop in temperature might do much more than simply freezing the virus in its tracks. It might damage the catapult beyond easy repair.

It isn't as if we could rely on the virus to help us, he thought, as the mist started to flow out of the compartment. The liquid beneath his fleet crackled as it turned to ice. *It's too dangerous to take lightly.*

Alerts flashed up in front of him as the temperature continued to drop. Tiny pieces of hail cracked against his mask, making him jump even though he *knew* they were largely harmless. The air was starting to clear, revealing a scene out of hell itself. Host bodies lay on the deck, steadily freezing to death. The pustules seemed to have been frozen in the midst of bursting. Colin felt sick, reminding himself—again and again—that the host bodies had been beyond salvation. Their very souls had been stolen by the virus. He hoped they hadn't been aware of what had happened to them, as their bodies were taken over and controlled by an alien intelligence. The reports from the handful of people who'd been freed were somewhat contradictory. And none of them had been infected for long.

He tongued his throatmike. "Deploy the remainder of the drones," he ordered. The atmosphere was gone. The viral particles were either dead or frozen. "I want the entire complex swept with UV light before we risk sealing the gash and pumping the atmosphere back inside."

"Aye, sir."

Colin allowed himself a tight nod as the platoon resumed its sweep, feet crunching through pools of frozen virus as they made their way through the complex. The virus didn't seem to have fitted airlocks, somewhat to his surprise. It might not *want* to start cutting off pieces of itself, but it was going to lose them anyway. Colin had been warned he might have to cut off his own arm to save the rest of him…he snorted at the thought. He'd always assumed the virus would be *less* concerned about the concept. Closing the airlocks would be roughly akin to pulling out a hair or two.

Which would still be painful, he thought, again. *And the virus probably wants to avoid it if possible.*

He smiled, briefly, as they completed their search. The complex didn't have as many nooks and crannies, let alone hiding places, as its human counterpart. If there were any host bodies still alive, they were very well hidden. Colin let out a breath. They'd completed *their* part of the mission. It all relied on the techs now.

"Mission completed, sir," he said, formally. "The catapult is in human hands."

CHAPTER EIGHTEEN

SUSAN SMILED AS THE REPORTS FLOWED IN from the landing parties. Twenty-five of thirty catapults had been taken intact, with seventeen either in usable condition or repairable with parts scrounged from the remainder. The techs were already swarming over the devices, replacing the biomechanical software with human computer nodes and datacores. They insisted the catapults could be brought online within two days, once they'd completed repairing the damaged units. Susan hoped they were right.

Her eyes lingered on the starchart, silently tracing the jumps back to New Washington and Alien-One. They were on the far end of a tramline chain, well beyond the flicker network. An entire enemy fleet could be bearing down on them and they wouldn't have the slightest idea, at least until it showed itself. It would be frustrating as hell to have to blow up the catapults and run for their lives, after spending so much time capturing them, but there might be no choice. The enemy might have shot a warning up their own flicker network, if they had one. It wasn't clear if they'd established one.

She frowned as she glanced at the post-battle reports. The fleet had completed its first mission with flying colours, but a handful of escort ships had been destroyed and a number of capital ships had been damaged. She was lucky the enemy hadn't managed to ram one of her battleships…she grimaced at the thought. The virus had been caught by surprise, once. It wouldn't take it long to deduce what she intended to do with the captured catapults. She just hoped it wouldn't have time to reposition its forces to cover the rear.

If nothing else, it will have to recall ships from the front, Susan thought. The briefing from New Washington had made it clear that the defences were starting to crumble. The Americans couldn't spare any more ships to extract the fleet if it ran into something it couldn't handle. *We'll win time to resupply our defences and give our people some rest.*

She finished reading the reports, feeling her scowl deepen. Damage control teams were working overtime, replacing armour and reloading missile tubes and pods. A handful of replacement starfighters had been rushed out of storage, the reserve pilots pulled from their regular duties and hurled into the cockpits. They were going to be spending the next two days training, but…it wouldn't be enough. Susan wanted to supervise personally, as if her presence would make the difference between success and failure… she understood, suddenly, why so many admirals became micromanagers. It was easier to direct tiny aspects of the whole than sit back and allow one's subordinates to do their jobs. Easier, but not right. She knew she'd picked a good command team. They could handle it.

Her wristcom bleeped. "Admiral," Richardson said. "The command conference will be online in five minutes."

"Understood," Susan said. She silently blessed all the gods she didn't have a political commissioner—or even a politician—looking over her shoulder. Not now. "I'll take it in my office."

She took one final look at the display, checking that the contingency plans were in place. If they couldn't make use of the catapults, for whatever reason, they'd make damn sure they were destroyed before they fought their way back to New Washington. She'd had nukes emplaced amongst the framework as soon as the battle had ended, just to be sure. The analysts weren't sure why the virus hadn't destroyed the catapults itself—their suggestions ranged from the virus being caught by surprise to a new sensitivity to losses—but she had no intention of making the same mistake. They'd destroy the remnants of the catapults after they completed the jump, just to be sure. If there was an alien fleet *en route* to the catapult system, it was going to be disappointed.

The thought cheered her as she stepped into her office. Her steward passed her a mug of coffee and retreated, leaving her alone. Susan sat in her chair, trying not to look at the stream of messages on her terminal. Most of them could be handled by her staff—she winced, inwardly, at a reporter's request for an interview—but she wouldn't know until she looked at them. She was tempted to ignore the messages, even though she knew it would be setting a bad example. If the mission was a success, she could handle them during the voyage home; if the mission failed, she'd have worse problems. Her lips thinned as the terminal bleeped, informing her that the conference was about to begin. The discussion would be a formality, and yet...

If the mission fails, they'll go through our logs with a fine-toothed comb to make sure the blame is assigned to the right person, she thought. *And anything we say may wind up being used against us.*

She straightened as the holograms flickered into existence. She'd always preferred holoconferences, if only because she could use a filter to look perfectly normal while lying in her bunk or taking a shower. Every month, there was a scandal about someone forgetting to use a filter and giving their viewers an eyeful, a scandal that always faded because everyone knew everyone did it...she smiled in welcome, wondering how many of her command staff were using filters. General Sampan and Admiral Li looked just a little *too* well turned out.

"General," she said. "I trust the marines have returned to their ships?"

"Yes, Admiral," Sampan said. He looked pleased, as well he might be. His part of the operation had been the most delicate, made worse by the lack of actionable intelligence, and yet he'd pulled it off with style. "Decontamination procedures are still underway, as you may expect, but preliminary reports suggest we don't have to worry about infection."

"Good," Susan said. Seven marines were dead…she promised herself she'd look at their records, when she had a chance. She owed it to them to remember their names. "The techs assure us the catapults can be pressed into service, so…"

She looked from face to face. "We should be able to jump the entire fleet into enemy space," she said. "It is my intention to proceed with Phase Two as soon as the catapults are online. Do any of you have any objections?"

The words hung in the air for a long, cold moment. It wasn't an entirely fair question. They'd been through the pros and cons time and time again, discussing all the potential options well before the fleet had assembled and departed. Now…she scowled, inwardly. A fleet could not be run by committee, yet she had to pay heed to their opinions. The CO of a multinational fleet had to be a diplomat as well as a military officer. She supposed it was a good thing they were so far from home. They all knew there was no way they could sit on their butts and wait for orders. Either they moved ahead with the plan or they destroyed the catapults and ran.

"As long as the catapults are usable, I see no reason we cannot proceed," Li said, finally. "The plan was authorised before we left Earth."

"We should proceed," Sampan put in. "How long do we have before they realise what we've done?"

Susan shrugged. "We haven't been able to locate a flicker station," she said. "However, that doesn't prove there *isn't* one. The warning might already be halfway to the alien homeworld."

"Or they might not have the slightest idea we blew their fleet to hell and took the catapults," Sampan pointed out. "None of their ships escaped, did they?"

"As far as we know," Susan said. "We have to assume the worst."

She made a face. Standard naval doctrine insisted that a cloaked picket should be positioned well away from the fleet, watching from a safe distance. If something went wrong, the picket could break contact and sneak away without being detected. The virus might have copied the idea, and if it had…she shook her head. There'd been so much sensor distortion during the battle that an entire fleet of cloaked ships could have escaped detection, if they'd existed in the first place. There was just no way to *know*.

"We'll proceed, if we manage to get the catapults up and running before the enemy fleet arrives," she said. "If you have any objections, you have two days to file them before we jump."

She smiled, briefly, as she ended the conference. A handful of her own pickets would remain within the system, to record the jump and then sneak home. Her crewmen would have one last chance to write letters to their families, their parents and partners and children…she wondered, idly, just how many letters would be carefully crafted to imply subtle disagreement with her plan without coming right out and saying it. Victory might have a thousand parents, but defeat was an orphan. The survivors would do their level best to escape blame for the disaster.

It won't be a disaster, she told herself, firmly. The enemy might have thought about a giant fleet materialising in their backyard—they'd certainly come up with the idea themselves—but they'd have problems responding to the threat. Whatever they did, the human race would come out ahead. *We're going to win.*

• • •

Tobias breathed a sigh of relief as the gunboat docked, a dull *clang* echoing through the craft as airlocks matched and mated. He'd hoped to return to the ship as soon as the battle came to an end, but fleet command had other ideas. The gunboats could remain on station longer than the starfighters and the admiral intended to make use of it. Tobias rubbed his forehead as he fumbled with his straps, all too aware he was drenched in sweat. He wanted to go for a shower, then climb into his bunk and sleep. It was all he could do to take off his helmet and place it beside the seat.

Marigold stumbled to her feet and removed her helmet. She looked terrible, her hair hanging down in sweaty ringlets. Tobias knew he didn't look any better. He was probably at least as smelly as she was, perhaps even worse. Thankfully, he'd gotten used to the smell of too many humans in too close proximity. He glanced at the washroom, wishing he'd had a chance to use it before they'd flown into battle. It was worse for starfighter pilots... he thrust that thought out of his head. He didn't want to think about it.

"Grab something to drink," Marigold said. "We're going to need it."

Tobias made a face as he fumbled through the drawer and removed a pair of nutrient drinks. His fingers refused to cooperate, forcing him to bite his way into his tube and drink it like a child. The flavour—it was supposed to be orange juice—revolted him. He'd had to drink something similar at school and it had never gone down well. He had to admit it made him feel better, but at what cost?

"We'd better move," Marigold said. "They'll expect us in the briefing room."

"They're so unreasonable," Tobias said. He knew he sounded like a whiny social queen and he didn't much care. "I want to sleep."

He forced himself to stand and follow her towards the hatch. His body ached, as if he'd been locked in place for hours...he had, he supposed. It *had* been hours since the battle began, yet it felt like days. His legs felt as if they were made of rubber. He gritted his teeth as he half-walked, half-fell, through the hatch. The battlecruiser felt like home, the air fresh and clear...he had a sudden impression of a cloud of filth surrounding him. The CAG would take one sniff and order him fumigated. The thought would have made him smile, if he hadn't been so tired. It became clear, as they walked into the briefing compartment, that he wasn't the only one. The entire squadron—the entire surviving squadron—looked exhausted.

"Grab yourself a mug of coffee and sit down," Bagehot ordered. The CAG looked tired, although it was hard to know why. He'd been sitting on his arse while the gunboats had flown against the alien hordes. "We'll begin as soon as you're ready."

Tobias poured two mugs of coffee, passed one to Marigold and crashed into a seat. It tasted vile, but it jerked him awake. He'd never been much of a coffee drinker before he'd joined the military—his mother had loathed the stuff—yet the squadron couldn't survive without it. His thoughts slowly cleared as he sipped the coffee, reminding him that part of the squadron *hadn't* survived. He felt a pang of bitter guilt. He didn't know the names of the dead men and women. He barely even remembered their faces.

They're your fucking tribe, you arsehole, a voice said at the back of his head. It sounded an awful lot like Colin. *You probably knew them online a long time before you actually met them.*

The thought mocked him. Colin had once demanded Tobias attend a football match and cheer the school's team, even though Tobias hadn't given a damn who won and lost. It had never mattered to him. Why should he support a team that had treated him like dirt? Why should he cheer for a school that didn't care about him? And yet, the dead pilots had presumably been recruited like himself. They'd been computer gamers, not…Tobias winced, inwardly. They hadn't deserved to die.

"The SAR teams did a sweep, but they found nothing," Bagehot said, without preamble. "Frank, Judy, Karen and Adrian are missing, presumed dead."

Presumed dead, Tobias thought, sarcastically. It was beyond belief the pilots wouldn't have activated their locator beacons, now the fighting was over. The PLBs could be activated remotely, if one had the right codes. The SAR teams would certainly have tried to activate them. *They are dead and any suggestion…*

He stopped himself, feeling another pang of guilt. They were dead and they'd deserved better and there was nothing he could do to *make* it better…he wondered, morbidly, if he'd be called upon to empty their drawers. He didn't want to do it and yet…better the gunboat pilots than a complete stranger. Bagehot would probably do it. He, at least, knew the dead better than Tobias himself.

"We'll review the rest of the engagement later," Bagehot continued. "For the moment, you did well. You handled the mission perfectly, killing a brainship and a fleet carrier. The admiral sends her congratulations."

Tobias kept his face impassive, somehow. Bagehot wasn't his old headmaster, the Beast. The CAG wasn't anything like as fond of the sound of his own voice. He should understand what he was putting his crews through, that they were tired and wanted sleep and…

"Go get some rest," Bagehot ordered. Tobias wondered, in a moment of horror, if he'd dozed off in the middle of the briefing. He'd zoned out completely. "I'll see you all tomorrow."

"And pray no one attacks while we're asleep," a pilot said. Tobias wanted to strangle him with his bare hands. "We need our rest."

"Yes, you do," Bagehot agreed. "Go."

. . .

Colin emerged from the decontamination chamber feeling uncomfortably naked, even though he was wearing a shipboard tunic. The medics swore blind that the decontamination procedure was intended to ensure that not a scrap of alien viral matter remained on their skin, but Colin suspected it was *really* designed to torture its victims. They'd bathed his suit in UV light, then insisted he remove it and be bathed again before subjecting him to an endless series of increasingly invasive tests. He understood the importance of ensuring that an unwitting host didn't board the ship, but still…

Sergeant Bowman met him outside. "Good work, Corporal."

"Thank you, Sarge," Colin said. He had a feeling the meeting wasn't coincidence. The fact he was being quietly steered towards a private room merely proved it. "The decontamination team took my hair!"

"What little you had left," Bowman said. He closed the hatch and turned to face Colin, his face a blank mask. "How did Kevin perform?"

Colin frowned. He'd had no time to think about the engagement, let alone write his report. It was unlikely the sergeant *really* needed to know immediately, unless he wanted Colin's unsullied responses. Not for the first time, Colin wondered who was backing the entire program. Bowman was way too junior to be in overall charge. He was surprised it wasn't being handled by the company CO himself.

"He did well, Sarge," Colin said, finally. "Handled the flight well, boarded the alien structure and coped without a breakdown…frankly, he did better than many of us on our first deployments."

"He would be used to alien environments," Bowman pointed out. "He's on this ship."

Colin nodded in understanding. "We're all alien to him, aren't we?"

"Yes, and compared to the virus, Kevin is practically human," Bowman said. "Are you happy to keep him under your command?"

"Yes," Colin said. It was true. "He handled himself well. I'd be happy to keep him."

"Very good," Bowman said. "He'll remain with you, for the moment."

Colin leaned forward. "Sergeant…is there something about this I should know?"

"Not really." Bowman frowned. "The blunt truth, corporal, is that it is important that Kevin does well—and that he does well on his own merits. We cannot afford to reject him, for political reasons, but we cannot afford to push him forward either. Do you understand me?"

"I'm not sure," Colin confessed. "Why is this important?"

"Politics," Bowman said. "Believe me, this could still go horribly wrong."

CHAPTER NINETEEN

"CAPTAIN," STACI SAID. "WE'RE TETHERED."

Mitch nodded, feeling torn between concern and an unholy glee. They were going to jump into enemy space and take them from the rear...he smiled, despite himself, at the double meaning. The virus was going to be taken completely by surprise and yet...he scowled inwardly as he studied the display. *Unicorn* was tethered to *Lion* and the rest of the squadron. If they ran into trouble now, his ship would be a sitting duck. So would the rest of the fleet, but they had the armour to take it long enough to disentangle themselves and fight back. *Unicorn's* main defence lay in speed, manoeuvrability and stealth. They were all denied to his ship as long as she remained within the mesh.

They just have to hold off long enough for us to make the jump, he thought. The admiral had deployed scouts up the chain. It was quite possible an alien fleet would sneak past them, but they'd have to go quite some distance out of their way...assuming, of course, they realised the scouts were there at all. *There's no hint there are any other alien squadrons before New Washington.*

He put the thought out of his head as he checked the countdown. The catapults had been charging for weeks, well before the human fleet had arrived to take control. It looked as if the virus had been fine-tuning the systems, readying them to hurl a fleet into human space and beyond. Mitch had checked the reports carefully, but there was no hint where the virus had intended to send its fleet. The command and control network hadn't survived the engagement. The techs had had to insert human-designed nodes into the system to take control. Mitch feared the worst, but—he told himself—it didn't matter. They'd won the race to the catapults. Whatever happened, the virus would have to start from scratch if it wanted to try again.

A thrill ran through him as the countdown continued to tick down to zero. He'd recorded a message to his family, then another to Charlotte. *That* was a risk—a censor might normally ignore a sexually-charged message, but *this* one was to another officer's wife—and yet he hadn't been able to keep from sending *something*. He had no idea how it would end, but he found it hard to care. He'd never really expected to rise any higher. *That* demanded good connections and he had none. Unless one counted Charlotte...he snorted at the thought. Charlotte might be an aristocrat, but she had no connection to the Old Boys Network. She might be able to influence someone, yet...they'd want to know why.

Staci glanced at him. "Captain?"

Mitch frowned. "Just thinking about our options, after we complete the jump," he said, rubbing his forearm. The medics had given them all shots to prepare them for the jump, but they'd been unable to swear convincingly that they'd work. The last time a catapult—a *human* catapult—had been used, the entire crew had been knocked out. "And where we're going to go."

"Better hope we make it through the jump, first," Staci said, practically. "And that we don't find ourselves in Virus Central."

"True," Mitch agreed. "And that we're not stunned beyond all hope of recovery."

He gritted his teeth. The virus *might* have devised a solution...assuming, of course, it knew it *needed* one. It had probably captured thousands upon thousands of war memoirs from the Second Interstellar War—there were so many that Mitch was certain that *everyone* who'd been there had written a book about it—but would it have read them? There was no way to know. *Mitch* would have, but he wasn't an alien virus. It was possible to learn a great deal about a culture from its books—he'd heard stories about an admiral who'd learned to understand his foes by studying their artwork—yet there was no sense the virus particularly cared. And yet...

If it gained access to the memories of a senior naval officer, he thought, *it will have learnt everything he knew about tactics and technology.*

He shook his head. The virus wasn't human. It wasn't remotely human. And it had used catapults before, just on a much smaller scale. Either it had a solution or it didn't need one. The end result was still the same. He rubbed his forearm, muttering a quiet prayer to gods he didn't really believe in. If they completed the jump as planned, they should materialise in a minor system. The real question—he didn't want to think about it, but he had no choice—was what might be waiting for them. Even a relatively small ship could do one hell of a lot of damage if it was firing on a bunch of sitting ducks.

"We'll make the jump, then see what we find," he said. The spooks insisted they'd be very close to a major alien system. Mitch hoped they were right. "And then we'll fight our way home."

Or keep probing the rear of their territory, his thoughts added. The idea of cruising around in the alien rear, blowing their way through every shipyard and industrial node they found was attractive, although he knew they'd run out of supplies sooner or later. *We could give them one hell of a fight until we ran out of missiles and supplies...*

The timer clicked a warning. Mitch smiled and settled back in his chair, putting all thought out of his mind. The die was cast. There was no time to back out now, even if he wanted to. And he didn't. He wanted, he needed, to strike as deep into the alien vitals as possible. It was what he'd been trained to do. He had a ship, a crew that would follow him, and a cause. It would be done.

He allowed his smile to grow wider. It wouldn't be long now.

• • •

"Signal from the flag, Captain," Commander Donker said. "We're to perform the jump in twenty minutes."

"I'll be on the bridge in ten," Thomas said. He sat in his ready room, studying the jump projections. "Inform me if anything changes."

He closed the connection, then turned his attention back to the projections. Theoretically, if they jumped together, the odds of accidentally crashing into each other were minimal. It was hard to be sure. The arrival zones were carefully spaced out in hopes of avoiding disaster, but no one had ever tried it before. The boffins had run thousands of projections, then concluded that there were too many uncertainties to say anything for certain. Thomas suspected they'd wasted their time. No one really believed the operation would come off without a hitch.

There's no way to jump back too, Thomas thought. The virus might have a few dozen additional catapults on the far side, but no one knew for sure. No one knew *anything* for sure. The fleet would be going where no man had gone before...a thought that had been rather more appealing before humanity had discovered a number of hostile alien races. *We'll have to fight our way through their lines.*

Ice ran down his spine as he brought up the starchart. He'd seen it time and time again—they'd discussed their options so many times he was thoroughly sick of hearing them—but it hadn't felt quite real until now. They were going to pass through at least twelve transits, before they made it back to friendly space. *And* they'd be heading directly towards the fleets besieging the border stars. *That* wasn't going to be fun. Running towards the enemy forces struck him as thoroughly stupid.

We have to do it, he told himself. *There's no other way to win.*

His console bleeped, a reminder he had yet to record a message to his wife and daughters. He hesitated, unsure if he wanted to say anything. He'd recorded a message before the fleet left Earth, along with checking his will to make sure there'd be no problems passing the estate to his older daughter. There wouldn't be much inheritance tax, not after the last tax revolt. His younger daughter would get his savings and nearly everything else he owned, that wasn't either entailed or gifted to someone else. Charlotte would have his pension and...

The thought cost him a pang. He was fond of Charlotte, in his way. He'd certainly been relieved she'd taken to estate management like a duck to water, allowing him to continue his military career without worrying about his duty to his family. Charlotte had been…fun…and yet…he sighed, inwardly. They'd never been particularly close, for all that they had two daughters together. She'd always tried to convince him to come home, to leave the military behind, and he'd always resisted. His country needed him, he'd said. It was true, but it wasn't the whole truth. His career gave his life meaning. He knew he'd lose it if he put his uniform away and took his seat in the House of Lords.

And you might discover she nags you, time and time again, he thought, sourly. *She's always demanding that you do things…*

Thomas banished the thought as he keyed the terminal. "Charlotte," he said. "By the time you receive this message, the operation will be well underway."

He paused. The censors would blow a fuse if he made any reference to the operation itself. Charlotte presumably knew some of the details—she had contacts at all levels of government—but that argument wouldn't cut any ice with the censors. Thomas would receive a sharp reprimand, perhaps even a court-martial. It would set a terrible example, the censors would point out, to let him get away with leaking information even if the person on the receiving end already knew it. They'd insist that there was no guarantee that Charlotte was the only person who'd hear the message. Hell, *they'd* hear the message. And being in line to the throne would cut no ice with them. They'd see it as a reason to demand even *harsher* punishment.

"I hope to make it back to you," Thomas said. He wasn't sure that was true. How long had it been since they'd slept together? Months? Years? His career hadn't taken him away from home for *that* long. "I think we should try to visit the Highlands again."

He snorted. He'd taken his new wife to the Maldives for their honeymoon, but that had been before the virus had brought international travel to a halt. The beaches had bored him to tears and…in hindsight, maybe it had been a mistake to make that clear. Charlotte had been looking forward to lying on a beach, soaking up the rays. Britain was cold and wet and largely gloomy…he shook his head. She'd known what she was getting, when she married him. They'd both known they had to produce children, for the family, and then…

"We'll discuss other matters when we return home," he said. He didn't want to discuss his daughters getting married, not in front of the censors. They weren't meant to gossip, but…who knew? He'd often suspected they leaked more information than they covered up. "I should be home for our special date and we can discuss it then."

He hit the terminal in frustration. The message sounded *terrible*. He'd never been good at writing about his feelings, let alone his frustrations. He certainly couldn't complain to her about the planning sessions, about how everyone from Admiral Onarina on down seemed intent on plunging into the unknown and to hell with the dangers. The Admiral might even be reliving her glory days…Thomas felt bad for even thinking it, as if he'd crossed the line into treason, but it was true. Admiral Onarina's naval career had been shaped by daring thrusts into enemy space, as well as a willingness to risk everything on one throw of the die. She'd practically committed mutiny against an aristocrat and gotten away with it…

She had no choice, Thomas thought. He'd read the private files, the ones his father had buried under the manor. The old man had backed Captain Blake and discovered, too late, that he'd made a dreadful mistake. *Captain Blake nearly got a lot of people killed.*

The timer bleeped. Thomas keyed the console, deleting the message. He didn't have anything like enough time to put together something Charlotte might actually *like*, let alone…he snarled in frustration. She wanted him back home, living up to his rank and title. And yet…his lips quirked. She was his agent. She spoke with his voice, as long as he was away from home. She wouldn't have *that* if he came back home.

He stood and composed himself, then walked through the hatch onto the bridge. *Lion* floated within the catapult, tethered to the rest of the squadron. Thomas's eyes lingered on the data code representing *Unicorn*, his lips thinning as he remembered just how enthusiastic Captain Campbell had been about the plan. Risking a frigate was one thing; risking over fifty capital ships was quite another. His eyes found HMS *Thunderous*, holding position at the other side of the mesh. Admiral Onarina was taking the plunge with them. Thomas had to admit it was impressive, but still…it didn't sit well with him. The fleet's CO should not be risked.

"Captain," Donker said. "All stations report they're ready for the jump."

No one is truly ready, Thomas thought. He'd seen the recordings from HMS *Vanguard* and the rest of her squadron. *There's no way to prepare for this.*

He took his seat. "Put the countdown on audio," he ordered. "And brace yourself."

· · ·

Susan sat in her chair and watched as the countdown ticked towards zero. She knew, unlike most of her subordinates, what it was going to be like. She'd been through it once before, back when she'd been a captain. She'd done her best to prepare her crews for the shock, but she knew her words had fallen on deaf ears. No amount of explanation could convey the coming impact, a shock that would hit them hard…she rubbed her forearm, cursing the medics under her breath. The transit shock would be painful, but it wouldn't kill them. The claim the medics could keep the crew from being shocked might be worse, when it sank in that the medics had been wrong. Susan couldn't believe they might be right. If they couldn't explain why people were shocked, how could they devise countermeasures?

She studied the starchart, bracing herself. The operation had seemed a simple concept, when she'd come up with the basic idea, but in war the simplest things were often the hardest. It would have been a great deal easier to destroy the catapults, sending the virus back to stage one…it wouldn't have offered the prospect of winning the war, but it would have kept her from having to face the prospect of losing it. A handful of analysts had even argued the catapults were a deadly trap, intended to lure the humans into taking them intact…she snorted in dismissal. It would have been a great deal easier to build a hundred battleships than thirty catapults. The very idea was absurd.

"Communications," she ordered. "Get me a link to Commodore Yagami."

"Aye, Admiral."

Susan leaned forward as the Japanese officer appeared in the display. "Admiral?"

"We'll be jumping in ten minutes," Susan said. "You understand what you have to do?"

"Yes, Admiral," Yagami said. "Record the transit, destroy the remaining catapults and escort the personnel transports to New Washington."

"No heroics along the way," Susan ordered. She was fairly sure the transits would be unobserved, but there was no point in taking chances. "If you encounter the enemy, do everything in your power to avoid a direct confrontation. Your objective is to return home, not to engage the enemy."

"I understand," Yagami said. "The techs cannot be risked."

Susan nodded. The Royal Navy was steadily running out of talented yarddogs, engineers, techs and researchers. The Admiralty had flatly refused to allow her to take the techs any further than the catapult system. She knew she was lucky to even get *that* concession. The government was trying to train more, but…she grimaced. It took too long to train new techs when you had to assign older techs to training duties, taking them away from the shipyards.

Something else we have to buy time for, she thought, grimly. She'd seen the figures. And the new weapons, which would give the human race a decisive advantage if they lasted long enough to put them into production. *A year or two of relative peace would give us enough time to get back on our feet and punch our way back into enemy space.*

"Good." Susan raised a hand in salute. Yagami had argued to be allowed to accompany the fleet, but his government had insisted he remain behind. She wasn't sure which of them was luckier. "See you on the other side."

Yagami saluted, then vanished from the display. Susan let out a breath as the countdown ticked onwards. It hadn't been *that* long since she'd commanded a fleet, she told herself. She still had it. And she hadn't done badly in her first engagement…she put her doubts aside as the final seconds ticked down to zero. It was time to put everything on the line. It was time…

"Five," Richardson said. Susan wanted to scream at him to shut up. The rest of her staffers were looking nervous. But it was far too late. "Four. Three. Two. One…"

Susan braced herself. The world went black…

CHAPTER TWENTY

SOMEONE WAS SCREAMING.

Mitch had the uncomfortable feeling it might be him, as he struggled back to wakefulness through a haze of pain. His head hurt dreadfully, as if he'd been on a three-night bender…as if he was still a teenager with more money than sense. He thought he saw a woman—he didn't know her—lying next to him, her body fading into nothingness as he returned to himself. His bridge had become a dark and shadowy place, a field of nightmares…

He stumbled to his feet, alarm shooting through him as he remembered where and when they were. The spooks had sworn blind the catapult was going to hurl the fleet into an uninhabited system, but there was no way to be *sure*. A desolate system could still serve as a transit point between two more useful systems, cutting weeks or months off travel times. For all they knew, an entire enemy fleet was bearing down on them. He keyed his console, bringing up the near-space display. The fleet was in formation—it could hardly be scattered, when all the ships were linked together—and seemingly alone. But, again, there was no way to be sure.

"Report!" His voice sounded odd, even to himself. His words rasped in his throat. "Status report!"

Staci looked as if she was still half-asleep. "No enemy contacts detected,

Captain," she said, slowly. Her words came out one by one, as if she had to think about each one separately. "We've lost contact with all decks."

Mitch gritted his teeth as he fumbled through his pockets for the injector tab and pressed it against his neck. He disliked using stimulants in battle situations, even though there were times when it was necessary. It was all too easy to wind up seeing things that weren't there...a surge of energy shot through him, clearing the cobwebs out of his mind. He reminded himself, sharply, that he had to be careful to question everything. The stimulant made it hard to think clearly.

"Pass the word," he ordered. His voice sounded high-pitched, as if something was wrong with the air. He checked the life support automatically, just to be sure. "Everyone on the alpha crew is to take one dose of stimulant, just one."

"Aye, Captain." Staci injected herself, then turned to the rest of the crew. "I'll go through the ship."

Mitch nodded as the remainder of the bridge crew came back to life. The display was still empty, thankfully. They were in no state for a fight. He glared at the empty stimulant tab, feeling an odd desire for more even though he *knew* it was a bad idea. The stimulants gave energy, for a short while, but they also took away good judgement. He'd be spending too much time checking and rechecking himself, all too aware that his ability to monitor his thinking was also impaired. If the universe was changing and all of the tools he used to measure it were changing as well, his instructors had warned, how would he know the universe was changing?

Your mind is wandering, he told himself severely. He sat at the console and scowled at the display. *You have to check yourself.*

He felt sweat bead on his brow, even though the bridge was cool, as reports came in from the rest of the ship. The crew was in no state for a fight, with the beta and delta crews already heading to their bunks. They'd have to recover naturally—hopefully, they'd be ready to take over when the alpha crew started feeling the effects of the stimulants wear off. That wouldn't be too long. Mitch hoped—prayed—that they'd have a day or two before they had to engage the enemy. The odds were going to be bad enough without the crew being stoned out of their minds.

His lips quirked. *Didn't that happen to Stellar Star once?*

He bit his lip. It wasn't funny. Stellar Star's scriptwriters didn't know how the universe actually worked. Anyone who tried such tactics in real life would be blown to atoms before they realised their mistakes. It was tempting to believe the enemy would be too busy laughing to open fire, but...he snorted, despite himself. The virus had no sense of humour. It would just blow the crazy ship away before it could do something stupid.

Staci returned to the bridge. "Captain, the alpha crewmen are at their stations."

Mitch nodded, stiffly. The fleet was coming back to life, sensors sweeping space in hopes of spotting a cloaked ship before it slipped into attack range. Admiral Onarina had ordered the fleet to bring up its sensors as quickly as possible, on the grounds there was no way to hide their arrival from prying eyes. The gravity waves would be visible halfway to the nearest star. There was no hope of avoiding detection, if there was someone watching and waiting under stealth. The display was empty...Mitch gritted his teeth. The warning could have already been sent up the chain. A major alien fleet might already be on its way to their location.

"Disengage from the fleet, then take us to point position," he ordered. He knew what they were *meant* to do, upon arrival. Admiral Onarina hadn't issued any countermanding orders. "And ready us for transit to the next star."

He sat back in his chair as a dull quiver ran through the ship. It felt good to be free of the tethers, even though they were *deep* in hostile space. The tramlines on the display led back to human territory, but they'd have to sneak their way through a dozen systems first...he shook his head. There was no way they could get the entire fleet through so many systems without being detected, unless they added weeks—if not months—to their transit time. If the enemy didn't know they were there...

"We have to assume they do," he told himself.

Staci glanced at him. "Captain?"

"Just thinking out loud," Mitch said. "We have to assume they know we're here."

. . .

Colin sat bolt upright as he heard a hissing sound, one hand grabbing for a handgun that wasn't there. The platoon had been ordered to stow their weapons in the lockers before the jump, just to make sure one of the marines didn't go crazy and gun down his comrades before he realised what he was doing. Colin had thought that wasn't likely to happen, but…there was no point in arguing. The lockers weren't sealed. They just required a degree of intelligence and dexterity to open.

He yelped as he slammed his head into the overhead bunk, the pain snapping him back to reality. Kevin was on the deck, hissing loudly as he kicked and beat at the air like an oversized spider. Colin stared, unsure what to do. The stimulants in his pack, the drugs they'd been cautioned not to use unless they were desperate, were intended for human use only. At best, they'd be completely useless if he injected them into the alien; at worst, they'd kill him. Colin cursed the uniformed politicians under his breath as he stood and stumbled towards Kevin. How did one help an alien through jump shock? They didn't even have a workable sedative!

Something else to put in the report, he thought, sourly. *We need…*

He ducked a wildly-flailing fist and caught hold of the alien, pushing him onto the deck. Kevin had a gangly look, as if whoever had designed him didn't quite know what he was doing, but he was surprisingly strong. Colin gritted his teeth and held him down, all too aware the alien wasn't in his right mind. Hitting a superior officer was a serious offence, even if one used the term *officer* lightly. There'd been a skit once about a private who'd attacked a senior officer and discovered, too late, that he'd attacked the one and only officer who'd actually earned his medals. It had been hilarious, at the time. It wasn't so funny now.

"It's alright," he said, although he wasn't sure it was true. Kevin's teeth were snapping at the air. They looked sharp enough to bite through a human arm. "I've got you."

He glared at the rest of the platoon as they staggered to their feet. The sergeant was going to kill them…probably. Colin had no illusions about what would have happened if they'd stumbled back to base drunk off their heads, unsure if they'd made it back in time, but here…he shook his head. They'd known jump shock would be bad. The sergeant was probably suffering the effects himself.

Kevin stared up, blearily. His eyes rolled, peering in different directions. Colin couldn't help feeling a twinge of unease, as if he was in the presence of something unnatural. Kevin and he were practically brothers, compared to their races and the virus, and yet…they were two different species. And Kevin was completely alone. There was no one for hundreds of light years who'd understand him.

"Most Highest Lord," Kevin said. "General…"

"Corporal," Colin corrected. The poor bastard was coming out of it, but it would be a while before he completely recovered. "We do all the real work around here."

The alien blinked at him. Colin silently kicked himself. It was no time for jokes…although, he had to admit, calling a corporal a general was pretty funny. Somehow, he didn't think the major would be too amused. He let go of Kevin and stood, silently daring the rest of the platoon to say something. They looked as dazed and unsure of themselves as Colin himself. None of them were in any state for a fight.

"Fuck," Willis muttered. "What was I *drinking* last night?"

"My head feels like there's a Frenchman living in it," Davies finished.

"Stow that chatter," Colin ordered. His eyes swept the compartment. "If any of you lot need the medics, say so now or forever hold your peace."

"Hold your piece," Willis said, with a giggle. "That's funny."

Colin helped Kevin to his feet, then checked the display. The battlecruiser—and the rest of the fleet—appeared to be safe, for the moment. There was no immediate danger, as far as he could see. The rest of the marines would be recovering, probably stumbling to the exercise compartments unless their services were required elsewhere. Colin hoped they wouldn't be needed. His hands felt as if they'd cramped up, to the point he couldn't so much as operate a datapad. He prayed, silently, that it wouldn't be permanent. He didn't like the thought of being invalided out of the marines.

"We'll go put in an hour or so on the machines," he said. "Some exercise will do us all good."

He ignored the handful of good-natured complaints as the platoon opened the hatch and started down the corridor. That was a good sign, he supposed. If they were complaining, nothing was actually wrong with them. Probably. He kept a wary eye on Kevin as they made their way into the exercise compartment. The alien seemed to have taken the jump shock badly. There'd been no way to know what to expect, of course, but Colin still felt as if he'd failed. It would have been wiser, perhaps, to sedate Kevin before the jump.

If we had a working sedative, he reminded himself. The xenospecialists hadn't focused on the Vesy, when it came to devising alien medicines. Anyone with any skill in the field was trying to devise a vaccine against viral infection and possession. Colin understood the logic, but it was hard not to resent it. *We don't know what we have to do if he gets really hurt.*

He made a face. He'd taken courses in battlefield medicine, of course. He knew what to do if one of his comrades got hit. He'd even studied the files on Vesy biology, although he was grimly aware he'd barely scratched the surface. The Vesy themselves had barely scratched the surface. Reading between the lines, he'd had the impression they hadn't known much about how their bodies worked until they'd made contact with humanity. And the xenospecialists had been severely hampered by their reluctance to *force* the Vesy to let themselves be studied.

We'll just have to do what seems best, he thought, glumly. *And hope it works.*

• • •

Susan had never been a fan of alcohol. Her father had banned her from touching the stuff, as a girl, and she'd never had the funds to indulge herself as she grew into a young woman. Her one experience with getting drunk had been enough to convince her not to do it again and yet…she felt, now, as if she'd been bullied into drinking enough cheap rotgut to kill herself. She rubbed her forehead, remembering how the girls of Hanover Towers had celebrated their eighteenth birthdays. That wretched Ethel had forced her to drink…

She shook her head. "Report!"

"The fleet is coming back to life, Admiral," Richardson said. He looked surprisingly unbothered by the jump shock. "However, right now, we appear to be operating at seventy percent of…"

Susan nodded, cutting him off. The reports flitting across her display were all too clear. A handful of crewmen were dead and a number of others were in urgent need of medical treatment…she wondered, sourly, just how the *virus* had intended to survive. The shock might have killed it outright, except it wasn't the *first* time it had used a catapult. It had to have some kind of solution…perhaps its mentality was just too big to feel much in the way of shock. Or maybe it was just quicker at recovering than the average human.

"We're safe, for the moment," she said. The display was clear. There was nothing within attack range, unless the virus had invented a whole new line of cloaking devices. "But that will change."

Her eyes narrowed as she studied the tramlines. The captured files insisted there was a major alien settlement on the far side. It was only a matter of time before *someone* popped their heads through the tramline, if only because they were using the desolate system as a shortcut to somewhere more populated. Susan had few illusions. The fleet could go straight back into cloak now and still risk detection, given how much energy they'd been pumping out. And it was quite possible the virus had picketed the system. Human navies kept a watchful eye on systems adjacent to their core systems, just in case. The virus might have the same tactical doctrine.

"Order *Unicorn* to make transit and confirm our survey data," she said. "And prepare two more frigates to follow in her footsteps."

"Aye, Admiral," Richardson said.

Susan nodded, returning her attention to the status display. The fleet was recovering, but was it recovering quickly *enough*? They were in no state for a fight...she glanced at the starchart, silently calculating how long it would take the virus to mobilise a reaction force. It was impossible to come up with any solid figures. They were deep in the enemy rear. It was quite possible the virus didn't *have* any heavy forces on standby, ready to react to a potential threat...

That's wishful thinking, she told herself. *They won't rely on fixed defences alone.*

She leaned back in her chair, feeling every one of her fifty years as her fleet came back to life. They'd been lucky, luckier—perhaps—than they'd deserved. They'd taken one hell of a risk. She rubbed her forehead, wishing she could go for a nap. Her body clock insisted that she'd been awake for days, even though she knew it wasn't true. She would start seeing things soon enough.

"Admiral, the remainder of the fleet command network is back online," Richardson said, calmly. "All units report ready for action."

"We'll wait for *Unicorn*," Susan said. She understood the value of aggression, but she disliked the idea of jumping blind. They'd done quite enough of *that* already. Besides, she couldn't come up with any real operational plans until she got a picture of what was waiting for her. "And then we'll decide how to proceed."

She stood, telling herself she needed to move. There was nothing for her to do, not until they engaged the enemy. Her staff had the CIC under control. She issued orders for them to alert her if something happened, then stepped through the hatch into her office. There was no sign of her steward. She'd told him to stay in his cabin, at least until the jump was completed. She poured herself a mug of coffee—she'd known officers who would have been horrified at the thought of pouring their own coffee—and sat at her desk. The warm liquid made her feel better...

Her eyes narrowed as she studied the starchart. They were alone, hundreds of light years from the nearest friendly star. And there was no way to hop back…they'd have to fight their way home. She shivered, suddenly feeling the weight of command crashing down on her. She was the fleet's commanding officer, completely alone…*she* was alone. She relished the challenge and yet she quailed at the thought of everyone relying on her. She hadn't been so alone since her stint on a survey vessel. And she hadn't had to worry about hostile aliens then.

But this time I have an entire fleet under my command, she told herself. She switched the display to tactical view and studied the fleet. The formation looked ragged, but she knew it would be effective if they ran into the enemy. *And we have enough firepower to give the enemy a very hard time indeed.*

CHAPTER TWENTY-ONE

"TRANSIT COMPLETED, CAPTAIN," Lieutenant Sam Hinkson said. "The drive is recycling now."

Mitch nodded, stiffly. His head still felt fragile, but a quick power nap and a bite to eat had done wonders. He was going to pay for the stimulant later, yet that had been deferred. For the moment. Staci was already keeping an eye on him, ready to insist he went to his cabin when the after-effects finally began to bite. Mitch hoped they'd wait a few hours longer. He needed to be on the bridge as they began their mission.

"Sensors," he said. "Report?"

Lieutenant Hannah Avis looked pale, although she'd taken the jump better than most. "The system is big, Captain," she said. "There are a *lot* of sensor emissions."

Mitch bit down the urge to make a sharp remark about Underling's Basic Descriptive Inability Syndrome. "How big is it, compared to Earth?"

"I'd say the system is *bigger* than Earth," Hannah said. "It's on roughly the same scale as Tadpole Prime."

"Fuck," Staci said, quietly.

Mitch understood. Tadpole Prime was the most heavily-industrialised system in known space. Earth came close—and he'd been told there was more redundancy built into Earth's industrial halo—but the Tadpoles still had the edge. It helped, he supposed, that they hadn't spent an awful lot of time trying to outdo or simply kill each other. And yet…his eyes narrowed as the display started to tighten up. There were so many energy signatures around a single world—and one of the gas giants—that it looked as if the entire planet was encased in a globe of industrial nodes.

His mind raced. Earth's industrial base was spread across the system. The asteroid belt housed a sizable number of industrial nodes, as well as mining stations and independent habitats. There were larger stations orbiting the gas giants as well as Earth herself. He'd been told it helped make life harder for anyone attacking the planet, although he wasn't sure that had worked out so well in practice. It was also hard for the defenders to cover each and every potential target. The virus had gone the other way. It had concentrated everything on a couple of planets. There was no way to be sure, but it looked as though the asteroid stations were nothing more than mining camps.

"Helm, take us closer," he ordered, grimly. "But keep us well clear of their sensor platforms."

He frowned as *Unicorn* started to glide deeper into the system, the sheer scale of the virus's activity becoming all too clear. The virus hadn't given a damn about the risks of massing so much industry above a habitable world. It looked as if it had practically turned the world into…into something. There were three orbital towers and dozens of space elevators, including a number that had been established well clear of the equator. Mitch had seen plans for turning uninhabitable planets into giant factories, but they'd always struck him as pointless. Why bother when it was easier to establish the factories near the asteroids? The virus, it seemed, disagreed.

"Captain," Hannah said, breaking into his thoughts. "Please, could I deploy probes?"

Mitch frowned. The probes were designed to be stealthy, and he knew from experience that they were very hard to spot, but the entire planet was practically glowing with sensor emissions. The probes might be detected, through inference if nothing else; they might alert the enemy to the fleet's presence. Assuming, of course, the enemy didn't already know the fleet was there. Mitch wanted to think the virus was ignorant, but he didn't dare count on it.

"Keep them a safe distance from the planet," he ordered. "And make sure they're as powered down as possible."

"Aye, Captain."

Mitch kept his eyes on the display as more and more data flowed into the sensors. The planet's mobile defences were strong, centred on a sizable force of battleships and heavy cruisers. There were no carriers, but Mitch was fairly sure the orbital battlestations were crammed with starfighters as well as missile tubes and energy weapons. The virus seemed to be far more paranoid than any other known race, although Mitch conceded it had good reason to be concerned. Anyone who deduced its true nature wouldn't hesitate to sterilise an infected world. Alien-One had been reduced to radioactive ruins a decade ago.

His skin crawled as he studied the planet. The world had been habitable, once. Now...it was all too clear the atmosphere was deadly. The virus was *everywhere*. The planet itself was practically alive, seas and clouds teeming with viral particles...he felt sick, just looking at the reports. There weren't as many details as he'd hoped, but he didn't need them to know the danger. Anyone who set foot on the world without a suit of heavy-duty armour would be turned into a zombie within hours.

And if they did wear armour, he thought, *the zombies would tear it off them*.

The sheer scale threatened to make even *him* quail. He was looking at a giant living thing, a single mind in billions of bodies...no, a single body composed of billions...his head hurt just trying to think about it. The flashes of light within the storm might be part of the virus's mentality or...he shook his head. How could they fight something so big? It was beyond them, beyond anyone. It was hard to believe the BioBombs would be effective. The virus was just too big.

We can kill it, he told himself. *It might be powerful, and alien, but it isn't God.*

"Captain," Staci said. "How close do you intend to go?"

Mitch shrugged. They'd noted and logged all the industrial nodes. The virus had dragged hundreds of asteroids into high orbit, strip-mined them for raw materials and finally turned them into more orbital nodes. He could see a dozen shipyards, concentrated rather than spread out; he could see a handful of ships in varying stages of construction. It was hard to be sure, but the operational tempo looked impressive. He tried to tell himself that the virus didn't need to worry about such things as life support, computer datanets and everything else the human race needed to keep its ships running, but it wasn't convincing. It wasn't good news either. The virus could churn out more ships if it didn't have to worry about the fiddly little details.

"We'll make one final sweep from a distance, then check out the gas giant," he said. He'd once read a proposal to ignite a gas giant and turn it into a sun. It had proven impractical, from what he could recall, but the idea had lingered. It would make one hell of a weapon, he'd thought at the time. And it would make taking out the industrial node a great deal easier. "And then we'll return home."

Unless we find something that demands closer inspection, he thought. The roiling storms pervading the planet's atmosphere hid a great deal of the surface. Who knew *what* lurked beneath those clouds? What little they could see wasn't encouraging. The virus didn't seem to care about fouling its own nest. *Or they realise we're watching.*

He forced himself to sit back and relax as *Unicorn* inched forward, maintaining a healthy distance between herself and the nearest alien ship. The virus had been extremely paranoid. Mitch rather feared there was an entire network of stealthed sensor platforms surrounding the planet. It was what *he* would have done. And there was no way they could be detected without bringing his active sensors online, ensuring their detection. He shrugged. As long as they were careful, it was unlikely they'd blunder into a trap.

Hope for the best, he reminded himself. It wouldn't be long now. *And prepare for the worst.*

• • •

"I feel like the man who went fishing for minnows and wound up catching a whale," General Sampan commented, as the report came to an end. "Do we have enough nukes to make a mark on that…that mess?"

"The BioBombs should spread rapidly in that atmosphere," Admiral Li said. "Even if they don't, the surface will be bombarded with thousands upon thousands of chunks of debris."

Susan nodded, tightly. Admiral Theodore Smith had fought a clean war. He'd insisted that the navy do everything in its power to refrain from committing atrocities, a tradition that had lingered until the virus's true nature had been revealed. Susan wasn't blind to the horrors unleashed on Alien-One, and the grim truth of what would happen as the BioBombs detonated, but she saw no other choice. There was no hope of coming to terms with the virus. It had to be destroyed, or every known and unknown intelligent race would be turned into soulless zombies.

"At worst, we can push asteroids into the atmosphere ourselves," Susan said. She felt a twinge of horror at how casually they were discussing genocide, then put it aside. "That isn't the issue now."

She studied the sensor records, thoughtfully. There was no hint the virus knew the fleet had arrived, although she suspected that was meaningless. The enemy fleet wasn't big enough to challenge hers in open combat. There was no reason to expect it to come charging through the tramline, blood in its eye. *She* wouldn't stray from the planetary defences, not until reinforcements arrived. And yet, staying so close to the planet would make it easier for an attacker to take the defences apart from a distance. The virus was caught between two fires.

Her fingers danced over the console, drawing up an operational plan. It looked remarkably slapdash, compared to the dog-and-pony shows she put on for politicians, but her audience was composed of military officers. They'd understand the harsh realities of war, including the simple fact they couldn't plan for everything. The enemy had a say in how things would turn out. Susan stroked her chin as the plan unfolded. It was workable, she hoped. And, at worst, it would let them land one hell of a blow and break contact before the enemy could pin her ships down and destroy them.

"We'll depart in one hour," she said, once the plan had been discussed, modified and passed to the staff officers for implementation. "If anyone has any problems, I want to know about them now."

There was a pause. The fleet had recovered, mostly, from the jump shock. A handful of crewmen remained in sickbay, but the remainder had either resumed their duties or bedded down for a few hours. They'd be ready to fight, when the fleet crossed the tramline. Or before. Susan's eyes lingered on the near-space display. If she was in command of the enemy fleet, she would be screaming for help and reinforcements. How long would it be before the planet's reinforcements arrived? Susan didn't know. There was no *way* to know.

"Dispatch scouts along the tramline, as planned," she ordered, quietly. The survey ships had been reconfigured, when it became clear the war wouldn't be over in a hurry. They could survive on their own for years, if they managed to avoid contact with the enemy. If worse came to worst, they could sneak back to the human sphere and report to their superiors. "If there are any enemy ships within one or two jumps of our position, I want to know about them."

Her eyes hardened. "Admiral Li, I want the fleet train to sneak into cloak as soon as we start to move," she added. "They are to remain hidden until the battle is decided, one way or the other."

Li saluted. "Yes, Admiral."

Susan grimaced. The fleet train was vitally important—and terrifyingly vulnerable. The freighters had been designed to keep pace with warships, and armoured as heavily as they could bear, but she had no illusions. They'd be sitting ducks if an enemy warship come into missile range. The virus would cripple her, if it took out the freighters. And it would cripple humanity's transport network as well.

All the unsexy details, she thought, with a flicker of amusement. *The freighters might be ugly as hell, but we couldn't fight a war without them.*

She sighed, inwardly. If the battle went badly, the fleet train would have to make its way home…that wouldn't be easy. Of course not. The freighters had cloaking devices, but they weren't cutting edge…she put the thought out of her head. They'd worked through all the contingencies while they'd been planning the operation. Her crews knew what they had to do.

"Our priority is killing that industrial node," she reminded them. "The enemy fleet is secondary to the node itself. Once the node is gone, we can either destroy what remains of the fleet or break contact."

She frowned. Her training insisted the enemy fleet was a priority target. It would take months, if not years, for the virus to replace the ships, if they were destroyed. And yet, she was all too aware that they weren't fighting a conventional war. The virus had just too much industry for anyone's peace of mind. It had to be weakened, before it steamrolled humanity and the allied races.

And we're going to be feinting at the fleet anyway, she thought. *We can take a bite out of them, even if we keep the range open.*

"We can do it," she said. Her subordinates were experienced officers. They didn't need a pep talk. Her lips quirked at the notion. She still thought her high school's team had lost the lacrosse game after the gym mistress had given them a pep talk that hadn't been remotely peppy. "Good luck to us all. Dismissed."

She smiled, coldly, as the holographic images vanished. The die was cast…but, in truth, it had been cast the moment they'd captured the alien catapults. That had been pretty much their last chance to back out…

"We can do it," she told herself, as she stood and headed for the hatch. "We *must* do it."

• • •

"And that is the plan," Bagehot finished. "Are you all clear on your roles?"

Tobias gritted his teeth. He'd thrown up, badly, in the first seconds after the jump. He hadn't been the only one. Marigold had been the only gunboat pilot with the presence of mind to run to the head, before expelling the contents of her stomach. Tobias wasn't looking forward to returning to his bunk, after the mission. Bagehot had arranged for it to be cleaned, while the pilots braced themselves for combat, but it was going to *stink*. And the crew would probably make snide jokes. Again.

Now, that's not fair, he told himself. *They stopped being snide when we proved ourselves.*

Marigold stuck up a hand. "Sir, what happens if they don't take the bait?"

"We go in anyway," Bagehot said. "It is vitally important we take out the node."

Tobias nodded. He'd seen the sensor reports. The planet was covered in industry. He hadn't seen anything so challenging since the final level of...he snorted at himself. The real world was different. People actually had to *pay* for things. And yet, the virus could and did encircle a world in industrial stations. The projections suggested a truly insane output. The system, alone, might be able to outproduce the entire human sphere.

Which raises the question, Tobias mused, *of precisely why the virus hasn't crushed us.*

He contemplated it, for a moment, as the pilots raised a handful of other issues. The virus could be expanding in all directions, waging war on multiple fronts simultaneously. Tobias had studied enough history to know that was suicide, although the virus might be powerful enough to do it. Or it might regard the war as an idle diversion rather than a life or death struggle. Tobias found it hard to believe, but looking at the sheer scale of the enemy system...he shook his head. The plan was sound, he'd been told. Their part of it certainly was.

And the rest relies on factors beyond our control, he thought. They'd gone over contingencies, but there was little to say. It would work—or it wouldn't. *If it doesn't work, we back off and try again.*

"To your ships," Bagehot ordered. "Good luck."

Tobias felt his stomach churn as they made their way to the gunboats. *Lion* was picking up speed, heading directly for the tramline. The remainder of the fleet was holding back, leaving the battlecruiser and her gunboats alone. Tobias felt abandoned, even though it was part of the plan. They had to get into position before the main body of the fleet arrived.

"I feel wretched," Marigold said, as soon as they were in the gunboat. "How about you?"

"At least you threw up in the toilet," Tobias said. He'd had a shower and changed his clothes and he *still* smelt vomit on his skin. He wasn't sure who'd thrown up first, but the stench had triggered everyone else. "Do you think they'll bill us for ruined uniforms?"

"They're designed to cope with blood," Marigold reminded him. She took her seat, running her hand down the console. "I don't think a little vomit is going to leave a stain."

Tobias nodded as the hatch closed. The gunboat came to life, the displays lighting up. Tobias checked their position—*Lion* was still ten minutes from the tramline—and then sat down. The straps had never felt *quite* so restrictive. They could have boarded their craft after the jump...

Hurry up and wait, he told himself. He wanted to stand and kiss her, but the smell would probably put her off him for life. It was funny how those details never made it into the books and films. He supposed they'd discourage people from joining the military. *That's the way it goes now. Hurry up and wait.*

CHAPTER TWENTY-TWO

"TRANSIT COMPLETED, CAPTAIN," Lieutenant Michael Fitzgerald said.

"No enemy contacts detected," Lieutenant Commander Sibley added. "There's no hint they know we're here."

Thomas kept his face impassive. He'd studied the reports, of course, but he hadn't really believed them. Not emotionally, at least. Intellectually, he'd known the sensor records were accurate—it wasn't as if Captain Campbell had made them up out of whole cloth—but it was hard to wrap his head around what he saw. A massive energy source orbiting a planet, another orbiting a gas giant…the scale was beyond his comprehension. It was the sort of target, he conceded privately, that gave planners fits. How could they hope to do enough damage to matter before the defenders drove them away?

Through cunning, he thought. *And as long as we get a BioBomb into the planet's atmosphere, we'll do one hell of a lot of damage even if we don't hit anything else.*

"Helm, take us into position," he ordered, quietly. "Tactical, prepare to launch gunboats at the slightest hint we've been detected."

"Aye, Captain."

The tension on the bridge started to rise as they crept into the alien system. Thomas studied the reports, feeling as if someone had hit him with a club. The system was just too large. He understood, now, what the Aztecs had thought when they'd looked up and seen the Spanish sailing towards them. They would have understood boats, even if they didn't have ocean-going vessels, but the Spanish ships would have been an order of magnitude bigger than anything the Aztecs had ever seen. Earth's massive industrial network had grown in fits and starts, each industrial node added to a greater whole. The virus's system looked somewhat more organised.

Thomas frowned as he ran his eye down the list of recommended targets. The analysts had picked out a number of possible weak spots, nodes that—if destroyed—would put a crimp in industrial production. There were one hell of a lot of them. The system might not have immense layers of redundancy, unlike Sol, but it was big enough that it probably didn't matter. Thomas had the nasty feeling they were going to run out of missiles and ballistic projectiles before they ran out of targets. And the targets probably had point defence weapons emplaced to protect them. It was what *he* would have done.

His eyes lingered on the alien ships, a handful of light codes holding station near the target. They were alert, but not *very* alert. Thomas suspected they were surrounded by a network of stealthed sensor platforms, allowing them to step their weapons and drives down without fear of being attacked at point-blank range. *Lion* could land a solid blow, if she caught them by surprise, but...he pushed the thought out of his head. It would be too great a risk.

Sweat beaded on his back as the seconds ticked on. They'd planned it carefully, in hopes of ensuring *Lion* was in position before the remainder of the fleet crossed the tramline, but there'd been too many variables. If they were caught...the virus had to be aware of the risks, surely. It had to know humans could build catapults of their own, even if it didn't know a handful of its own catapults had been stolen. Thomas felt alone, in the midst of his crew. It was hard to escape the sense they were being watched, that the virus was just biding its time before it reached out and took them.

It doesn't have mental powers, he told himself, sharply. *It can't read our thoughts and see us coming.*

The timer pinged a warning. They had only ten minutes before the main body arrived. Time enough, if the projections were accurate. Time enough…

"Launch the gunboats," Thomas ordered. "And prepare to launch missiles."

"Aye, Captain."

• • •

"We have our orders," Marigold said. A dull clunk ran through the gunboat as she disengaged from the hull and set out on a ballistic trajectory. "We'll be within engagement range in twenty minutes."

"Got it," Tobias said. He checked the laser links automatically, all too aware of what would happen if they lost contact with the rest of the gunboats. They couldn't risk turning on their radios to regain contact. "I'll be ready."

He forced himself to stay calm as the tiny craft picked up speed. It was hard to escape the impression that *Lion* was throwing eggs at a solid wall—and that *they* were the eggs—but the odds were in their favour. They were certainly better than flying into a mass of enemy battleships, each one crammed to the gunwales with energy weapons and missile tubes. And yet…his heart sank as he studied the enemy position. The planet was bristling with potential defence platforms. If each of the industrial nodes mounted a single point defence weapon…

"If we get out of this alive," Tobias said, "where do you want to go?"

Marigold snorted. "Bed."

Tobias nodded in understanding. They'd caught a short nap, after the jump, but it hadn't been anything like long enough. He felt…on edge, as if it was just a matter of time before he got tired. Sleep was important… he put the thought out of his head. He wanted to distract himself, not…

"And when we get home," he pressed, "where do you want to go?"

"I don't know." Marigold turned and winked at him. "Where do *you* want to go?"

Tobias thought about it. He'd *like* to take her to a fancy restaurant, if he'd had the money. Naval crewmen had an excellent chance to save money—the military paid their living costs—but he'd sent half of his wages to his mother, then spent the rest on their last holiday. And then...he shook his head. He could never take her somewhere near his home, for fear someone would recognise him. Colin had told him that some of Colin's former cronies were still assholes. They hadn't changed at all.

If they even joined the military in the first place, Tobias thought. It had taken him a long time to get over the idea of the military as nothing more than a pool for thugs, uneducated delinquents and losers. His father had died well, he supposed, but...he'd left his family behind. *I suppose some of them were too stupid even for mine-clearing details.*

"Perhaps we could try somewhere new," he said. "Do you think the Jupiter run is still open?"

"It might be," Marigold said. "I..."

She broke off as the console bleeped an alert. "They're launching missiles now," she said, curtly. "They'll be past us in fifteen minutes."

Tobias nodded, not trusting himself to speak. The system was glowing with sensor emissions. The gunboats *would* be detected, no matter how stealthy they were designed to be. Hell, the missiles were only a *little* smaller. His eyes narrowed thoughtfully as the display updated. If they were spotted ahead of time...

"We'll be ready," he said. "I thought the distraction was about to arrive."

"It's probably already here," Marigold said. "They just don't know about it yet."

• • •

Susan watched, grimly, as HMS *Thunderous* plunged through the tramline and into the alien system. The mischievous side of her mind insisted it was a moment for dramatic music, perhaps something composed by an artist out of his mind on drugs; the remainder of her mind was all too aware she was breaking tactical doctrine that had been shaped in the fires of the First and Second Interstellar Wars. She could have crept into the system, making sure no one knew the fleet—as big as it was—was even there until she shortened the range and opened fire. Instead, she'd practically announced her presence to the entire universe.

"The fleet's completed its transit, Admiral," Richardson reported. "They're forming up as ordered."

"Good," Susan said. She hadn't expected trouble. The transits had been spaced out enough to ensure that none of the ships collided upon emergence, yet…she put the thought out of her head. Nothing had gone wrong. Yet. "Order the fleet to deploy as planned."

She studied the display, silently running the calculations through her head. They were ten light minutes from the alien fleet. It would be ten minutes before the fleet saw them, then another ten minutes—or longer—before she knew if they'd decided to challenge her before she could threaten the planet. They had no choice, but the virus might think differently. It might even prefer to take the risk of her bombarding the planet, rather than let its ships face her alone.

They probably felt safe, this far from the front lines, she thought. The system was hardly undefended—she wouldn't have wanted to stumble across it in a survey ship—but it didn't have anything like enough mobile forces to drive her out of the system. *So they drew down their mobile forces here.*

Her lips twitched as more and more data flowed in front of her. The analysts were hard at work, telling her things she didn't want to know about the system's industrial capability. They weren't trying to hide the probes now. The virus had to know the haze was being stripped away, piece by piece. Susan already knew enough to plan an offensive, but more data never hurt. She wondered, idly, if the virus was hoping she'd be intimidated and back off. The more she learnt about what was waiting for her, the greater the chance she'd decide to break contact…

And we can do that at any time, she thought. *If we encounter something we can't handle…*

"Captain," Richardson said. "Their fleet is moving onto an intercept course."

Susan nodded. The virus knew it was outgunned—unless it hadn't seen *all* of her ships, or thought some of them were decoys—but it didn't want her hurling missiles anywhere near the industrial nodes. Even if she hadn't wanted to hit the planet, the odds of her doing so were far too high. The virus would probably prefer to batter her ships as much as possible, even if it cost their entire fleet. It might dissuade her from pressing the offensive against the planet itself.

The display sparkled with red lights. "Report!"

Richardson stared down at his console as the red lights blurred into a single mass. "Admiral...they launched every last shuttle at us."

Susan blinked. Her sensors were having trouble figuring out precisely how many shuttles there were...she hadn't seen that since the *last* war, when sensor tech hadn't been so advanced. The virus was desperate. It had to be. There were so many shuttles that a number were bound to get through the point defence and crash into her ships, weakening her formation before the capital ships arrived. It was a neat tactic, she conceded, even if it *did* damage the system's industrial base. But it would be easy enough to borrow shuttles from other systems until they could be replaced.

They didn't have time to cram nukes and missile racks into the craft, she told herself. The virus had planned and executed an effective counterattack, far quicker than any human could match. *But if they start ramming our ships, it isn't going to matter.*

"Launch starfighters," she ordered, calmly. She'd hoped to keep the pilots in their launch tubes for a little bit longer, but it couldn't be helped. "We'll go with Tango-Two."

"Aye, Admiral."

Susan nodded as the alien shuttles raced past the capital ships and roared towards her formation. Tango-Two would hold back a third of her starfighters to cover the bigger ships, while the remainder engaged the alien shuttles. They'd expected to face enemy starfighters, but the principle was the same. Susan frowned, wondering what had happened to the alien starfighters. They should have been launched by now. She didn't dare believe they didn't exist. The virus had had plenty of time to assemble a truly awesome force to cover its industrial node.

She nodded to herself as the alien craft materialised, keeping pace with the capital ships. Clever, she supposed. There were so many shuttles ahead of them that the starfighters would be more dangerous to their allies than their enemies. They'd let the shuttles absorb her fury, then swoop in to take revenge. She wondered, idly, if the virus would have problems coordinating so many craft. There were no brainships in the oncoming fleet.

Not that they're needed, she mused. *They're not that far from the planet.*

"Reprogram a handful of shipkillers for counter-fighter detonations, then fire them into the alien shuttles," she ordered. It wouldn't do much damage, but it was worth a try. If nothing else, it would keep them on the hop. "And then let the starfighters have their fun."

"Aye, Admiral."

Susan leaned forwards. The tidal wave of incoming shuttles looked like an unstoppable juggernaut. She was too experienced an officer to believe they'd smash her fleet to atoms, but they'd do a lot of damage. The shipkillers didn't slow them down for more than a second or two. There were just too many of them. She frowned as the starfighters crashed into the alien shuttles, shooting hundreds of them out of space. The remainder just kept coming. It didn't look as though they were armed.

"Admiral," Richardson said. "The point defence is going live...now."

The alien shuttles started to evade, whipping back and forth like crazy as they closed the range. Susan wasn't surprised. It was a standard starfighter attack technique, although not one she'd seen from shuttles. She doubted they were designed for such rapid shifts in course and speed. Marine shuttles were, but even they would have trouble matching the alien craft. A handful lost their drives and spun out of control, heading away from the fight. They'd die in interplanetary space, unless the virus won the battle and deigned to pick them up. The remainder kept coming, closing rapidly. Susan watched hundreds upon hundreds evaporate as the point defence picked them off. And...

She cursed under her breath as the shuttles started to ram. They were concentrating on the bigger ships…a blessing, although she didn't *feel* that way. The damage started to mount rapidly. Seven shuttles crashed into USS *George Bush*, crippling the carrier; thirty-nine crashed into *Stalin*, blowing the Russian battleship into a cloud of debris. Susan glanced at the *Bush's* damage report and swore, again. The carrier would have to be abandoned and scuttled. There was no way in hell they could repair the ship without a proper shipyard.

Thunderous vibrated, just for a second. Alarms howled. Susan studied the display, feeling oddly detached from the crisis. The damage wasn't that bad. The damage control teams were already on their way. If it had been her ship…she shook her head. Captain Bushier could handle his command. It had been a long time since she'd taken command of *Vanguard* in the middle of an engagement. *Thunderous* had a captain who knew what he was doing. Susan had made sure of *that* before asking him to serve as her flag captain.

"The enemy starfighters are advancing, Admiral," Richardson warned. "They'll be engaging our pilots in two minutes."

"Recall the pilots, have them merge with the CSP," Susan ordered. If she was any judge…yes, the virus's fleet was picking up speed. They'd be coming into weapons range in five minutes. "Signal the fleet. They are to launch ballistic missiles in one minute."

"Aye, Admiral," Richardson said.

Susan watched the last of the alien shuttles die, silently assessing the damage. Five ships destroyed, damaged beyond easy repair…the remainder hurt, but still intact. The damage control teams would be able to seal the breaches in the hulls, then wait for peace to return before they started replacing the destroyed weapons and sensor nodes. It looked as though she'd come out ahead. And yet, she knew it was an illusion. The shuttles had sold their lives dearly. They might have done enough damage to force her to break off.

"Missiles away, Admiral," Richardson reported. "Decoy drones launching…now."

"Signal the fleet," Susan ordered. They had to keep the enemy off balance, long enough for everything to get into place. "Prepare to come about on my mark."

"Aye, Admiral."

Susan nodded, counting down the seconds. Let the virus think it had driven her off, just for a few more seconds. It had overcommitted, sending its ships too far from the planet for its own good. She hadn't given it much choice, but still...

"Mark," she ordered, quietly.

She braced herself, half-expecting disaster. They'd put the fleet through countless manoeuvres in the simulators, but they hadn't had *time* to try them in real life. The odds of one ship crashing into another were very low, yet...not zero. She waited, not daring to breathe, as the fleet started to bank away, the alien ships altering course to match. Susan couldn't help a hot flash of resentment. The virus's formation was ruthlessly practical, without even a hint of elegance, and yet it worked. There was nothing cumbersome in its movements at all. A single intelligence was directing every movement.

The virus might not be life as we know it, she told herself. *But it is intelligence.*

"Admiral," Richardson said. The display updated, rapidly. "The manoeuvre has been completed."

"Let it think it has us on the run," Susan said. If she'd timed it right... the fleet should have exposed its flank. "And order the missiles to go live in ten seconds."

"Aye, Admiral," Richardson said.

And hope Lion *is in position, as planned*, Susan thought, grimly. *This could still go horribly wrong.*

CHAPTER TWENTY-THREE

TOBIAS HAD THE UNEASY FEELING, as the seconds ticked away, that he was trying to sneak up on someone who knew perfectly well he was there. There was nothing he could point to that suggested they'd been detected, no sensor pulses sweeping across the gunboat's hull, but he couldn't help feeling naked and alone in the darkness of interstellar space. The planet was growing in front of him, a tiny blue-green orb that belied its immense size; he felt, as he kept a wary eye on the sensors, that the entire planet was alive and watching him. It was no consolation to know that an uncountable number of alien starfighters had been hurled at the fleet, currently several light minutes from the planet. He was entirely sure the virus had kept some starfighters in reserve. It was what *he* would have done.

Marigold cleared her throat as the countdown ticked towards zero. Tobias nearly jumped out of his skin. He had no idea how the video stars managed to stay so calm, as their fleets flew towards starships straight out of nightmares. They were probably used to it...it helped, he supposed, that the enemy goliaths weren't actually *real*. Tobias had initially been blasé about combat simulations, even though he'd been ordered to take them seriously. The first real taste of combat had ended poorly.

"We'll be in engagement range in two minutes," Marigold said. "Are the missiles primed and locked?"

Tobias glanced at his console, although he already knew the answer. The gunboat sensors had located hundreds of targets, from immense orbital fortresses to industrial nodes built on the remains of asteroids. He'd seen the sensor images from *Unicorn*, during the mission briefing, but he hadn't grasped the sheer *scale* of the system until he'd seen it with his own eyes. It was so huge he had the feeling they could take shots at it for years and not even scratch the surface. The analysts claimed that taking out a relative handful of the facilities—and hitting the planet itself with the BioBombs—would render it effectively useless, but Tobias wasn't so sure. The virus might have to rebuild the machines to rebuild the machines to repair the damage, yet it wasn't short of resources or time. It could probably put things back together at terrifying speed.

"Yes," he said. The process was largely automatic. "The missiles are ready to go."

The timer hit zero. Tobias jabbed a finger at the console, watching in awe as the sensor decoys came online. Hundreds—thousands, millions—of targets suddenly sparkled to life, an endless tidal wave of destruction heading towards the alien planet. The vast majority of the targets were nothing more than sensor ghosts, but the virus would have to take them all seriously until it devised a way to separate the ghosts from the real contacts. It wasn't going to be easy. The decoys looked much more dangerous than the *real* missiles.

He sucked in his breath as the enemy point defence came to life. The virus had concentrated an *insane* amount of firepower around its planet, hundreds of stealthed platforms revealing themselves as they opened fire. Beyond them, Tobias saw a relative handful of starfighters launching from the orbital fortresses...not enough to make a difference, he thought, but enough to take out the gunboats as they reversed course and tried to escape. He kept a wary eye on them, noting how the virus seemed more interested in using them as mobile point defence platforms then hunting down the gunboats. It was ruthlessly practical. The gunboats were largely immaterial now. All that mattered was protecting the system.

A human might not be quite so practical, he thought, as the gunboat altered course and headed away from the planet. *He'd want to hunt us down even though the missile ships don't need us any longer.*

He watched, grimly, as the missiles lanced into their targets. The navy had spent a great deal of time and effort devising newer and better nuclear warheads, including a cluster designed to smash asteroid settlements to rubble. It was hard to believe *anything* could survive so much megatonnage, that the blasts would *not* do staggering damage to everything in orbit. And yet…he frowned as he saw orbital fortresses and even a handful of industrial nodes survive direct hits. It was hard to tell how much damage they'd done, although it looked as if one of the fortresses had been disabled. And yet…

A handful of missiles lanced past the fortresses, plunging into the planet's virus-ridden atmosphere. Tobias had seen the recordings of viral clouds drifting through the air, of seas tainted with viral cells, but…he shuddered as the surviving missiles began to detonate. The mission planners claimed that infecting the virus clouds would disrupt the virus's ability to coordinate its defences, although they'd been cagey on just how long it would take for the BioBomb to spread over the entire world. Tobias suspected it would be several days, at the very least. The fleet would have to hit the world time and time again if it wanted to speed the process up.

His terminal bleeped an alert. "They're coming!"

"Understood," Marigold said. "Open fire as soon as they enter range."

Tobias nodded as the enemy starfighters boosted their drives well past the point of sanity. He was no expert, but he was fairly sure the enemy ships would burn out their own drives well before they could return to their bases. If, of course, their bases survived. The system was dying. The virus probably wanted to hurt the invaders as much as possible before it was too late. Tobias gritted his teeth, feeling the gunboat starting to vibrate as Marigold pushed the drives to the limits. They didn't dare boost their own drives. The risks of losing power were just too high.

His hands darted across the console as the datanet came online, linking the gunboats into a single entity. There was no point in trying to hide any longer, not now the enemy starfighters had their scent. Their world was dying. The enemy would try to ram the gunboats, if he was any judge. Why not? They had nothing to lose.

"Enemy craft entering range now," he said. "Firing...now!"

• • •

"Captain, the first wave of missile strikes caused immense damage," Sibley reported. The tactical officer kept his eyes on his console, as the display updated time and time again. "I have passive locks on the enemy point defence platforms."

"Target them with railguns and open fire, then launch the next salvo of missiles," Thomas ordered. The enemy was alert now, spitting fire in all directions. The railguns would hopefully weaken their defences long enough to let the missiles get through. "Do we have an impact assessment on the planetary strikes?"

"No, Captain," Sibley said. "Projections suggested it may be some time before the virus begins to die."

Thomas scowled. A handful of analysts had insisted the shock of being infected would be enough to disrupt the virus's defences, although Thomas had thought that fanciful. The virus wasn't linked *that* closely together, not outside the planet's atmosphere. The remainder had suggested it would be several days, perhaps several *weeks*, before the infection spread out of control. There was even a possibility of the virus dropping shipkiller warheads on its own world, trying to cauterise the wound and burn out the counter-virus before it was too late. It might have no choice. And yet, in doing so, it would do a hell of a lot of damage to itself.

"We'll hit the planet again, if we have to," he said. The gunboats were under attack, but they were no longer necessary. The planetary defences and installations were a known factor now. They couldn't hide from his missiles or guns. "Continue firing."

"Aye, Captain."

• • •

"Admiral, the enemy fleet is coming about," Richardson reported. "They're altering course…"

"Too late," Susan said. She felt a surge of heavy satisfaction. "They can't escape us now."

She smiled as the torrent of missiles roared down on the alien ships. Her long-range sensors had reported that *Lion* had begun the planetary bombardment, forcing the virus to decide between trying to run down her fleet and breaking contact. It looked as if the virus had decided on the latter, despite the chance to do her ships some real damage. And yet, it was too late to completely evade contact. She waited, expecting the enemy fleet to swing back to its original course. It was just a matter of time.

They should have sent a brainship with the fleet, she thought. The enemy battleships weren't stupid, but they lacked the flexibility of the brainships. *It's too far from the planet for direct command and control.*

"Order the antishipping starfighters to begin their attack runs," she said, as the enemy point defence started to open fire. "And prepare the battleships to go in behind them."

"Aye, Admiral."

Susan leaned forward. The enemy warships staggered under the weight of her missile bombardment, unable to separate the decoys from the real missiles until it was far too late. Their starfighters were being worn down, unable to cope with the sudden appearance of an antishipping strike. As she watched, the enemy starfighters broke contact and screamed back to their fleet in hopes of covering the ships long enough to let them escape. Too late, she told herself. Too late…

"Signal from *Lion*, Admiral," Richardson said. "The planet has been hit. Repeatedly."

"Good." Susan wasn't too concerned about the planet itself. It wouldn't be *that* hard to find an asteroid and shove it into the planet, if they ran out of other weapons. The remnants of the orbital defences would fall into the planet's atmosphere, a handful striking the surface and causing immense devastation. "Order him to concentrate on the orbital facilities."

She put the matter out of her mind as her fleet converged on the enemy ships, spitting wave after wave of missiles as they came. The starfighters were already hitting the enemy defences, torpedoes lancing beams of deadly energy into their hulls and plasma cannons targeting weapons emplacements and sensor nodes. Susan felt no pity, beyond a grim awareness that countless host bodies were about to die. It was hard not to feel sorry for them, even though most of the hosts had probably been born and bred to serve the virus. They could have been intelligent. They could have lived their own lives...

We're putting them out of their misery, she told herself. *And that is all we can do for them.*

Thunderous vibrated as she launched another salvo of missiles. The rate of fire was dropping now—the battleships were threatening to shoot themselves dry—but the enemy defences were too weak to stop them. Susan felt a flicker of cold glee as a missile plunged into a gash in an enemy hull and detonated, the resulting blast blowing the entire ship into a cloud of expanding plasma. The ship must have taken a great deal of internal damage already, she noted absently. Battleships were designed to take multiple hits and keep going. Or maybe the virus hadn't felt able to risk closing the hatches...

"Admiral, the enemy ships are picking up speed," Richardson reported. "They're trying to close the range."

"Order the starfighters to target their drives," Susan said. The enemy ships were trying to ram. They had no other choice now, but to sell their lives as dearly as possible. It might work, too. She was all too aware she was deep in enemy space, unable to take the time to repair a damaged ship. The virus knew they were there now, she was sure. They'd have to head home as quickly as possible. "And order the fleet to evade as much as possible."

She felt her heart pounding as the range continued to close. The enemy battleships kept coming, directing their escorts to shield them as long as possible. Susan watched calmly as they died, one by one; their weapons raking her hulls and damaging her ships. They might have the last laugh, she noted grimly. They'd weakened her to the point she couldn't risk another engagement, at least until she'd rearmed her ships and made what basic—very basic—repairs she could. And if enemy reinforcements arrived in time...

The starchart glowed in front of her, mocking her. How close *were* enemy reinforcements? They'd have a flicker station somewhere along the tramline or she was a midshipwoman with delusions of grandeur. The captured files weren't *that* good...she had no idea what was waiting for her as she cut her way back into human space. The virus would do everything in its power to block her retreat, even if it meant abandoning the front. *That* wouldn't be bad for the human race, she thought, but it would be bad for her personally. And for the rest of her fleet.

She forced herself to watch, impassively, as the damage continued to mount. An American battleship lost two drive nodes, a Japanese cruiser was disabled and swatted aside, a Chinese carrier took four direct hits and only survived through sheer luck...a Tadpole superdreadnaught stood her ground against an alien battleship, the two ships converging until they collided and exploded with terrifying force. There was no time to mourn, Susan told herself. The last of the enemy ships were still coming...

"Admiral," Richardson said. "They're closing on us."

"Understood," Susan said. She was just a spectator now as the alien ships bulled through her fire. There was no point in trying to evade. "Alert the datanet. Prepare to transfer command to Admiral Li."

Her mind raced. Did the virus know *Thunderous* was the flagship? It was impossible to be sure. The decision hadn't been made until shortly before the fleet had left Earth. She supposed it was possible the virus had infected someone in a position to know, but...she shook her head as the alien craft staggered under her fire, losing speed as it was blasted to atoms piece by piece. It was probably just a coincidence. She'd been reluctant to place herself in the middle of the fleet. She owed it to her people to put her life on the line too.

Richardson looked up. "Admiral," he said, formally. "The enemy fleet has been destroyed."

Susan nodded, curtly. There were a handful of remaining starfighters, but none of them posed any significant threat. Her starfighters would hunt them down before they could escape...if, of course, they had anywhere to go. She frowned as she studied the display. The system was a big place. It was quite possible there were stealthed resupply facilities within reach, if the enemy starfighters set out before it was too late. There were a couple of automated starfighter tenders holding position near Earth.

"Signal the fleet," she ordered. The datanet had already resorted her fleet, ensuring that the damaged units were pulled out of their formations and replaced. She disliked relying on the computers to handle it, but she didn't have time to handle it herself. "Task Force Omega is to head to the gas giant and destroy the facilities there. Task Force Alpha is to head to the planet and link up with *Lion*. The remainder of the fleet is to hold position here."

"Aye, Admiral," Richardson said.

Susan took a moment to study the damage reports. Twelve ships had been destroyed outright. Four ships would probably have to be abandoned and scuttled, unless their crews thought they could make it back on their own. There was no way they could keep up with the fleet, let alone defend themselves when they ran into enemy forces. And the remainder were damaged...she frowned as new icons popped up on her display as the damage control crews started to file their reports. They could repair most of the damage, if they had time. She just didn't know how much time she had.

"Signal to *Unicorn*," she ordered. "She is to proceed through Tramline Two and sweep the system, then return here."

"Aye, Admiral."

"And detach two destroyers," Susan added. "I want them to peek through Tramlines Three and Four."

"Aye, Admiral," Richardson said.

Susan could hear the doubt in his voice. She understood. Destroyers were tough little ships, but they weren't designed for survey or recon missions. Their sensors were nowhere near as sharp as *Unicorn's*. They'd still be good enough to pick up a major fleet rushing towards the alien system, she told herself. The virus wouldn't be wasting time with stealth, if it thought it could save something...she smiled. It was too late. The system had been crippled beyond easy repair.

She glanced at the live feed from *Lion* as the fleet commenced repairs. The planet's orbital installations had been destroyed, crippled or rendered effectively meaningless. There was no point in wasting missiles on orbital battlestations that no longer had anything to defend. The atmospheric sensors reported that the counter-virus was spreading rapidly, killing the virus as efficiently as it killed its hosts. Susan knew they were committing genocide, but...she shook her head. The virus had made it clear that it intended to create a universe where it was the only intelligent life form. There was no choice. It had to be destroyed, whatever the cost, or it would destroy everything else.

And now we complete our repairs and start running, she thought. *It'll be coming for us...*

"Admiral," Richardson said. "There's an odd report from the planetary survey. They're requesting permission to deploy a landing party."

Susan blinked as she ran her eye down the report. The thought was madness. There was no way they could be *sure* the enemy world was safe. Hell, it *wasn't* safe. And yet...

"Volunteers only," she said, firmly. "Make it clear. This is a volunteer-only mission."

CHAPTER TWENTY-FOUR

"YOU KNOW, IF WE GET HOME, this story is bound to impress the girls," Davies said. "How about you, Kevin? Are you planning to impress the girls?"

Colin scowled behind his mask as the shuttle plummeted through the planetary atmosphere, the hull groaning and creaking as if it were being pummelled by an angry god. He hadn't been so scared since his very first parachute jump, when he'd wet himself. It wasn't the first time he'd set foot on an infected world, but this world had been infected from top to bottom before the BioBombs had been dropped. They couldn't trust anything, from the air they breathed to the very trees themselves. They'd be spending the entire mission in their suits, praying desperately they didn't spring a leak...

"What about it?" Davies leaned forward. "What do you see in a woman?"

"Knock it off," Colin growled. The marines had plenty of experience integrating people from different cultures, but alien races? *That* was something new. Kevin might be hideously offended—or simply bemused—by Davies's comments. Colin didn't have time to deal with any of it. He was too busy kicking himself for volunteering. "We'll be landing shortly."

The shuttle rocked, something crashing against the hull hard enough to make him think—just for a second—that they'd touched down. The boffins on the ship had insisted the weather was completely unpredictable, pointing to the combination of dying viral matter and thousands upon thousands of pieces of debris falling into the atmosphere to explain why they couldn't see much of anything. Colin wished, just for a moment, that the boffins were accompanying the marines. He knew he was being unfair, but he was starting to feel as though he'd made a mistake. The shuttle was being pushed to the limit as it dropped through the atmosphere. There was little hope of recovery if they crash-landed on the alien world.

He glanced at the four figures at the rear of the compartment. The xenospecialists had insisted on accompanying the marines, despite the danger. Colin admired them for taking the risk—they could have easily stayed on the ship—but, at the same time, he wished they'd been a little less brave. Close-protection duties weren't really his forte, even on Earth. Here, on a dying world, he was all too aware they could be overrun at any moment. The LZ was dozens of miles from the nearest alien city, but that was meaningless. The entire planet was riddled with the virus.

The intercom crackled. "Landing in five minutes," the pilot said. "Bend over and kiss your arse goodbye."

Colin promised himself a long *talk* with the pilot when they were back on the ship. His platoon knew the risks, and knew what pilots considered amusing, but the xenospecialists had to be terrified. The turbulence alone was quite bad enough, without the risk of being knocked out of the air or stranded on an alien world. Colin sighed inwardly, wishing he'd thought to suggest the xenospecialists stayed on the ship. Not that they'd have listened, he supposed. Their careers would be *made* if they came up with something new...

He braced himself as the pilot counted down the last few seconds. The shuttle crashed down hard, hard enough to set off the alarms. Colin unbuckled himself and stood as the deck shifted, wondering—for an insane moment—if the pilot had accidentally landed them in the ocean. He'd been through survival training, but he didn't give them good odds if they *had* landed in the water. The suits were so heavy they'd sink the moment they got out of the shuttle.

Alerts flashed up in front of him as he stepped into the airlock, the inner hatch hissing closed and locking before the outer hatch opened. It was supposed to be midday, but the sky was gloomy and overcast and flickering with eerie lightning. Rain splattered down around him, dripping off the shuttle and crashing to the ground. The landscape looked terrible. He hadn't seen something so vile in his entire life, even the muddy bogs they'd used for exercises…

His radio crackled. "What does it look like out there?"

"Like snot," Colin said. "You sure we've come to the right place?"

"Yes," the pilot said. "I put us down right on target."

Colin frowned as he jumped to the ground. It felt squidgy under his armoured boots. He tried not to think about the dying virus, about how it might have taken the entire planet with it. Perhaps the world could be terraformed at some later date or…he put the thought out of his head as the rest of the platoon and the xenospecialists joined him. The latter seemed surprisingly eager to proceed. Perhaps they'd come to realise that the longer they spent on the surface, the longer they'd have to spent in their suits.

The lead xenospecialist—Doctor Simpson—pointed east. "That way," he said. "Follow me."

"Follow *me*," Colin corrected. "Let me take point."

He ignored the doctor's irritation as he started walking. The sky grew more ominous as they moved, billowing yellow clouds dripping poisonous rain on their suits. His sensors warned him that the rain was dangerous, as if the brown liquid didn't already look horrible. The landscape didn't grow any better, as they kept moving. He couldn't help thinking that the entire planet was decaying into sludge. The platoon moved in silence, without any of their normal jokes or banter. The landscape was just too oppressive for jokes.

It was nearly twenty minutes before they reached the city. Colin held his rifle in one hand as he crested the hill and peered down at the alien buildings. They looked odd, the proportions completely out of shape. The virus tended towards the strictly functional, when it built planetary installations, but there was something oddly whimsical about *these* buildings. Colin felt a shiver running down his spine. It wasn't a human place.

The xenospecialists didn't seem bothered. They launched a set of drones, then started to search the buildings one by one. Colin kept a wary eye on his sensors, half-convinced the complex wasn't as abandoned as it looked. The buildings seemed to have been abandoned ages ago, yet…a chill ran down his spine as they peered into a small chamber and spotted hints of long-gone machinery. The complex had been something, once upon a time. But what?

Davies put the feeling into words. "What do you think this place is?"

"We don't know, yet," Doctor Simpson said. "We spotted it during the planetary survey. The virus didn't seem to have paid it any real attention."

Colin frowned. He'd seen the live feed from the alien world before the counter-virus had begun to devastate the population. The host bodies had represented three or four different races, but one had been predominant. "You think this place belonged to the original natives?"

"It's a possibility," Doctor Simpson said. "We're not sure how long the world has been infected, but…this place survived. We want to know why."

"It might have been useless," Davies pointed out. "The virus doesn't really give much of a damn about food and shelter."

"It normally makes use of everything it finds," Doctor Simpson corrected, stiffly. "It captures homes—it uses homes. We're unsure if it's drawing on some legacy from the host body's memories or if it's just being practical, but it does. This place seemingly remained untouched for decades, perhaps centuries. We want to know why."

Colin kept his thoughts to himself as they quartered the tiny settlement. It was hard not to feel the weight of ages pressing down, yet…there was so much *missing* that he couldn't decide if their excitement was remotely justified. The aliens who'd built the place might have intended it to be anything from a retirement village to a military barracks. The virus might not have cared enough to make use of it, once the original host bodies had died out. It had been much more interested in turning the world into an industrial powerhouse.

Lights flickered and flared in the distance as more and more junk fell out of orbit. The orbital towers had been knocked down long ago, vast pieces of debris crashing to the ground and blasting dust into the atmosphere. Nuclear winter was a very real possibility, along with everything else. He grimaced at the thought. Shipkillers were tiny, set against the immensity of deep space, but on a planetary scale they were utterly devastating. He didn't think shipkiller-sized nukes had been tested on a planetary surface, at least until the attack on Alien-One...

"Come look at this," a xenospecialist called. "I found something!"

Colin followed, trying not to get too excited. The settlement was little more than a hollow shell. The buildings themselves had been designed to survive—the techs hadn't been able to determine what they were made of—but the contents had decayed long ago. Colin tapped his suit, wondering if some far-future xenospecialist would find the suit and wonder who and what had worn it. Would the xenospecialist be human or alien? Would they even recognise the suit for what it was? Or...who knew?

"I found a chamber under the building," the xenospecialist said. She stood next to an opened hatch. "Can we go down there?"

"Me first," Colin said. He clicked on his suit's flashlights, shining them down into the chamber. The floor wasn't that far down, although it looked as though it was going to be a tight squeeze. "There should be enough room."

He braced himself, then clicked off the lights and dropped down. Darkness enveloped him as he landed. The suit's sensor suggested the air was breathable, but rapidly becoming less so. Colin frowned as he clicked the lights back on and looked around. The chamber was filled with odd pieces of machinery, all beyond his comprehension. He'd never seen anything like them. Chunks of raw matter, worked into...into what? A sense of disorientation ran through him. He had to fight the urge to jump up and run for his life.

"I think we're going to need more people," he said. "Whatever this is, it's important."

"Got it," Doctor Simpson said. "You let us handle it."

"No worries," Colin said. The chamber looked as if it had been designed for children, rather than grown adults. There weren't many adults who could have fitted into the chamber without constantly scraping their heads against the ceiling. "You're welcome to it."

He clambered out, keying his radio to call the ship and make a full report. The major would have to decide if it was worth risking additional marines...no, it wouldn't be the major who'd make the final call. Colin's eyes swept the upper chamber as Doctor Simpson and his team dropped into the lower chamber. In hindsight, it was blindingly obvious that the designers had been child-sized. Colin suspected that they'd never grown higher than a metre.

And none of the known host-races are so small, he thought. *What does that mean?*

• • •

Susan was almost grateful to receive the report, even though it threatened to open up a whole new can of worms. She'd had nothing to do, not personally, since the battle had finally come to an end. Her crews knew what to do, leaving her to wait for them to complete their tasks before she could take the fleet back home. She couldn't do anything else. She knew from grim experience that nagging and micromanaging only slowed things down.

She looked up as she finished scanning the report. "Are you telling me that an incredibly advanced race set foot on that world and...left behind a batch of their technology?"

Doctor Simpson looked tired and worn. He'd be back on the shuttle now, if Susan was any judge. Landing the research craft couldn't have been easy. It had probably started to sink in that he might never be allowed back onto the fleet, not without going through an intensive decontamination procedure. And even then...Susan told herself, sharply, that they hit the planet with a dozen BioBombs. It was unlikely, to say the least, that the virus was in any state to even notice the landing party was there. She'd seen the footage from the infected cities. The planetary ecosystem was coming apart at the seams.

"Yes, Admiral," Doctor Simpson said. "Their technology is clearly more advanced than ours."

Susan frowned. "And what does it *do*?"

"We don't know," the xenospecialist confessed. "Our investigations have started to map out some of their systems, but…we haven't yet been able to determine what they do. The technology is powered down and we have no idea how to start it up again."

"And the virus didn't manage to infect the colonists," Susan mused. "It certainly didn't discover how to duplicate the tech for itself."

"The colonists might not have known," Doctor Simpson pointed out. "With all due respect, Admiral, do you know how to build a Puller Drive from scratch?"

Susan shook her head. The modern world had been growing increasingly complex for decades. The days in which someone could repair a car with their bare hands or basic tools were long gone. She commanded a fleet she didn't understand and couldn't rebuild…she had to admit he had a point. The colonists might not have understood how their tech functioned. The virus couldn't have forced them to tell it something they didn't actually know.

"Point," she said. She glanced at the live feed from the repair crews. "Can you strip the settlement of everything you can and transport it to the freighter?"

Doctor Simpson blinked. "Admiral, we cannot ensure that the technology will remain intact," he said. "Moving it may destroy it."

"We cannot stay here," Susan said. The remaining settlements within the system were effectively meaningless, at least until the virus started to rebuild, but it wouldn't be long before the alien reinforcements arrived. "And we cannot guarantee that we will return to this system."

She rubbed her forehead. There would be political implications, of course. The Great Powers—and their alien allies—would insist on having a look at the technology. Britain couldn't keep it for itself, no matter how much certain people might wish otherwise. And yet, there was no guarantee the research programs would produce anything useful. The tech gap might be just too wide. Neil Armstrong would be freaked out by a modern-day battleship. Lord Nelson would be completely baffled. It was unlikely he'd even recognise it as a ship. Back then, they hadn't even had the concept of interplanetary travel.

"You have your orders," she said. "See to them,"

"Understood," Doctor Simpson said. "If we could just have a day or two…"

"Doctor, if a major enemy fleet arrives, we will have to depart the system at once," Susan said, tartly. "We will barely have time to yank you and your fellows off the planet. If we get caught badly out of place, we won't even have time for *that*. Get everything you can move out of the complex and into the shuttles, then launch it into orbit. We just don't have time for anything else."

She winced, inwardly, as she broke the connection. She understood his position. Archaeology wasn't easy, even when humans had built the ancient buildings. It took time and care, painstaking care, to dig the old ruins out of the ground without damaging them still further. Susan had been fascinated, once upon a time, by the concept of studying the past, although she'd never considered making it a career. The future had called to her instead.

Her eyes darted to the near-space display. The fleet was working desperately to patch its wounds and reload the missile tubes before all hell broke loose. Again. Susan could practically *feel* the enemy fleet bearing down on them, although the long-range sensors were clear. There was probably a cloaked ship somewhere in the system, reporting up the flicker network to the relief fleet. Susan wouldn't have cared to bet against it. The virus had had enough warning to detach a picket, relying on sensor jammers and decoys to allow the ship to sneak away without being detected. And, so far, she hadn't located and destroyed the flicker station.

She tapped her terminal. "Set up a command conference to be held in one hour," she said. If she was any judge, word would have already reached the rest of the fleet. She had to head any trouble off at the pass, before it led to problems she couldn't handle. "And alert me if there are any new discoveries."

"Aye, Admiral," Richardson said.

Susan frowned as she sat back in her chair. The boffins had always speculated the virus wasn't natural. There'd never been any proof, one way or the other. Whoever had designed it, if it was a bioweapon that had gotten out of control, had known far more than humanity about designing bioorganisms from scratch. And yet, if they'd designed and released the virus, they'd either been irredeemably stupid or outright evil. She wondered, idly, if the creators had released the virus on the planet below. Or... if they'd merely been the first to die at the creation's hands. She could see why someone might consider the virus an effective weapon. And yet, she could also see the risks of unleashing something that might easily get out of control.

And I may never know, she thought, as she called for coffee and a snack. She had enough time to consider what she was going to say to her officers, by the time their holograms assembled. Hopefully, they'd agree to put the alien artefacts aside until they got back to Earth. *The truth may be lost forever.*

CHAPTER TWENTY-FIVE

"THIS SYSTEM APPEARS TO BE A WASTE OF TIME," Staci commented. "There's nothing here."

Mitch nodded. It was hard to disagree. The system—it had a number, but no name—was seemingly barren. There were no planets, no asteroids... nothing of interest, apart from two tramlines. Mitch frowned as he studied the display, silently calculating the tramline's path back towards the human sphere. If the captured data was accurate, that was the way to go.

And yet, we don't know for sure the data is accurate, he mused. *The virus hardly needs computers to store vast amounts of information.*

His eyes narrowed as he studied the display. There could be an entire fleet of cloaked starships lurking in the system, completely undetectable as long as they didn't do something stupid like activating their sensors. It was possible, but—hopefully—unlikely. The projections certainly suggested the virus would do everything in its power to save the industrial system, yet it was already too late. Mitch didn't see any point in fighting for a system that had been blasted to scrap, then infected with the counter-virus. The admiral certainly had no intention of trying to hold the system. There was nothing there to defend.

"Deploy two stealthed sensor platforms," he ordered. "Once they're in position, bring us about and take us back to the fleet."

"Aye, Captain."

Mitch settled back in his chair, feeling oddly exposed. The enemy fleet *had* to be on its way, but…how long did they have? The projections were little more than guesswork. He'd seen simulations that insisted the enemy fleet was about to come crashing into the system with blood in its eye and simulations that insisted it would be weeks, if not months, before the virus gathered the power to crush the human intruders. They *had* to be deep within the enemy's rear area. The virus might see no point in basing vast fleets nearby. One might as well position warships at Tunbridge Wells.

He snorted at the thought, although it was far more likely to encounter a fleet of starships here than submarines in an inland town. There was nothing *stopping* the virus—or another race—from sneaking a fleet through the tramlines and hitting a core world or two. The virus couldn't risk leaving its rear completely bare, even if it was trying to bring everything to bear on humanity's defences. There would be other ships within range, probably trying desperately to concentrate into a fleet before the human fleet arrived. The flicker network would see to that, he was sure. The virus wouldn't regard it as a pain in the butt.

"The platforms are emplaced, Captain," Lieutenant Hannah Avis reported. "Their stealth systems are up and running."

"Good," Mitch said. "Helm, take us back to the fleet."

"Aye, Captain."

Mitch glanced at the other tramline as *Unicorn* rotated and headed back to the first tramline. Who knew what was on the far side, waiting for them? A massive fleet? An inhabited world? Or another barren system? He wanted to reverse course and poke his head through long enough to check, but he had to report back to the admiral. She'd send him back soon enough, he was sure. *Unicorn* was the finest scout in the fleet.

And completely expendable, he mused, thoughtfully. *No one will give much of a damn if we get blown away.*

He braced himself as the frigate jumped through the tramline. The display blanked, then returned to life as it downloaded a status report from the stealthed platform they'd left behind when they'd jumped. There was no sign of the enemy fleet. He breathed a sigh of relief. It hadn't seemed *possible* that Admiral Onarina and her fleet had been jumped—and slaughtered—while he'd been gone, but the worry had nagged at his mind. They were just too deep within enemy space. He had no idea how hard they'd have to fight to get home.

Perhaps we should consider taking the long way home, he thought. *If nothing else, we wouldn't be following a predictable flight plan.*

"Local space is clear, Captain," Staci reported. "There's no sign of the enemy."

"No," Mitch agreed. "Send our report to the admiral, then hold position."

"Aye, Captain."

. . .

"*Unicorn* has returned," Admiral Onarina said. The holoconference was very quiet. "The next system is apparently barren."

Thomas frowned as he studied the report. Captain Campbell had gone to some pains to remind everyone that he didn't know what was on the far side of the *other* tramline, a fact that could hardly have been unknown to anyone on the fleet...except, perhaps, the reporters. *They* couldn't be expected to know anything. His message list was already full of requests for interviews, with long lists of pointless questions he didn't have the time or patience to answer. A handful made sense, he supposed, but the remainder...what on Earth had they been drinking? They couldn't be that ignorant, could they?

He dragged his attention back to the holoconference. "We cannot remain here much longer," Admiral Onarina said. "Once we have completed the transfer, we'll head through the tramline as quickly as possible."

"That will leave us no time to survey the remainder of the planet," General Sampan pointed out, tightly. "We don't know what else might be there."

"And we shouldn't leave it for the virus," Admiral Li added. "If it learns to make use of advanced technology..."

"We've removed what we can," Admiral Onarina countered. "Do any of you think the virus can wave a magic wand, deduce how the technology works and put it into active service?"

"We shouldn't take the chance," Admiral Li argued. "The risk is too great."

Thomas winced, inwardly. The truth, as far as he could tell, was that no one knew what had *really* been recovered. It could be anything from a secret stash of high-tech superweapons to an alien barrel organ. The xeno-specialists were sure they'd unravel the mystery sooner rather than later, but there was no way to be sure. For all they knew, the process of removing the alien artefacts had broken them beyond repair. The facts were clear and yet...everyone seemed to think they'd recovered something that would win the war in a heartbeat. It was going to be a disappointment when it sank in that they didn't even know what the artefacts did.

If anything, Thomas thought. *We might have stumbled across a patch of alien fool's gold.*

"The conditions on the surface are growing worse by the hour," Admiral Onarina said, calmly. "We do not have the resources to sustain a position down below and, even if we did, it would be exposed to attack as soon as the enemy retakes the high orbitals. We'll pull the team up once they've collected everything that can be moved, then destroy the site with shipkiller missiles. There will be nothing left for the virus to find."

"That will not sit well with the politicians," Admiral Li warned. "They'll be afraid the mystery aliens pose a threat..."

"They may already have died out," General Sampan objected. "Or simply progressed to the next plane of existence."

"If it exists," Admiral Onarina said. She shook her head. "Do either of you—do any of you -believe we can hold this system indefinitely?"

"No, Admiral," Admiral Li said. "However, it is my duty to make you aware of the implications."

Thomas nodded, thoughtfully. There had been a great deal of debate, ever since humanity had first encountered the Tadpoles, over why they hadn't spotted any signs of far more advanced races. The quest for alien life beyond explored space had turned up almost nothing, certainly no hints of a race significantly more advanced than humanity. He'd read papers that suggested there were no more advanced races, for reasons that ranged from the sensible to the crazy, and papers that argued that superior races regularly transcended into godlike creatures that stayed well clear of the lesser races. He had no idea which, if any, of the theories were actually true. There were standing orders regarding artefacts from more advanced civilisations. None of them included blowing the artefacts up.

But we have no choice, he thought. *The virus cannot be allowed to recover them itself.*

He frowned. "It makes no sense."

Admiral Onarina's holoimage turned to look at him. "What makes no sense?"

Thomas flushed. He hadn't realised he'd spoken out loud. "The artefacts were present on an infected world," he said. "The virus practically turned the world into a single entity. Surely, it would have known the artefacts were there."

"They were some distance from its settlements," General Sampan said. "Planets are *big*."

"Yes, General," Thomas said. "But...the virus infected the entire ecosystem. It would have known it was there, just as we would know we were wearing clothes. It could hardly *not* have been aware of the artefacts."

"A mystery for another time," Admiral Onarina said. "For the moment..."

She cleared her throat. "We will proceed as planned, unless any of you have any objections. We need to put some distance between ourselves and the system before we cloak and try to sneak our way home. And we have to be ready for when we'll meet the enemy."

When, not if, Thomas thought. *Time is not on our side.*

"We'll be ready," General Sampan said.

"I want my objections to go on the record," Admiral Li said. "The artefacts should not be destroyed."

"I understand," Admiral Onarina said. "But my orders stand."

Thomas nodded. Admiral Li had a point, but they had no choice. They could neither hold the system nor guarantee they'd be able to regain control before the virus found the artefacts and made use of them. If, of course, it could. It might have simply noted their presence and ignored them. Thomas found it hard to understand, but if the virus had found the artefacts incomprehensible it might just have chosen to leave them alone. And yet, the virus had vast brainpower...more computing power, some analysts believed, than a full-scale datanet. It could reason its way to comprehension, if it was prepared to devote the time and effort to the study...

"I want to be ready to depart as quickly as possible," Admiral Onarina said. "Dismissed."

The holoimages blinked out of existence. Thomas rubbed his eyes. The lack of sleep was starting to catch up with him. He'd had to leave Commander Donker in charge of the rearming—thankfully, the enemy hadn't fired on *his* ship—so he could attend to his other duties, but he just had too much to do. It hadn't been so bad during the last operation, when they'd been operating alone. Admiral Onarina must be having problems commanding an entire fleet, with hundreds of personalities brushing against each other...

The intercom bleeped. "Captain, fleet command has *requested* we embark a few dozen survivors from *Mao*," Donker said. "They'll be redistributed once the fleet is back underway."

"Then bring them onboard," Thomas said. "Find them berths, if you can. If not, sort out bedding in the hold."

"Aye, Captain."

Thomas stood, trying not to rub his eyes again. It was never easy taking on refugees from other ships. The Chinese crewmen would presumably speak English—every spacer was certainly *supposed* to speak English— but they wouldn't be used to serving on a British vessel. There would be problems, even with the best will in the world. And Thomas would have to handle them without causing a diplomatic incident.

We can do it, he thought, curtly. *We have no choice.*

. . .

There weren't *many* advantages to being a gunboat pilot, Tobias had discovered. They didn't have the glamour of starfighter pilots and they didn't have the long-term career security of crewmen and officers alike. Indeed, it was unlikely any of them would ever be considered for serious promotion. They just didn't have the training to fit into a more demanding role on a starship. Bagehot had hinted there might be a CAG position in their future—they knew, intimately, what gunboats could do—but Tobias wasn't convinced. He didn't resent the navy for being reluctant to promote them. Hell, he wasn't sure he *wanted* to stay in the navy.

He smiled as he spooned against Marigold, holding her tightly. The only real advantage was that no one expected them to help out after the battle, once they'd swept local space for starfighter pilots who'd had to eject. They'd tried to volunteer, only to be told they had to remain within their section and stay out of the way. Tobias hadn't been too upset, although some of the younger pilots had been offended. They didn't *like* the idea of doing nothing while the rest of the crew worked their asses off. Tobias knew better. He knew from grim experience that they'd just annoy people if they got in the way.

Marigold shifted against him, one hand taking hold of his and directing his fingers to the place between her legs. He'd fumbled a lot at first, back when they'd started sleeping together. It had taken him longer than it should to learn how to take direction, to realise she knew her own body better than anyone else. In hindsight, he should have known porno movies weren't *real*. The men and women in the films were actors, faking it. He still blanched at his own stupidity. He should have known better than to believe what he was seeing. Or the bragging he'd overheard in the changing rooms.

He felt her shift again as his fingers went to work. She twisted, turning around to face him. Tobias drank in the sight, admiring how she'd slimmed down in the months since he'd first met her. He'd never really thought he could slim down either...he grunted, despite himself, as she took him in her hand...

The alert rang. Tobias froze, caught between the grim awareness they had to get to their stations and a suicidal desire not to go. He wanted her, yet…Marigold let go of him and jumped off the bed, snatching up her underwear and donning it with desperate speed. Her bare bottom winked at him as she yanked her panties up her legs, nearly falling over in her haste to get dressed. Tobias cursed as he forced himself to grab his trousers, leaving his pants behind. He didn't need them, not really. He yanked on his jacket and ran for the hatch, pausing long enough to check Marigold was decent before he keyed in the code. The hatch hissed open, revealing a scene of absolute chaos. It felt as if the entire crew was running around like headless chickens.

"Fuck," he said. His face reddened. They'd been in the privacy tubes. Everyone would know what they'd been doing. No one seemed to be paying any attention to them, but…he knew they knew. It wasn't fair. "Fuck it!"

"Move," Marigold said. She looked as frustrated—and as embarrassed—as he felt. "We have to get to the boat."

Tobias nodded. Bagehot didn't care what they did off-duty, but they'd been on-duty from the moment the alert sounded. Thankfully, the privacy tubes weren't *that* far from the launch ring. He hurried through the corridors, breathing a sigh of relief when he realised the rest of the gunboats hadn't been launched. The ship wasn't under attack, not yet. He felt unclean as he jumped though the hatch and took his station, idly wondering if they had time to use the washroom. They hadn't had time to wash.

"Check the sensors," Marigold ordered. "What happened?"

"Incoming enemy ships," Tobias said. The display sparkled with red light. "That's not good."

"No," Marigold agreed. "But at least we have someone to blame."

• • •

"Long-range sensors are picking up an enemy fleet transiting Tramline One," Richardson reported. "At least seven battleships and carriers, if our sensor readings are accurate."

Susan frowned. They were a *very* long way from the tramline. The enemy fleet had had plenty of time to complete its transits and then drive on the planet. It hadn't moved to block their escape, yet, but that would change shortly. Her eyes narrowed as more enemy ships appeared on the display. She had the firepower to take them, she was sure, but it would weaken her badly. She might not have enough firepower to take them out and get home afterwards.

She glanced at her aide. "Have the landing parties returned to the ship?"

"Yes, Admiral," Richardson said. "They're going through decontamination now."

Poor bastards, Susan thought. Decontamination got worse with every passing month. *But better that than carrying an infection onto the ship.*

She put the thought out of her head. "Signal the fleet," she ordered. "The monitors are to commence planetary bombardment, as planned. The remainder of the fleet is to depart orbit and thrust for the tramline on my mark."

"Aye, Admiral," Richardson said.

Susan said nothing for a long moment as the monitors launched a spread of shipkillers towards the planet, then started tipping chunks of debris into the atmosphere. It was overkill—and, worse, it would deprive her of missiles she feared she'd need later—but it would hopefully conceal what they'd been doing. The virus didn't need to know what they'd found. She wasn't blind to the theories that insisted it already knew...

She snorted. Right now, that wasn't the problem. The real problem was the alien fleet that was going to be snapping at their heels, at least until they crossed the tramline. Who knew what they'd encounter on the far side? Another fleet, trying to pull off an impossible pincer? It might not be quite so impossible with the flicker network. They still hadn't found the stations they knew had to exist. And that meant they had to move, now, before the odds got any worse.

"Mark," she ordered. "It's time to start the voyage home."

CHAPTER TWENTY-SIX

THOMAS KEPT HIS THOUGHTS under tight control as the fleet thrust away from the planet. The enemy had managed to reach the system quicker than they'd feared, barely giving the invading ships a chance to rearm before they were forced into another battle. Admiral Onarina was trying to evade, it was clear, but Thomas wasn't sure it would work. The warships could outrun the alien starships, if they tried. The fleet train didn't have a hope of outrunning its foes.

He watched the display, silently assessing their chances. They could take the alien fleet. The multinational fleet had enough firepower, even with half its units damaged, to take on the aliens and win. He was sure of it. And yet, they'd take more damage in the process. Their escape would be slowed, perhaps stopped altogether. The virus might hope to expend a handful of ships to delay the fleet, long enough to muster the force necessary to tear it apart for good. There was no way to know what the virus was thinking, but…it rarely showed any concern for individual ships and men. It was quite happy to expend units in pursuit of a larger goal.

And we're leaving a mystery behind, he mused. He'd studied the preliminary reports from the xenospecialists. They'd said little of value. The recovered tech could be anything from a home entertainment system to a set of military tactical datacores, if indeed they were anything within human comprehension. *Who left that tech behind, and why?*

He mulled over the problem as the fleet picked up speed. The alien ships seemed content to keep their distance, rather than trying to close the range. Thomas hoped that was a good sign, that the enemy ships were the only ones within the sector, but he feared they hadn't been anything like so lucky. The alien flicker network could be working overtime, trying to coordinate a trap...the sort of trap that had been the preserve of bad novels based on impossible tech, before the FTL communications network had been invented and put into widespread use. Thomas gritted his teeth as his eyes flickered to the starchart. Their course was predictable. They *had* to pass through two particular systems, if they wanted to follow a least-time course back to Earth. And the virus knew it.

Unless there's something wrong with the tramline projections, he reminded himself. *We never quite get them right.*

He put the thought out of his mind as the minutes started to turn into hours. Someone with advanced tech—*very* advanced tech—had set up a base on the infected world. Why? Did they think they could study the virus from a safe distance? Did they not realise the world was infected so completely it was—it had been—practically a single mind? Or...had they been infected, the moment they breathed the air? Thomas shook his head. There just wasn't enough data to make any real judgements, certainly nothing beyond guesswork. It was hard to believe the virus could infect an advanced society without anyone noticing, but no one had predicted an intelligent virus before it had first been encountered. The original contact team had been infected precisely because no one had known what to expect.

It was a mystery. Cross-species viruses were vanishingly rare. *The* virus was perhaps the only one that could infect multiple races, if only because it created command and control structures within the victim's bloodstream rather than taking direct control of their brains and muscles. And yet, humanity had been aware of *that* danger ever since *The War of the Worlds*. Bioscanners had been in operation long before First Contact. Thomas found it hard to believe a more advanced race, one with awareness of other civilisations, had been so careless. Perhaps they'd believed their immune systems were superior. God knew there'd been humans who'd believed themselves intrinsically superior to their fellow humans. The idiots had rarely managed to grow out of it before reality slapped them in the face. And yet...

Too many people forgot the truth about the world, Thomas thought. The world was red in tooth and claw and utterly merciless to people who took it for granted. *And that bit us on the backside time and time again.*

"Captain," Commander Donker said. "The marine platoon is returning to the ship. Their CO requests permission to skip decontamination, on the grounds they were already decontaminated on the research vessel."

Thomas considered it for a moment, then shook his head. It was probably overkill, but—in his experience—there was never enough kill. The virus was just too dangerous to take lightly. It might have been dying, but the dying could prove the most dangerous of foes. They already had nothing to lose. Thomas could envisage it packing itself down into a tiny mass, then clinging to a marine's suit—or inching its way into his air supply—until it had a chance to breed again. Maybe he was being paranoid. The combination of bioscanners, biofilters, blood tests and UV lights should be enough to keep the virus from getting a foothold. But he didn't want to take it for granted.

"They go through full decontamination," he said, flatly. "Have the missile tubes completed resupply?"

Commander Donker looked pained. "Yes, Captain," he said. "The logistics staff want to transfer additional supplies to the cargo holds."

"If we have the room, then go ahead," Thomas said. "Just remember we have guests aboard, too."

"Aye, Captain," Donker said.

Thomas looked back at the display, cursing under his breath. Resupplying while underway was dangerous at the best of times. It was a great deal harder when an enemy fleet was breathing down his neck. The freighter crews were dangerously exposed to enemy fire...if the enemy had the wit to realise it, taking out the freighters could make it impossible for the fleet to fight its way through the coming ambush. And that would mean…

You knew the job was dangerous when you took it, he thought, dryly. He'd argued against the plan, but there was no point in arguing anymore. *We have to get home fast or we'll be ground down and destroyed.*

• • •

"You know," Davies said. "I'm starting to think Captain Hammond hates us. Did someone sleep with his wife or something?"

Colin shot him a sharp look as they made their way into the decontamination chamber and undressed under the harsh UV lights. There was little privacy on a warship, outside the privacy tubes, but there was *no* privacy whatsoever in the chamber. The entire section was so closely monitored that a fly couldn't pass wind without being noticed. Davies would be in deep shit if someone reported his comment to the major, let alone the captain. Colin was as annoyed as the rest of the platoon, but he understood the danger all too well. The virus could not be allowed to infect the ship.

He felt an odd little chill run down his spine as Kevin walked past. The alien was just…alien. His body bent in all the wrong places. Looking at him made Colin feel as though something was fundamentally wrong. It was hard to tell where to hit, if one wanted to take the alien down quickly. Vesy were apparently less vulnerable to groin attacks. Colin rolled his eyes at the thought. It wasn't something anyone wanted to think about. The idea of aliens who could cross-breed with humans had been absurd long before humanity had encountered *real* aliens.

The decontamination process was as uncomfortable as ever. Colin kept his mouth firmly closed as foul-smelling liquid splashed down around them, leaving him feeling as if his skin had been thoroughly scrubbed by a wire brush. The light seemed to grow brighter and brighter as they moved into the next compartment, where their blood and hair were sampled repeatedly. Colin heard two of his mates grumbling under their breaths and snorted inwardly, trying not to admit he wanted to agree. The process was extreme, to say the least. But the danger was equally so.

It could be worse, he thought. The xenospecialists hadn't been bothered. Colin had been impressed until he'd discovered that intensive decontamination procedures were part of their job. They'd even told him that had been true well before they'd encountered *the* virus. *We could be doing this every day.*

He stepped through the final hatch into a changing room, breathing a sigh of relief when he saw the pile of clothes on the far side. The basic shipsuits were hardly BDUs, but they were better than nothing. Besides, they'd provide a little protection when—if—the ship was holed. He checked the mask automatically, then waited for the rest of the team. They'd already filed their reports while they'd been on the research ship, but—if he was any judge—his superiors would have questions. The significance of what they'd found wouldn't have been lost on any of them.

And yet, there's nothing I can tell them that wasn't in the reports, he thought. The idea he could just *look* at a piece of alien technology and determine what it did—and how it worked—was absurd. *We don't even know what we found.*

A dull quiver ran through the battlecruiser as she picked up speed. Colin stepped into the corridor and keyed the nearest terminal, trying to pull up a status report. The fleet was accelerating, leaving the planet behind. Colin shivered, despite himself. The planet had looked ghastly, even before the orbital bombardment had *really* started. It would be decades, perhaps centuries, before the planet could be settled, if indeed it ever could be. Colin knew retired military personnel could practically write their own tickets, if they agreed to settle newly-colonised worlds, but he wouldn't settle *that* world for anything. It wasn't even clear the biosphere would survive. The combination of dying viral matter and bombardment might kill the entire world. Perhaps that wasn't a bad thing. The world could never be fully trusted, not ever. The virus could easily go dormant and wait.

He glanced back into the changing room. "Come on," he said. "It won't get any easier."

Kevin joined him, looking tired. Or Colin thought he looked tired. The drooping feathers were meant to signify tiredness, but…it was hard to read the alien body language. Colin had tried to draw Kevin out, to talk to him as more than just NCO to ranker, yet…Colin shook his head. They had very little in common beyond the marines. Human jokes—the funny and the puerile alike—meant nothing to the Vesy. Colin had asked Kevin to tell him a joke, something his people would find funny, but Kevin hadn't been able to answer him. It was difficult to believe the Vesy didn't have a sense of humour…

They are completely at our mercy and they know it, Colin thought, as they made their way back to Marine Country. Dozens of crewmen rushed past them, transferring weapons and supplies from the shuttles to the hold. *They don't want to offend us.*

He shook his head at the thought. The Vesy jokes probably meant nothing to human ears. It was hard to explain human jokes to them, not without stripping out the humour. They depended on cultural and stereotypical references the aliens simply lacked. And even when they were explained, they were still meaningless. He rubbed his forehead as they stepped through the hatch. It would be a great deal harder with his fellow humans. Familiarity would make it harder to believe there might be differences, at least until it was too late.

Sergeant Bowman met them inside the hatch. "I hear you had an exciting time down there?"

"No, Sarge," Colin said. "We were on duty."

Bowman snorted. "You can probably put in a claim for a share of salvage rights," he said, dryly. "Just remember to remember me in your will."

Colin laughed. "Sure," he said. "I'll write a note right now. I remember Sergeant Bowman."

The sergeant grinned. Kevin looked unsure of himself. Colin sobered as he remembered his earlier thoughts. The joke wasn't funny unless one understood the context. Hell, the joke lost a lot of its humour if one assumed the sergeant was *serious*…

He frowned. "Can we really put in a claim?"

"You should be able to," Bowman said. "But it may be some time before they work out how much you deserve."

"A kick up the backside, probably," Colin said. "What we found is either worthless or priceless."

"They'll put a price on it," Bowman said. "They can put a price on anything, these days."

. . .

Susan would almost have preferred it if the alien ships had been launching starfighters and closing the range as much as possible. An enemy who was giving her all the time in the world to prepare to meet the offensive, an offensive everyone knew was coming, was being suspiciously accommodating. She studied the display, wondering if there was an enemy fleet waiting for her in the next system. It wouldn't be *that* hard to set up an ambush, using the flicker network. *Unicorn's* survey had found no trace of enemy presence, but that was meaningless. A star system was big enough to conceal every starship in human service and still have room for a Death Star or two.

Her lips twitched at the thought, before she dismissed it with a flash of annoyance. There were only two tramlines in the next system. They *had* to pass through them if they wanted to get home. She briefly contemplated reversing course and doubling back, perhaps hiding under cloak in a desperate bid to avoid contact, but she knew it wasn't likely to work. They wouldn't have anything like enough time to get organised, let alone evade the enemy starships long enough to break contact completely. She was all too aware they hadn't killed *every* last enemy facility within the system. The cloudscoops, shipyards and industrial nodes might have been smashed beyond repair, and the planet itself was dying, but the remainder of the enemy presence remained intact. It would die on the vine, given time. It would still survive long enough to tattle on her to marauding starships.

"Admiral," Richardson said. "The scouts are preparing to transit."

"Order them to report back as soon as possible," Susan said. They were going to have to evade the enemy ships long enough to reach the next tramline, yet…a least-time course would be completely predictable. She just didn't have the time to be clever. "And ready the fleet for transit."

Her eyes returned to the display. The enemy fleet wasn't making any attempt to slow her down. It was what *she* would have done, particularly if she was trying to buy time. The enemy fleet could have harried her ships, without closing the range to the point she could crush it. And that suggested it knew something she didn't. There had to be another fleet, forming somewhere ahead of her.

She studied the starchart for a long, chilling moment. The tramline projections were supposed to be complete, although no one knew for sure. It hadn't been *that* long since humanity had realised the early projections were wrong because alien-grade tramlines had less of a gravimetric presence. The survey ships had been updating starcharts for years, including scouting within enemy territory, but…she shook her head. They didn't have time to conduct their own surveys. She'd have to risk it.

"They'll know where we're going," she mused. "Perhaps we can take advantage of that."

Richardson looked up. "Admiral?"

Susan rotated the starchart. "When we make the second transit, the least-time course for New Washington would run through Tramline Two, right?"

"Yes, Admiral," Richardson said. He'd accepted the role of sounding board—and devil's advocate—when they'd started to work together. "That would cut several weeks off the voyage."

"But we could still get home if we went through Tramline Three," Susan mused. "It'll just take a little longer."

"A couple of extra weeks, Admiral," Richardson confirmed. "It would depend on our speed."

"And what we encountered along the way," Susan agreed. The tramlines were relatively easy to predict, but everything else…? She shook her head. They were so far from the Human Sphere that no one had so much as looked at the alien stars through telescopes. Shipboard sensors just didn't have the resolution to pick out planets, let alone starships. "We could feint towards Tramline Two, then head directly to Tramline Three…"

She frowned. It depended on unknown unknowns. How many enemy ships were waiting for them in the third system? How many of them would be in position to watch as the human ships made transit? And how many of them would be close enough to notice a fleet of drones being deployed to create the impression the fleet was heading straight for Tramline Two?

Her fingers danced across the console, tapping orders into the system. *Unicorn* could operate independently, if necessary. Captain Campbell and his crew could loop through Tramline Two, passing through three other systems before they linked up with the fleet again or made their own way home. Susan disliked the idea of splitting her fleet any further—she'd already detached too many survey ships—but she knew the fleet needed hard data. They had to know as much as possible about the enemy interior, if they wanted to resume the offensive. The virus would find it a great deal harder to move or conceal industrial bases and shipyards. The navy would move to destroy them as soon as they knew the industrial nodes were there.

"Get me Captain Campbell," she ordered, putting her doubts aside. "I have specific orders for him."

"Aye, Admiral."

CHAPTER TWENTY-SEVEN

THERE WAS NOTHING MORE DEPRESSING, Mitch had often felt, than a barren and desolate star system. It was the second time *Unicorn* had transited into the system and it hadn't improved. If there was any alien presence within the system, it was keeping its head down and trying not to be noticed. Mitch eyed the console, wondering if there were unseen eyes close enough to track the fleet. It was quite possible. The fleet's stealth systems weren't powerful enough to conceal it while maintaining flank speed. And they didn't want to risk activating the cloaking devices just yet.

He leaned back in his command chair and mulled over the orders he'd been given. He wasn't blind to how much trust the admiral had placed in him, although she'd been honest enough to admit the scheme had only a fifty-fifty chance of working. It depended on too many factors that couldn't be easily controlled. If the enemy had a starship close enough to watch as they transited the next tramline, the entire scheme would be worse than useless. He forced himself to wait as the remainder of the fleet entered the system, sensors sweeping for stealthed or cloaked ships. They found nothing. He knew, all too well, that proved nothing.

"Captain," Staci said. "The fleet is setting course for the tramline."

"Good," Mitch said. The transit would take seven hours, assuming none of the starships lost a drive node or two. Warships were designed to keep going, even if they took a great deal of damage, but freighters were much more vulnerable. "Are the drones ready to deploy?"

"Yes, Captain," Staci said. "The decoy emissions are already programmed into their cores."

Mitch nodded as he studied the display. He would have preferred to have two or three other ships accompanying *Unicorn*, even if that meant being under someone else's command, but the admiral couldn't spare any more ships. *Unicorn* was expendable. The admiral had warned him to be ready to make the trip back home himself, if he lost contact with the rest of the fleet. He didn't want to abandon his comrades, but he knew he might not be able to link up with them again. He tried not to consider the possibility that *Unicorn* might be the only ship that made it home.

The display sparkled with red icons. Mitch leaned forward. The enemy fleet was making transit, moving with an unhurried pace that suggested it knew the human fleet was heading straight into a trap. Mitch hoped the admiral was right about where that ambush might be, although a cursory glance at the starchart had suggested several other possibilities. Hell, they might be intercepted in *this* system. The only thing that argued against it was the simple lack of starfighter attacks. The virus seemed more interested in maintaining contact, in making sure it knew where the fleet was, than in bringing it to battle.

He stood. "You have the bridge," he said, formally. "Inform me if anything changes."

Staci took the command chair. "Aye, sir."

"And get some rest yourself," Mitch added. "We both need our sleep."

He allowed himself a flicker of amusement at the hypocrisy as he walked from deck to deck, touring the ship. The crew looked ready for anything, although some of them looked tired and worn. *Unicorn* didn't have enough crew to ensure that *everyone* was well-rested at all times...Mitch directed some of the crew to catch up on their sleep, so they'd be ready when they made the second transit. It was quite possible the alarm would yank them from their bunks, leaving them feeling worse, but...Mitch shook his head.

The last thing he wanted or needed was the crew abusing stimulants. He'd be completely understanding, if he caught a crewman drugging himself, but that wouldn't stop him from arranging a dishonourable discharge for that unwitting crewman. He just couldn't take the risk of someone opening fire on something that wasn't there.

Perhaps a bigger ship would have an easier time of it, he mused. *But how could her captain know every inch of her?*

He smiled at the thought as he returned to his cabin and checked his inbox. There weren't many messages, all of them routine fleet business that was—somehow—still carrying on in the midst of a battle. He felt a pang of...*something*...at the absence of anything more personal, then brought up the message from Charlotte and watched it again before heading for his bunk. Common sense told him he should delete the message, before someone else saw it, but he couldn't bring himself to do so. It would be like erasing something that had been placed in his trust.

You're being silly, he told himself. *Do you think you mean anything to her?*

Mitch turned off the light, then closed his eyes and tried to sleep. It wasn't easy. He'd long since grown used to snatching what sleep he could, even with an enemy fleet bearing down on him, but this time...he tossed and turned, trying to clear his head long enough to go to sleep. His dreams were strange, flickering images that refused to remain in his mind when the alarm rang. He practically hurled himself out of bed, his head spinning as he looked at the display. It was clear.

He keyed the terminal. "Report!"

"We are one hour from the tramline," Staci said. She sounded refreshed. "The drones are updated and ready to deploy."

Mitch frowned. He hoped Staci had rested, but she couldn't have slept any longer than he had. Hell, she wouldn't have abandoned the bridge in a hurry. Command experience was not to be sniffed at, not when she was in line for a promotion to captain herself. He made a mental note to insist she got more rest once they were through the tramline, then poured himself a mug of coffee and drank it. There weren't any stewards on *Unicorn*!

Having his own coffee pot in his cabin was as close as he'd get to having a servant, unless he was kicked upstairs to a capital ship. Or flag rank... he shook his head. *That* was a terrible thought. He would no longer be in command of his own ship.

He finished his coffee, splashed water on his face and returned to the bridge. The tactical display looked unchanged. The enemy fleet was still keeping its distance, close enough to the human ships to maintain contact while remaining far enough to ensure it could evade the fleet if it turned and tried to bring the alien ships to battle. Mitch was fairly sure that wasn't good news. The virus might be concerned about losing more ships, but if it was biding its time...

"The fleet will make transit in twenty minutes," Staci reported. "Their cloaking devices are already powered up, ready to go online."

Mitch nodded. The timing wouldn't be a major headache, unless the virus had a starship close enough to monitor the transit. There was no way to be sure. If the timing worked, the fleet would go into cloak while the drones headed to the next tramline...hopefully, leading the enemy fleet in the wrong direction. Mitch wasn't sure how long they could keep up the deception, or how the enemy would react when it discovered the truth, but it didn't matter as long as it bought them some time. The admiral needed time to make her escape.

"Take us through the tramline as planned, then deploy drones," Mitch ordered. "Fuzz our emissions as much as possible."

He tensed as the tramline grew nearer and nearer. If there *was* something on the far side, *Unicorn* was going to fly straight into their fire. A thought crossed his mind as they readied themselves for the transit. It might be possible to spring an ambush...if not now, then later, when they linked back up with the fleet. The countdown began, ticking down to zero. Mitch's stomach lurched as they transited, the display blanking and rebooting with commendable speed. There were no incoming missiles, just...empty space.

"Activate the drones," Mitch ordered. "Fuzz everything."

"Aye, Captain," Staci said.

Mitch leaned forward as more and more data flowed into the display. The system had five planets—unless there were more on the other side of the primary—but there didn't seem to be much settlement. The rocky worlds could have been terraformed, and biological packages introduced, yet the virus didn't seem to have bothered. Mitch didn't understand it. The only industrial presence in the system was a pair of cloudscoops, orbiting the gas giant. A fuelling station? It was possible, but odd. There hadn't been any need for the station, at least not until the previous system had been devastated. Perhaps the virus had just thought it was building a great deal of redundancy into the system.

"The fleet is making transit," Staci said. "They're cloaking...now."

Mitch nodded. The drones *should* look like starships—like the entire fleet—if the enemy hadn't been watching carefully. The sensor fuzz should have made it hard for the virus to spot the switch, but its mere presence should have warned any watching eyes to be careful. Why would anyone bother, unless they had had something to hide?

"Bring us about, then set course to the tramline," he ordered. "Make sure the drones follow us."

"Aye, Captain," Staci said. She grinned. "Do you think they'll follow us right through the transit?"

"Good question," Mitch said. He grinned back. "A pity we can't count on it."

He leaned forward as the cloaked fleet—the *real* fleet—departed, heading towards the other tramline. There wasn't much time before the enemy fleet arrived, although it would have to think carefully before making transit. Standard tactical doctrine—and there was no evidence the virus thought differently—insisted one shouldn't follow an enemy fleet through the tramline. Not too closely, at least. There was too great a risk of being caught with one's pants down, with sensors and weapons offline as the enemy reversed course and pounded your hulls at point-blank range. Mitch would have urged an ambush if he'd thought the scheme workable. In theory, it was. In practice, it only worked if one had a friendly scriptwriter.

Someone tried it at the academy, hoping it was such a dumb concept no one would expect it, he recalled. *It didn't work.*

His lips twitched at the memory—the instructor had been particularly sarcastic—then thinned as the enemy fleet began to make transit. The virus had pushed its luck to the limit, balancing the desperate need to get through the tramline with the grim awareness the human ships might be lying in wait. Mitch had to admit it had done well. It had come through close enough to track the fleet—or the decoy drones—without running straight into a wall of fire. And it was taking its time, too. The fleet was coming through piece by piece. It clearly didn't intend to rush straight into the fire.

"Keep us on course," he ordered, quietly. "Let them get our scent."

"Aye, Captain," Staci said.

Mitch studied the display, silently calculating the vectors. The enemy ships *could*—in theory—run the drones down. *Unicorn* could break contact, at the cost of losing the drones and revealing the deception ahead of time. And yet...he felt his heart start to race as the alien fleet assembled before it started to advance. Had it seen through the deception already? Had it realised it had been conned? Or was it biding its time, allowing the human ships to fly straight into an ambush? There was no way to tell. The system might not be as empty as it looked. There could be *anything* between the decoy fleet and the tramline, lying in wait for them.

"Captain," Lieutenant Hannah Avis said. "The enemy fleet is starting to move. It's coming after us."

"Oh, what a pity," Staci said, with a deadpan look on her face.

Mitch snorted. It was good news, but still...millions upon millions of tonnage bearing down on a single frigate—and a fleet of ghosts—didn't really *feel* like good news. How long would it be before the virus realised it had been fooled? The deception wouldn't last, once they ran into the enemy fleet. Even a complete idiot wouldn't miss the simple fact that the ships weren't returning fire. They were drones. They *couldn't.*

"Hold us on course," he ordered. The *real* fleet was heading away from them, so sharply that the icons on the display were nothing more than guesswork. By the time the enemy realised they'd been had, the admiral and her ships should have broken contact completely. "And deploy two additional sensor drones. If there's something waiting for us, I want to know about it first."

"Aye, Captain."

Mitch forced himself to relax as the two fleets—the ghosts and the real ships—crawled towards the tramline. The enemy thought they were outgunned, but…he was still a little surprised they hadn't tried to close the range. There was just no way to know what they were thinking. They didn't seem to have a brainship with them, but mounting antishipping strikes didn't require one. The more he thought about it, the more he recalled being forced to go shooting on Captain Hammond's estate. The game-beaters had driven the pheasants towards the shooters, providing all the targets they could possibly want. It hadn't struck Mitch as funny at the time—drugging the poor birds would have been kinder—and it was even less funny now. He had the nasty feeling *he* was the one being driven towards the shooter.

At least the rest of the fleet is safe, he thought. There was no way to be sure they'd get through the tramline without revealing the deception, but the enemy would be badly out of position once they realised they'd been conned. *They'll have plenty of time to make their escape.*

He sent Staci off for a quick nap, then waited—grimly—as the hours ticked by. The enemy fleet kept its distance, not even trying to close the range as they neared the tramline. Mitch ordered the ghostly fleet to alter course, randomising the precise location they'd pass through the tramline. The enemy fleet started to accelerate, too late. Mitch breathed a sigh of relief, then started to snap orders. There was only one thing that could have convinced the enemy to speed up, now. They'd been flying straight into an ambush.

"Fuzz the drones again," he ordered. They were too far from the remainder of the fleet to be sure they could signal it…and, of course, the virus might start wondering who he'd been signalling. "And then take us through the tramline."

The display blanked, then rebooted. A cluster of red icons held station on the tramline, far too close for comfort. Mitch allowed himself a grin, even though the enemy fleet was already turning towards them. The admiral would have been in deep shit if she'd flown straight into their welcoming eyes. He had to admit the virus had very nearly pulled off an unprecedented ambush. And it might just have worked if the admiral hadn't seen it coming.

"Alter course, then redeploy the drones," he ordered, tracing a line on the display. They might just have enough time to put some distance between them before it was too late. If they were really lucky, they might convince the virus the fleet had cloaked. Better that than the virus realising the fleet hadn't existed at all. "And prepare to deactivate the drones on command."

"Aye, Captain."

Staci rejoined them as the ship—and the drones—picked up speed. The alien carriers were launching starfighters, but the ghostly fleet was right on the edge of their effective range. Or were they? The virus might see value in expending the fighters, as long as they kept contact with the fleet. Mitch cursed under his breath. They'd suddenly run out of time. The deception couldn't be sustained for much longer, if at all.

"Deactivate the drones and trigger their destruct cycles, then take us into cloak," he ordered, calmly. The Admiralty would reassign him to an asteroid mining station in the middle of nowhere if he allowed a drone to fall into enemy hands. The decoys were designed to be difficult to open, without the proper codes, but there was no way to be sure. "And then set course for the next tramline."

"Aye, Captain," Staci said. "Drones deactivated...now."

Mitch grinned. The virus was going to be in a real mess. If it thought the fleet had cloaked, it was going to waste a lot of time searching for it. Even if it realised the truth, it was going to have to relocate the *real* fleet or...or what? He didn't know. His ship quivered as she accelerated, speeding away from the alien position. It was unlikely anything would get in their way, he thought. They could carry out a series of brief surveys as they passed through the enemy systems, noting targets for later destruction.

The admiral would be pleased…and, even if they didn't make it back to the fleet, they could take their information all the way back to Earth. And who knew? They might come across targets they could destroy.

"They're blundering," Hannah commented. "They don't know what happened to the fleet."

"They may not want to admit they were fooled," Mitch said. He'd met humans who allowed themselves to be tricked time and time again because they didn't want to admit—even to themselves—what had happened. "Or they simply haven't realised what we've done."

He leaned back in his chair. "And now we've lured them away, we can proceed as planned."

CHAPTER TWENTY-EIGHT

"LONG-RANGE SENSORS ARE CLEAR, CAPTAIN," Sibley said. "We appear to have broken contact."

Thomas nodded, curtly. They'd jumped through the tramline into another uninhabited—as far as they could tell—system. The enemy ships hadn't returned in time to track them down, suggesting they were still chasing *Unicorn* and her escort of decoys. Thomas had to smile at the thought, although it wasn't funny. That much firepower would atomise the frigate if the virus realised what had happened, if she didn't manage to break contact in time. Captain Campbell had a remarkable talent for getting on Thomas's nerves, but that didn't mean he deserved to die.

"Good," he said. He glanced at the fleet status display. The admiral was ordering them to maintain course and speed, hidden under the cloak. If they were lucky, they could remain undetected until they reached the war front...or, more likely, they encountered a target worth attacking. Thomas would have liked to believe they'd given the virus a black eye, and perhaps destroyed its ability to make war, but that was wishful thinking. "Hold us in formation."

"Aye, Captain."

Thomas sighed, inwardly. It was going to be a long time before they reached the next tramline, let alone made it back to safety. The fleet was still undergoing repairs—the endless series of alerts and updates suggested the Chinese personnel would be shuttled to another ship soon enough—but some of the ships needed a shipyard. He wondered, morbidly, what he would do if he was ordered to abandon and scuttle his command. Obey orders? Or beg for permission to try to sneak home? It wasn't as if he'd get another command. Given his age, and social rank, it was far more likely he'd be promoted, even if he didn't want it. His experience was valuable, he'd be told; it was important that he shared it with up-and-coming officers who needed to learn from his mistakes, before they went off and started making their own. Thomas was morbidly sure they would. God knew he'd made quite enough mistakes, too.

"I'll be in my ready room," he said, standing. "Commander Donker, you have the bridge."

"Aye, Captain."

• • •

The porno movies, Tobias reflected sourly, hadn't been a very accurate depiction of real life at all. They hadn't shown just how hard it was to fit two people into a washroom, let alone have a quickie without one or both of the participants developing a cramp or otherwise embarrassing themselves. He had no idea how Stellar Star had managed to have sex in an even smaller compartment, unless it had been dimensionally transcendent or *something*. Just getting inside and lowering their pants had been quite hard enough.

He groaned as he slipped out of the washroom and back to the bunk. Marigold needed to wash first, just in case the alarm sounded again. The privacy tubes had been closed and locked ever since the fleet had begun to move, even though they were needed. Tobias knew he should be relieved they'd made it out of the system, but as time started to tick by…he shook his head in annoyance. They could be attacked at any moment. It wasn't as if they could wait until they got back home. There was no way to be sure they *would* get back home.

His back cramped. He bit off a curse, hoping he hadn't damaged himself badly enough to need a doctor. Bagehot would laugh his arse off, before screaming at them both for fucking around—literally—in the face of the enemy. Tobias groaned at the thought. It was sheer goddamned luck no one had said anything about their hasty emergence from the privacy tubes, when they'd sat in their gunboat for hours without being actually launched. He scowled in frustration. If only they'd dared to do it there…

Don't be a fool, he told himself. *You'd get in real trouble if you were caught fucking in a gunboat.*

He rubbed his eyes, tiredly. It had been five days since they'd broken contact with the enemy fleet, but it felt like the virus was still breathing down their necks. The admiral had insisted on maintaining full stealth protocols, powering down everything that wasn't strictly necessary even though the cloaking device should have been able to compensate. Tobias didn't blame her. They'd passed through two systems, both of which had been effectively uninhabited. The slightest hint of radiation—even something as tiny as a radio beacon—might lead the enemy to the fleet. Tobias would have been glad of the break, if it hadn't left the gunboat pilots with little to do. He was fairly sure he and Marigold weren't the only ones who'd partnered up. It wasn't as if there was anything else to do.

Exercise, he thought. There were things he could do, but he didn't want to do them. He was meant to study textbooks, in preparation for *something*, yet…he shook his head. It seemed pointless. If they got back to New Washington, he could study on the way to Earth. *Or even go see Colin.*

The thought comforted him more than he'd expected, although he knew he couldn't actually go. The marines were training too, readying themselves to board an enemy ship or repel an enemy boarding party. Tobias wondered, idly, who'd they'd gotten to help them. The gunboat pilots had other concerns right now. They might have to launch at any moment.

Marigold stepped out of the shower, a towel wrapped around her. Tobias had no time to stare. He had to wash before something—anything—happened. He smiled, blew her a kiss and hurried past her into the washroom.

There'd been no hope of taking a shower together. The compartment was barely large enough for a grown man. He was glad he'd lost weight over the past six months. He'd seen men fat enough to get stuck if they tried to use the shower.

And they wouldn't have a hope of getting into a gunboat, Tobias thought, as he stripped and turned the water on. *They'd be stuck on Earth.*

He frowned as he washed quickly, not daring to stay under the water for more than five minutes. He hadn't expected to join the navy. He'd worked desperately to earn one of the coveted university slots, in hopes it would keep him out of the military. God knew there was no way he'd get into a decent billet, when he was conscripted. He'd thought he'd be lucky if he didn't find himself digging ditches for his National Service. It had never crossed his mind the navy might want him, that it might have a role for him...and that it would turn his life around.

Someone banged on the hatch. "Are you decent in there?"

"Just coming out," he called back. He intended to turn a blind eye if any of the other pilots wanted to use the washroom for a quickie. They'd hopefully do the same for him. "Give me a moment."

He shook his head. No, it wasn't where he'd expected to find himself. Yes, the thought of being blown to bits still scared him. And yet...he was glad he'd accepted the offer. He wouldn't have met Marigold, not in real life, if he hadn't joined the navy. She made a great many things worthwhile.

And when we get home, we can go somewhere nice, he thought. They'd have more money in the bank, when they returned to Earth. It wasn't as if they had to spend anything while they were on active duty. *Somewhere where it will be just the two of us.*

• • •

Susan could *feel* the tension pulsing through the immense battleship, even though it had been over a week since they'd sighted the enemy. The crew might have been happier if they'd known where the enemy was, even if the enemy happened to be bearing down on them with enough ships to crush

FIGHTING FOR THE CROWN

them effortlessly. Susan had to admit she would be happier, too, if she knew what the enemy was doing. How much time had they wasted, trying to track *Unicorn* and her ghostly fleet? It was hard to believe they were still fooled. The drones simply wouldn't have lasted long, even if the ghosts had maintained their distance from the enemy fleet. Susan's best-case estimate, which she admitted—privately—was almost insanely optimistic, was that the drones would have started to fail five days ago. The virus would know it had been conned.

She sat in her office, looking at the starchart without actually seeing it. They'd gone through the details time and time again, hashing out the plan—and a series of contingencies—until they were practically dreaming of the coming struggles. She was almost sick of looking at a chart she'd memorised, a chart that was useful and yet not useful enough. There was no way to know what was waiting for them, no way to be sure there wasn't an entire enemy fleet in their path. She hadn't dared order the fleet to take the time to search for the flicker stations and destroy them. The virus would have known *something* had happened to the stations, even if it hadn't known precisely *what*. It wouldn't have found it hard to guess, she reflected. It might well have assumed she'd detached ships from the fleet even if it *hadn't* realised it had been had.

And we're taking the long road home, she mused. She was a little disappointed the fleet hadn't encountered any major enemy worlds. *We might be accidentally evading their fortifications...*

The intercom bleeped. "Admiral, Doctor Simpson is requesting permission to speak with you," Richardson said. "Should I put him through?"

Susan glanced at the near-space display. It was blank. The next tramline was slowly coming into view, suggesting the fleet would begin transit—again—in less than an hour. She had time to speak to the xenospecialist, even though she doubted he had anything useful to say. The last report had been completely uninformative. She'd schooled herself to accept they might not learn anything useful from the mystery artefacts.

"Put him through," she ordered.

CHRISTOPHER G. NUTTALL

Doctor Simpson materialised in front of her, wearing a civilian tunic rather than a shipsuit. Susan's eyes narrowed in disapproval. The research ship—a modified survey cruiser—might be fast, but she wasn't fast enough to escape the enemy if they caught her with her drives offline. The doctor should wear a shipsuit at all times, even if he was in his bunk. Better to put up with some mild annoyance than get killed if someone blew a hole in the hull.

And if someone had to vent the ship to kill an infection, she thought. She'd have to raise the issue with the ship's commanding officer. *He wouldn't have time to get dressed before it was too late.*

She pushed her annoyance aside. "Doctor," she said. "Have you made any progress?"

"We believe so," Doctor Simpson said. "We're still nowhere near understanding how the alien tech actually works, but we're getting a sense of what it can *do*."

"Interesting," Susan said, slowly. One didn't have to understand technology in order to use it. Human history made that all too clear. "What does it do?"

Doctor Simpson leaned forward. "We reviewed the records from the landing parties as well as the sensor drones and whatnot," he said. "The level of viral matter in the air was quite high when we first landed, even though it was either dead or dying. Its cohesion had been shattered beyond effective repair..."

"I am familiar with the BioBombs," Susan said, cutting him off. "What does this have to do with the alien tech?"

"The level of viral matter in the alien basement was actually quite low," Doctor Simpson explained. "It was actually live, at least until the hatch was opened and it was exposed to the contaminant outside. And yet, if the bioscanners were accurate, the viral matter was...effectively inert. It wasn't part of the planetary mind. The biological researchers think it was in a form of stasis."

Susan frowned. "And that had something to do with the alien tech?"

"We think so," Doctor Simpson said. He looked discomfited, just for a second. "I…we…feel slightly unsure of ourselves, when we look at the alien artefacts. We thought that it was sheer incomprehension, that there was at least fifty to a hundred years between their tech and ours. Or, perhaps, that the artefacts *are* alien, that they repel us on a very primal level. But this isn't true when we view them through sensors. It only affects us if we're in close proximity."

"I see." Susan stroked her chin thoughtfully. "It's not uncommon for people to find aliens disconcerting."

"Aliens," Doctor Simpson said. "Not alien tech, just aliens."

Susan wasn't so sure. Tadpole technology tended to look more than a little *odd* to human eyes. It was all too clear it had been designed and built by creatures that had a very different way of looking at the universe. The laws of physics didn't change—science worked as well for aliens as it did for humans—but viewpoints *did*. She doubted she'd ever be truly comfortable on an alien ship and suspected they felt the same way. They just weren't designed for humans.

"We believe the artefacts were designed, at least in part, to keep the virus away from the settlement," Doctor Simpson explained. "It may explain why the virus seemed content to ignore it."

"You believe the artefacts put the virus to sleep, whenever it gets too close to them," Susan said. "Are you sure?"

"No, Admiral," Doctor Simpson said. "We've run tests. There is a slight, a very slight, effect on the brainwaves of anyone who spends more than a few minutes next to the artefacts. It appears to be harmless—as far as we can tell, it doesn't actually do anything—but it is very definitely there. The viral particles, being a lot smaller than human brains, may be more strongly affected."

"Interesting," Susan mused. "How does this actually work?"

"We don't know," Doctor Simpson admitted. "There are some…neural weapons designed to interfere with brainwaves, for want of a better term, but they have detectable effects."

Susan's eyes narrowed. "You just told me you could detect an effect."

"I beg your pardon," Doctor Simpson said, with a frown. "I can detect the effect, but I can't detect what's actually *causing* the effect. The artefacts are doing something, we just don't know how."

"I see." Susan stared down at her hands. Radios worked, but humans couldn't detect radio waves. Not naturally. It required a radio set to pick up the messages…she looked up at the doctor, feeling a flash of paranoia. If the artefacts could cause flickers in someone's brainwaves, what *else* could they do? She didn't want to find out the hard way. "I assume you're taking all precautions?"

"Yes, Admiral," Doctor Simpson said. "The artefacts are isolated from the rest of the ship. The handlers who inspect them directly undergo full decontamination as they enter and leave the isolation sector…"

"Good," Susan said, when he'd finished. "I'll discuss the matter with my staff and get back to you."

She closed the connection, then muttered a curse under her breath. The fleet was approaching the next tramline. She didn't need more problems, not now. And yet, there was no way to be *sure* the artefacts didn't pose a threat. The virus had been content to ignore them…perhaps the planet-wide mind hadn't noticed a tiny fraction of its body had gone to sleep. Or…she wondered, suddenly, if they were a trap. Had they been meant to pick the artefacts up? Or…she shook her head. Anyone with the power to predict the future so perfectly wouldn't need to arse around playing games. They could have brushed humanity's navy aside and blown Earth to dust any time they liked.

The thought mocked her as the fleet drew closer and closer to the tramline, the scouts hopping ahead to make sure the coast was clear. The uncertainty gnawed at her. She thought she could trace a line from Sir Francis Drake and Lord Nelson to her command, but…in truth, neither of the two would really have understood her world. Even Sir Theodore Smith would have been astounded by *Vanguard*, *Invincible*, and *Lion*. They were light years ahead of the old *Ark Royal*.

Worry about it later, she told herself, as the scouts began to return. *Right now, we have other problems.*

The intercom bleeped. "Admiral," Richardson said. "The scouts have returned. They've located a major alien base."

Susan nodded as the sensor records were downloaded into her terminal. The alien world was nowhere near as intensely developed as the previous target, but...it wasn't an opportunity she could afford to turn down. There didn't seem to be many defending starships...she frowned, wondering where the ships had gone. They couldn't be the fleet they'd evaded unless they'd missed a whole string of tramlines. *That* fleet had seemed to come from behind them, unless they'd sneaked through the system...no, the timing didn't work out. And yet...if that were true, where were the defenders? The orbital fortresses weren't enough to protect an entire world.

She shook her head. There was no time to worry about it. The virus had to know, by now, that it had been conned. She couldn't risk giving it time to reinforce the defences, not here. She had to blow through the system and then make her escape, before it was too late.

Susan tapped her terminal. "Command conference, twenty minutes," she ordered. "We have an operation to plan."

CHAPTER TWENTY-NINE

TOBIAS HAD AN UNCOMFORTABLE SENSE of *déjà vu* as the gunboats hurtled towards their targets on a ballistic trajectory, exactly the same tactic they'd used during the previous battle. The planet ahead of them was neither as heavily industrialised or defended as the last target, but it was wrapped in a glowing haze of active sensor emissions. The virus might not know the fleet had entered the system—it wasn't clear if they'd managed to evade the enemy fleet—but it clearly wasn't taking anything for granted. Tobias was all too aware they were going to be detected quite some time before they entered missile range.

He scowled as he peered down at his console. The missiles were flying beside the gunboats, passively waiting for orders. It struck him, not for the first time, that the Royal Navy considered the gunboats completely expendable, perhaps even more so than the unmanned missiles. Their targeting sensors, which would be used to point the missiles at their final destinations, would draw fire to *them*, rather than the missiles themselves. Tobias knew the odds—it wasn't as if the navy had tried to lie to the gunboat pilots—but it still bothered him more than he wanted to say. He knew, deep inside, that he wasn't very brave.

"The sensor emissions are getting stronger," he said. The virus would spot them soon, if it hadn't already. It could have caught a sniff of the gunboats and artfully avoided doing a sensor focus, ensuring the gunboats didn't realise they'd been detected. "They may have us already."

"We should see it if they launch starfighters," Marigold reminded him. "They'd have to launch them openly if they wanted to catch us."

Tobias nodded. Starfighters were designed for ballistic launches—he'd seen it done—but they wouldn't be able to move at speed until they brought up their drives. He glanced at the overall display, calculating the odds. The enemy would have had to have seen them a *long* time ago if it wanted to get starfighters into position to ambush them, unless they'd come up with something completely new. He frowned as his sensors picked up more and more industrial activity. The virus could have used shuttles to tow the starfighters into position, then leave them lying doggo until the gunboats came within range. It would have required an extreme dose of paranoia, but the virus had already lost a major industrial node. Tobias didn't care how many dozens—perhaps hundreds—of such worlds the virus possessed. Losing the planet's industrial base *had* to hurt.

Red light washed across the display. "Fuck," Tobias swore, as enemy sensors focused on the gunboats. "They have us!"

A quiver ran through the gunboat as Marigold flash-woke the drives. "Bring the sensors online," she snapped. There was no point in trying to hide now. Red icons flared around the enemy positions as they launched wave after wave of starfighters. "Pick your targets now!"

"On it." Tobias worked his console. The virus might have realised the gunboats were escorting missiles, but it would still have to find them... not an easy task, when the missiles were tiny on an interplanetary scale. They weren't designed for stealth, not exactly, but as long as they didn't bring up their drives they were relatively safe until they got a great deal closer. "Targeting...now."

He smiled, grimly, as the display rapidly narrowed. The enemy orbital industry had the same weaknesses as the previous world, with a handful of installations that couldn't be replaced in a hurry...if, indeed, at all. Once they were taken out, the world would be a great deal less useful to the virus.

And, beyond the world…there were no orbital towers or elevators this time, but the BioBombs would still do a great deal of damage. Tobias remembered the images from the last world and smiled again. This planet was just as thoroughly infected with the virus. And the infection was doomed.

The red icons swooped closer. Tobias gritted his teeth as he forwarded the targeting data to the missiles. They should be able to reach their targets alone, going live only a few moments before they actually struck home. It was never easy to maintain the balance between speed and stealth, between the need to get into striking range without being detected and the need strike their targets before anyone could react and start shooting them down. The missiles were programmed to deploy sensor decoys the moment they were detected, but it would probably be too late. They'd be so close to their targets that the enemy point defence could fill space with plasma bursts. A single hit would be quite enough to take out the missile.

"Here they come," he said. The gunboats linked together into a single entity, their point defence readying itself for the duel. "Prepare to reverse course."

"Two minutes," Marigold said. "Let them come after us first."

Tobias nodded, sweat beading on his back. He understood the logic—they had to lure the starfighters onto the gunboats, in hopes of keeping them away from the missiles—but he didn't like it. The gunboats were supposed to be tougher than the average starfighter, according to the techs, yet a single plasma bolt in the wrong place would be enough to disable or destroy them. They'd practiced emergency escape procedures, but he was all too aware that they might not have *time* to grab their survival packs and jump. The gunboats were too big for proper ejector seats…

The enemy starfighters swooped down on them, their plasma guns already firing madly. Tobias watched, knowing the engagement was already out of his hands. The gunboat datanet was the only thing that could spot opportunities and make use of them, snapping off a shot in less time than it took a human to notice the opportunity was there. The lower half of the display filled with tactical notes, the computers assessing enemy patterns and trying to predict them. They weren't that good. The virus might not think along the same lines as its human foes, but it understood the virtue of randomness. A pilot who flew a predictable flight path was a dead pilot.

He smiled, despite everything, as four enemy starfighters vanished. The host bodies were dead...he wondered, suddenly, if they'd ever been alive at all. It was impossible to imagine sharing his body with an intelligent virus. There'd been a lot of jokes about the concept, when humanity had first realised the truth. The jokes had grown steadily less amusing as the virus ground its way towards Earth. Tobias couldn't help thinking that they were doing the host bodies a favour. They didn't deserve to live as nothing more than hosts for a virus...

"Reversing course...now," Marigold said. The compensator field shivered, just slightly, as the gunboat spun around. It wasn't anything like as manoeuvrable as a starfighter, but it made up for that by bristling with point defence weapons. There were no blind spots that would allow an enemy a clear shot at the hull. "The starfighters should be on their way."

Tobias nodded. The fleet had launched starfighters the moment the enemy sensors had picked up the gunboats, but they were still quite some distance from the planet. It would be quite some time before they reached the gunboats...not long at all, in an objective sense, but quite long enough for him. The enemy starfighters redoubled their efforts, even as the enemy commander—he guessed it was the planet itself—unleashed its remaining defenders. A wall of shuttles and starfighters emerged from the planet and rocketed towards the gunboats.

Marigold let out a sound that was half-laugh, half-gasp. "All that for us?"

"And the fleet," Tobias said. The virus couldn't be in any doubt about the fleet's presence *now*. The starfighters weren't even trying to hide. It wouldn't require a genius to deduce there were at least five carriers lurking in interplanetary space...and, if there were carriers, there were probably battleships and cruisers, too. The days when carriers had mounted raids on their own, or with only a handful of escorts, were over. "They're trying to keep them away from the planet."

He glanced at the missile status display. They had to hold out for a few more seconds, just long enough to let the starfighters and shuttles roar past the missiles. Once they were past, the missiles could go live, forcing the enemy to decide between reversing course or continuing to attack. If they hesitated, even for a few seconds, the choice would be made for them. They might not even manage to do anything at all. The admiral's briefing, passed down from officer to officer until it finally reached the gunboat crews, had suggested she would be quite happy to blast the planet from a distance and leave it—and its defenders—to die on the vine.

An alert sounded. "The missiles are going live," he said. "Let's see what they do…"

He allowed his smile to widen as the missiles showed themselves, their drives coming online and boosting them towards their targets. The enemy formation seemed to shudder—for a moment, he genuinely believed the virus was a telepathic entity—and hesitate, before it reversed course and started to spit fire at the missiles. It had already lost its best chance to strike them down, he noted; the missiles were faster than any shuttle or starfighter. The window of opportunity was closing.

"Our starfighters are here," Marigold said. "I'm setting course for the barn."

Tobias nodded. The gunboats were no longer important. The missiles would do a hell of a lot of damage—and, if they didn't, the fleet could either snipe at the defenders from a safe distance or simply withdraw, having given the enemy one hell of a fright. They'd been caught out of position… their starfighters were already moving to challenge the human starfighters, rather than waste time trying to track down the missiles. The operation couldn't have gone better.

A pang of guilt struck him as he noted two gunboats were missing, presumed destroyed. He hadn't seen them go. He didn't even know who'd crewed them. He kicked himself mentally as the gunboats picked up speed, heading back to *Lion*. They didn't deserve to die. They didn't deserve to die and be forgotten. Their names would be honoured, briefly, and then…no one would remember them. Except their families…

"Fuck," he muttered, more to himself than anyone else. "War is hell."

• • •

"Admiral," Richardson said. "Fifty-seven percent of the missiles reached their targets."

Susan nodded, concealing her displeasure behind an emotionless mask. She'd hoped the missiles would do better than *that*. The enemy had clearly learnt *something* from the previous engagements, perhaps enough to make the missiles less and less effective until the Royal Navy had to go back to plasma weapons. The boffins kept *talking* about more powerful energy weapons, but—so far—they'd only managed to make slight improvements to battleship guns. Susan knew, better than most, that the promises of more and better weapons were often broken.

She pushed the thought aside as the display continued to update. A dozen enemy installations had been smashed, the debris spinning out in all directions or raining down on the planet below. The planetary defence installations were trying desperately to smash the debris into smaller chunks before they could hit the surface, the shower distracting them from the real threat. The BioBombs were on their way. They'd enter the atmosphere and detonate, sentencing the entire planet to death. Susan wondered, morbidly, if nuclear weapons or massed asteroid strikes would be kinder. The planet was so thoroughly infected that it might be completely beyond recovery.

"Check with the sensor departments," she ordered. "Are there any mystery installations on the surface?"

Richardson looked up. "None as yet, Admiral," he said. "However, they caution us that they haven't been able to get good visuals of the surface."

Susan shrugged. It wasn't as if they had time to land marines and recover more artefacts...if, indeed, there were more artefacts to find. The surface was consumed by the virus, the landscape studded with industrial centres operated by countless host bodies...she cursed under her breath. Last time, the counter-virus had clearly spread up the orbital towers and taken out a chunk of the orbital facilities. Here, there were no towers. The remnants of the system would have to be left to die, even though it ran the risk they'd be recovered and repaired by the virus. She just didn't have the time to destroy them all. The virus might not have known they'd broken contact, before they'd shown themselves, but it sure as hell did now.

And some wanker back home will insist I could have kept the fleet under cloak and crept all the way to safety, she thought. It probably wasn't true, but she could see why the thought would appeal to an armchair admiral. *They know we're here now. They'll be coming for us.*

She watched, grimly, as the enemy shuttles and starfighters fell on her ships, their movements powered by a determination to make her pay for what she'd done. They ran straight into the point defence, but kept coming anyway…Susan shivered as a trio of shuttles rammed a destroyer, setting off a chain of explosions that blew the destroyer to atoms. Another shuttle crashed into a battleship, damaging her armour…Susan shuddered, even though the giant ship had survived. The damage was starting to mount up, each and every blow making it harder and harder for her to repair her ships before time ran out. And she didn't have the slightest idea just how much time she had. Whatever she did, she was entirely sure someone—with the advantage of hindsight—would criticise her.

"Deploy two destroyers to the tramlines," she ordered. "One of them is to launch missiles to locate and destroy the flicker station. The other is to jump though the tramline and recon the next system."

"Aye, Admiral," Richardson said.

Susan nodded. The flicker stations weren't easy to find—it was quite possible she'd just wasted a handful of missiles—but it was worth a try. If they took out the FTL communications station, the virus would lose a chunk of its flicker network. It wouldn't keep the rest of the alien system from knowing her fleet was there—and where it had been—but it would deprive them of realtime data. She might just have enough time to put some distance between herself and the avenging alien fleet.

Richardson cleared his throat. "Signal from the forward recon units, Admiral," he said. "The BioBombs have detonated."

"And the planet is doomed," Susan said. Millions—billions—of host bodies were about to die. There was nothing she could do for them. The resources under her command wouldn't scratch the surface, even if she had time to try. And it was quite likely there was nothing to recover. She felt sick. Cold logic told her they had no choice, that they were fighting a war in which quarter could neither be asked nor given, but still…"Deploy a pair of recon drones to monitor the collapse."

"Aye, Admiral," Richardson said.

Susan frowned. The counter-virus was designed to spread at immense speed. The virus, she'd been assured, was uniquely vulnerable to the counter-virus. The biological weapons would burn themselves out, if they were deployed against humans, but not against the virus itself…or so she had been told. She wasn't so sure. The virus had to know what had happened now, time and time again. It *had* to be looking for a counter.

It'll come up with something, she thought, grimly. *It's just a matter of time.*

She cleared her throat as the last of the alien starfighters died. "Recall our starfighters and gunboats, then prepare to boost for the tramline," she ordered. "And get me a complete damage report."

"Aye, Admiral," Richardson said.

Susan let out a breath. The battle had been pretty much one-sided, but that was about to change. The virus knew where they were. She studied the display thoughtfully, silently gauging how it would react to their presence. It didn't have many options, not if it wanted to keep her from getting her fleet home. The virus probably didn't understand the concept of morale, or the importance of boosting civilian faith in eventual victory, but it sure as hell understood the danger of letting her *keep* her ships. It had a chance to destroy them before she got them home. She found it hard to believe it would just let the chance go.

And we're flying right towards the war front, she thought. There was more than enough enemy tonnage along the front lines to destroy her fleet, if it concentrated and then brought her to battle. *They really don't want us punching our way back into New Washington.*

"The damage control teams believe the damage can be fixed, given time," Richardson reported, breaking into her thoughts. "However, *Copenhagen's* cloaking device is offline and requires replacement."

Susan cursed under her breath. Carrying out repairs underway was difficult enough without having to keep the ships under cloak too. The slightest mishap might be enough to alert a prowling enemy ship or trigger a remote sensor platform. And yet, she didn't want to abandon a ship if it could be avoided. The fleet needed every unit it could muster.

"Have them replace the cloak, if possible, and align the ship with another if not," she ordered, finally. Flying in tandem was a pain in the arse even if the fleet wasn't under attack. "We don't want to leave anyone behind."

"Aye, Admiral."

CHAPTER THIRTY

"CAPTAIN," COMMANDER DONKER REPORTED. "The surviving gunboats have returned to the ship."

The surviving gunboats, Thomas thought. He'd made sure to glance at the personnel files, during the voyage from Earth to New Washington. The gunboat pilots might not be...*traditional*...naval personnel, but they'd done their work well. He hadn't been sold on the concept, when he'd first heard of it, yet...he had to admit it had worked. *Poor bastards.*

He promised himself he'd hold a proper ceremony for them, when they had some free time, and then put the thought out of his mind. The fleet was picking up speed as it fled the dying world, leaving the remaining enemy installations behind. There was nothing they could do to impede the fleet now, save—perhaps—for shaking their fists in the fleet's general direction. Thomas smiled at the thought of hundreds of host bodies doing just that, then sobered. They'd just killed millions—perhaps billions—of host bodies. They'd just committed mass murder, if not outright genocide. And yet...what choice had they had? The thought taunted him. There were no alternatives. The virus's mere existence was beyond the pale.

His mind churned as the fleet glided away from the planet. He'd met enough aliens to know that they were intelligent, that they were as deserving of life as the human race itself. The thought of mercilessly sentencing them to death, just for existing, was appalling. They were different—they certainly didn't *think* like humans—but their mere existence didn't pose a threat. The idea of a war that could only end in the complete destruction of one side appalled him. And yet...he couldn't think of anything better. The virus would never come to terms with the rest of the universe. It *had* to be destroyed.

And there's nothing we can do for the hosts, he thought, numbly. They'd been infected from birth. It was unlikely they'd developed any intelligent personality of their own. How could they? The virus might regard their brains as yet another source of food. *Killing them might be the only thing we can do for them.*

He dismissed the thought as the fleet picked up speed, altering course the moment it slipped into cloak. The virus would know they were heading for the tramline—reversing course would add several months to their journey, if they didn't run into the fleet they'd decoyed away—but it wouldn't know precisely where they intended to jump. Hopefully, they'd remain undetected long enough to sneak through the tramlines to reach New Washington before it was too late. Thomas wasn't afraid to encounter the enemy fleet again, but he knew how easily the fleet train could be destroyed. The virus could take it out first, weakening the rest of the fleet. And then they'd wear the ships down and destroy them.

"Signal from the flag, Captain," Lieutenant Cook reported. "The recon destroyer just returned from the tramline. The next system isn't particularly developed."

"Good," Thomas growled. The fleet had barely been tested—they hadn't shot themselves dry attacking the *last* system—but the longer it took to encounter the enemy fleet, the better. The repairs needed to be completed as quickly as possible. "Keep us in formation."

He sighed inwardly, feeling as if he were losing control. *Lion* was too big a ship to fly alone—he felt a sudden stab of envy for Captain Campbell—but she didn't have to be part of a *huge* fleet. The admiral was making the real decisions and directing operations and...in a way, Thomas felt almost powerless. He might be the admiral's second, at least as far as the Royal Navy was concerned, but he wouldn't inherit her position if she died. He understood, now, why so many younger scions of the aristocracy turned into drunkards, fops, or outright villains. They had almost no real power over their lives. They might live in luxury, but it wasn't *their* luxury.

It could be worse, he told himself, dryly. *They could have no control and no luxury.*

He keyed his console, bringing up the latest simulation reports as the fleet prepared to make transit. The tactical staff had studied the last set of engagements and suggested minor improvements, although a handful of their more complex ideas would have to wait until the fleet got home. Thomas wasn't going to have the missiles torn down and rebuilt while the fleet was in transit. The thought was absurd. They might need to fire the missiles at any moment. The enemy was still out there, somewhere...

"Signal from the flag, Captain," Cook reported. "The transit zone is clear."

Thomas nodded. "Helm, take us through on command," he ordered. "Tactical, prepare to bring up weapons and defences if necessary."

"Aye, Captain."

Commander Donker glanced at him. "Captain? Do you expect trouble?"

Thomas shrugged. "We're deep in enemy space," he said. "I'd be more surprised if we didn't run into trouble."

He let out a breath as the timer reached zero. The virus shouldn't have been able to track them, but...there were over a hundred ships in the fleet. Thomas knew from grim experience that the cloaking devices weren't *that* good. There were so many ships in such close proximity that there was a very real chance one of the cloaking devices would interfere with another, causing a hint of disturbance that might draw attention. If the virus knew where they were going, it could have set up an ambush. The odds were against it, as spacers reminded themselves on every transit, but if there was any power that could pull it off it was the virus.

The display blanked, then rebooted. Thomas felt his heart clench as the aftershock of the jump claimed him. He was getting old...he shook his head, reminding himself that the admiral was pretty much his age and *she* was riding starships with the young bucks. The thought was silly. He had many decades to live, unless he died in combat or in a hunting accident. It wasn't as if he *liked* hunting, but it was expected of him. And no one had thanked him for pointing out that it was stupid.

"Captain," Sibley said. "Local space is clear."

Thomas nodded. The system was clearly inhabited—the display was starting to fill with icons—but not particularly industrialised. It reminded him of an early colony, with little spacefaring presence beyond an orbital entry station and a cloudscoop positioned above the local gas giant. The virus had infected the system—the sensors had no trouble picking out its drive fields—but never bothered to develop it. Thomas suspected it hadn't considered the system particularly important. There were several more developed systems within a few short jumps.

The system might have been settled by an old enemy, before the virus overwhelmed it, he mused. *And the virus never bothered to expand on their work.*

"Signal from the flag, Captain," Cook added. "We are to launch a ballistic BioBomb towards the planet, then continue towards the tramline."

Thomas frowned. It would take days for a ballistic missile to reach its target...he supposed it didn't matter. The virus might not even *notice* the missile until it slipped into the atmosphere and detonated. And it might even assume the fleet had proceeded onwards without bothering to bombard the planet. It might not see death coming until it was too late...

"Tactical, launch the missile as ordered," Thomas said. It wouldn't be hard to get closer to the planet, but the admiral's briefing had made it clear time was not on their side. "And then continue to monitor the system."

"Aye, Captain."

Thomas settled back in his chair, feeling a deep abiding tiredness threatening to overwhelm him. He'd been in the navy for most of his adult life and yet he'd never been so unable to stand and leave the bridge to his subordinates. They were so deep in enemy space that the situation could go to hell in a heartbeat…he knew, intellectually, that the odds of being discovered were low, but he didn't really believe it. And yet…

He forced himself to stand. "Mr XO, you have the bridge," he said. The period of maximum danger would be when they crossed the next tramline. He had to be rested before then or he'd start making mistakes. Dangerous mistakes. "I'll be in my ready room."

"Aye, Captain," Donker said.

• • •

Tobias allowed himself a moment of relief as a dull *thump* echoed through the gunboat, confirming they'd docked safety with the mothership. He'd feared the worst, when they'd been ordered to escort the battlecruiser once they returned to the—relative—safety of the fleet; he'd feared they might be picked off by enemy starfighters, intent on making the human fleet pay a price for invading their system. The tactical display warned that the fleet had taken damage…it was just a matter of time, he knew, before they hit something vital.

"Life isn't a computer game," he muttered. "You can shoot a handgun at a tank all day and it won't do any real damage."

Marigold stood. "What?"

"I was just thinking," Tobias said. "A terrible habit."

"A very bad habit," Marigold said. "Penny for your thoughts?"

Tobias laughed. "Can I charge you a pound for my thoughts?"

"You could try." Marigold considered it. "I wouldn't pay, mind you, but you can try."

"I think I've priced myself out of the market," Tobias said. "I…remember those games, where you can line up a row of soldiers and take pot-shots at a tank with handguns until it explodes? It doesn't work in the real world."

Marigold frowned. "I don't think that thought is worth a penny," she said. She removed her helmet and ran her hand through her sweat-sodden hair. "What's your point?"

"I was trying to convince myself the shuttles and starfighters wouldn't do any real damage to the fleet," Tobias said. "But that isn't true."

He yawned as he stumbled through the hatch. They needed some rest, quickly. He had no doubt they'd be going back into action shortly, perhaps very shortly. The alien system was inhabited, if not particularly industrialised. The virus would feel a certain inclination to protect it. Tobias had no doubt it was just a matter of time before the main body of the alien fleet arrived. And who knew what would happen then?

Marigold stepped up beside him as they made their way to the wardroom. Bagehot was already there, drinking coffee. Tobias felt a hot flash of naked hatred that surprised him, given that Bagehot had been the very epitome of a reasonable authority figure. He'd been so much better than anyone else Tobias had met that there wasn't any real competition. And yet...Bagehot passed them both cups of coffee, then motioned to chairs as the remaining pilots flowed into the compartment. Tobias sat, feeling as if he was going to fall asleep at any moment. He hadn't felt so bad since the day he'd stayed up half the night studying for an exam... which he'd failed.

And if I hadn't failed the exam, I might never have joined the navy, he thought. *And I would never have met Marigold.*

"The mission was completed," Bagehot said. "However, Callam, Johan, Penny and Alana were lost."

"Soften the blow, why don't you?" Tobias didn't realise he'd spoken aloud until Bagehot looked at him. "They're dead. They..."

"Yes." Bagehot looked pained. He'd spent more time with the new pilots than Tobias, even though Tobias had been meant to show them the ropes. "Their deaths weren't in vain."

Tobias wasn't sure that was true. How many people would remember the dead pilots? Hell, how many people remembered his dead father? How many people would mourn him, if he died? His mother and sister? Who else? Marigold would probably die with him. Colin? The thought would have made Tobias smile, if he hadn't been so tired. His former bully might just be relieved if Tobias died, just because Tobias was a constant reminder of the person he'd been. Tobias knew he was being unfair—he *hoped* he was being unfair—but his thoughts were a mess. The sooner he hit the bunk, the better.

"We will remember them," Bagehot said. "And the mission was a success."

Marigold leaned forward. "How much damage did we do?"

"Enough, we hope," Bagehot said. "The planet itself was struck by BioBombs and hopefully devastated. The orbital industries got hammered. It will take months, if not years, to repair the damage and replace the destroyed nodes. The knock-on effects will be considerable. Their supply chains should be thoroughly disrupted."

Tobias nodded. He'd studied the topic in school. A shortage of any-thing—iron, for example—meant a shortage of anything that *needed* iron. There'd be a whole string of endless problems caused by the lack, all of which would be hard to solve until more iron was found...he grimaced. It was hard to be *sure* just how much damage they'd done. Or how hard it would be for the virus to replace the losses. It was quite possible it wouldn't take very long at all.

He yawned, again. "Can we go to bed?"

"That's *can we go to bed, sir?*" Bagehot grinned. "Yes, go to your bunks. Hopefully, you should have at least a few hours of sleep before we find ourselves having to fight again."

"Thank you, sir," Tobias managed. His teachers had never been quite so merciful. But then, the teachers hadn't known their lives depended on Tobias's ability to stay awake. "We'll see you tomorrow."

"Sleep well," Bagehot said. "I'll sound the alarm if all hell breaks loose."

• • •

Susan felt, as the fleet crawled across the first system and transited into the next, as if someone was peering over her shoulder. It was hard to put it into words, certainly hard to put it into words someone would take seri-ously. She hadn't felt quite so exposed since her schooldays, when there had been no hope of keeping her former classmates from realising that her skin was darker than theirs…she scowled at the memory. She'd punched a boy out for peeking at her, many years ago. She had the sense she was being watched now, too.

She spent fitful nights in her bed, then days on the flag deck alternatively watching the empty displays, running simulations and reading reports from her subordinates. The crews were being pushed to the limit, all too aware there'd be no safety until they made it back home. She wasn't too surprised at the problem, although it hadn't been anything like as bad on *Vanguard*. But then, the virus was a very different problem. Defeat meant the end of the world. She recalled, grimly, the proposals to flee the human sphere and set up a hidden colony somewhere on the other side of the galaxy. None of the proposals were remotely practical. If nothing else, the virus could simply follow them.

But the virus isn't as curious as we are, she mused. The reports suggested it had been a spacefaring entity for far longer than any of the other known races. If it had expanded at the same rate, it would have discovered Earth at roughly the same time Columbus had discovered America. *It might never even realise we'd tried to flee.*

The thought tormented her as the days crawled onwards. They passed through two more systems, taking the time to launch ballistic missiles at the planets before proceeding again. Susan felt almost blasé about it now, even though she knew she was condemning millions of host bodies to death. The horror of what she'd unleashed was matched—and exceeded—by the sheer horror of the virus's existence. She wanted another option—she wanted a solution that didn't involve genocide—but she knew she didn't have one. The virus could not be battered into submission. She wasn't sure it could even be contained. The proposals to allow the virus to remain alive, infecting an unindustrialised world, struck her as thoroughly unpleasant. The virus would have to be allowed to keep a multitude of host bodies…

We know it can produce blobs and brains, she thought. *Perhaps, if we deny it the host bodies, it will be forced to rely on them.*

She paced the decks, taking the time to explore the battleship even though—technically—she was supposed to remain on the flag deck. She just couldn't stay still. She wished she could demote herself back to captain, to take command of a ship and set sail for the edge of explored space. She wished…she put the thought out of her head. It wasn't going to happen. The best she could hope for was collecting enough prize money to buy her own ship. *That* wasn't likely to happen unless she somehow found herself in possession of an advanced alien starship. The prize money for that would…

The alarms howled. She jumped, then keyed her wristcom.

"Report," she snapped.

"Admiral," Richardson said. "Long-range sensors have detected alien starfighters on search vector."

Susan sucked in her breath. She'd felt as if someone was peeking at her. Had an alien ship shadowed them from the last system? It was quite possible one had, keeping the human ships in sensor range long enough to signal ahead for reinforcements. "Do they have us?"

"Not yet, I think," Richardson said. "But they'll have solid locks on us within twenty minutes, at best."

"Understood," Susan said. Her mind raced. Starfighters meant carriers…somewhere far too close to her ships for comfort. "I'm on my way. Bring the fleet to alert status, but do *not* launch fighters."

"Aye, Admiral."

CHAPTER THIRTY-ONE

SUSAN TOOK A MOMENT TO COMPOSE HERSELF, then stepped through the hatch and into the CIC. The main display teemed with red icons, the enemy starfighters darting around as they quartered space with active sensors. They were easy to spot, but she was morbidly certain there were stealthed or cloaked starfighters and starships in the empty space beyond. The enemy might not have gotten a *precise* location on the human ships, not yet, but opening fire on the visible starfighters would reveal their exact position to any watching eyes.

"Admiral," Richardson said. "Our current projections indicate they'll have us within ten minutes."

"They must have shadowed us from the last system," Susan said. Her mind raced as she considered the possibilities. The enemy could have had a starship in the system, one with the presence of mind to keep an eye on the human fleet from cloak rather than expend itself in a futile attack. "They already have a rough idea of our position."

She frowned. The odds against the enemy having stumbled across them by accident were astronomical. They would have had to have a carrier—or more—in the vicinity, then…she shook her head. No, they'd been spotted and shadowed until they'd been ambushed. It was sheer luck they hadn't blundered right into a trap. The enemy shadow must not have clung *too* closely to them. Or the decoys had worked better than she'd thought.

Her eyes narrowed. The enemy starfighters were drawing closer and closer. If the human fleet remained on its current course, it was going to be uncovered; if they risked altering course, there would still be a very good chance they'd be spotted. She considered, briefly, powering everything down and pretending to be a hole in space, but the enemy were just too close. If they filled space with active sensor pulses, they'd find her ships and blow them away before they could raise their defences and return fire.

"We're going to have to locate their carriers," she said, grimly. There were no enemy bases within detection range. There had to be a carrier, probably more than one, holding station somewhere near. "Signal *Lion*. She is to prepare the gunboats for a search and destroy mission."

"Aye, Admiral," Richardson said.

Susan keyed the terminal, bringing up a set of probability spheres. The starfighters had a strictly limited range. The virus probably had extension packs, and it might have decided to write the recon fighters off anyway, but the carriers *had* to be somewhere within the sphere. Unless, of course, the virus had come up with something new...she narrowed the cone a little as she projected the starfighter flight paths backwards, trying to guess at their rough location. The carriers had to be cloaked. She'd have spotted them by now if they hadn't hidden themselves.

And the starfighters might have already found us, she mused. *They could be playing dumb to lull us into a false sense of security.*

The enemy starfighters moved closer and closer. There was no *sign* they'd detected the human ships, yet the odds of detection were increasing by the second. Susan ran the simulations, again and again. She could take down the starfighters, at the price of revealing her exact location. And yet, it was just a matter of time before they were revealed anyway. The enemy were already closing in on them.

She drew a line on the display. "Signal the lead escorts," she ordered. "They are to fire on the starfighters when they cross the line."

"Aye, Admiral," Richardson said.

"As soon as the starfighters come under fire, we are to bring up our active sensors and launch the gunboats," Susan added. "I want a shell of recon drones in place, covering every possible angle of attack. Push two more along our direct course. The enemy carriers might well be lurking there."

"Aye, Admiral."

Susan felt her heart race as the enemy starfighters approached the line. It was hard to believe—it was impossible to believe—they didn't know the human ships were there. They were almost *taunting* her, mocking her. And yet, they wouldn't have been so fat and happy if they'd known…unless, of course, the virus considered the recon starfighters expendable. It was quite possible, she supposed. Starfighters were cheap, compared to warships…

The display changed, sharply, as the enemy craft picked up speed and launched themselves right into the heart of her formation. Susan gritted her teeth as the escorts opened fire, picking off four enemy starfighters before they had a chance to realise they were under attack. The remainder kept coming, ducking and weaving through her formation instead of trying to attack her ships. They were picked off, one by one, but their deaths hadn't been in vain. The virus knew where she was. Worse, it had a fairly complete list of her ships.

And we still don't know where their carriers are, she thought. *They could be anywhere within the sphere.*

"Admiral," Richardson said. "The gunboats are away. Drones are launching now…"

He bit off a curse as the display filled with red icons. "Enemy starfighters approaching on attack vector," he said. "I say again…"

"I heard." Susan shook her head. "Launch all starfighters on CSP duties. The gunboats can handle the search for the enemy carriers."

"Aye, Admiral."

Susan frowned as the enemy starfighters hurtled towards the fleet. The ambush hadn't been timed perfectly, she supposed, but it had been done well enough to pin her before she spotted their carriers. There was no hope of avoiding action, not even if she reversed course. She had no idea what might be coming up behind her. The enemy had had more than enough time to contact the fleet she'd decoyed away, earlier, and order it to catch up and put a knife in her back. Captain Campbell couldn't do anything about *that.*

He might have gotten halfway to the RV point by now, Susan thought. She hadn't been able to give him any specific timetable. It was quite possible that Captain Campbell would reach the RV point, wait a few days and then head to New Washington. His orders were clear. He was not to risk his ship if he had vital intelligence, intelligence the Admiralty would need to plot a final offensive. *There's nothing he can do to help us.*

She silently counted the alien starfighters, noting there had to be at least three carriers lurking somewhere nearby. Perhaps four...she wondered, absently, if the virus had started converting freighters into makeshift carriers. The Royal Navy had a small fleet of freighters that could carry a couple of squadrons of starfighters, once they were refitted. The virus had probably seen them in action. If it hadn't come up with the idea itself, it could easily have copied it...

"Admiral," Richardson said. "The enemy starfighters are engaging ours."

Susan nodded, putting her thoughts to one side. The display looked like a demented game, with green and red icons dancing around, but she knew what it meant when one of the icons vanished. The alien starfighters were splitting into two groups, one concentrating on engaging the human starfighters while the other fell on the capital ships like wolves on sheep. *These* sheep were well-armed, Susan reflected, but there was no way they could avoid the starfighters. The enemy craft bored in, launching torpedoes as well as raking her hulls with plasma fire. The point defence couldn't stop everything.

And the closer the action, the harder it is to tell the difference between friends and enemies, she thought. Blue-on-blue incidents were a fact of military life, but they still hurt. *No wonder they're pressing us as hard as they can.*

Her people knew what to do. There was no point in giving orders. And yet…she wanted to do something, anything, beyond watching as the damage started to mount. The enemy starfighters seemed intent on tearing through her formation, rather than concentrating on a handful of targets, but…in the long run, she supposed it might work out for them. The damage would be spread out enough to slow the fleet, rather than force her to abandon a handful of ships to save the rest. She checked the live feed to Admiral Li's flagship as the alien storm converged on *Thunderous*, just in case he had to take command at short notice. It should be fine…

"Admiral," Richardson said. Red icons blinked into existence, right on the edge of the probability sphere. "We have located the alien carriers."

Susan frowned. The carriers were in position to block her, if she took a least-time course to the next tramline. *That* was odd. The enemy carriers didn't seem to be assault carriers, let alone something akin to *Ark Royal*. They weren't designed to stand in the line of battle. If she closed the range, her battleships could tear them apart before they could escape. Either the enemy were stupid, which struck her as unlikely, or they had something else up their sleeve. Her eyes lingered on the space beyond the carriers. What could be hiding there?

"Signal *Lion*," she ordered. "The gunboats are to engage the enemy. *Lion* is to provide missile support upon demand."

"Aye, Admiral," Richardson said.

Susan nodded, curtly. She was short of options. Closing the range would work, but she had no idea what might be lurking past the carriers. *Opening* the range would buy them some time, yet not enough to take out the enemy starfighters. The ambush, if indeed it was an ambush, had been better timed than she'd thought. The virus was either trying to lure her into a bigger mess or bluff her into leaving the carriers alone.

The gunboats will take out the carriers, she mused. She frowned as the gunboats circumvented the alien starfighters, then lanced towards the carriers. *And if there's anything beyond them, they'll see it too.*

. . .

"I wish I'd stayed in my bunk," Tobias commented. He'd managed to get some rest during the voyage, but he still felt as if he were being pushed to the limit. "There are four carriers out there."

"Keep an eye on the sensors," Marigold warned. "There might be something else out there too."

Tobias nodded, curtly. The enemy starfighters had largely ignored them, preferring to target the capital ships, but that was likely to change. There was probably a CSP waiting for them too. The enemy would have learnt from the human tactic, if they hadn't come up with it on their own. They certainly wouldn't want a cluster of gunboats blowing hell out of their carriers.

His eyes narrowed as he studied the sensor records. Bagehot had pointed out how unlikely it was the enemy carriers would just *sit* in the fleet's path, without even bringing up their drives and preparing to move. Tobias couldn't disagree with his logic. The virus had lost two heavily-industrialised worlds in quick succession. It *had* to be leery of taking heavy losses. And yet, it seemed to be putting four carriers at risk. Tobias wasn't sure how long it would take the virus to replace them, but…it couldn't be less than a year. Could it?

The display bleeped an alert. "They're launching starfighters," he said. It wasn't exactly a surprise, but it was still disconcerting. "I'm sending the missile targeting data to *Lion* now."

"Understood," Marigold said. "The formation is closing up…"

She broke off. Tobias glanced at the display as another alert sounded and swore. The sensors had just burned through the enemy cloaking field. There were ships out there…*lots* of ships. He had the nasty feeling he'd just flown right into a trap. His heart pounded as more and more ships were located and identified. Battleships, carriers, cruisers…and, beyond them, a brainship. The enemy trap hadn't snared the fleet, thankfully, but it had come pretty close to snaring their ship.

His fingers danced over the console, forwarding improved targeting data to the missiles. It was *just* possible they'd get a clear shot at the brainship, although the odds were poor and growing worse by the second. The enemy were launching more starfighters, an endless tidal wave of death and destruction flying towards them. Tobias felt like an egg thrown at a brick wall. They were about to be smashed for nothing.

The gunboat squadron reversed course. Tobias worked his systems, steering the rest of the missiles towards their targets. The enemy fleet was shedding its cloaks now—there was no longer any point in trying to hide—and bringing up its drives. The carriers seemed torn between recalling the CSP to cover their hulls and relying on the point defence to protect them. Tobias hoped they'd make their mind up quickly. The remainder of the missiles were going live, lancing towards their targets...

"Four direct hits," he said. An enemy carrier staggered out of position, bleeding plasma from its drive section; another blew up so violently he was tempted to wonder if it had been crammed with antimatter. No one had produced antimatter outside the lab, from what he'd heard, but it was the Holy Grail of weapons technology. "Their point defence is getting better."

"Yeah." Marigold yanked the gunboat back, just in time to dodge a starfighter that had been intent on ramming them. "I think they know what we can do now."

Tobias's console bleeped. "*Lion* is launching more missiles," he said. "We have to guide them in."

"I'll keep us as steady as possible," Marigold said. Another starfighter shot towards them, only to be blown to dust. "Just see if you can hit that brainship."

"I'll try," Tobias said. His heart sank. The brainship was surrounded by so many escorts, each one pulsing with sensor emissions, that he doubted they could slip a single missile into attack range. "But I don't think we can."

"Do or do not," Marigold quoted. "There is no try."

"There is now," Tobias retorted. "We can do everything right and still get fucked."

• • •

Susan had braced herself for bad news, as the gunboats and drones swooped towards the alien carriers, and she'd expected to discover more ships lurking in cloak, but even *she* hadn't expected *quite* so many ships. The virus had assembled nine battleships, five carriers and at least fifty-nine smaller ships, then laid a trap that had come far too close to succeeding. She knew she was damn lucky and yet…

There was no time to waste. "Bring the fleet about," she ordered, tracing out a new line on the display. They had one thing in their favour. The virus had had to power down its drives, just to ensure it remained undetected. It was powering up now, of course, but her ships would have some room to manoeuvre. "We have to put some distance between us and them before we run out of time."

"Aye, Admiral," Richardson said.

Susan nodded as she studied the in-system display. There was a flicker station somewhere…she'd bet her paycheck on it. Where? As long as it remained intact, the enemy fleet could keep signalling ahead. It would only be a matter of time before they were driven into another ambush, with one fleet ahead of them and another behind. The first wave of alien starfighters were breaking off and streaking back to their carriers, but the second wave was flashing past the gunboats and heading straight for her. She had too many problems she couldn't solve before she ran out of time…

"Detach two destroyers and order them to find the flicker station," she ordered. It meant weakening her point defence, but two destroyers wouldn't make *that* much difference. Not in the grand scheme of things. "We'll continue to evade here until the station has been taken out."

She didn't need to look at her staff to sense their sudden alarm. The obvious tactic was to make a beeline for the tramline. Susan understood, yet…there was no better way to run straight into another trap. No one had tried a tramline assault in real life—no one had ever been stupid enough to try, when it was so blatantly unnecessary—but she'd seen simulations that suggested any attempt would turn into a bloody slaughter. They were just too close to the front for the virus *not* to be tempted to redeploy an entire fleet to block them, using the flicker network to coordinate. She had to take the network out before she showed her hand.

The display updated, again, as the aliens protected their brainship. Susan cursed under her breath. She could reverse course—again—and close the range, but whoever won the engagement would be so badly weakened they'd be wiped out effortlessly in the next engagement. She couldn't take the risk, not now. The fleet had to be preserved intact, as much as possible. There was no hope of inflicting enough damage, here and now, to ensure total victory.

And there's no way to take out the brainship otherwise, she thought. The marines had boarded brainships before…this time, the virus would know what to expect. The boarding party wouldn't get far enough into the hull to plant a nuke, set the timer and run. *We'll just have to stay alive long enough to take out the flicker station and break contact.*

She winced, inwardly, as the enemy starfighters closed once again. Her pilots were waiting, but they were already reaching the limits of their endurance. They needed to rearm under fire, something that was never easy. And yet, they had no choice. She couldn't afford to draw down the CSP, not now. They were already far too exposed.

We can get out of this, she told herself. She didn't have to beat the enemy fleet to win. *We just have to stay alive.*

CHAPTER THIRTY-TWO

STACI LOOKED PALE, in the half-light of the bridge. "Do you think this is the virus's homeworld?"

Mitch shrugged. They'd passed through three star systems after they'd lost the enemy fleet, flying deeper and deeper into unexplored space. He'd made sure to keep the ship under cloak, determined not to give the virus any hint of their course and speed. It made it harder to gather data, but he considered it a small price to pay. The longer the virus remained in the dark, the better. And then they'd flown into yet another system and discovered...

He sucked in his breath. The system was *immense*, an order of magnitude bigger than Sol or Tadpole Prime or even the *last* infected system they'd seen. Every planet within sensor range was pulsing with emissions, while hundreds of ships made their way from the gas giants to the asteroid belts and the facilities orbiting the rocky planets. All four of them looked to have been terraformed, to the point the system practically pulsed with malevolent life. The sheer scale of the infection was beyond his comprehension. It was impossible to look at the figures and grasp what they really meant. They were nothing more than statistics.

"If it isn't, I don't want to see their homeworld," he said, shortly. There were a surprising number of starships and installations orbiting one of the gas giants. Could the virus have been born on a gas giant, instead of a rocky world? It seemed unlikely and yet…the virus itself was pretty damn unlikely. "How do we attack a system like this?"

His eyes narrowed as he studied the live feed from the sensor drones. He'd seen no choice but to launch them despite the risks. And yet, as they revealed more and more about the system, he wished he hadn't. The planets were surrounded with so many sensor nodes that it was all too likely the drones would be detected, even though they were designed to be practically invisible. There were just too many watching eyes. Mitch had spent enough time working with cloaking devices, as both the hunter and the hunted, to be certain there was no way to get a cloaked ship into striking range. No cloaking device ever built could compensate for so many sensor pulses. Someone would notice and all hell would break loose.

Hundreds, perhaps thousands, of enemy starfighters cut through the orbital space above the planet, ducking and weaving in a manner that suggested the system was already under attack. The virus was taking nothing for granted, Mitch decided: it clearly hadn't assumed the invading fleet really *had* gone in the other direction. Mitch wished, just for a moment, that the rest of the fleet *was* with him, then told himself not to be stupid. The fleet would bleed itself white trying to break through the planetary defences and lay waste to the surface. There were so many facilities that even the BioBombs wouldn't be decisive.

"We need a supernova bomb," he muttered. "Or some other way to blow up the whole system."

He gritted his teeth as more and more data flowed into the display. There was a small armada of ships holding position near the planet, including something that looked strikingly like *Lion*. A missile-heavy battlecruiser? Mitch cursed under his breath. If the virus had managed to duplicate the design after it had first seen *Lion*, a mere nine months ago, it suggested frightening things about its ability to see a design, reverse-engineer it and put its own version into production. Even if *this* battlecruiser was a one-off, a test model rushed into service…Mitch hoped, deep inside, that the virus's R&D efforts had been on the brink of producing battlecruisers before *Lion* had entered service. The alternative was worse.

I could be wrong, he told himself. The ship *looked* like a battlecruiser, but there was no way to *know* until she opened fire. *She might be something else altogether.*

He put the thought out of his mind as the display continued to update. The world—he *hoped* it was the enemy homeworld—was surrounded by so many icons, some hazy to suggest a level of sensor distortion, that it was hard to believe the surface got any sunlight. He'd seen proposals to put a shell around a planet, but...he couldn't believe anyone would actually *do* it. And yet, the virus seemed to be trying. Perhaps it just didn't care. Or maybe he was wrong. The sheer volume of orbital industry was terrifying.

"We could sneak a ballistic missile down to the surface," Staci suggested. "If we struck the world with the BioBomb..."

Mitch considered it briefly, then shook his head. There was no way to *guarantee* striking the surface, while trying and *failing* would reveal their presence to an entire system of watchful eyes. Mitch thought they could evade contact, if they were careful, but they'd still alert the enemy. The virus would *know* they'd stumbled across its homeworld. If it truly *was* the virus's homeworld. There was just no way to be sure.

For a moment, even Mitch's nerves quailed. He wanted to turn and run, to flee through the tramlines to New Washington and scream for help. And yet, he feared the massed power of humanity and its allies would be insufficient to reduce the enemy system. There were just too many defensive installations...his eyes roamed the display, jumping from a chain of orbital battlestations to hundreds, if not thousands, of automated defence platforms. He'd never seen anything like it. They could throw thousands of missiles at the orbital facilities without scoring a single hit. Compared to the infected system, Earth was practically naked.

We thought they spent everything on building fleets and offensive weapons, he thought, numbly. *But they spent just as much on planetary defences.*

"We wouldn't be able to hit the surface," Mitch said. "Even if we did, the BioBomb wouldn't spread far enough to do real damage."

He sighed, inwardly. The system's installations weren't linked together. Not physically. The counter-virus would get up the orbital towers and elevators, if the virus didn't shut them down in time, but it wouldn't get any further. Vast numbers of industrial nodes and defensive platforms would remain utterly untouched. And then…who knew what would happen then? The virus might continue, largely unharmed…he'd read, once, a paper that argued that spacefaring humans would be better off without the planet-bound masses. The virus might be the first intelligent race to actually put theory into practice.

"Helm, take us on a recon course around the gas giants," he ordered. "And then we'll head for the tramline back home."

He leaned back in his chair and forced himself to think. Their discovery *had* to be reported to higher authority, although he wasn't sure what they could do with it. Massing enough firepower to crack the alien system would take months, if it was doable at all. Maybe they'd get orders to go back and start harassing the virus, ensuring it didn't have a chance to resume the offensive. The sheer scale of the enemy industry would concentrate a few minds. Mitch was no expert, but it was fairly obvious the virus could out-produce the allied races if it put its mind to it. The hell of it, he conceded ruefully, was that the allies should be grateful that the virus had devoted so much effort to defending itself. It could have won the war by now if it had invested those resources in ships.

The display kept updating, time and time again. There were thousands, perhaps hundreds of thousands, of asteroid settlements, ranging from simple mining facilities to industrial bases. A handful of asteroids were even being moved to the planet, ready to be converted into raw materials… Mitch was tempted to try to capture one of the asteroids and turn it into a dinosaur-killer, even though he knew it would be futile. The virus would see the asteroid coming well before it struck the planet and blow it into rubble. And yet…he was torn between the urge to sneak away as quietly as possible and the desire to do something, anything, to hamper the aliens before he departed. He wanted—he needed—to do something, even though it was futile. The idea of bowing his head and bending his knee had never sat well with him. He'd gotten into a lot of fights because he'd never been able to back down.

His heart sank as the ship approached the nearest gas giant. There were a dozen cloudscoops within detection range, which suggested there were more on the other side of the planet. The handful of moons were thrumming with life...his eyes lingered on an icy-rocky world, wondering if the virus had set up home under the ice. Hell, it might have been *born* under the ice. Humans had discovered very basic life on Jupiter's moons...his imagination suggested a humanoid race setting up a mining operation, only to discover—too late—that they'd dug too deep and awoken something truly nasty. There were hundreds, perhaps thousands, of movies with that exact plot. They didn't seem so thrilling now.

Staci turned to look at him. "I don't think we can get much closer, Captain," she said. "They're bringing more and more sensor arrays online."

Mitch frowned. Had they caught a sniff of *Unicorn*? It didn't seem likely—the frigate had remained well clear of any active sensor installations—and yet, it was hard to believe it was a coincidence. He stared at the near-space display, wondering what might be hidden in the trackless reaches of seemingly-empty space. Had they passed too close to a passive sensor platform. The navy had decided, long ago, that such platforms were a waste of resources, but...Mitch could imagine the *virus* establishing entire networks of stealthed platforms. And, after the human fleet had materialised in their rear, the virus would have to be concerned about the rest of its industrial nodes. They wouldn't let a sensor flicker go unchallenged.

"Helm, pull us away," he ordered. There were no enemy starships on his sensors, but that didn't mean they weren't there. It was vitally important they kept the virus from realising what they'd discovered, if possible. "Take us up and above the system plane, then set course for the tramline."

"Aye, Captain."

Mitch tried not to wince. The idea of running from a fight was alien to him. His thoughts kept insisting they hadn't actually been detected, let alone brought to battle. The enemy couldn't have set up an ambush unless they'd been able to see through the cloaking device from day one, in which case they would have made far better use of the technology. Mitch had served in engagements that would have gone the other way, if they hadn't been able to rely on their cloaks. He wanted to think they hadn't been detected, that the enemy hadn't so much as gotten a sniff of their presence. And yet, he knew he couldn't take the chance.

He felt weirdly detached from the universe as the frigate picked up speed, looking down on the enemy system as she made her way towards the tramline. The virus had turned the entire system into a giant industrial node…he found it hard to believe what he saw. His tactical staff had tried to estimate the system's industrial capability and…Mitch shook his head. The numbers were just too high. And yet…he snorted. Human communism had failed because of human nature. The virus was a single entity, although one that existed in many parts. It wasn't in constant competition with itself.

Mitch didn't relax, not completely, until they were through the tramline and into the next system. The virus had set up facilities there too, although—thankfully—not on as grand a scale. Mitch brought up the starchart and studied it for a long moment. They'd seen three major enemy industrial nodes, widely separated. It looked odd to him—despite decades of investment, Earth still had more industry than New Washington or Britannia—but he supposed it made a certain kind of sense. Alien-One had been on the edge of the virus's empire, as had the system they'd just attacked. It could muster forces to react to a threat—and support those forces—quicker than any other interstellar power.

He frowned as he stood and headed to his cabin. The human race had trouble supporting colonies—and fleet deployments—hundreds of light years from Earth. It wasn't *easy* to assign an entire fleet train to a fleet, let alone establish industrial nodes orbiting planets that couldn't make use of them—let alone pay for them—for decades. There were dozens of systems along the edge of explored space that barely had any contact with Earth, simply because they were too far away. The pre-war projections had suggested it would be years before they were brought closer to the homeworld. In hindsight, it would have been wiser to establish naval bases and depots along the border. But the politicians would never have gone for it. They'd spent too much of the nation's GNP on the fleet.

Mitch sat in his chair and stared at the terminal without really seeing it. He knew he should sleep, now they were clear of the infected system, but…he felt too keyed up. He wanted to stand and tour the ship, just to make sure every last station was ready for trouble, yet…his crew knew their jobs. They didn't need him peering over their shoulder, bothering them. They didn't need…

The hatch bleeped. Mitch looked up. "Come."

He smiled as Staci stepped into the cabin. "I just completed the tactical analysis of the previous system," she said, holding out a datapad. "It's not good news."

Mitch nodded as he ran his eye over the summery. The alien system was effectively impregnable, unless they massed a far larger fleet or invented a whole new war-winning superweapon. There were just too many starships, battlestations and automated weapons platforms orbiting the planets. He glanced at her tactical concepts and nodded, again. It would take a *lot* of firepower to grind the system into dust.

"No," he agreed. "We're lucky they didn't spend all those resources on ships."

He opened a drawer and removed a bottle of shipboard rotgut, then poured them both a glass. He wasn't supposed to condone anyone brewing on his ship, but—as per tradition—he was prepared to turn a blind eye as long as things didn't get out of hand. He didn't mind his crew having a glass or two, when they were off duty, but he'd crack down hard if someone turned up to their duty station as drunk as a lord. His lips quirked into a smile as he passed Staci a glass, then lifted his in a toast.

"To humanity," he said. "And to our allies."

"To humanity," Staci echoed.

Mitch took a sip. It tasted foul. Charlotte would probably detest it. And yet…Mitch recalled the sweet wines and expensive liqueurs he'd sampled on her estate. He had no idea how someone could drink them, but…he shrugged. It was unlikely Charlotte—or her husband—had ever had to drink the cheap stuff. They'd happily spend more money on a tiny bottle than the average person earned in a month.

He let out a breath as he put the glass on the desk. "We'll have to see what the admiral thinks, before we come up with any real plans. Unless they really *have* invented a supernova bomb."

"They *did* have a theory involving compressed gravity fields," Staci said. She shook her head, curtly. "But if someone did blow up the star, wouldn't that play merry hell with the tramlines?"

Mitch frowned. No one had ever *really* accounted for the tramlines. It seemed logical enough that stars, easily large enough to warp the fabric of space itself, could produce lines of gravimetric force linking them together, but…no one knew for sure. There were people who believed the tramlines had been created by a long-gone alien race, so advanced they were almost gods…he remembered what they'd discovered on the infected world and scowled. That theory seemed almost believable now. And yet…he shook his head. If something happened to a star, it seemed likely the tramlines would shift in response.

"No way we can test it," he mused. He shrugged. "It isn't as if we have such a weapon anyway."

"No, sir," Staci agreed. "We have to find a way to take out the system."

Mitch glanced at the datapad, again. "We need more firepower," he said. "If we rain missiles on them like water, sooner or later we *will* get something through the defences. And if we do…we still won't infect the entire system. We may have to destroy every last facility within the system before we can declare victory."

He keyed his terminal, bringing up the starchart. How many other infected worlds *were* there? The virus didn't *need* a full-scale invasion to establish itself. Once it got into the biosphere and started to turn the locals

318

into hosts, total conquest was just a matter of time. They might never complete the task of exterminating the virus. For all he knew, it might have infected another STL starship and sent it to a system that—apparently—lacked tramlines.

"We are learning more all the time," Staci said. "Sooner or later, we'll come up with a working vaccine."

Mitch nodded. "We'll reach the RV point in a few days," he said. "And then…if we don't link up with the fleet, again, we'll head straight to New Washington. And then"—he smiled, coldly—"we'll find a way to take the war to the enemy one final time."

CHAPTER THIRTY-THREE

"CAPTAIN," SIBLEY SAID. "We have incoming starfighters."

"Stand by point defence," Thomas ordered, stiffly. "Prepare to repel attack."

He gritted his teeth. The fighting had raged across the system for the last two days, with the enemy fleet—keeping its distance—hurling wave after wave of starfighters at the human ships. The tactic was cowardly as hell, but he had to admit it was working. The damage was starting to mount rapidly, particularly after the enemy had taken out a handful of freighters. Thomas had barely managed to snatch any sleep over the last day or so and he knew it wasn't much better for anyone else. The starfighter pilots were being pushed so badly they'd been forced to resort to stimulants just to keep themselves in the game.

Which is going to bite us pretty damn hard, he thought, as the red icons swooped into his point defence envelope. *The poor bastards will start shooting at each other soon enough.*

He watched, numbly, as a handful of red icons vanished. The remainder kept coming, launching torpedoes towards the hull before breaking off and fleeing back to their mothership. A couple more died—they made the mistake of flying in a straight line for more than a second or two—but it hardly mattered. The point defence had to hit the torpedoes, blowing them out of space before it was too late. A dull thump echoed through the ship as the survivors reached their target. Thomas glanced at the status display—the damage control teams were already on their way—and then looked away. He trusted his crew to handle the repairs, while he concentrated on the overall situation. They'd been damn lucky the missiles hadn't struck the gunboat ring.

His heart sank. The gunboats had feinted at the alien capital ships twice, but their point defence was just too good. Thomas's missiles hadn't gotten anywhere near the brainship, either by stabbing at the brainship directly or trying to grind down the escorts first. He was all too aware the fleet could probably crush the alien ships, even now, if it was prepared to take horrendous losses in the process. The virus probably had reinforcements already on the way. The fleet might win one encounter, only to lose the next.

He wanted to order the fleet to alter course, to run for the tramline, but he knew it couldn't be done. Not yet. They had to find the flicker station, the station they knew was there even though they hadn't found it in two days of intensive searching. Thomas was all too aware the enemy could track the fleet, that there was no hope of breaking contact. If the enemy could signal ahead...

"Captain," Donker said. "We took damage to sectors..."

"Evacuate the section, if it cannot be repaired," Thomas ordered, curtly. They'd already lost a handful of resupply shuttles. They couldn't afford to lose more. The fleet train was the fleet's greatest weakness and the virus knew it. In hindsight, they needed a new breed of freighters, ones that were mounted on military hulls. "And then seal the compartment completely."

He cursed under his breath as more red icons swooped into attack formation. If the host bodies were starting to wear themselves out, like their human counterparts, they weren't showing any sign of it. The wear and tear on their equipment had to be staggering and yet they were—somehow—maintaining a remarkable operational tempo. Thomas would have been impressed, if they hadn't been attacking *him*. It was just a matter of time before the tech started to break down, but…he doubted it would happen quickly enough to save the fleet. They needed to get out of the trap before it was too late.

And that means finding the flicker station and destroying it, he reminded himself, sternly. *We cannot jump through the tramline until it's gone.*

• • •

"Move, move, move!"

Colin forced himself to keep moving as the entire battlecruiser shuddered violently. The deck shifted under his feet, the gravity field flickering before it reasserted itself. Alarms howled in the distance, emergency lights coming on everywhere. The battlecruiser was under heavy attack. Colin hadn't felt so exposed since his first time on the training field, when he'd encountered incoming fire for the first time. It had been a grim reminder of just how fragile the human body truly was.

The ship lurched again as he stumbled towards a hatch. The light overhead was green, but the display beside the hatch blinked a warning. The compartment directly behind the hatch was fine; the compartment beyond *that* was in serious risk of decompression. Colin glanced at his platoon, then checked his mask and keyed his access code into the hatch. It opened, revealing an empty corridor. Colin led the way forward, making sure the entire team was inside before closing the hatch and setting it to airlock protocol. The interior hatches weren't proper airlocks, but they'd do. He hoped. They were short on options.

He frowned as they reached the second hatch. The light was red, the display warning of slow decompression. Colin keyed the hatch, then switched on his helmet light as the airlock hissed open. Beyond, the compartment was dark. A handful of people were making their way towards him. Colin stepped to one side to allow them to enter the makeshift airlock, checking their masks as they moved. The shipsuits should keep them alive long enough to get them to safety, if anywhere was truly safe now. He'd spent far too long helping evacuate sections and repair the damage to be confident.

His blood ran cold as a couple of injured crewmen stumbled towards him. He snapped orders to his men, ordering them to take the wounded to the triage centre as he continued poking into the compartment. The temperature was dropping rapidly, suggesting the leak was growing bigger. Colin stepped through a hatch that was badly damaged, too badly damaged to keep the air inside, and looked around. The compartment was blasted beyond recognition. He saw a pair of bodies lying on the deck, both charred to the point he couldn't tell if they'd been male or female. He logged their position, then turned slowly, allowing his suit's sensors to log the damage. The gash in the hull would have to be patched, sooner rather than later, but the rest of the compartment would have to wait. The crews just didn't have time to fix the damage.

If it's even possible, Colin thought. He peered through the gash, staring out into empty space. Lights twinkled in the distance…enemy ships? Friendly ships? Or stars? He didn't know. *We could die here.*

He pushed the thought out of his head as he swept the remainder of the damaged section, noting and logging three more bodies. One of them had been bisected, an attractive young woman who was missing everything below her waist; the remainder were battered beyond easy recognition. He looked around for the missing legs, then decided it was pointless. If they weren't on the deck, they'd probably been sucked out into space. It wasn't as if the crewwoman needed them any longer. She was dead.

Poor bitch, he thought, as another quiver echoed through the hull. *She deserved better.*

Colin kept speaking, recording his report, as he made his way back to the airlock. The medics had arrived and taken control, hastily checking the survivors to see who could be treated effectively and who would have to be given painkillers and told to wait until they could be treated properly. Colin knew the score—not *everyone* could be treated immediately, not in the middle of a battle—but it still made him feel sick. There were crewmembers who were about to die…crewmembers who could have lived, if they'd received the proper treatment. He didn't envy the medics. Whatever choices they made, people were about to die. And someone was sure to blame the medics for their choices.

He breathed a sigh of relief as he stepped through the airlock, even though he knew the safety was nothing more than an illusion. The starship was under constant attack. A single missile in the right place would be more than enough to ruin their day, once and for all. He wanted to remove his helmet and sit down, but he knew he couldn't. He had too many duties to perform.

And it's just a matter of time until we're completely worn out, he thought. *What'll happen to us then?*

He kept a wary eye on his platoon as they continued their duties. They weren't used to being helpless. He'd heard some of the higher-ups float plans to board the alien starships, plans that struck him as demented and yet were better than sitting around and waiting to die. In his experience, aggressors couldn't be allowed to get away with it or they'd *keep* doing it…he shook his head. The sensor reports were all too clear. A boarding party would be vaporised well before it reached its destination. Colin knew himself to be brave, but…boarding the ship would be nothing more than suicide. He'd throw his life away for nothing.

"I could have been an accountant, like my mother wanted," Davies said. "It would have been far safer."

"And to think you can't count past twenty without taking off your pants," Willis put in. The normally affable marine sounded tired, as tired as the rest of them. "I'm sure you keep miscounting the number of drinks I owe you."

"Hey!" Davies laughed. "I'll have you know my counting is perfect. I verified it myself."

"Hah," Willis said. "I bet…"

The deck shook again. "Focus," Colin ordered. Light banter was one thing, even though civilians would see it as stupid or irredeemably offensive, but there were limits. The banter was starting to develop a harder edge. "Concentrate on your duties."

"Yes, boss," Davies said. "You think we'll get out of this in less than twenty pieces?"

"We better had," Willies said. "You can't count past twenty without..."

"I said *focus*," Colin snapped. "We want to get out of this in *one* piece!"

He glanced at Kevin, wishing he could read the alien's emotions through his suit. If the constantly shaking hull, and passages through damaged sections, were unsettling him...he hated to think what it must be like for Kevin. He'd never enjoyed moving into different environments...he shuddered, remembering the first time he'd set foot on a boat. His instructors had informed him that commandos had to have a sailing ticket...it was funny, in hindsight, that he'd never realised it before joining the marines. The boat had been disconcerting and the rickety old aircraft they'd used for parachute jumps had been worse, but at least they'd been human. Kevin didn't even have *that* consolation.

Alarms howled. He gritted his teeth, forcing himself to move faster. There was no time to rest. If he got out of this alive, he promised himself, he'd spend his entire leave in bed. He'd hire a hotel room and arrange to have his food delivered to his bedside, perhaps by a young woman who'd be impressed by his service...he bit his lip, hard. His mind was wandering in all directions. There was no time to think about life after the mission, let alone after the war, either. And that meant...

"Come on," he said, as he opened the next airlock. The hatch ahead of them was shut, the light overhead glowing red. "We have work to do."

• • •

Commander India Khan kept her face under tight control as INS *Nehru* poked her way down the tramline. It was hard to escape the impression that another starship, human or alien, would materialise on top of them, but that wasn't what was bothering her. They were light-hours from the rest of the fleet, yet her sensors could see far too much of the battle. The fleet was under heavy attack.

It wasn't a pleasant thought. India's father had died in the brief

Anglo-Indian War. She'd grown up in a navy that looked forward to a rematch, even though India had quietly acknowledged that there were better ways to reach Great Power status. The Second Interstellar War—and then the *Third* Interstellar War—had cautioned them against fighting their fellow humans while genocidal aliens were prowling towards them. She hated the thought of abandoning the fleet, or being seen to run from battle, even though she had her orders. She *had* to find the flicker station.

She studied the empty display, wondering if they'd been tricked. The flicker station couldn't be *that* close to the star, could it? She'd had her staff run all sorts of simulations, trying to determine where it could be hidden, but they'd drawn a blank. The tramline was tiny, compared to the system, but that was a relative term. They still had to search a volume of space large enough to hide every starship in human service and still have room left over for the combined alien fleet.

If they mounted the station on a starship, we might never find it, she thought. It shouldn't be possible, but the virus itself shouldn't be possible either. *If they managed to cloak the station instead...*

She winced as her sensors picked up another energy flare. A starship had died...she tried to tell herself it was an alien ship, even though she knew better. The last update had stated that the admiral had ordered the fleet to defend itself, rather than going on the offensive. India disliked *that* thought, although she understood the logic. If the Indian Navy had played it a little more carefully, nearly two decades ago, the war might have gone very differently.

And we would have run into the virus anyway, she thought. *There's no time to worry about our petty human scrabbles...*

The display pinged. "Captain," the sensor officer said. "I've located an enemy structure."

India frowned. The enemy structure was surprisingly close to the primary star. Not close enough to melt the station, whatever it was, but close enough to disrupt its radio links to the rest of the tramlines. She could understand the reasoning—it cut down the time it would take to send a radio signal from one station to another—yet it struck her as odd. The virus would be better off accepting the downsides of positioning the station further from the primary...

"Tactical, lock weapons on the structure," she ordered. There was no time to worry about it. She'd study the reports later. "Fire!"

The destroyer vibrated as she launched a pair of missiles towards the alien installation. India watched, half-expecting to see the structure come to life and start spitting plasma fire at her missiles. The virus seemed to like installing point defence on anything and everything it could. But the missiles reached their target, detonating with terrific force. The structure, whatever it was, vanished in the blaze.

"I picked up a gravimetric shudder," the sensor officer reported. "That was the station."

"Signal the fleet," India ordered. She studied the sensor display for a long moment. Flicker stations were expensive, to the point that even the Great Powers clubbed together to operate them, but if there was any race that could build multiple stations in an isolated system it was the virus. "Inform them that we have taken out the station, and that we are currently checking to make sure there are no others."

"Aye, Captain."

• • •

"Signal from *Nehru*, Admiral," Richardson said. His voice rose in excitement. "They killed the flicker station!"

Susan allowed herself a moment of relief. The enemy had battered her fleet constantly, steadily wearing her people down. She'd been on the verge of ordering the fleet to alter course anyway, of taking the risk of jumping through the tramline even though the enemy might have been waiting on the far side. Her people needed rest, something they weren't going to get. Not yet. She had to get them out of the fire before it was too late.

"Signal the fleet," she ordered. *Nehru* had warned there might be more than one station. She didn't have time to wait for them to finish their survey.

The fleet was on the verge of breaking. "All units are to alter course, as planned, in twenty minutes."

She frowned as more and more warnings flashed up in front of her. "The ships that are no longer capable of making flank speed are to be evacuated, then set on automatic and abandoned," she added. She doubted the automatic ships would slow the virus for more than a few seconds, if they were lucky, but every moment counted. "If they can be stripped of anything useful in that time, it is to be taken. If not...leave it."

Richardson sounded shocked. "Aye, Admiral."

Susan understood. It went against the grain to abandon ships, particularly ships that could be repaired if they reached a shipyard. But there was no way they could get them out before it was too late. The fleet *had* to put some distance between themselves and the enemy. A combination of abandoned but still firing ships and sensor decoys would probably—hopefully—confuse the enemy long enough for her to break contact. And then they could rest.

A thought crossed her mind. It would be risky, and costly if it went wrong, but it might buy time. Might. There was no time to organise it properly. And yet, she was short on ideas. It had to be tried.

"And signal *Nehru*," she added, after a moment. They would have to put the operation together on the fly. "I've had an idea."

"Aye, Admiral."

CHAPTER THIRTY-FOUR

"AND TO THINK I THOUGHT WE WERE GETTING A REST," Willies grumbled. "Fuck me."

"You'll be getting arrest in a moment," Davies teased. "Arrest? Get it?"

"Everyone got it," Colin said, crossly. He wanted to rub his forehead. The stimulant coursing through his system had left him feeling uncomfortably sweaty—and permanently on edge. "They just didn't think it was funny."

He scowled around the shuttle. They'd been on the ship moments ago... he supposed he shouldn't have been surprised. Whenever Fleet Command scented trouble, the very first thing they did was call for the marines. And yet...sweat beaded on his brow as the shuttle plunged through space. They were supposed to be stealthy, but he knew the enemy could see them. One enemy starfighter would be more than enough to blow the shuttle into dust.

"I don't understand our orders," Kevin said. "Why are we being sent to drag the crew off their ship?"

Colin sighed, inwardly. The admiral had ordered that every ship that couldn't hope to escape had to be abandoned, left to their fate. He understood the logic, but he hated it. The idea of leaving one of his mates behind, while he ran for his life, *really* didn't sit well with him. He could understand spacers being reluctant to abandon their ships, even though their ships were doomed and they'd die with them if they remained on the hulks. It was quite possible that some of them might think they could break contact and make their way back home without being hunted down and destroyed. But it wasn't likely. The human race was desperately short of trained manpower. They couldn't afford to leave anyone behind.

"We need them back home, ready to crew the next generation of ships," Colin said. He made a mental note to discuss the issue later, when they had more time. It would be interesting to compare traditions. Did the Vesy have boats? He couldn't recall. "And we don't have time to argue."

He took a breath as the shuttle altered course. The interior felt oddly deserted, the platoon crammed into a tiny handful of seats. The remainder of the company had been dispersed over the other shuttles, or held back to provide interior security. Colin's hand dropped to his belt, checking to make sure his shockrod was firmly in place. He disliked the idea of using it on an allied crewmember—that was how diplomatic incidents got started—but there might be no choice. If the shit hit the fan, he was damn well going to put a stop to it before matters got out of hand.

"Contact in one minute," the pilot called. "Brace yourself!"

Colin gritted his teeth as the shuttle crashed against the Russian cruiser's hull. The gravity field seemed to grow stronger for a moment, then subsided. He'd once heard a rumour the Russians liked to keep their shipboard gravity stepped up a notch, just to ensure their crewmen grew stronger, but he'd always thought it was silly. And yet...he shook his head. Medical research had discovered, a long time ago, that variable gravity fields caused health problems. They could be handled, with genetic engineering, but such cures tended to lead to more problems further down the line. It was unlikely the Russians would bother.

He stood as the hatch slammed open. His mask blinked up an alert, warning him that the air was slightly contaminated. He stepped through the hatch and saluted a pair of officers standing on the far side. They wore Russian national uniforms with their own rank insignia, rather than GATO-approved designs. Colin cursed, inwardly. He understood the value of nationalism—that had been battered into him at school—but there were limits. He had no idea who he was addressing, or what rank he held. Or if he was in command of the vessel.

The Russian glared at him. "I am in command of this ship."

Colin nodded, as he saluted. A junior officer, almost certainly. Probably someone far enough down the chain of command not to expect to assume command, not under normal circumstances. His English was heavily accented. The briefing, such as it had been, had stated the Russian ship—with an unpronounceable name—had been badly damaged. How many officers had died to put this young man—he didn't look *that* much older than Colin himself—in command? Colin didn't think he wanted to know.

"You have orders to evacuate," he said, carefully. "We can take what remains of your crew off before it's too late."

"I cannot abandon the ship," the officer insisted. He hadn't so much as given Colin a name. "I cannot leave her behind."

"You have no choice," Colin said. He was tempted to stun them both, but that would start a fight as well as a diplomatic disaster. "This ship is doomed."

He winced, inwardly. The idea of *him* taking command of the company, let alone the regiment, was absurd. He wondered, grimly, how he'd handle it if he did find himself in command. The shock of losing so many officers wouldn't do him any good at all. And yet...he forced himself to meet the Russian's eyes, willing him to understand. His superiors back home wouldn't punish him for losing the ship. It had been lost well before he'd taken command.

"We can take your crew to safety, where they can be transferred to a new ship," he said, carefully. "If they stay here, they'll die for nothing."

He allowed himself a moment of relief as the Russian conceded without further argument and summoned his crew. The marines had been warned they might have to search the hulks for survivors, if they had time. Colin suspected they wouldn't have time to give the ships more than a cursory search. If someone was trapped in a sealed compartment, unable to get out or to call for help, they would be left behind to die. The virus might blow the ship away from a safe distance, just to be sure, or it might dispatch boarding parties. Colin's blood ran cold as he turned back to the shuttle. It was all too likely the abandoned ships would be set to self-destruct. If the virus caught and infected the survivors, if there *were* survivors, it would know everything they knew.

The Russian caught his attention as he stepped back onto the shuttle. "You have an alien on your ship."

"He's one of us," Colin said. He kicked himself, mentally, for not warning the Russians ahead of time. The British crew had grown used to Kevin, but the Russians hadn't even known he was there. "Is there anyone left onboard?"

The Russian looked pained. "Not as far as I know."

Colin checked the timer, but it was just a formality. The fleet was already altering course. If the shuttle stayed much longer, they wouldn't be able to get to the ships before it was too late and they got left behind. His heart sank as they disengaged. A standard cruiser, according to the briefing, had a complement of two hundred officers and crew. They'd saved forty-seven. The remainder were either dead or wishing they were.

"We'll get you home," he promised the Russian. The enemy starfighters were coming in again. "And then we'll get you to a new ship."

The Russian said something in Russian. Colin didn't understand. He'd taken French in school, but he'd never been particularly good at it. Russian had never even been a possibility. It struck him as odd—the Russians were a Great Power—but there was no point in worrying about it now. He'd ask his old headmaster, if he ever got asked back to tell the students about the military life. Given what had happened last time, it was unlikely he'd ever be asked back.

He leaned back in his chair and forced himself to rest. He'd done all he could. There was nothing he could do about the incoming starfighters. Either they blew the shuttle to hell or…it didn't matter. He closed his eyes. All he needed was a little sleep…

• • •

"The shuttles have disengaged, Captain," Commander Donker reported. "They're on their way back now."

"Good," Thomas said. The fleet was altering course, steadily picking up speed as it drew away from the cripples. The automated ships were turning to face the enemy, but no one really expected them to do anything more than delay the inevitable. Their self-destruct systems were already engaged, ready to blow the ships to atoms if they survived the enemy onslaught. "Helm, keep us moving with the rest of the fleet."

He forced himself to sit back, all too aware the nightmare was far from over. The enemy might not be waiting for them on the other side of the tramline, but there was nothing stopping the ships behind them from continuing the assault. There would be a few moments of grace, then... then what? Thomas glanced at the starchart, although he'd studied it time and time again over the last two weeks. There was too great a chance of encountering ships making their way back from the war front. They needed—they desperately needed—enough time to rest the crews and make repairs before they ran into the enemy again.

Lion picked up speed, her hull quivering slightly as she paced the remainder of the fleet. The fleet train was holding steady, but it was just a matter of time before the freighters started losing speed. Thomas made a mental note to suggest they transferred more supplies to the warships, before it was too late. The warships weren't designed to serve as freighters, and transferring the supplies again would be a pain, but it would be better than nothing. Right now, the enemy was all too aware of the fleet's weaknesses. It could just keep battering away at them until something broke.

Bagehot's face appeared in front of him. "Captain, the gunboat crews are ready for deployment."

Thomas nodded, keeping his face carefully blank. He'd been aware of the simple fact the gunboats were expendable ever since he'd first been briefed on the design, but it had never sat well with him. God knew the gunboat crews weren't *regular* naval personnel, after all; they'd never really intended to spend their lives in uniform. But he couldn't see any choice. The gunboats were far more expendable than the rest of the fleet. And there was at least a slight chance they'd survive.

"Deploy them when we reach the first waypoint," he ordered. "And tell them I said good luck."

"Aye, Captain."

The display cleared. Thomas sat back in his chair and waited, the seconds ticking away as the alien starfighters redoubled their attacks. They had to feel as though they'd been conned. They'd kept the range open so far that they couldn't bring up their own carriers, not soon enough to make a difference. Either they'd continue the attack until they ran out of life support or they'd pull back, giving the fleet a break. He wasn't sure which one he wanted. Taking out the enemy starfighters, or letting them take themselves out, would probably save more lives in the long run.

He frowned as the alien starfighters reversed course. That wasn't a good sign. The brainship knew the human ships were heading towards another ambush, even if they'd evaded the risk of being caught on the hop. Thomas felt the relief rippling around the bridge and sighed, inwardly. They'd made it out of the frying pan, perhaps, but they might well be about to fall into the fire. Who knew *what* was on the far side of the tramline?

The admiral will dispatch scouts ahead of the fleet, he told himself. *We should have a few seconds to deploy, before the shit hits the fan.*

Somehow, he didn't find the thought very reassuring.

• • •

"Signal from *Pinafore*," Richardson said. "Captain Corcoran sends his compliments, Admiral, and confirms the transit zone is clear."

As far as his sensors can determine, Susan thought, coldly. She kept that to herself. Any officer worthy of the name would already know it. *The enemy might have a rough idea where we'll make transit even if they don't know the precise location.*

She dismissed the thought. "Order the fleet to begin making transit, as planned," she said. "Deploy drones, then rotate them to suggest we're preparing to make a last stand."

"Aye, Admiral," Richardson said. "*Lion* reports the gunboats are ready to deploy."

"Deploy them," Susan ordered.

She smiled, despite her bone-wrenching tiredness. The virus wouldn't believe she *intended* to make a last stand, of course. It was unlikely to believe it had managed to keep her from jumping out, not when the majority of her ships could still make the jump. It would see her bluff for what it was, she hoped; it would see weakness and rush to the attack before she could make her escape. And if she was lucky...

. . .

Tobias hadn't felt as if he'd been set up for disaster since...since his school-days, when he'd been ordered to join a team that didn't want him and charge up and down a muddy field that offered plenty of opportunities for everyone else to trip him up or kick his backside whenever the PE teacher wasn't looking. Or when he was looking...the arsehole had openly favoured the sporty kids and penalised the rest for not taking the match seriously. He might as well have covered Tobias in steak sauce and thrown him into the lion's den. This time, at least, their deaths might be in a good cause.

Fuck, he thought. They'd been given a chance to rest, when it had become clear the gunboats couldn't hit the alien carriers, but he felt as if he hadn't slept. *This could end really badly.*

The gunboat drifted in interstellar space, close enough to the tramline to jump through it...if, of course, they'd had a Puller Drive. The boffins kept promising to come up with a miniature FTL drive, but—so far—they hadn't managed to devise a working model and put it into mass production. Tobias felt weirdly exposed, even though they were under stealth, as the remainder of the fleet made transit. The sensor ghosts surrounding their position wouldn't fool anyone. He'd been told the plan involved *not* fooling the enemy, that it would be better if the virus thought it had seen through the deception, but it seemed to him as though the admiral was trying to be clever. His instructors had warned him that trying to be clever was a good way to get killed.

Which is true, he thought, ruefully. *I was always smarter than Colin. It didn't stop him beating me up all the time.*

"Pick your targets," Marigold said. "But don't fire until you see the whites of their eyes."

Tobias nodded, not trusting himself to speak. The enemy fleet was picking up speed, launching missiles at the drifting hulks instead of trying to bypass them. Tobias hoped that was a good sign, as he selected his targets. The brainship was obvious, but there were others. If he could take out the carriers, which were recovering their fighters in preparation for the jump, the fleet would have a good chance of keeping ahead of the battleships until they reached New Washington. If...

Marigold cleared her throat. "Tobias?"

"Targets locked," Tobias said. "I'm uploading targeting data to the missiles now."

He sucked in his breath. The enemy fleet seemed to be trying for a hard transit. They'd be vomiting on the decks if they made transit at speed, if—of course—the host bodies actually vomited. The thought bothered him, although he wasn't sure why. Perhaps the catapult transit had been so rough because the virus didn't *need* to worry about jump shock. Perhaps...

"I've programmed the missiles to fire when the ships reach Point Alpha, unless they scan us first," he said. "We don't want them sweeping the missiles out of space."

He braced himself as the seconds ticked down. They'd unloaded hundreds of missiles—almost the entire reserve—into space. If they were spotted before they went live, the entire exercise would be worse than useless. He didn't want to die for nothing! His eyes narrowed, sweat trickling down his back as enemy sensors swept over their position. The decoys should distract them, but it was growing more and more obvious that the decoys were just sensor ghosts. They weren't shooting at the advancing ships.

The display flashed red. "They have us!"

He hit the firing key, as Marigold flash-woke the gunboat and yanked it around on an evasive pattern. The enemy seemed stunned as hundreds of missiles came to life, screeching towards their fleet at point-blank range. He cursed under his breath as they cut their drives...they'd probably damaged their drive nodes, hitting the brakes like that, but it would keep them from impaling themselves on the missiles. Their point defence came to life seconds later, sweeping dozens of missiles out of space. But the remainder kept coming...

It might have been a mistake, targeting the brainship, he thought. *It's the most heavily protected ship in the fleet.*

He felt his heart leap as a handful of missiles made it through, tearing into the enemy ship. For a moment, he feared the worst...and then the brainship exploded. The remaining ships seemed to flinch, their coordination falling apart as they fought desperately to survive. A carrier fell out of formation, a destroyer was vaporised...

"We got the bastard," he cheered. "We got him!"

"Don't get too pleased," Marigold advised, as she set course for *Nehru*. "The rest of the fleet is still coming."

"Yeah." Tobias grinned. "But we bought the fleet some time."

CHAPTER THIRTY-FIVE

"ADMIRAL, *NEHRU* JUST CROSSED THE TRAMLINE," Richardson said. "The ambush worked."

Susan nodded, stiffly, as the report blinked up on her display. She hadn't expected much from the ambush. She'd only consented to deploying so many missiles because she'd believed she'd lose them shortly, when the virus resumed its attack on the fleet train. And yet, it had worked. The gunboats had taken out the enemy brainship, then barnacled themselves to the destroyer so she could carry them back through the tramline. Susan told herself she shouldn't have been so doubtful. The virus had been so desperate to keep her from escaping that it had impaled itself on her missiles.

Which should buy us a little time, she thought, grimly. *But will it be enough?*

She studied the display as the fleet moved off the tramline and plunged further into the deserted system. They were only two jumps from the RV point—and four from New Washington—but that only ensured the chances of interception were a great deal higher. Susan wanted to believe the Americans would launch a spoiling attack out of New Washington, forcing the virus to decide between intercepting the fleet and knocking the Americans back onto the defensive, but she knew it wasn't likely to happen. The Americans didn't have any way to know what was happening on the far side of the tramline. And even if they did, they had to put the safety of New Washington first. There were millions of people on the surface.

"The fleet is to cloak, as planned, before we alter course," she ordered. She was tempted to follow a least-time course, on the assumption it would be the last thing anyone would expect, but there was such a thing as out-smarting herself. The brainship was gone. The virus's ships might follow an unimaginative course and wind up winning by complete accident. "And then we begin a dog-leg to the next tramline."

She stroked her chin, hoping—praying—that her crews would have a chance to rest. If they managed to lose themselves somewhere within the trackless wastes of interstellar space, they might just be able to take a break and perform repairs before they forced the next tramline. The repair crews were already hard at work, patching holes in hulls while the transhipment teams emptied the freighters into the warships. Susan suspected a number of the freighters would have to be abandoned, sooner rather than later. They were becoming a serious liability. Her lips twisted in annoyance. Losing the freighters would be a liability, too.

Her eyes turned to the starchart. In theory, if the survey crews hadn't missed anything, there wasn't any major enemy presence between the fleet's position and the RV point. In practice, who knew? The virus had presumably established a flicker network that ran as far corewards as New Washington. It could be deploying its forces to stop her…she silently ran through the calculations, asking herself where *she* would put the ambush. *She'd* strike in the last system, bar one. It wouldn't do to accidentally alert the Americans to her fleet's survival. The virus would have to assume the Americans would come to her aid.

We could use the 5th Calvary coming over the hill right now, she thought. She'd watched a bunch of cowboy movies as a young girl, although it hadn't taken her long to notice they all followed the same basic formula. *I'd even settle for a squadron of battleships.*

She dismissed the thought as the fleet continued into the empty system. Questions spun around and around in her mind. How long would it take the fleet to make transit, without the brainship? What would it do? Was there enough viral matter on the ships to make up for the lost brainship? Would the fleet try to hunt them down? Or would it proceed to link up with the next enemy fleet, then turn to face the human ships? She just didn't know.

The hours started to tick by, one by one. Susan kept a wary eye on the reports, breathing a sigh of relief when it appeared she wouldn't have to abandon any more ships. Even powered down, they might have served as a trail of breadcrumbs that would have led the enemy right to her. And... she keyed through a series of reports, watching grimly as the datanet noted and logged the evacuees, then suggested placements for them. There would be Russian engineers in Chinese engine rooms and French pilots flying off American carriers and...she shook her head. They'd cope. They had to.

"Admiral," Richardson said. "We've reaching the passive sensor limits. We won't be able to monitor the tramline for much longer."

"Understood," Susan said. She hadn't placed much faith in the passive sensors. The fleet was already too far from the tramline to be *sure* of spotting a cloaked ship, when it made transit. If the enemy fleet had finished licking its wounds, it could already have jumped through the tramline and started searching for them. Doctrine suggested deploying a handful of drones to monitor the tramline, but she didn't have any to spare. "Order the sensor crews to keep an eye on it."

She sat back in her chair, forcing herself to think. Their options had narrowed significantly in the last two days. She could alter course radically and dart back through the tramline, taking an extremely long route home, but she didn't have the supplies. The logistics report was grim. They were short on everything from ammunition to spare parts. The starfighter and gunboat crews had been pushed to the limit. She was no longer confident of victory if she reversed course and engaged the pursuit fleet, let alone whatever might be waiting for them further up the tramline. She had to admit the virus had played its cards well. It had forced her into a situation when she *knew* there was a trap waiting for her, but she had to spring it anyway.

Our only chance is to sneak through as carefully as possible, she thought. *And it knows that, too.*

She stood. "Get some rest," she ordered, addressing the entire compartment. "That's an order."

"Aye, Admiral," Richardson said.

Susan smiled, then headed into her cabin and closed the hatch. Her head was starting to hurt. She'd drunk too much coffee…she was going to pay for that, even if she hadn't risked taking anything stronger. Half her starfighter pilots were in for a world of pain once the stimulants finally wore off. They'd be in no state for a fight, at least until they got a day or two of rest. And…

Her heart sank as she kicked off her boots and clambered into bed. It wasn't easy to forget that the fleet was being hunted, that the enemy might stumble across them at any moment…that they might blunder straight into a trap because they didn't dare risk using the active sensors. Susan could imagine all sorts of horrors, from the enemy copying her missile trick to simply laying a minefield in her path. The Royal Navy generally considered minefields a waste of resources—it was impossible to be *entirely* sure the enemy would remain on a predictable flight path—but if there was any interstellar power that would feel differently, it was the virus. And if Susan was worried, the people under her command would be worried as well.

They're not the ones responsible for getting us out of the mess, Susan thought. The entire mission concept had been her idea. She'd get the blame if the mission failed, although—if it did—it was unlikely she'd live long enough to face a court-martial. *I'm the one who has to get us clear.*

She closed her eyes and lay back, but sleep was a long time in coming.

• • •

Tobias couldn't move.

The gunboat was docked safely on the ring, the hatch blinking green, but he couldn't force himself to get up and stagger to the hatch. He wasn't sure what was wrong with him—he hadn't taken *that* many stimulants—yet…

he felt as if he was simply unable to move ever again. Marigold didn't sound any better, from what he could hear. He couldn't turn his head to see her.

He coughed, loudly, as he stared down at his console. His shipsuit felt grimy. He was uncomfortably aware he probably stunk like…his imagination failed him. They'd been in the gunboat for hours, during the brief engagement and then the transit through the tramline and the flight back to *Lion*. The battlecruiser hadn't waited for them. Tobias understood, intellectually, that the battlecruiser was far more important than the gunboats, but it still felt like a betrayal.

The terminal pinged. "Are you two decent in there?"

Tobias flushed and tried to speak, but nothing came out. It was hard to muster the energy to care. He wanted to sleep and yet he was too tired. The hatch hissed open behind him, something that should have worried him…he'd learned the hard way not to ignore someone behind him, but… he just didn't care. He didn't even jump when he felt strong arms fiddling with his straps, pulling him free.

"Richard?" Colin. It was Colin. Tobias was almost too tired to be alarmed. "Tobias?"

"…Fuck," Tobias managed. He felt as if he was about to slop out of his seat and turn into a puddle on the deck. "What…?"

"I've got you," Colin said. He finished freeing Tobias, then hauled him out of the seat and slung him over his shoulder. "It'll be fine."

Tobias's awareness blurred, as if he'd fallen into a fever-dream. His worst nightmare was coming true, right in front of him. Colin was carrying him through the hatch…he saw a green-skinned alien, right in front of him; he saw the bulkheads start to shimmer, bending and twisting in ways no human could comprehend. He wanted to run, but his legs refused to work and…

His awareness snapped back to normal. He was lying on a bed, staring up at an intimidating array of machinery. It looked like a set of dentist's tools or…his head spun as he realised he was in sickbay. Someone had stripped him, then covered his body with a sheet. He started to sit upright, even though the deck seemed to be heaving like a ship caught in a storm. Bile rose in his throat. It was all he could do not to be sick.

"Welcome back," Doctor Haugen said. "How are you feeling?"

Tobias coughed. He'd seen…he wasn't sure *what* he'd seen. His stomach felt uncomfortably empty, as if he hadn't eaten for days. Hunger had never really been part of his life, whatever else one could say about his childhood. Ration bars were free, even if no one wanted them. And yet…he felt dazed rather than sore. How much of what he'd seen had been real?

"The stimulants have burnt their way out of your system," the doctor assured him. She held out a mug of water, her dark eyes watching him intently as he sipped. "You slept through most of the aftermath, for which you should be grateful. I saw fit to keep you under until the last of the effects left your system, too."

"Thanks," Tobias managed, somehow. He felt woozy, as if he hadn't had anything like enough sleep. "What…what happened to Marigold?"

"She's in the next bed," the doctor said. "She took more stimulants than yourself and the after-effects were considerably worse. She should be fine, once they've worked their way out of her system. I'd prefer to keep an eye on her, and you, but…we're in a pickle. You might have to go back on duty at short notice."

Tobias stared at Marigold. It wasn't the first time he'd seen her sleep, but…she looked unhealthily pale. Her freckles stood out so clearly he half-thought she was dead. She was naked, her modesty preserved by a towel… he wondered, suddenly, who'd undressed them both? The doctor? Or…he didn't want to think about it. He'd heard enough changing room bullshit to last a lifetime.

"I…fuck," he managed. He put the mug to one side, then wobbled to his feet. "Can't I stay with her?"

"Not until she wakes up," the doctor said, bluntly. "For the moment, I advise you to get something to eat and then go back to your bunk. You should try and get as much sleep as possible before you have to go back into battle. Do you understand me?"

Tobias nodded. "Yes," he said. "I do."

He found a spare shipsuit in the locker and pulled it on as the doctor went about her business. It was a size too large, but it would have to do. He'd have to change when he returned to the wardroom anyway, just in case...he took one last look at Marigold, then forced himself to step out of the compartment and into the corridor. It was lined with makeshift beds, crammed with personnel...Tobias swallowed, hard. Some of them looked badly hurt. They were the ones who should be in sickbay...

And if we'd been a little less lucky, he thought numbly, *we could have been badly injured, too.*

He shuddered as he made his way back to pilot country. He'd known that war meant death and destruction. His *father* had died in the war. And yet, he hadn't quite understood what it *meant*. His father had been vaporised. The gunboat pilots he hadn't let himself get to know had been vaporised. The men and women in the corridor had survived, but they'd been badly injured. Modern medicine was good, yet...they'd bear the scars for the rest of their lives. It was hard to believe they would ever be the same again.

Poor bastards, he thought. Oddly, looking at the wounded made him more fearful than reading the lists of the dead. The lists were just...words. The men in front of him were all too real. *They deserve better.*

He forced himself to keep moving. There was nothing he could do for them, except...he swallowed hard. All he could do was refrain from staring, just to let them keep what little dignity they had left. And he knew, deep inside, that it wasn't enough. But it was all he could do.

• • •

"I'll be fine, Captain," Senior Crewwoman Elaine Winslow said. "It's just a flesh wound."

Thomas kept his face under tight control. Crewwoman Winslow had lost a *leg*. She was going to need months of treatment before she returned to something close to normal, even though the navy would pay for a cloned or prosthetic leg. The awards she'd receive for saving her subordinates, at the cost of being wounded herself, hardly seemed to make up for it. Her file had made it clear she'd never seen herself as one of the navy's lifers. It hardly seemed fair to take such an injury, shortly before her enlistment came to an end.

"You did your part," he said. "Rest now."

He felt almost pathetically useless. He'd had deportment classes and etiquette lessons, but he'd always been uncomfortable dealing with wounded crewmen. It was never easy to know what to say. He'd never even exchanged pleasantries with Crewwoman Winslow before she'd wound up in sickbay. Her subordinates spoke well of her, but...Thomas felt a stab of guilt. He should have made time to get to know her before the ship went into battle. She'd been wounded, badly, while she'd been under his command. And he hadn't even known her name!

The sense of uselessness grew stronger as he walked from bed to bed, exchanging a handful of words with his wounded crewmembers. Some of them were asleep, or pretending to be asleep; others were polite, yet distant. The prospect of being injured wouldn't have seemed quite real, not until it actually happened. A handful had probably just seen their careers draw to an end. No one would give them a hard time for being given a medical discharge, but still...

Thomas spoke briefly to the doctor, then turned and left the compartment. The fleet had managed to break contact, but they all knew it was just a matter of time before the virus found them again. His crew were working desperately to repair the damage, patching holes in the hull and slapping new point defence mounts into position...*Lion* had been lucky, compared to some of the other ships. A couple of battleships and a carrier had been so heavily damaged it was a minor miracle they'd managed to stay with the fleet. The admiral had already given orders for all nonessential personnel to be evacuated, just to ensure the remainder could be pulled off if the ships had to be powered down and abandoned. Their captains weren't pleased...

A chill ran down Thomas's spine as he made his way back to his ready room. It would be at least two days before they reached the tramline, then a week before they made their way back to New Washington…anything could happen in that time. There was a major enemy fleet somewhere in front of them and another at the rear. He stepped to one side as a team of crewmen hurried past, conveying spare parts to the repair crews. Their efforts might be futile. Thomas was all too aware they wouldn't be out of danger for a *long* time.

This is just a pause in the storm, he told himself. *And we have to make use of it before they find us again.*

CHAPTER THIRTY-SIX

"TRANSIT IN TWENTY SECONDS, CAPTAIN," Lieutenant Sam Hinkson said. "Nineteen...eighteen..."

Mitch waited, bracing himself. They were, technically, in explored space, but the virus had infected it heavily. They'd passed through a couple of systems that had been explored and settled before the war, yet they'd picked up no signs of human life. They hadn't been able to tell if the colonies had been infected or simply bombed from orbit, but...he knew that was wishful thinking. The virus didn't need to land troops to capture the colony and then keep the locals under control. It could just infect the colony, then turn the colonists into host bodies. Resistance would be not only futile, but inconceivable.

It's been nearly a decade since the system fell, he thought, grimly. *The only thing we can do for the colonists is turn their planet into radioactive dust.*

The thought would have sickened him, once upon a time. Now...it was just a fact of life, just something they would have to accept, that they would have to *do*, just to win the war. He wanted to win before anyone started questioning their morality...he wanted to win, just so his people would live long enough to start questioning their morality. Mitch was a student of history. The great victims of the past had always been beaten, ground under so thoroughly they couldn't hope to recover, before the victimisers and their descendants had started to wonder if they'd done the right thing. It was hard to believe, sometimes, that the victims had ever been a threat. But they had been...

He put the thought out of his mind as *Unicorn* made transit. His eyes lingered on the display as it blanked and came back to life, reporting a handful of sensor emissions closer to the system primary. A handful of ships, holding station near Tramline Four...the tramline that led down the chain to New Washington. They didn't look anything like numerous enough to take the fleet in a straight fight, although Mitch knew better than to allow them to come within firing range of *his* ship. *Unicorn* had no place in such an engagement and everyone knew it.

"Captain," Staci said. "I'm not picking up any hint the fleet passed through the system."

Mitch wasn't too surprised. His best-case estimate had suggested *Unicorn* would reach the RV point at least a day before *Lion* and the rest of the fleet. It was why he'd agreed to spend so long surveying the alien system, poking his nose into every nook and cranny he spotted on their voyage home. The sheer wealth of tactical data he'd amassed had made him seriously consider continuing the flight, rather than waiting to link up with the fleet. There was so much data that he knew he couldn't allow it to be lost. GATO was going to need it to plot a—hopefully—war-winning offensive.

"Helm, take us to the RV point," he ordered. "We can give the fleet a couple of days before we proceed on our own."

He frowned as he peered at the tramlines on the display. Tramline Three looked as innocuous as any other tramline, but he knew the fleet was somewhere on the far side. It had to be. The alternative was unthinkable. And yet...he wished he knew what the fleet had encountered, during its long voyage. The tramlines were predictable, to a certain extent, but what about the alien planets, installations and fleets? There was no way to know what they'd find until they went looking.

His thoughts churned. He didn't *want* to abandon the fleet. His orders weren't *that* clear, he told himself; the tactical data he carried was vitally important, yet a week or so of delay in getting it to Earth wouldn't make any difference. It had been hard enough to assemble the ships for Operation Lightning Strike. Putting together the sort of firepower necessary to smash the virus's homeworld—he hoped to God it *was* the alien homeworld—was going to take months, if not years. He could give the fleet a few days without risking anything...

"Captain," Hinkson said. "We are closing on the RV point."

"There's still no sign of the fleet," Hannah added.

"Hold position," Mitch ordered. He wanted to believe the fleet had already passed through the system, but—his thoughts reminded him, again and again—it was unlikely. "We'll wait."

He brought up the tactical records and studied them thoughtfully. There weren't *that* many systems between New Washington and the alien homeworld. They didn't have many mobile units attached to their defences, unless they'd been lurking under cloak. And yet...his mind raced with schemes, each one more impractical than the last. The enemy defences would have to be reduced sharply, yet the only way to do *that* was through force. There were no fancy tricks that could be used, no feints that might distract the enemy long enough to let a covert force land a major blow. It would be force against force and he feared, deep inside, that the combined navies couldn't amass enough firepower to crack the planet's defences.

We can't even hit the planet with BioBombs, he thought. *Anything stealthy enough to pass through the defences without being detected won't survive the passage through the atmosphere.*

The display bleeped. Mitch thought, just for a moment, that the fleet had arrived...before realising two ships had entered the system from entirely the wrong direction. It was hard to tell what they were, but they looked as though they were heading down to New Washington rather than turning to engage the fleet. Mitch sighed inwardly, trying not to show his annoyance. He'd always been happiest doing something, rather than sitting patiently for someone *else* to do something. The idea of hurrying up and waiting had never sat well with him.

He stood. "XO, you have the bridge," he said. His head was starting to hurt. He'd worked the problem from a dozen angles and drawn a complete blank. His plans to attack the alien homeworld required ships that didn't exist or technologies that had never been made practical. It was starting to look like an exercise in wishful thinking, not tactical planning. "I'll be in my cabin."

"Aye, Captain," Staci said.

Mitch felt a flash of affection as he made his way through the hatch and into his tiny cabin. Staci would have a command of her own, sooner rather than later...he felt a flicker of irritation at the thought of losing her, combined with the dull awareness it was going to happen one way or the other. He'd known a commanding officer who'd constantly blocked promotion for his subordinates, on the grounds he didn't want to train up replacements. The idiot hadn't realised his subordinates would resent it, then seek ways to get out from under his thumb. Morale had been in the pits well before the Admiralty started asking awkward questions. Naval service could be dangerous, and promotion could be slow outside wartime, but only a fool would make it worse out of petty stupidity. A discontented crew was one that would start looking for ways to make its feelings known.

He lay back on his bunk and closed his eyes. They could wait two days, perhaps three, before they had to make their way to New Washington. It would mean abandoning the remainder of the fleet, but...he shook his head. *Unicorn* was unlikely to make any real difference, if the fleet ran into something it couldn't handle. The frigate was designed for surveillance, missile targeting and stealth insertions, not open combat. She'd be blown away in seconds if the enemy concentrated their fire on her.

A thought crossed his mind. *What if we set up a base in the alien system and start grinding down their defences? Either they send their mobile units to fight us, allowing us to take them out without crossing the fixed defences, or they let us get set up and lay siege to the system without interference...*

He started awake as the intercom bleeped. He'd been asleep...how long had he been asleep? Were they under attack? The alarms weren't howling...

he rubbed his forehead as he sat up, one hand fumbling for the terminal. Staci knew what to do, if they came under attack. He wouldn't fault her for snapping orders when he wasn't on the bridge. *Unicorn* wasn't tough enough to wait for him, if the shit really hit the fan…

"Report," he snapped.

"Captain, a large fleet of ships just transited the tramline," Staci reported. "They're heading towards us."

Mitch frowned. "Admiral Onarina?"

"No, Captain," Staci said. "These ships came from Tramline One. They're heading towards us—and Tramline Three."

"…Shit." Mitch stood, keying the terminal. A horde of red icons was bearing down on their position. The enemy fleet was big enough to swat *Unicorn* without even noticing. He counted a dozen battleships and carriers, surrounded by a swarm of starfighters. Either they feared attack or they'd caught a sniff of his presence. And yet, that was far too much firepower for one little frigate. "They're heading down the chain, towards the fleet."

He brought up the starchart. The enemy might have a rough idea where the fleet was…no, there was no doubt about it now. Mitch's most optimistic estimate had suggested the decoys wouldn't fool the enemy for more than a couple of days at most…and that, he conceded privately, was probably *too* optimistic. Assuming the enemy had reversed course immediately, it might just have made it to the next tramline in time to track down the fleet and bring it to battle. Or simply maintain contact until reinforcements arrived.

"I'm on my way," he said. "Helm, move us out of their way. We don't want them catching a sniff of us."

If they haven't already, his thoughts added. It didn't seem likely—*Unicorn* had plenty of time to evade contact, given that the enemy hadn't tried to sneak up on them—but it was possible. *Where do they think they are going?*

He pulled on his jacket, then returned to the bridge. The alien fleet looked larger than ever on the main display, sweeping space with sensor pulses as it made its way towards the tramline. It might not have been *looking* for *Unicorn*, but it was likely to find her if they got lucky. Mitch took his seat and nodded in approval as the frigate glided to one side, keeping the range open as much as possible. The alien ships stormed past, without so much as focusing their sensors on *Unicorn*. Mitch guessed they were pumping out so many sensor emissions that they were actually confusing their own sensors. They'd get a return off every piece of space junk in the vicinity.

Not that there's anything worth noticing, he thought. *Apart from us, of course.*

"Captain," Hannah reported. "They're bringing stealth systems online. I think they're planning to cloak."

Mitch frowned, then felt his blood run cold. There were enough ships in the fleet to give Admiral Onarina and her fleet a very hard time. No, there were enough ships to destroy her...particularly if they combined the first fleet with the second. He had the impression he was watching the jaws of a giant trap steadily starting to close. One fleet would drive Admiral Onarina into the other's waiting arms. And then...

His mind raced. Admiral Onarina and her ships were *not* expendable. He liked and respected her too much to even consider abandoning her to her fate. And yet...he cursed under his breath. If *Unicorn* was lost, all her tactical data would be lost with her. The allies wouldn't know where to send their fleets, not until they found the alien homeworld for the second time. Mitch squirmed mentally, torn between two competing priorities. He had to save the fleet and, at the same time, he had to get the information home.

He keyed his terminal, drawing lines on the display. Perhaps they could rush to New Washington and then double back...no, even on a least-time course, it would take three days to reach New Washington. The Americans would probably have the enemy system under observation—it was standard practice, if one had the ships to spare—but Mitch had no idea where to find the American pickets. They might not even accept his message. They'd fear *Unicorn* had been captured and her crew infected. God knew it had happened before.

We have to warn the admiral before she flies right into a trap, Mitch thought. The enemy fleet could be avoided, if there was enough warning. *We have to warn her...*

"Helm, take us after the alien fleet," he ordered. "Hold us as close as you can without compromising the cloaking field."

"Aye, Captain."

Mitch took a breath. "I am about to bend our orders to breaking point," he said, addressing the bridge crew. It would be more accurate, he conceded privately, to say he was about to violate his orders. The Admiralty would not be amused, although it might be grateful if they saved the fleet. "If any of you have a problem with that, this is your one chance to say so. It will be noted and produced in evidence during the formal inquiry."

There was a pause. No one spoke.

Mitch relaxed, slightly. He'd put the crew in a terrible spot. Breaking orders—or bending them to the point they were effectively broken—was frowned upon. So was mutiny. A Board of Inquiry could reasonably decide that anyone who did more than file a formal objection was guilty of mutiny, even if they—technically—had right on their side. And it could—probably would—be the end of someone's career if they tried. The navy regarded the chain of command as sacrosanct. A captain would have to commit a serious offence before his subordinates were allowed to relieve him of command.

Which is what I am about to do, he thought. *And they might wind up being hung beside me.*

"XO, file a protest anyway," he said, curtly. If they succeeded, the log could be quietly ignored. He'd happily testify that Staci had protested his orders on his orders. He smiled at the thought. That little logic bomb should upset the beancounters. If they failed…there was no reason Staci's career should go down the toilet with his. "Everyone else, see to your duties."

Staci looked thoroughly displeased. Mitch understood. No matter what he said, during the inevitable Board of Inquiry, there would be people who thought Staci had put a knife in Mitch's back. Bastards. There were the ideals of naval regulations and the messy realities of wartime service. Staci was caught between two fires, just like everyone else. Mitch would do what he could for her, but he knew it might not be enough. Hopefully,

357

the admiral would go to bat for her, too. God knew *she* understood what it was like to face such a painful dilemma.

Mitch settled back into his chair as the frigate picked up speed, silently considering his options. The enemy, damn them, would know where to go. They'd know where they'd meet Admiral Onarina and her fleet. Mitch didn't. His best guesses were still guesswork. He could accelerate and circumvent the enemy ships, to carry the warning to the admiral, but...he didn't know where to go. It would be quite easy to take the wrong tramline, or accidentally inform the enemy that their planned ambush had failed. If they got it wrong...

He forced himself to wait as the enemy fleet started to make transit, without slowing down at all. Mitch had suspected the virus was largely immune to jump shock, or at least able to continue operating despite the pain, but it was still disconcerting to see it confirmed. He tried to tell himself the virus knew it was jumping into empty space, yet...it was hard to believe. The virus should be more vulnerable, not less. It was just another thing about it that didn't quite make sense.

"Take us through the tramline," he ordered. They'd be making the transit far too close to the alien fleet for his peace of mind. "Communications, prepare an emergency transmission. If they target us, I want a warning screamed to the entire system."

"Aye, Captain."

Mitch took a breath. He had few qualms about risking his life, yet... he would never know, if the virus spotted them and opened fire, if his death had saved the fleet. The thought cost him a pang. He'd always thought he'd die in battle, perhaps blown away by enemy missiles or ramming his small frigate into an enemy battleship to save a larger ship, but he'd always seen his death as being meaningful. Here...he had no way to know, now or ever, if there would be anyone in the system to hear his final words. The scream might fade hours—or days—before Admiral Onarina made transit. He might have thrown his ship and crew into the fire for nothing.

The display blanked. Mitch forced himself to project an appearance of calm. They might die before the display rebooted, the hull evaporating under the fire of nearly a hundred enemy ships. He counted down the seconds, each one feeling like an hour. He heard a breath echoing around the bridge as the display came back to life. The enemy fleet, hidden under cloak, was heading away at terrifying speed.

"Helm, shadow them," Mitch ordered. "Sensors, can you spot the admiral?"

"No, Captain," Hannah said. "The system appears to be as dark and silent as the grave."

Poor word choice, Mitch thought, as they picked up speed. *Very poor word choice.*

CHAPTER THIRTY-SEVEN

SUSAN WASN'T FOOL ENOUGH TO THINK they'd lost the enemy ships completely. They'd moved too far from the least-time course to be certain the system was empty, and the need to keep their sensors powered down made it harder to spot any watching eyes, but—as they prepared to jump into the next system—she felt almost optimistic again. The enemy hadn't spotted them...probably. They might just make it through the next system—and the next—before they ran into real trouble.

She took one final look at the fleet's status as the countdown began. They'd repaired everything that could be repaired, at least without a ship-yard. She had no illusions about how long they'd last, when the enemy found them again, but they'd have a fighting chance. And her crews had had a rest, even the damage control teams. They were about to be pushed to the limit, but...she shook her head. There was no way they could get a *proper* rest. That wouldn't happen until they reached New Washington—or, perhaps, travelled all the way back to Earth.

We have to get to New Washington first, she thought. *If we don't do that, we won't be getting home at all.*

"Admiral," Richardson said, as a yellow icon appeared on the display. It turned to green as he spoke. "*Pinafore* just made transit. Local space beyond the tramline is clear."

"Take us through, as planned," Susan ordered. The enemy fleet wasn't waiting for them…where *was* the enemy fleet? She wanted to believe she'd escaped contact, but she knew it was unlikely. "And deploy four additional recon drones as soon as we're through the tramline."

She braced herself as the countdown reached zero. *Pinafore* was a good ship, and Susan knew her commander personally, but it was quite possible she'd missed something. Space was immense. The entire enemy fleet could be lurking a short distance from the tramline, far away enough to escape detection while close enough to move in for the kill. She let out a breath as the display rebooted, displaying a star system that hadn't been particularly developed even before the virus had swept down from Alien-One in the early days of the war and taken possession. There was no sign of the enemy fleet.

"Transit completed, Admiral," Richardson reported. "Local space appears to be clear."

"How…convenient," Susan said. She stared down at the display for a long moment. Her experience told her to expect trouble. "Signal the fleet. We will proceed as planned."

She let out a breath as the fleet started to shift onto its new course. It would add several hours to the journey, but—hopefully—it would keep them clear of any ambushes. The virus would have to shift position if it saw them coming—if it was out there, waiting for them—and that would give her sensor crews a chance to spot it. She checked her remaining drones obsessively, cursing the shortage under her breath. If she had more, she could surround the fleet with an entire flotilla of drones. It would be a great deal harder for anything to sneak up on her.

The minutes continued to tick by, each one feeling like an hour. Susan bit her lip to remain alert, all too aware they might be lulled into a false sense of security. She knew she should be resting, that her alpha crew should be resting too, but she'd never forgive herself if she was off the deck when the alarms howled. Her lips twitched. She'd have worse problems if the alarms woke her when she was fast asleep. The headache would leave her wishing the virus would hurry up and put her out of her misery.

She kept a wary eye on the display as she worked her console, trying to calculate the odds of being intercepted. It was impossible to draw any real conclusions…she deleted her projections in a flash of irritation. They told her nothing she didn't know already. The fog of war had enveloped the fleet, leaving her guessing…she hoped, deep inside, that the virus was guessing, too. It might have a rough idea of where she was, but that rough idea encompassed a whole series of star systems. Who knew? Maybe it had given up the chase.

We're still in its territory, she reminded herself. *It won't let us go so easily…*

"Admiral," Richardson said. "The drones are picking up sensor distortions."

Susan kicked herself, mentally, as she stood and studied the reports. Sensor distortions didn't always mean a prowling enemy fleet, but they were so deep in enemy space she couldn't afford to ignore them. They were in an odd place, further from the system primary than she'd expected… she frowned, wondering if the enemy had simply gotten lucky. Or if they'd tracked the fleet ever since it had broken contact and jumped through the tramline.

Or we have an infected person onboard, she thought. It should have been impossible—the bioscanners, blood screenings and UV lights should have revealed any zombies—but she couldn't dismiss the thought completely. *They could be calling the enemy fleet right to us.*

"Divert two drones towards the contact," she ordered. The enemy ships—if they were ships—were already too close for comfort. Their sensors would probably be able to detect her fleet, even though they were cloaked. There were just too many ships in too close proximity. "And put the starfighters and gunboats on alert."

"Aye, Admiral."

Susan watched, gritting her teeth as the seconds ticked away. The longer she waited before launching starfighters and altering course, the greater the chance the enemy would land a solid blow on her ships. But if she launched starfighters, which couldn't cloak, the enemy would know she was there. It crossed her mind to wonder if she was poking at a decoy, something intended to flush her out of hiding. The virus was perfectly capable of being subtle. It just didn't bother very often.

"Crap!" Richardson cleared his throat. "Admiral, incoming starfighters!"

"I see them," Susan said. The drones had picked up the carriers, too late. The virus looked to be copying its earlier tactics, hiding the battleships behind the carriers. Did it expect the trick to work twice? Or was it trying to trick her into thinking it was repeating itself? "Launch starfighters, then bring us about. Try to widen the range as much as possible."

"Aye, Admiral."

Susan's mind raced as the carriers started to launch starfighters. The virus had found them, which meant...what? Her fingers danced over the console. It was possible the virus had just gotten lucky. The fleet they'd evaded two systems ago could have caught up with them. Or...she keyed a command into the console, as the cloaking devices were deactivated. A sensor focus might reveal an unwelcome travelling companion...

"Admiral, the drones have isolated a number of enemy drive signatures," Richardson reported. "They're the ships we encountered earlier."

"Good," Susan said. It wasn't really good news. The drones were revealing more and more ships behind the carriers. The enemy was clearly coordinating its assault, even though there wasn't a brainship in sensor range...perhaps the enemy ships had simply used the flicker network to ask for orders. It was hardly impossible. "Deploy the gunboats to deter them from getting any closer, then alter course again. We have to get through that tramline."

"Aye, Admiral."

Susan sat back in her chair, trying to project an image of calm. This time, they couldn't afford to hunt down and destroy the enemy flicker station. This time, she couldn't risk a long, drawn-out engagement. This time...

They could have gotten their fleet past us without us noticing, she told herself. *If they had some way to track us, they didn't need to risk an engagement...*

She groaned, inwardly. The virus wasn't closing the range. Again. It was forcing her to defend herself, expending her supplies for nothing. And she had no choice, but to play its game until she could get through the tramline...

...

Tobias felt uneasy as the gunboats lanced away from *Lion*, heading towards the enemy carriers. They weren't maintaining a CSP, somewhat to his surprise, but they'd moved enough escorts forward to protect the carriers. It was a crude tactic, yet workable. The gunboats could evade the escorts— they were far faster than any starship—but the missiles couldn't. The enemy were pumping out so many sensor pulses that even ballistic missiles were unlikely to remain undetected long enough to get into striking range.

He gritted his teeth as the range closed sharply. The remainder of the gunboats were spread out, a grim reminder of the simple fact there were only four gunboats left. He wanted to feel guilty at forgetting the dead—at not really knowing them at all—but it was hard to feel much of anything. He'd gone beyond horror, beyond anything save for the need to stay alive for one more day. They could make it home and then...

"I have missile lock," he said. The carriers weren't really trying to hide. The haze surrounding them wouldn't be enough to shield them from detection, although he supposed it would make it harder for anyone to lock missiles directly on their hull. The gunboats were close enough to see right through it. "Missiles targeted, ready to go live."

"Go live," Marigold said.

Tobias nodded and tapped the console. The gunboats reversed course, spitting out a handful of sensor decoys as they fled. He left her to handle the piloting as the missiles went live, picking up speed as they flashed towards their targets. The salvo should have been larger, he noted grimly. Only one missile survived long enough to strike a carrier and it didn't do anything like enough damage. It looked as if the carrier had lost a single flight deck, but so what? There were three more.

A handful of enemy starfighters swooped down on them. Tobias watched, helplessly, as the automatics handled the engagement. The battle was just moving too fast. A lone gunboat was blown to atoms, wiped out too quickly for the crew to escape. Another...

The gunboat shook. The gravity field flickered and died, the displays blinking out of existence seconds later. Tobias froze in horror as he heard a whistling noise echoing through the craft. They'd been holed! There was a gash in the hull! He felt liquid trickling between his legs as he realised they were about to die, unless they got very lucky. His fingers were suddenly clumsy, terribly clumsy. It was all he could do to pull himself free of the straps as the gunboat careened out of control. Marigold was caught in her seat, unable to get free. Tobias shivered, the cold starting to get to him as he yanked his helmet into place, pulled down his mask and stumbled towards her. She was trapped...

He pulled at her straps for a second, then realised his mistake and disengaged the whole chair. The installation came apart, leaving her drifting in the middle of the compartment. Her eyes were wide with fear. Tobias managed – somehow—to get her mask into place and yank her towards the gash in the hull. The stars beyond were spinning in circles...he took her masked hand, wrapped his arms around her and dragged them both into interplanetary space. He could feel the cold, even through the shipsuit. Panic yammered at the back of his mind as the gunboat vanished into the distance, a sparkle of light suggesting it had exploded. They were screwed. They were dead. Their only hope for rescue was the virus and *that* would rescue them only to infect them. Tobias wondered if he'd have the nerve to commit suicide, if the virus would let him. He couldn't bring himself to pull his mask free and start sucking vacuum.

Marigold pulled herself up towards him. Tobias almost giggled as they tried to line their helmets up. They looked absurd. They *really* had to look absurd, as if they were fighting and hugging at the same time. Her mask had tinted automatically, but he could see her eyes behind it. She was scared, as scared as he...the cold was starting to leech into his bones and drain his energy. Bagehot had sworn blind the shipsuits would protect them from the vacuum, but Tobias was starting to think he'd exaggerated. A few seconds might be fine. Hours or days...he didn't want to think about it.

He clicked his PLB on, hoping it would attract attention. The *right* kind of attention. Someone would be on SAR duty, right? Someone might pluck them out of space before it was too late...he swallowed, hard. There wasn't much time, not for them...not any longer. And if they died...

I'm sorry, he thought, although he wasn't sure who he was talking to. Marigold? Bagehot? Colin? His mother and sister and dead father? *I just wish...*

• • •

Mitch awoke as the alarms howled, cursing under his breath as he rolled out of his bunk and hit the terminal with his bare hand. The alarms quieted, but didn't stop. He'd given strict orders, as the ship shadowed the alien fleet towards the second tramline, that the alpha crew was not to be awoken unless the shit had really hit the fan. He hoped someone had jumped the gun, or screwed up so badly the rest of the crew would hate their guts. The alternative was worse.

"Report," he snapped. Staci should be in her cabin, leaving the bridge in Lieutenant Hinkson's hands. "What's happening?"

"Captain," Hinkson said. "We just detected an engagement. Preliminary projections suggest our fleet was jumped by an undetected enemy fleet."

Mitch keyed the terminal. They were quite some distance from the engagement, but certain things were clear. Admiral Onarina had run into a *second* enemy fleet, which was...Mitch's blood ran cold. The admiral didn't know about the *first* fleet. She couldn't. It was waiting for her, readying itself for the kill while the second fleet drove her into its waiting jaws. The sheer enormity of the trap made Mitch stare in disbelief. They'd been cautioned, time and time again, not to be clever on an interstellar scale. Boring but practical was far superior to awesome but impractical. And yet, the virus had pulled it off. The scale of the trap was probably why the admiral hadn't seen it coming.

They pulled ships off the front line and sent them here, he thought, numbly. The jaws were steadily closing. It wouldn't be long before the admiral was caught between two fleets, unable to break contact with one without running into the other. *If she could get past them...*

"I'm on my way," he said. They had to act fast. "Power up the transmitters and send a warning, then start evasive patterns. I want everyone to hear the warning."

Hinkson didn't hesitate. Mitch silently promised him a commendation. He knew they'd draw attention to themselves the moment they started to transmit. The cloak wouldn't protect them, not when they were screaming in the enemy's ear. They'd be fired upon before they had a chance to start repeating the message, unless they were very lucky. But they might just save the rest of the fleet.

Grabbing his jacket, he ran for the bridge. If he was going to be blown out of space, he was going to do it on his bridge. And if they'd saved the fleet, it would be worthwhile...

"Start dumping our sensor records, too," he snapped, as he burst onto the bridge. "Copy everything. Make sure they know about the alien world."

And hope to God enough ships survive to get home, he added, silently. The alien fleet was coming to life. *Unicorn* was dropping back, but she was still far too close to the enemy ships for comfort. *If we don't get the fleet out, and the message home, no one will know what we've done.*

· · ·

"Admiral, I...my God!"

Susan started. "Report!"

"Signal from *Unicorn*," Richardson said, as the display started to sparkle with red icons. "We're flying right into an ambush."

For a moment, Susan refused to believe what she was seeing. An enemy fleet was right in front of her, dangerously close...too close. How the fuck had it gotten so close to her without being detected...she looked at the first fleet and knew the answer. She'd been so intent on avoiding action that she'd let herself be driven straight into an ambush. A second ambush. And yet, *Unicorn* had saved her arse. The frigate shouldn't even have been there, but she'd won the fleet a moment of time. It might just be enough...

Her mind raced. The enemy fleet had been crawling towards her, sacrificing speed for stealth. It would need some time to bring up its drives to full power, even if it took the risk of flash-waking its systems. It was barely starting to launch starfighters towards the human ships. Susan had a window of opportunity. She could not afford to waste it.

"Alter course," she snarled. "Ramp up the drives to full power"—she drew a line on the display—"and loop us around the enemy fleet. If any of our ships can't keep up"—her words caught in her throat—"they are to be evacuated and abandoned. Launch two drones towards the fleet and two more along our flight path..."

And hope there isn't a third enemy fleet also waiting for us, she added silently, as she continued to issue orders. She knew just how badly her fleet had been weakened. *If that happens, we're dead.*

CHAPTER THIRTY-EIGHT

UNICORN SHOULDN'T EVEN BE HERE, Thomas thought, numbly. *What the fuck is Campbell doing here?*

He told himself, sharply, not to look a gift horse in the mouth. The enemy fleet was far too close for comfort, but it wasn't close enough. The admiral was already snapping orders through the datanet, commanding the ships to alter course and steer their way out of the trap. It was going to be close, as the enemy ships realised they'd been rumbled and started to pick up speed, but not close enough. They might just make it out of the trap.

The display sparkled with red icons. Missiles. Long-range missiles. Thomas shuddered as he saw the sheer weight of the enemy broadside, fearing the worst if the enemy had also improved their missile designs. They might have configured them to slip through the human defences and ram into their hulls…he put the thought out of his mind as the enemy carriers launched their starfighters. They intended to slow the fleet long enough to let the battleships close and batter it into submission. It could not be allowed.

"Captain." Bagehot's image flashed up on the display. "The gunboat crews have activated their beacons."

Thomas cursed under his breath. The pilots would not have risked activating their PLBs unless there was no other choice. They had to have

371

abandoned their craft, something they wouldn't have done unless they'd been hit…he cursed again as he studied the display. The fleet was turning away, trying to put some distance between itself and the enemy fleets. There was no time for a pickup and yet he couldn't risk abandoning his pilots. He was their CO. He had a duty to them.

"Launch marine shuttles on SAR duty," he said, finally. He would have preferred to assign starfighters to the task, in the middle of a major engagement, but none could be spared. And besides, they'd have to make sure the gunboat pilots were their own men before they risked bringing them back onboard. It wasn't likely the virus had managed to capture, infect and release them in the space of a few short minutes, but it had managed to pull off the impossible before. "And make it clear that this is a volunteer mission only."

"Aye, sir," Bagehot said.

Thomas scowled, inwardly. The marines *would* take up the mission. He had no doubt of it. Peer pressure, as well as the need to live up to their reputation, would see to that. And yet, he'd never liked pushing someone to do something they didn't want to. It had always struck him as blatant foul play. Better to let a coward, or even someone who rationally calculated the odds, leave of their own accord then risk putting them on the front lines. He'd heard enough horror stories to know it was better to keep such people well away from danger.

The marines went through commando training, he reminded himself, dryly. The Royal Marines were an all-volunteer force. It was the Home Guard that had to make do with unsuitable conscripts, men who shouldn't really have been accepted into the military. *They wouldn't have passed the final exercises if they weren't up for it.*

He sighed—it was a little too much like throwing good money after bad—and concentrated on the display as the wall of missiles advanced on their position. *Lion* was returning fire, as were the remaining battleships, but their combined firepower wasn't anything like enough to overwhelm the enemy point defences. Thomas calculated the odds of scoring a single hit and decided they were far too low. The fleets were just too close—now—for any clever tricks. They were going to be banging away at each other uselessly until the range closed still further...

We're going to be shooting uselessly, he thought, as the enemy missiles entered attack range and started to speed up. *They're the ones who are going to be scoring the hits.*

. . .

Susan kept her face impassive as the battle continued to unfold. The enemy fleets were picking up speed, trying to bring their main body into range before the human ships could escape the trap. They might just succeed too, she thought, as the enemy missiles roared into her formation. Hundreds died, but hundreds more made it through. The damage started to mount rapidly. A battleship fell out of formation, unable to keep up with the rest of the fleet. There was no time to evacuate. Her captain brought her about, intent on selling his life dearly in hopes of winning the remainder of the fleet time to escape. Susan was all too aware it wouldn't be enough.

She felt her heart sink as the enemy fleet closed on her position. She needed more time, damn it. She needed more time, the one thing the enemy wasn't going to give her. The virus had gambled by pulling ships off the front line—her tactical staff had identified a handful of enemy ships, last seen laying siege to New Washington—and it had paid off for them. The Americans wouldn't have the slightest idea the virus had given them a window of opportunity to push the front lines back, not unless someone alerted them...she shook her head. By the time a messenger reached New Washington, it would already be too late. The virus would have beaten her fleet and rushed its remaining ships back to the front lines.

The enemy starfighters fell on her ships like wolves on the flock. They ducked and weaved through a web of point defence fire, launching torpedoes as they closed to attack range before strafing her hulls with plasma fire. The latter did little damage to the hulls themselves, but they weakened her point defence and sensor nodes beyond immediate repair. Susan cursed as another ship fell out of formation, followed rapidly by a carrier exploding into a ball of expanding plasma. Thousands of lives had been wiped out in a split second…she told herself she'd mourn later, if there was a later. The enemy fleet was still narrowing the range at terrifying speed. By the time their battleships brought their main guns to bear, her ships would barely be capable of spotting targets, let alone engaging them.

There was no point in issuing orders, no point in distracting her crews. Her mind raced as the seconds ticked away, her thoughts spinning in circles. Had the plan been flawed all along? Had she been wrong to attack the second enemy world? Had she made a mistake by not breaking contact and sneaking through the tramlines? Or had the outcome been inevitable, right from the start? She'd always known she'd have to break through the front lines to get back to safety. Her court-martial was going to be the shortest formality on record.

"Admiral, *Clinton* is taking heavy fire," Richardson reported. "Her captain is requesting additional cover."

"Granted," Susan said, curtly. She might keep the assault carrier alive for a few moments longer. Its point defence, in turn, might keep the fleet going for a little bit as well. "And try to rally the starfighters…"

She cursed under her breath. The enemy had forced her to exhaust her pilots before showing its hand. Her starfighter squadrons had been shattered, makeshift formations hastily thrown together long enough for a single mission and then restructured—again—from the remnants of the previous formations. British pilots flew with French, Russian and Chinese wingmen, their differences forgotten in the desperate need to survive. It would have pleased her, if she hadn't known they were trapped. She was only going to save a handful of her ships…if she was lucky. The odds were good that *her* ship wouldn't make it out.

They'll be able to blame me in peace, she thought, ruefully. The hell of it was that that might be for the best. *If they blame everything on me…*

"Admiral," Richardson began. "I…"

He broke off. "My God!"

• • •

Mitch had the uncomfortable feeling, as he put more space between *Unicorn* and the enemy fleet, that he had a ringside seat to the greatest naval disaster in human history. Human fleets had been beaten before—the Battle of New Russia had been a one-sided slaughter—but this was different. The enemy had outsmarted the human commanders, getting their ships into position for a hastily-planned ambush without being detected. It had deserved to win, Mitch reflected sourly. The only thing that had saved the human fleet from being crushed was sheer goddamned luck.

And yet, we might not have saved the fleet, Mitch thought. His sensors were blurred, their readings distorted by weapons fire and sensor jammers, but he didn't need precise details to know the fleet was taking a battering. The admiral was doing the only thing she could—evading the two fleets in hopes of breaking free—yet the virus knew it had her ships on the ropes. *It just needs to keep pounding at us until we go down.*

Every instinct he had called for a charge into the teeth of enemy fire, to launch his ship into the enemy formation in hopes of buying time. And yet, cold logic told him he'd get himself killed for nothing. *Unicorn* would be swatted out of existence, as casually as a man might swat a fly...if the virus condescended to notice her at all. It might simply ignore the frigate, confident she could do nothing to harm it. The virus would be right. Mitch could ram his ship into a brainship, taking both ships out...for nothing. The remainder of the brainships would continue to direct the engagement until the human fleet had been crushed.

*Unless...*A thought crossed his mind. *They don't know we went the short way around, do they?*

He forced himself to think. The virus knew *Unicorn*—or someone— was behind them. It just didn't care. The fleet was a far more important target than a lone frigate. And yet, the virus didn't know *Unicorn* had been attached to the fleet. It might assume she'd been dispatched from New Washington instead. It might assume...

"Deploy the sensor drones," he ordered. "I want the virus to see a fleet advancing from the rear."

"Aye, Captain," Staci said. "It won't fool them for long..."

Mitch shrugged. He couldn't sit on his arse and watch the human fleet die, not if there was something he could do. The beancounters would bitch and moan about expending so many drones, but they'd whine more about losing the fleet. If the virus allowed itself to be tricked into thinking there was about to be smashed with a frontal attack on its rear...his lips twitched, remembering the joke about the deserter who ran the wrong way and got the VC. Right now, he'd happily put up with all the jokes as long as it got the fleet out of the trap.

"Deploying the drones now," Staci said. "They'll go live in two minutes."

"Good," Mitch said. He silently counted the enemy ships, asking himself—grimly—if they'd keep their nerve. The drones would *look* like they were threatening the brainships...the virus wouldn't want to lose them, would it? And yet, all the virus had to do to win the engagement was to do nothing. "Direct the ghosts right at the brainships."

"Aye, Captain."

. . .

Richardson found his voice. "Those ships aren't real!"

Susan was inclined to agree. The Americans had no reason to launch a probe so far into enemy space. If they had, they'd muffed it. They'd given up the chance to hit the brainships...she shook her head. The fleet *had* to be nothing more than sensor ghosts, keeping their distance to provide an explanation for why they weren't pouring fire into the enemy rear. And yet...

The virus flinched. Its fire slackened as it hastily redeployed ships and starfighters to stand against the new threat. Susan understood. The brainships were the only thing holding the enemy formation together. If they were taken out, the remainder of the fleet would have serious problems. And she thought the virus, for the first time, was feeling the pinch. It might just be unwilling to risk engagement against vastly superior forces…forces that didn't exist. The illusion was unlikely to last more than five minutes at most.

"Long enough," she said. She raised her voice as she drew out a trajectory on the display. "Signal the fleet. All units are to accelerate and punch through into interplanetary space, heading straight for the tramline."

"Aye, Admiral."

Susan smiled, grimly. The enemy ships were already starting to show signs of hesitation, suggesting they'd started to wonder if they were being tricked. She wondered, idly, if it would take the risk of finding out the hard way. It was what *she* would have done…perhaps, if she'd been sure the sensor ghosts really were illusions. Or that the damage she'd take would be worth it, in the long run. The virus might fold its hand, rather than risk a victory that might easily become a defeat…

Just a few more seconds, she thought. *Just a few more seconds and we can turn this around.*

• • •

Space, Tobias reflected sourly, was cold. Very cold. He could feel it seeping into his bones as they tumbled through interplanetary space, despite the heating elements worked into his shipsuit. He tried to tell himself, as he clung desperately to Marigold, that he was imagining it, but it didn't work. His fingers were slowly turning to ice. He held her tightly, wishing he could kiss her one final time. They were together, and yet they were alone. They couldn't even talk.

He saw flickers of light in the distance, tiny glimmers that suggested the battle was still going on. There was no way to know what was happening, who was winning…he was uncomfortably aware that his PLB was pinging frantically, screaming for help. If the virus won, Marigold and he would be yanked out of space and infected…he wondered, grimly, if they'd be able to kill themselves. They hadn't thought to grab their service pistols before abandoning ship. He kicked himself, mentally. He'd tried to strangle himself, five years ago, and it hadn't worked. He hadn't really wanted to die.

His heart started to race as he spotted a light moving towards him. A missile? A plasma bolt? He didn't feel any better as the light took on shape and form and became a shuttle...he wasn't reassured. It was a human design, but that was meaningless. The virus's fleets included ships from a dozen races, known and unknown. He tensed as the shuttle slowed, its hatch snapping open to reveal a man in a suit. A line snapped out towards them, yanking them into the airlock. Gravity asserted itself a second later, sending them falling to the deck as the hatch closed. He grunted as he hit the hard metal surface.

The suited man removed his helmet. Colin? Tobias felt a flicker of panic, combined with the dull sense that Colin had saved his life. Or had he...? The shipsuit mask could tell him if the air was breathable, but not if it was infected. Colin might already be a mindless slave. The nasty part of Tobias's mind insisted Colin had always been mindless. And a slave to his baser appetites.

Colin knelt beside him and carefully disconnected the mask. Tobias choked. The air smelt...unclean. The virus? Or...or what? He was breathing it already! He was...

"You're safe now," Colin said. "Welcome home."

Tobias coughed, then blacked out.

· · ·

"Admiral," Richardson said. "I think they've caught on."

Susan nodded. "But they were fooled just long enough."

She allowed herself a moment of relief as she calculated the vectors again and again. The decoy fleet had won her *just* enough time to extract her ships, then race for the tramline—and New Washington—before the enemy fleet could slam the door shut once again. They'd already fired off most of their missiles, ensuring they couldn't do much more than annoy her as she ran. She knew she was leaving too many dead behind, along with a handful of ships that could no longer move under their own power, but... it was better than the alternative.

Unless they have a third fleet, somewhere ahead of us, she thought, grimly. It didn't seem likely. The virus wouldn't have needed to pull so many ships off the front lines if it had more ships to spare. *We should be well on our way home.*

The virus evidently agreed. Its fleet slowed, taking the time to pick off the stragglers and start recovering its starfighters. Susan winced, knowing there was nothing she could do to save the wounded ships. They'd evacuated some of their crews, but...she shook her head. The virus had won the engagement, even if it hadn't managed to destroy the fleet. There was nothing to be gained from pretending otherwise.

And yet, it allowed itself to flinch, she thought. If the virus had kept its nerve, it would have run the engagement outright by destroying her fleet. *Why did it allow itself to be fooled?*

The thought tantalised her as the fleet picked up speed, heading straight for the tramline. *It was reluctant to risk serious losses*, she thought. The virus had always been cold and calculating, willing to sacrifice starships and squadrons without hesitation if it seemed necessary. *Could it be that it doesn't have the ships to spare?*

She knew it might be wishful thinking, but the thought refused to go away. *If we can take advantage of their sudden reluctance to risk everything*, she asked herself, *can we win the war?*

CHAPTER THIRTY-NINE

NEW WASHINGTON LOOKED BUSIER than Mitch recalled, he noted, as the shuttle made her way towards *Thunderous*. The Americans had been astonished when the remnants of the multinational fleet had limped through the tramlines to safety, but their astonishment hadn't stopped them from hastily putting together a major attack on the next system. The virus hadn't bothered to put up much of a fight, suggesting that rumours of its weakness were far from exaggerated. The Americans had chased the enemy fleets out of the system, destroyed everything that couldn't be moved in a hurry and hit the planet with BioBombs. A new sense of optimism was starting to spread through the human worlds.

The shuttle docked. Mitch allowed himself a tight smile as the hatch opened, revealing a welcoming party. He stepped through the hatch, returned the salutes from a dozen officers and marines, then allowed himself to be escorted through a series of corridors to the admiral's office. He was mildly surprised she hadn't greeted him herself, although he knew she had a great deal of work to do. The milksops back home had taken five minutes to cheer for victory, then gone back to complaining about the cost. He snorted in disgust. They'd be complaining a great deal more if the fleet had been destroyed. If, of course, they'd lived long enough.

He braced himself, then saluted as he stepped into the admiral's office. She stood and returned his salute, before indicating he should take a seat. Mitch sat, gratefully accepting a mug of coffee from the admiral's steward. The admiral took a mug herself, then sat facing him. Her face was calm, very composed.

"I've recommended you for the Navy Cross," she said, without preamble. "I have no doubt there will be people back home who'll complain you disobeyed orders, which you did, but no one can quibble about the results. I don't know, yet, if you'll actually *get* the medal—I don't know how much influence I have, right now—but it should be enough to answer any stain on your record."

Mitch nodded, not trusting himself to speak. The admiral couldn't be sure of her standing, not after the mission had nearly turned into a complete disaster. It was unlikely the allied navies would be happy leaving her in command of the fleet, or what remained of it; it was unlikely the Admiralty would accept her recommendations without question. But, even if he didn't get the medal, the fact she'd put his name down for it would work in his favour. It had been *her* orders he'd disobeyed, after all.

"Without you, the fleet would have been destroyed," the admiral said. "I think we can afford to show a *little* gratitude."

"As long as I don't get promoted," Mitch said. It wasn't really a joke. He wanted to stay on *Unicorn*. "The medal will be gratitude enough."

The admiral smiled. "I quite understand," she said. "We'll see what the Admiralty has to say."

Mitch nodded and sipped his coffee. He'd taken one hell of a risk—two of them, really—but it had paid off. The fleet had been saved...he supposed there were officers who wouldn't be able to see past the simple fact he'd disobeyed orders, yet the majority of those officers had been killed or reassigned during the early years of the war. And besides, his commanding officer was in his corner. She could easily punish him by sentencing him to frigate command. Anyone who understood it wasn't much of a punishment would also understand that he didn't really *deserve* punishment.

"I've also forwarded your survey reports and your tactical concepts," the admiral continued, calmly. "The alien homeworld, if indeed it *is* the alien homeworld, will be attacked as soon as possible. That may be quite some time."

"Even if we go with my plan?" Mitch leaned forward. "At the very least, we'd put the virus on the defensive again. It would buy us time…"

"I intend to make that case to the Admiralty," the admiral said. "I've been recalled to Earth, as have you and Captain Hammond. You may be called upon to make your case to the Admiralty."

Mitch smiled. "I don't mind if I don't get the credit, Admiral."

The admiral grinned. "You're the highest-ranking officer who laid eyes on the alien world," she pointed out. "Never mind that your sensor records are already being studied on Nelson Base. Never mind there's nothing you can tell them that they don't already know. Never mind that the media wants to lionise you as the saviour of the fleet…"

"Ouch." Mitch stared at his hands. "Is that a good or bad thing?"

"It depends." The admiral was suddenly very serious. "Having the media on your side can be very helpful, if—when—you run into trouble. It saved my career a couple of times. On the other hand"—she met his eyes evenly—"reporters are like vampires. They can never be trusted. They'll suck you dry and then discard you. They'll raise you high and then drop you like a stone, the moment you don't meet their expectations. "

She shrugged. "You want my advice? Watch your back."

"Yes, Admiral," Mitch said.

He felt an odd little thrill. He'd never wanted promotion, not beyond command rank, but he did want fame and fortune. Military heroes had been rock stars—*real* heroes—since the Troubles, when Britain had learnt to respect her fighting men again. The idea of being lionised, of having his praises sung to the entire world, was seductive. His family would be pleased. No one would be able to shuffle him to the side again. Ever.

The admiral smiled. "For what it's worth, you have my gratitude," she added. "And that of the fleet's commanding officers. That may—or may not—work in your favour."

Mitch frowned. "How so?"

"I committed mutiny," the admiral said, flatly. "I had good reason. I saved the ship *and* the fleet. I made the right choice. Every commanding officer in that fleet agreed with me. But that made it harder for the Admiralty to decide what to do. If they rewarded me, it might be seen as giving in to international pressure; if they punished me, they might be seen as insulting their allies. It wasn't easy for them to steer a path through the storm."

"You did the right thing," Mitch said.

"Tactically, yes," the admiral agreed. "Politically...that depends on your point of view."

She finished her coffee. "Go back to your ship," she ordered. "We'll be departing shortly."

"Aye, Admiral."

Mitch stood and allowed himself to be escorted back to the shuttle. It was hard not to be excited about the chance of winning the Navy Cross, even though the admiral had warned him that nothing was certain. And yet... the mere fact he'd been nominated for the medal worked in his favour. It would make him look very good indeed. He wondered, idly, what Charlotte would make of it. The message she'd sent him had been exciting, and erotic, but short on actual detail. Mitch didn't mind. He wanted to see her again. No, he wanted to sleep with her again. He was sure she felt the same way, too. She'd already invited him to stay at the manor...

He allowed his smile to get wider. The future looked bright and full of promise.

. . .

"I'm starting to hate sickbay," Tobias muttered. "Can I get out of here now?"

Doctor Haugen shrugged. "I'm starting to think you don't like me," she said. "I am *very* hurt."

Tobias flushed, then realised he was being teased. "I like you, but I don't like sickbay," he said. "I don't want to be here."

"A very common attitude," the doctor said. She looked him up and down, then nodded. "You'll be pleased to hear I'm discharging you today. I've repaired the damage, and there shouldn't be any risk of long-term issues, but I expect you to take care of yourself. I've already spoken to your commanding officer. You'll be on light duties for the rest of the month. I suggest you spend the time studying."

Tobias frowned. "It isn't as if there are any more gunboats..."

He winced. Only two gunboat pilots—Marigold and himself—had survived the final desperate battle. None of the gunboats themselves had survived. He couldn't help feeling guilty for not knowing the gunboat crews a little better...he cursed under his breath as he wobbled to his feet. He'd have to empty their drawers himself, unless Bagehot had already done it. Marigold was still in the regeneration tube. The doctor had told him it would be at least a week before she could be discharged.

"Light duties," the doctor repeated. "You should be fit to return to duty by the time we reach Earth."

"Just in time to go on shore leave," Tobias said. "Wonderful."

"You'll have fun, I'm sure," the doctor said. She waved a hand at the hatch. "Good luck."

Tobias nodded and stepped through the hatch. The majority of the evacuated crewmembers had been sent elsewhere, or so he'd been told, but the corridors outside sickbay still looked a little scruffy. Bagehot would have thrown a fit if the gunboat pilots had left their wardroom in such a state. Tobias grimaced, despite himself. He hadn't shared the military obsession with neatness until he'd joined the navy himself and discovered its value. A spacer or a soldier who didn't take care of his equipment would find himself unable to rely on it.

Don't shit where you eat, Tobias remembered. One of his gym teachers had said that, during a forced march that had been a foretaste of hell. *And don't crap on people, because they might crap on you.*

The thought made him scowl. Colin had saved his life. Colin...the thought of being grateful to Colin was thoroughly unpleasant, even though

Tobias *knew* Colin had grown up a lot in the past few months. They might never be close friends, but...he shook his head, reminding himself that Colin had saved Marigold's life, too. He owed the bastard that, if nothing else. It wasn't as if there were any other girls who'd ever shown any interest in him.

He reached the wardroom and stepped inside. Bagehot was kneeling beside one of the bunks, unloading the contents of the drawers onto a cardboard box. Tobias opened his mouth to object, then remembered that the former occupant was dead. She'd deserved better. They'd *all* deserved better. And...he stepped forward, peering into the box. There was little *personal* about the contents. There was nothing to suggest anything about its former owner.

Bagehot looked up. "Do you want to help?"

Tobias shrugged. "Would it do any good?"

"There's a pile of old uniforms over there," Bagehot said, curtly. "Take some, if they'll fit you. Or put them aside to go back into general use. Anything that isn't on the naval list is to go back to the families."

"I see," Tobias said. He'd been told that starfighter pilots generally left their possessions to their surviving peers, but gunboat pilots didn't have to follow that tradition. "I ... fuck it."

"It's healthy to grieve," Bagehot said. "No one will fault you for it."

"I'm not grieving," Tobias said, a little sharper than he'd intended. "I didn't know them well enough to grieve and I feel guilty and...fuck it!"

"It's never easy to cope with loss," Bagehot said. He picked up the box and pushed it into Tobias's hands. "But you have to learn."

Tobias stared into the box. A handful of datachips. A couple of pictures. A single set of civilian clothes. Nothing else, not even...he shook his head, feeling tears prickling at the corner of his eyes. A life had been reduced to nothing and less than nothing...he wondered, suddenly, what Bagehot would say when he wrote to the pilot's parents. The truth? Or just boilerplate?

"Yes, sir," he said, finally. "I'll do my best."

"Take some leave, when we get home." Bagehot stood and patted Tobias on the shoulder. "You and Marigold can have fun, somewhere. And then you can consider taking my place."

Tobias smiled, although it wasn't funny. "Am I supposed to put a knife in your back?"

"No," Bagehot said. "But the gunboat program *is* being expanded. It's only a matter of time until someone gets promoted into my place. You might have a decent chance at the post, if you start studying now."

"If I want to spend my life in the navy," Tobias said, quietly.

"If," Bagehot agreed. "Look at it this way. You're enlisted for five years— or the duration, whichever one is shorter. You can keep flying gunboats, but there's a reason most starfighter pilots rarely stay more than two or three years in the role. Even if the odds don't catch up with you, and you wind up blown to pieces, you'll find you start losing your touch. And then the odds *will* catch up with you."

He shrugged. "And besides, retiring at a higher rank means a higher pension."

Tobias shrugged. "I'll give it some thought," he said. "Really."

"You should," Bagehot agreed.

• • •

"We cannot afford to relax," Bowman said. "The mission may be over, but we are far from safe."

"Yes, Sergeant," Colin said. He couldn't disagree. New Washington might be heavily defended, but it was on the front lines. The Americans had shoved the virus back, yet no one expected it to stay on the defensive forever. "We're still running drills and suchlike."

He nodded In some ways, the mission had been a little disappointing. He'd hoped for planetary invasions and boarding missions...he'd have settled for counter-boarding operations. He knew he should be glad the marines hadn't been deployed as often as he'd wished, but...he shook his head. No one joined the marines to do damage control duties or SAR missions. He could do them, but…it wasn't what he'd signed up for.

Bowman leaned forward. "We need to talk about Kevin," he said, and smiled as if he'd just said something funny. "There will be plenty of report writing in your future, I'm afraid, but for the moment…how is he coping?"

Colin took a moment to consider his answer. The sergeant wouldn't penalise him for telling the truth, or bawl him out for not being diplomatic, but…Colin was uneasily aware his words were likely to be sent up the chain. He might get in real trouble for mishandling the situation or just disagreeing with a politician he didn't know personally…

He braced himself. "On the surface, he's coped admirably. Perhaps more than *merely* admirably, as he is an alien amongst aliens. The environment must disturb him at a very primal level, yet…he copes. His training is good, he held up well…there are none of the issues that would come with training to integrate a Tadpole into the platoon. The only downside is that he's too stubborn to confess to injury or ignorance. That's not uncommon, of course, but we don't have any real baselines for his biology. We don't know what might prove a hindrance, in the long run."

"His biology is hardly a secret," Bowman pointed out, stiffly.

"No, Sergeant," Colin agreed. "However, it is very different from ours. It isn't easy to say, in the middle of a battle, what's lethal and what can be safely ignored. There will also be problems using human-keyed medical kits to tend to him, if he gets wounded. Our painkillers are useless to him. If they were injected by accident, he'd be killed."

He took a breath. "The platoon treated him as the average FNG. There was a little hazing, as always, but I was careful not to let it get out of hand. That we were separate from the rest of the company, perhaps a little detached from it, probably helped. We were allowed a great deal of latitude. How well this would have worked if we'd been expected to pull our weight as part of the overall company I don't know. It might not have gone so well."

"Perhaps not," Bowman agreed. "On the record, the decision will be made well above our pay grades. Off the record…do you think we could accept more Vesy recruits?"

Colin frowned. The question sounded casual. He had the feeling it was nothing of the sort.

"There would be issues," he said, finally. "Kevin is alone. He had to work hard to fit in with the rest of us. There was no shared society. If we added others, however, it would be harder to integrate them. They might even have problems getting along, if they happened to be of different castes or nationalities. Something that would appear to be nothing to us might be very serious to them. And if we made allowances, it would damage our cohesion in other ways. In short, Sergeant, I don't know."

Bowman nodded. "You can continue to work with Kevin and the rest of the platoon until we return home," he said. "At that point, I'm afraid the formal assessments will begin. Think about what you're going to say, before they start shouting questions at you. And pray you actually get some shore leave, in the midst of everything. The admiral is, apparently, already planning our next move. Rumour insists she intends to hit the enemy homeworld with a massive fleet."

Colin looked up. Rumour was normally unreliable, but if *Bowman* was repeating it…"Will there be a role for us?"

"We don't know," Bowman said. He grinned, showing his teeth. "But I hope so."

CHAPTER FORTY

"AND YOU'RE SAYING THE ALIEN ARTEFACTS are useless?" Admiral Hanson sounded thoroughly displeased. "That all the effort we expended on bringing them home was wasted?"

Susan bit down on her annoyance. The Royal Navy—and GATO—had every right to thoroughly investigate every last aspect of the mission, from the successful attack on the infected worlds to the near-disaster just two jumps short of New Washington. She'd spent a sizable portion of the voyage home writing detailed reports, reading the responses from the Admiralty and writing even more detailed answers to the questions they raised. She had the nasty feeling that GATO was breathing down the Admiralty's collective neck, demanding answers from her even as it sought insight from the foreign officers attached to her command. It would have been *nice* to have a few days of shore leave, before the Admiralty convened a formal Board of Inquiry, but…it was not to be.

"The artefacts are clearly from a more advanced civilisation than our own," she said, keeping her voice under tight control. "It cannot be denied they have an effect on the virus. That was confirmed when one of the artefacts was moved to the Biological Research Centre and exposed to viral matter. We don't know how they work, not yet, but knowing that something is *possible* is half the battle. We have every reason to think that, sooner or later, we will successfully duplicate the effect ourselves. Furthermore, their mere existence is proof that there *is* a more advanced society out there. We will not be surprised when we encounter it."

"A society that might have been responsible for creating the virus in the first place," Hanson pointed out. "Do we *want* to encounter them?"

"With all due respect," Susan said, "we may not have a choice."

Admiral Jackson cleared her throat. "Admiral, there is some feeling in GATO that the operation was a failure," she said. "How would you respond to that?"

Susan took a moment to organise her thoughts. Admiral Jackson was a pen-pusher, but she was charged with overseeing international cooperation and—as such—had probably taken the brunt of the international response. It remained to be seen just how *serious* it was. Her officers agreed the operation had been largely successful, but that wouldn't stop the foreign politicians from trying to use their doubts for political advantage. Susan would have smiled, if the situation hadn't been so serious. Who would have thought that foreign politicians would have had so much in common with their British counterparts?

"I would say, were I asked, that there are several points that need to be brought to their attention," Susan said. She made a show of ticking points off on her fingers. "First, we succeeded in keeping the virus from using catapults to hit us here. A direct strike on Earth would have been disastrous, even if it was beaten off. That alone made the operation worthwhile.

"Second, we successfully struck deep into enemy space and destroyed two major industrial nodes. We proved the BioBombs are devastatingly effective against worlds so heavily infected that the biospheres themselves are compromised beyond repair. We also proved that the virus is incapable of keeping the counter-virus from spreading, not without severely hampering its own effectiveness. In short, we did a great deal of damage to the virus's industrial base. It *must* have noticed."

She smiled. "Third, we located their homeworld—or, at the very least, a third major industrial node—without them realising what we have done.

We have already started devising ways to hit the system, to harass the enemy even if we cannot destroy their facilities immediately.

"And fourth, in the middle of extracting the fleet from a trap, we proved that the virus is showing a marked concern for losses. It could have won the engagement, and dealt us a devastating defeat, if it had had kept its nerve and thrust in for the kill. It did not. Indeed, when the Americans attacked from New Washington shortly after we made it back to safety, the virus withdrew rather than making any serious attempt to fight. Why would it have conceded a gateway system that opens up all sorts of possibilities, for us, if it felt it had a choice?

"I think the virus has finally been forced to take us seriously. We have hurt it, perhaps badly; we have done enough damage, I think, to force the virus to go on the defensive. This may well be our only chance to launch war-winning offensive of our own. At the very least, crippling or destroying the system we discovered will weaken the virus still further. I submit to you that we must move as quickly as possible. There may be no time to waste."

Her words hung in the air for a long moment. She waited, trying to gauge their feelings. She was a Lady Commander of the Garter, and yet she'd always been an interloper amongst them. She knew there were admirals and politicians who would sooner see her take early retirement than rise to the very top, even though they knew her to be a competent and experienced officer. They'd never seen her as one of them.

"We will consider your suggestion," Admiral Hanson said, finally. "However, it may be difficult to convince GATO—and our alien allies—to gamble everything on another deep-strike mission."

"Perhaps impossible," Admiral Jackson said. "It is unlikely the operation will be launched under *our* command."

"It does not matter, as long as it is launched," Susan said. She would have liked the command, but...she could give it up, if it meant the operation would go ahead. It wasn't as if it was hers by right. "Time is not on our side."

"We do understand," Admiral Hanson said. "For the moment, however, we suggest you take a week's leave."

Susan nodded, recognising the dismissal. It wasn't anything like as kind as it sounded. A week of leave for her would be followed by a month of interrogations, if the Admiralty found it politically expedient to throw her to the wolves. She wasn't alone—she had a number of high-ranking supporters—but they'd be pressured into remaining quiet if the operation was branded a failure. Her lips quirked, as she saluted and left the chamber. Captain Hammond had invited her to his estate. She'd have a chance to lobby some of the political and aristocratic leadership in person.

She sighed, inwardly, as she made her way down to the entrance hall. She knew she'd been lucky. The operation had come far too close to disaster. If Captain Campbell had obeyed orders…she kept her face under right control as she stepped into the lights. A small horde of reporters was standing on the far side of the road, pointing everything from cameras to distance microphones at her. Thankfully, a car was already waiting for her. Susan ignored the reporters as she climbed inside, then closed the door. The reporters wouldn't follow her, not yet. They were still waiting for their editors to decide how she was going to be handled.

As long as they let me have a week to breathe, she thought. *I'll be back soon enough.*

. . .

Mitch waved, as cheerfully as he could, as he made his way past the line of reporters and clambered into the limo. The news media had been telling the story of his exploits for weeks, ever since the first reports had been declassified. Mitch was mildly amused at just how much they'd gotten wrong, or blown out of all proportion; they'd—somehow—managed to run a story written by a girl who claimed to have dated him back in school. It hadn't taken the more cynical news sites long to work out that the dates didn't quite add up, but Mitch found it hard to care. Being a hero certainly had its advantages.

He smiled at the reporters as the limo roared to life and glided onto the streets. The admiral had warned him that it wouldn't last, and the hotel hadn't been too pleased to discover a small army of reporters on the doorstep, but he intended to enjoy it as long as he could. He'd already hired a publicity expert, just to make sure it didn't come back to bite him later. It was astonishing what people would tolerate in their heroes, as long as they *remained* heroes. He settled back in his seat and poured himself a drink as the limo picked up speed. The party was due to begin shortly.

His datapad vibrated, alerting him to new messages. Interview requests, party invitations, even marriage proposals...Mitch flickered through the latter, unsure if he should be amused or horrified. He'd never heard such blunt invitations in real life. The photographs attached to some of the proposals veered from tasteful images of girls wearing formal dress to outright pornography. He hoped—prayed—that the girls had at least *consented* to have their photographs sent to him. A handful of proposals hinted they'd actually been sent by the parents. He felt a stab of sympathy for their daughters. He'd often complained about his parents, but they'd never done anything like *that*.

He was still reading the messages when the limo reached the estate. This time, there was a formal gathering to welcome him. Captain Hammond didn't seem too pleased to see Mitch—he looked as if he'd bitten into something sour—but Charlotte winked at him as her husband turned away. Mitch told himself to be patient as he moved from guest to guest, shaking hands with people who hadn't so much as known his name the *last* time he'd visited the estate. They all seemed to want to speak to him, yammering endlessly about nothing in particular. He found himself getting antsy as the day slowly turned to night. He hadn't come to talk to people who wanted to look down their noses at him.

"I think Admiral Onarina did a good job," he said, when a particularly annoying armchair admiral questioned Admiral Onarina's tactics. "She handled her fleet well, she took advantage of the opportunities presented to her and she managed to get the majority of her fleet back to safety."

He regretted it, moments later, as a small army of armchair admirals and generals surrounded him. Some had actual military experience—one looked so ancient it was easy to believe he'd served alongside Lord Nelson himself—while others were clearly poseurs, unable or unwilling to put themselves in harm's way. A couple knew what they were talking about—they spoke about Theodore Smith in a manner that suggested they'd known him—while the others were ignorant idiots, unaware of the realities of naval combat. They wanted his opinion, as long as it accorded with their own. It was striking, really, just how many of them disliked Admiral Onarina. Mitch hated them for it. The admiral had saved their bacon from the wolves.

Charlotte rescued him, just in time to save the fools from a display of his temper. "How are you coping?"

"Poorly." Mitch felt his heart begin to race as she led him upstairs. "Do they really think they know what they're talking about?"

"Politics," Charlotte said. "As long as we keep them sweet, they'll vote the way we want them to."

She led him into a small bedroom and closed the door with a kick, then pressed her lips against his. The kiss was so greedy that Mitch was lost, his hands fumbling with her dress as he felt her undoing his trousers and pushing them to his ankles. She kissed him, time and time again, as they stumbled towards the bed. It was all he could do to keep from exploding as he started to thrust inside her...

It crossed his mind, just for a second, that they were taking an immense risk. The dinner party hadn't been formally dismissed. They'd sat through all the speeches, and socialised, and yet...he smiled as he started to move faster and faster. The risk was part of the thrill. He hadn't felt so excited since his teenage years, when he'd kissed and groped his first girlfriend in her shop, in the certain knowledge that her father would beat them both bloody if they were caught. Finding a place to do it in relative privacy hadn't been anything like as fun.

"Don't stop," Charlotte breathed. "Don't stop."

And Mitch was lost in her.

• • •

"Admiral Onarina did well," Thomas said. He had his own doubts about her tactics, but they were better discussed in private. The Admiralty would not thank him for badmouthing an officer in front of a bunch of gossipy armchair admirals. "I feel she coped admirably."

He sighed inwardly. The armchair admirals wanted to talk about the operation, while the armchair *generals* wanted to ask about the Vesy. Thomas had kept his distance from *that* particular affair on Charlotte's advice, knowing that there was no way it would make *him* look good. Better to let a junior officer do all the work and reap the rewards, if there were . Thomas wouldn't begrudge him the credit. The risks were just too high.

"I must say, using alien troops in combat does not speak well of us," another armchair general insisted. "We should have the courage of our convictions and put ourselves at risk."

Thomas bit down on a sharp response. Where the hell was Charlotte? She was supposed to save him from idiots who could barely string a coherent sentence together. Thomas allowed his eyes to roam up and down the bastard's outfit. The uniform was completely fictional, as far as he could tell. The wearer was so overweight that he'd be laughed out of a recruiting office, if he actually tried to put his arse on the line. The nasty part of Thomas's mind suggested that if he charged the enemy, the enemy troops would be paralysed with laughter.

That happened in Stellar Star, he reminded himself. *But it wasn't laughter that made them so stiff...*

He smiled at the terrible joke, then composed himself. "I believe the idea was to introduce them to modern technology and tactics," he said. "As such, it was a success. I don't think there are any large-scale plans to import Vesy to serve as soldiers, or work on Earth."

"That didn't work out very well last time," the armchair idiot said.

"And who'd want a Vesy to serve as a nanny?" Another man guffawed. He'd clearly had too much to drink. The poor woman beside him looked as if she wanted to die from embarrassment. "Can you imagine those claws picking up a baby? The very thought!"

Thomas snorted, then turned and walked away. He was just...sick of them. There was no point in pretending to *like* them. They were so dependent on him that he could make them jump through his hoops for his approval and they'd like it. Or say they liked it. His eyes swept the room, spotting a handful of senior military officers and politicians...even a particularly irritating scion of royalty. But there was no sign of Charlotte. His wife had vanished.

He hailed a maid as he left the hall. "Where's my wife?"

The maid flushed. "I...ah...I think she went to her rooms."

Thomas blinked. Charlotte *loved* parties and gatherings and social events where people with more money and rank than sense showed each other up. The idea of her leaving ahead of time was just absurd. There were hours yet, before the hosts formally withdrew and the guests could leave without giving serious offense. Not that Thomas, at least, would have given much of a damn. He turned and strode away, leaving the maid behind. She was probably new. It was rare for maids to last longer than a couple of years. They tended to move on to higher-paid jobs elsewhere.

He walked up the stairs, silence falling around him like a shroud. Charlotte really *didn't* like leaving early, unless she felt unwell. No, that wasn't like her at all. She rarely got sick. Her family had splashed out on all the latest genetic modifications, ensuring she never suffered from anything more unpleasant than the common cold. *The* virus might be able to bring her down. He couldn't think of anything else that could.

A flicker of unease ran through him as he reached the corridor leading down to his wife's suite. There should be two maids on duty at all times, but there was no sign of them. They wouldn't have been sent to help downstairs. Charlotte would sooner go hungry than stop keeping up appearances. He stopped, dead, as he heard a moan. It sounded like...

He crept forward, as quietly as possible. The noise was growing louder, feminine moans mingling with male grunts...ice washed through his system. Charlotte...it *had* to be Charlotte. His daughters were still at school. They wouldn't dare bring a lover home, not without prior permission. It was unthinkable. It was...Thomas stopped outside the door, unsure if he wanted to open it or walk away. And then he heard another, louder, moan.

Anger shot through him. He stepped forward and yanked the door open. The light was dim, but his eyes were good enough to make out Charlotte's pale skin. She was lying on her back, her legs wide open as she was ploughed…Thomas stared in horror. Captain Campbell was in bed with his wife? It was hard, so hard, to wrap his head around the sheer scale of the betrayal.

"You…" Thomas cleared his throat, angrily. "What the fuck do you think you're doing?"

But he knew the answer even before he spoke…

• • •

THE END
The *Ark Royal* series will return in:
Drake's Drum
Coming Soon.

Printed in Great Britain
by Amazon